Nemonymous Night

by

D F Lewis

Nemonymous Night
by D F Lewis

ISBN: 978-1-913766-28-3

Publication Date: 2024

Originally published in 2011 by Chômu Press

EibonVale

www.eibonvalepress.co.uk

“There is certainly a spiralling ominous weirdness here, a sense of shifting scales such as reveal to us the bizarre denizens of the world beneath a microscope, so much a part of our mundane existence but usually invisible to us (not to mention the possibly more bizarre world we would see through a macroscope), but the psychedelia of *Nemonymous Night* perhaps owes less to the sixties than it does to the lucid and lyrical ostranenie of writers such as Denton Welch. There is an understanding here of the piquant craft of strangeness that is the basis of all lasting fiction. The inside-out logic is Carrollian. The word-play, dare I say it, is Jungian; it is the wordplay of dreams.”

Quentin S. Crisp

“In a top front room of one of those grander houses, a young woman woke to find herself standing in the middle of a carpet. She often woke like this, and was not surprised; but she asked herself to what room the carpet belonged *this* time.”

–From ‘I Hear You Say So’, by Elizabeth Bowen (1945)

“I saw Elvis at the mall last night. He was eating pizza with DF Lewis. Can’t think why they’d ordered anchovies.”

–Karl Edward Wagner: ‘The View from Carcosa’ (Deathrealm)

Contents:

"You are not your name, not your body, not your various actions— not even your soul or self. Just dig and see, haul back what you find. And try not laugh or cry when, from the core of reality, you reveal the true nature of 'you'."

Lope de Vega (loose translation)

Prelude

This book is like a child clumsily finding its feet upon a carpet: a space and a foundation that seem to be its whole world. The book starts out to navigate this world, to become practised at walking, to become schooled, loved and loving, finally prepared for death.

Only later does the book discover that the world is quite a different world from the one for which it has been prepared.

Each page will therefore eventually grow up into another later page of the book. This process is the story. This is the truth of its fiction. The growing-up of a book in difficult times.

These words are not a pretentious authorial introduction to the book. They do not even represent the book's own intrinsic prologue. They are part of the growing-up process. They are part of the plot.

Nemonymous Navigation

The carpet was quite ordinary. Nobody around was an expert on the manufacture of carpets, so all that could be said about it was some reference to ordinariness. Even the stains were ordinary. Years of wine and grime. Years of mishandled vacuuming. The careless knees of toddlers as they scorched their model cars through the rough of tufts. The odd tread of strangers.

The pattern was non-existent since the carpet possessed a plain beige colour—originally with nothing to recommend it except its unpretentiousness. Yet, despite these various negatives, the items of furniture that pressed its pedestals, castors and broad-beam bases into the pile were rather pleasant in an antique fashion—but whether these represented genuine antiques was anybody's guess. They were rather down-market sticks of furniture in spite of the dusting by a previous owner who rather enjoyed the varnished or polished gleam of knotted wood more than the clean lines of a carpet's cleanliness.

The carpet itself had no mind of its own—obviously.

Nothing could be inferred about its soul. If it had thoughts, it kept them to itself. There is a theory that inanimate objects feel themselves to be so real that nobody—even with the wildest imagination—can imagine them as *imaginary*. And if anything is deemed unimagined or unimaginary or unimaginable then it is incapable of existing in fiction, fantasy or dream—but merely in real life. And it is true that many actual things yearn to be imagined rather than to exist for real... simply for the pleasure of being fantasised about. This carpet was no exception.

It must feel trapped not by the webbed stitching of its underlay, by its carpet tacks keeping it tight to the skirting-boards and by the downward press of the mock antique bric-a-brac and furniture, but also by the knowledge of its essential reality as a floor-covering, with no possibility of weird elaboration or of weaving into the character of something unreal... thus to make it worthy of imagining or dreaming about. For example, that day, there were deep misunderstood mumbles in large areas of the carpet's jurisdiction—come down to it together with the pad of two spread-soled solid feet and the prod of two sharp feet as they moved about amid the lugubrious talking that belonged to the feet's owners—or so the carpet would have assumed given the carpet's ability to have such assumptions.

"How are you today?"

The man who spoke was Mike. Deceptively heavily-built. Physically distracted, but he strode through the room as if he owned it. A lorry driver's face.

The woman followed him about, as far as she could follow someone in such a small room. In contrast to Mike, she appeared as if owned or, rather, controlled by the room while—with rather more panache than the situation demanded—she kept adjusting ornaments... also brushing dust into a pan: a secondary pursuit. Given name Amy. More a girl than a woman but with a woman's manners. She said very little. Only direct questions could stir her into response.

"Not so bad."

She had a pretty face, but when she spoke—even lightly, thoughtlessly—there was a frown that appeared and a deep divot within the frown's area. Hair a fashionable matted brown, so very her it would only be noticed if it suddenly wasn't there. Apron failed to hide her sexuality and high-heels seemed out of kilter with the dustpan.

Mike was definitely older: more in his mid-forties, compared to her mid-twenties. His own greying hair and stubbly beard were far more noticeable as distinguishable features—compared to the straight 'herness' of Amy's hair. Suit a bit bedraggled. Shoes solid brown with laces—the type men had worn for years, in and out of offices. The fact he was pacing about the room exposed his nervousness despite the aura of confidence and command that Amy only saw. Or only Amy saw.

Mike was a hawler, although he would have spelt it differently had he known the word at all. At this stage, it was unclear what a hawler was—or what a hawler did. But Mike knew he was one and probably knew what one was and what one did, even if he didn't know the name itself. Not a transporter of heavy goods along the roads, as that was a haulier. In the old days, a hauler (sic) was involved in moving coal from the coalface, coal that had already been worked by others: a lifetime of chip chip chip, only for the hauler to haul it off. An art in itself and one fraught with many logistical problems. Today, however, there were no coal-mines and therefore haulers had died out—or needed to diversify. Some claimed that butchering was now within a hawler's brief, even if they only dreamed of the word hawler and later forgot it. A brief for beef, and it is true that Mike loved to consume steak—there being a saying, almost a proverb, that everyone knew but failed to understand whilst otherwise consciously understanding it to the hilt—that Mike, and others like him, "were so voracious they ate beef till it was raw".

In many ways, when perspectives were collected at the end of the day, this did not mean anything and gave no clue as to the nature of hawling.

Mike had left the house. Amy was upstairs making the bed. He wanted to visit the pub but doubted if anyone he knew would be there and he hated drinking alone. The park was second best: a good place for thinking. Susan was on his mind and Susan may indeed be in the park with her two children, one of which was bewitched... or so Susan once told Mike. Mike had usually steered clear of married women especially if they had children, but life was never simple. The bewitched child was a case for a hawler... a nameless child who often dreamed most of the night. While most people dreamed throughout the hours of sleep, very few among them actually remembered all the dreams that had disturbed the felt equilibrium of their rest. But Susan's bewitched child remembered every single detail of what followed her and of what she followed, sometimes the same thing, follower and followed. The child was nameless and so were the inhabitants of her dreams. One day she'd have proper names for them. Proper nouns.

Susan had a name for her bewitched child but she did not tell Mike because if a hawler's magic was to work, he must not, in any circumstances, know the name of the child whom he was attempting to hawl. The child must remain nemonymous—which was a word for a sort of cross between anonymity (only wholly real things could be anonymous) and a subliminal or aspirational state of non-existence.

Much was inexplicable, yet it would become explicable when put into practice and seen for what it was. Mike suspected that this child in question (Susan's bewitched offspring) was named either Sudra or Sundra because he thought he had heard Susan calling the child by a similar name but, naturally, he tried to put the fact out of his mind, so that his hawling would be more effective when the time came. He even put the fact of his ability to <hawl> out of his mind. Yet another word that evidently had gone missing somewhere along the fading spectrum between two or more minds—but there was, so far, nobody narratively *compos mentis* around these parts to reconcile any differences.

He gingerly walked across the park ground. He wondered what stage of the housework Amy would by now have reached. Cleaning the bedroom carpet was never a joke and only attempted by Amy once in a while. He glimpsed Susan and her two children (including Sudra or Sundra) playing on the distant swings and he even thought he saw Susan waving at him. She wasn't always that friendly. Mike was a hawler, after all, and most people instinctively treated hawlers with a cold respectful shoulder—or, otherwise, they would have given away their presumptive knowledge of any hawler's identity. Mike, if he thought about it at all, believed himself to be the only hawler left in the country, if not the world, or the only *practising* hawler. He felt tears prick out at the thought of Amy. The ground was cousin to the carpet as he sensed his feet shudder, listen to his thoughts and plumb his sorrow. Others felt such shudders as imaginary earth tremors or, at least, that was the best thing to believe them to be. Upon any other way, lay madness.

Or a plate of sizzling beef. But, first, duty called as Mike plucked up enough courage to approach Susan and her children, leaving any residual thought of Amy to the vacuuming.

Amy talked to herself. She imagined knives and saws and axes, with blood along the tips of their edges. Mike often created images like these in her mind.

"What to do," she asked or stated. The carpet cleaner churned noisily, cutting out such thoughts before they hit the fuse with a deafening spark of the earth wire failing.

She was back a few years before. Mike had not come into her life as yet. She was still living as a child at home with her mother and brother. She recalled that her brother had always been a bit of a loner, non-expressive and wild. He concocted experiments with household goods, mixing them into a chemical syrup by means of adding garden mud to substances like washing-powder, disinfectant, flyspray. These misalchemies were alive—at least in her brother's eyes and Amy laughed as she remembered their mother's remonstrations of despair while she tried to talk sense into her son but merely ended up communicating with the "cowpats" of mixture he had left in his wake. At least he did the experiments outside. And indoor fireworks only came out of Christmas Crackers in those days, so they were not an all-year problem: those sizzling wormcasts on the seasonal carpet. That was a Godsend.

Amy couldn't remember her brother's name. It was as if he had never existed. Her mother was a Mrs Cole, Edith to her friends. Amy was *afraid* of remembering her brother's name because, by dragging it from the past, trawling it via the coarse-grained muslin of memory's filter, she could too easily tug or tussle through into the present more dangerous element of the past, undoing, in the process, everything Mike had since done up for her. Untying the nemonymous knot would release a booby-trap—and she continued scraping the lower surface of the vacuum across the grit in the carpet that had collected there like any dust collects there... from wherever dust and grit and, indeed, stains come from—a mysterious source only hawlers are able to fathom.

She couldn't really countenance that Mike had more than one job on the go at once. She wanted to be his only subject—because being a hawler's subject was not dissimilar to being in love. Unadmitted love, true, but love nevertheless. Dreams came from below, not above.

She shrugged, turning over the vacuum and emptying it of what it had collected. A scene of a park so cultivated its grass was more like a plush lawn for the toes of effete royalty or fairies. She saw it in her mind's eye, but failed to recognise the fey walkers that positively languished in its heady Proustian delights.

Amy had once been a child herself—self-evidently.

"Amy! Where's Arthur?" screamed Mrs Cole. Edith looked out into the garden where Arthur should have been at this time of day, especially bearing in mind his slippers on the floor and his coat gone from the door-hook. Amy was nowhere to be seen. The meat in the oven was burning, so she rushed off to adjust the temperature gauge—knowing that slowly-slowly-caught-the-monkey. Amy was never a worry, as she spent her time not worrying. Someone who didn't worry never gave worries, Mrs Cole knew this instinctively without articulating the thought. On the other hand, Arthur was a big worry—as he always worried about going out, worried about fulfilment, worried about the ever-increasing need to mix quantities of the world together to see what gave.

Mrs Cole, having finished with adjusting the oven, knew that one of her two children was bewitched and the evidence pointed to Arthur. She reached the apartment window again and eagerly scanned the inner square between the walls of the four blocks that formed it. There was a solitary fountain at its centre—and a few all-weather seats surrounding. Not much for children to do in the square but it was certainly better than the city streets amid which this square was a relatively safe oasis. She saw a huddled figure on one of the seats and, believing it to be Arthur, she called from the window for him to come in. She'd forgotten why she needed him to come in at this precise moment, but the need was one that had become a bee in her bonnet. The white face looked up. It was Amy. And Mrs Cole unaccountably shed tears... followed closely by desperation as she saw a taller figure enter the square. Anyone needed to enter the square via the apartment blocks—so the place was not exactly public but the security was lax. And where was Arthur? The figure in the square was too tall to be Arthur although he *was* growing too quickly these days.

Being at the higher end of the block, Edith Cole felt helpless, should there be any crisis moments in the square far below.

The head teacher had just announced his visit by the officious knock on the apartment door. He'd come up in the lift. No doubt there was some problem with Amy or Arthur. Or even both... at once.

"Hello, Mr Clare," said Mrs Cole, opening the door. She had put any problems to the back of her mind, as if she predicted even bigger problems arriving via Mr Clare. "I'm glad to catch you in," he announced, not waiting for an invitation to enter the flat.

Mrs Cole wondered why he hadn't made an appointment. This was the second time he had arrived this way. She planted her feet on the ground, expecting the worst, bracing herself for something dreadful she didn't really want to hear. But a carpeted floor several levels up in the air was hardly the *ground*, and she felt no assistance from this attempt to earth herself. "Get a grip!" she said quietly to herself between gritted teeth. She heard several conversations coming up to her from below—a cacophony of different groups of families in the cross-section of abodes beneath her feet. They spoke of frightening things, childish things, trivial things…

"What can I do for you? Would you like a cup of tea?" Mrs Cole was still an attractive woman and she knew Mr Clare better than he knew himself. She could see it in his eyes.

At this moment, Arthur arrived, Amy in tow. They must have spotted their head teacher arrive from wherever they had been in the building. Arthur's hands were covered in some sort of heavy-duty grease, as if he had been oil-changing a large truck. Amy dragged a tiny toy trailer behind her, in which was seated one of her dolls. A large ugly one, more in keeping with a punch-

and-judy show than one in a little girl's keeping: it almost looked knowing enough to be alive. Yet she loved it as if it were real plastic with mock synthetic hair and badly painted rosebud lips.

"Would you like to stay for dinner, Mr Clare?" Edith had advanced from offering tea to giving him the chance to share the meat sizzling in the oven. He had not really answered but had decided to occupy the armchair in front of the old-fashioned TV, without even a word. The fact he had caught Mrs Cole at home seemed in itself sufficient to create a successful mission.

The trouble was that not one of them knew what the others were thinking. Yet there had to be a lot of sympathy for all of them and that sympathy cost more sympathy, growing and growing cumulatively as the events overtook them at later stages some of which would never be known, let alone described. Each person would take turns to feel... to feel deeply... for the others and themselves. All that was needed was patience. Meanwhile they were simply playing at life, without understanding any of its rules.

Mike was quite ordinary and nobody around was expert on what made any man tick—so that all that could be said about him was his ordinariness. Not exactly nemonymous—in the true sense of that strange word we all grew to know... eventually... despite its difficulty to say or to understand, because that would have implied that he was anonymous to the point of non-existence. And Mike sure could lift a few spirits with just a few chosen words from beneath his mask of ordinariness. He lived a full and useful life because of his ordinariness rather than despite it.

Although ordinary, he felt responsible, more responsible for the world's affairs than he had the right to be. At an early age, he had felt the hawling power in his mind, in his hands: a power that actually was fed by the ordinariness that was his essential default. He saw—instinctively—layers of people passing down a lift shaft, spending time on each floor till they either reached the ground or the top. These layers of people were going both ways, in fact, not just down, passing each other, sometimes changing direction more than once, but staying, for a while, nevertheless, on each floor—getting to know the others on that floor, then proceeding on... downward, after all, or, yes, upward. Hawling was not dissimilar to being a liftman, pressing the buttons, allowing beings to board or disembark as each floor light flashed and resulted in the lift-doors sliding aside... new strangers coming in, old strangers leaving, but there was more to hawling than that—it was running a butcher's shop, listening to the carcasses crack as you lay in bed at night. He was also transporting fossil fuel from the depths of the earth (where the earth's soul was most attentive) to the surface for the fires of life to be lit and smoulder on... and eventually extinguish with a dying wink... which meant more fossil fuel was needed to be fetched from Mike's mine. It was all this... and more. Mike would only discover the 'more' when the time was ripe or if he became mine, if not me, himself.

He had just watched Amy Cole riding up and down the utility supply shaft of some inner city tower. Her brother, whose name was unknown or forgotten, was the one she was seeking, having lost him in childhood, when they were both suddenly orphaned. Their mother had been hauled off from them one unexpected day whilst they both played outside among the makeshift dams and rivers of slurry which pleased her brother so much. Amy even lost Amy, lost, at least, who she was and what her years were or bloodcourses were.

Mike had then watched someone else. Susan and her two children running through an unkempt, shaggy park, among stub-winged birds flapping from bush to bush, hardly using the air at all. They were all chased by a figure in a cape. Mike desperately wanted to help them but, temporarily, his hawling skills were stunted by the experiencing of the traumas of other families slipping through several dissolving floors towards a huge pit in the earth.

Mike woke in a cold sweat. He put one foot outside his bed to ensure at least his own bedroom floor was still there. Amy snored beside him, mercifully, it seemed, free of the dreams that had just beset him... or were still besetting him.

Mike often reminisced about the time he worked in an office, mostly as an administrator, but also as a consultant or salesman, a business that often concerned very complex financial matters. He used to entertain clients at sporting events or orchestral concerts, lunched important representatives from other Companies, attended Board Meetings across the country, driving all manner of distances in a day. He couldn't do this now, but, in those earlier days, he used to manage stress much better. It was almost like a dream. He had a family, then, too—Susan was his wife and his two children Amy and Arthur. Amazingly, they were still his family today, having put up with him all these years. The children had grown up, of course, and left home. It was just him and Susan now. Susan went out to work and he stayed at home: a token househusband. So, there was a lot of time for reminiscing.

His body was the most mysterious thing about him. He could easily fathom his own mind—but his body felt like impersonal meat on a base of bones: somehow disconnected from the ground that he—his mind—walked upon. Self-cannibalism did not occur to him, obviously, because, if it had, he would certainly have considered himself mad. Bad enough even to *skirt* such touchy subjects amid the other reminiscences, let alone delving into them.

Those corporate entertainments he remembered as uncomfortable sessions, when he often felt invisible. Eyes grazing him, edging even nearer but, just as quickly edging away to gaze elsewhere. He used to try to fathom the faces in the dance of business and artifice—and wondered if any real minds lay behind them, as they tried, like him, to balance a drink and plate, whilst making small talk before the concert started. Brahms' Double Concerto with Nigel Kennedy and Robert Cohen playing the violin and cello respectively—the concert music easing away the thoughts, as Mike merged with the rest of the audience who, eventually, clapped as one entity: one nemonymous creature of applause with the merged thought that they remained single entities.

The clues as to what a hawler really *is* sometimes come together piecemeal, often obliquely—rarely in great moments of clarity.

Amy had finished the vacuuming. The man she knew as Mike often popped in so as to see how she was doing. He evidently fancied her. She needed to be checked by someone at least and Mike was representative of the Letting Agents. He needed to follow the rules and rub a finger over a sideboard top to see if it collected dust. He turned a blind eye to the carpet. In any event, Amy's job did not reach beyond vacuuming it—and any deeper cleaning would have to be commissioned from a specialist steam-cleaning organisation. Mike usually trusted her to lock up after she finished. A good working relationship. No doubt, one day, he would try more than just fancy her from a distance—she knew. Men were like that, despite the existence of a wife and two children. He referred to his wife as 'the wife', but perhaps hawlers were allowed to have more than one wife; indeed, one day, believing X was his wife, whilst, the next day, believing Y was his wife—and on those separate days, he was only aware of either X or Y respectively, depending on what day it was. Hawlers were a confused bunch... if there were more than one hawler in the first place, and Mike may have been the only one.

Amy shrugged. She had her own two children to worry about and that's why she did these housework jobs for the Letting Agents. Mike gave the impression that he'd once had a job better than checking on skivvies like her. Amy put the vacuum into the broom cupboard and left for the lift. She was confused about Mike. She did not even know the existence let alone the meaning of the word hawler.

Often, she even wondered who *she* was. A busy life made her like that. She laughed at herself as the lift left the floor behind.

At the centre of the earth there exists the strongest power in the Universe. All life radiated from this centre, gradually becoming fossilier, bonier, meatier, livelier, airier in various stages of animation from dead to aethereal. At a certain stage between meat and life sat the people that revolved around and radiated from each other in a dance of fiction or friction. Only the real was excluded because nothing real could be imagined and, in turn, that was because imagination could only possibly imagine things that were unreal. Only hawlers knew of the various layers through which anything or anyone could travel.

Mike was at his golf course, during those heady days when he was a businessman. Susan was at home faithfully caring for the two kids whilst Mike surveyed the dips and dunes—almost *feeling* them with his golf mind—as he took stance for his first teeshot of the day. Golf was instinctive, knowing the contours, assessing the relief map between him and the hole... and as his arm swung back, he trawled the air with his clubhead for the invisible creatures that would eventually guide his tiny hard white ball above the alchemically magnetic layers of ley-line and geomantic quirk that only these creatures could fathom.

Susan was silent. It was too early to start preparing Mike's dinner. Her friend Amy had just left. The two women had a lot in common, both having two kids of similar ages and sexes. A good feminine chat whilst these kids were at school and the husbands elsewhere—that was always a good tonic. But now she was alone with her own thoughts. Often a dangerous thing to be sunk eye to eye with nemonymity. One needed other people to allow oneself to exist at all. And the potential of her family's homecoming was not strong enough to radiate back in time to stiffen the sinews of her existence. One of her children was currently non-existent as was one of Amy's children…

Susan shook her head. Two out of four children. She cried. She began to hear something breaking the silence, something she didn't understand equally as much as she didn't understand the words in her empty head. The sound of a cricket ball smacking the meat of the willow with a resounding echo... or, rather, a small white hard egg-pod being squashed to smithereens by the coal-pick beneath her feet, or between them.

Arthur Cole—despite all his damming games with the sand, earth, household chemicals etc.—became a bus driver. His sister, Amy, used to stand by his side, all the other passengers assuming this to be a flirtatious bus-driver groupie girl who often stood by the steering-wheel chatting about this, that and the other, fancying anyone in trousers especially if his control of a huge vehicle like a bus gave his manliness an edge it wouldn't otherwise have had. But in this case, it was the driver's sister disguised as a bus driver groupie, telling him surreptitiously when to turn left and right amid the maze of ratruns and back-doubles that the city had become in recent years. She was his 'brainwright': an old word for someone who acted as a brain for someone else.

Since the days they lived with their single mother in an apartment intended for fewer than three, there had been long periods when Arthur was in and out of Care Homes, especially ones specialising in their own variety of 'brainwrighting'... until Amy herself was old enough to take over such duties—their mother having vanished as had a replacement father figure who had been living with them for a while until eventually vanishing himself... gradually.

They couldn't remember his name. They couldn't even remember their mother's name or, rather, they had deliberately blocked it out. The man's name they had genuinely forgotten.

It was a miracle that Arthur managed to find a job at all, let alone such a responsible one as a bus-driver in the city. The fact that his sister was always at his side dressed as a flirtatious bus-driver groupie had been missed by the bus company's inspectors. Arthur was a good instinctive driver—despite all his driving documents being forgeries.

One day, he was destined to use his bus as a get-away vehicle (with passengers still on board) but that was irrelevant to the events that followed each other—at least semi-logically—in the guise of a story that stood by his side like a narrative thread he followed by means of the metaphysical steering-wheel of his life. Many of the events didn't directly affect Arthur at all, but those events were directly affected by Arthur.

Returning to his childhood days—when the shadowy mother and father figures were still shimmering like technical interference on a TV screen—his ability to get his hands dirty by actually delving the fingers deep into what he took to be the earth's crust (or rind) to obtain some purchase on its spinning (also as part of his messy damming river games for which he used the kitchenware substances) was really a dress rehearsal for driving a bus, although he did not realise that at the time, if he realised anything about anything. But certainly Amy—growing into a pretty girl and even prettier woman—knew instinctively that Arthur could control big things just with the flick of his finger.

Arthur dreamed one night of mixed ambitions competing with each other for the forefront of his brain (some eventually to be considered worthless and unmemorable by his waking mind) together with worries about death and guilt... and of crawling forward through a long hedge where it was relatively easy to proceed with only the slightest tear by plant-spike and sting by nettle, until he reached an impenetrable clump at the end edge of the hedge, whereby he had to retreat backwards with the spikes and nettles closing in quite violently as a result of the opposite direction of travel he was attempting to forge through the undergrowth which was resprung against his passage. The dream, however, was not quite so convoluted as the necessarily convoluted account of its own passage through Arthur's mind. The words for all this had been lost in transit. Maybe, if he retraced his footsteps, clarity could be hauled back, although, no doubt, with some difficulty. Another dream—this one more grounded in day-to-day life—was one of trying to park his bus each night outside his house, with Amy waving him into some very tight space between other vehicles. His back was once jammed right up to the vehicle behind, but it was only a small thing (a bubble car?) and this had quite a big gap behind itself to manoeuvre in reverse should it want to get out. Arthur's memory was of something even smaller than a bubble car, but this was probably a later twisting of the truth in the dream to match the verities of waking life.

Amy and Arthur lived together—and their neighbours must have assumed they were husband and wife or (more likely these days) boy friend and girl friend, rather than brother and sister. In real life, he was indeed a bus driver and didn't, of course, need his sister working as his brainwright (a word he hardly remembered, if at all, from somewhere or other, like hawler, weirdmonger and nemonymous)—and he did not, naturally, park his bus outside the flats, but left it at the bus garage at the end of his shift—a shift that usually entailed the night bus. Amy was a counter assistant at one of the local department stores—but sometimes she filled in (for extra money) as a supermarket shelf-filler of disinfectants, washing-powders, cleaning-fluids, fabric-conditioners etc. She was on carpets at the department store, spending most of the day arranging for fittings, after the customers—with her expert help—had chosen the pattern and quality of the carpet they wished to buy.

Still, then, the horrors hadn't yet started. Various strange words start to build up—as if against the dam of sanity: connections and misconnections which fracture and fragment dream and mix it with real life: an impending doom that gradually increases in sickly strength. In fact, little did they know, but the impending part of the doom was worse than the eventual doom itself.

Mike and Susan lived together on the other side of the city. Mike worked at a covered market—with his long-time caped colleague Crazy Lope (who should have been a Red Indian with a name like that but was more quite an ordinary girl-shafting ex-miner with an odd turn of corrupt phrase)—but it was the market itself that was the noteworthy element in the day's work. The area of the city where it was situated was not at all English in atmosphere but had a dark magical realism more akin to Eastern Europe. This is the first time—it has to be noted—that it has been made clear that most of the events under scrutiny took place in England. A fact that hadn't been realised until this comparison with Eastern Europe became necessary: i.e. inadvertently slipped out, as it were, in the cause of geographical context. All accomplished without any direct narrative intervention whatsoever…

The covered market had open sides but did have a robust roof, so it was not *strictly* open-air or covered. On some days—when the rain clouded in with untimely gloom—it looked more like a warehouse, especially after the market attendants closed down the sides with temporary wind-breaks: the entrances between these 'walls' looking more like the beginnings of downward spirals to underground railway stations where the peasants under-crossed the city between the various farms and smallholdings which employed them on the perimeter of the city. Mike dreaded going to work, in case he was dragged down and became mixed up with these transit groups who didn't belong to the city at all. The market work itself remained unclear, but Mike was good at it: he kept getting rises. Crazy Lope was not so lucky, if luck were indeed the cursor to success and failure in such settings.

Susan worked in a pub in an even more unsalubrious section of the city. It was the pub that many continually sought in dreams but forgot about seeking when they woke up. Well, it certainly fitted the bill, but she enjoyed working for the landlord called Ogdon. Anyone dreaming about this pub—unlike Susan who worked as a barmaid within its walls in real life—would be drawn towards it against their will, believing its regular drinkers to be rather low down in the scale of humanity. Both forbidding and attractive at the same time, but mainly forbidding most of the time; it was paradoxical that the attraction won when the forbiddingness was stronger than the attraction. But like all dreams, one couldn't quite get to the bottom of it. Susan, meanwhile, worked there—a real place she couldn't avoid as she needed the money.

Mike and Susan lived in a top floor flat in the city centre with their two children, Amy and Arthur. They just about made ends meet, with the help of Government tax credits. Anyone dreaming of this top floor flat would have the same feeling about it as the other dreamers felt about the pub where Susan worked and the same feeling as of yet more dreamers dreaming the covered/open-air market where Mike worked. A certain dread mixed with attraction: imagining the flat to be dirty, with threadbare carpets, rickety beds, greasy cookers, dubious bed-covers. And a feeling that sexual peccadilloes were rife with one or two men living there, one of these men the dreamer's friend in real life, so you did need to visit him (although this was a dream and you weren't really visiting your friend at all)—whilst, all the time, it was not dream for Mike and Susan who actually lived in that top flat, with their two children; it was their shelter, their life... where their ends met. Who had lived there before them was not relevant. Not relevant to Mike or Susan. Whether it be dream or real life.

When life is tough, most things take the backseat, everything, that is, except survival of oneself and of one's own. If buildings carried dreams (or, for that matter, if dreams carried buildings), it didn't matter because all one was concerned with was those buildings giving shelter or giving work.

Tonight, as the beginning of the drama is homed in upon, Mike and Susan are sitting on the couch in their top flat, ready to speak to each other: the children recently put to bed after TV's Children Hour: "Whirlygig" with Humphrey Lestocq and Mr Pastry. The Queen of England was still quite young and the end of the war was not more than about ten years old. The carpet was much older; and being new tenants they didn't know exactly how old or who had once trod its threads.

A vehicle—like a bus—doesn't touch the earth with its metal body but has a layer of toughened rubber-around-air between it and the road it treads.

Mike watched the bus turn the corner, its top blown off like a sardine can containing explosive sardines—just the bars of the seats being seen from where he stood. It must have just gone under a bridge too low for its height and those passengers seated on the top deck were either crouched low or decapitated. Mike winced. It would be in the newspaper tomorrow no doubt—but why hadn't the bus stopped? Or, rather, why had it now slowed? Not because of a bus stop, but because it had self-evidently just had an accident. A serious accident. Mike watched it wheel round the corner, thinking, as he did, of hit-and-run situations and where the bridge was likely to be. He couldn't think of a low bridge in the area. Hit-and-run. Like having children, then forgetting them... only for them later to become your friends and you don't remember them, so they are real friends, not your children, because your children can never be your real friends: too much customs duty to intervene…

He was on his way from work. He usually walked—and only caught the bus when it rained. Office work had its own life and customs; people who worked in offices were a certain breed. Mike wished he could work outside, like a labourer could or someone in an open-air market. Office-workers, on the other hand, not only watched 'Big Brother' on TV but talked about it in the office the next day. Office-workers had ambitions—of sorts. But the ambition usually involved jealousy rather than the intrinsic need to be promoted. Mike had been promoted beyond his own capabilities (as most office-workers were). He had the healing power—to make himself ignore how he was wasting his life in competing for petty duties... although, these days, he and his wife Susan were often invited to office receptions to entertain clients. This was a godsend to their social life and there was no obvious need for sitters, as nobody knew if they had children. They'd just watch TV otherwise—and bicker.

Mike's office was only round the corner whence he had just turned. It was an Advertising Agency with some really creative people—but Mike worked in Administration and only allowed creative jobs from time to time. One would never have known it was an Advertising Agency, because the building was a plain Sixties-built tower block with nothing to recommend it. It wasn't like that open-walled Eastern European market that plagued Mike's dreams as his real workplace but one he could never find afterwards. He wasn't paid much—hence the need to work overtime, as he had tonight. He shivered as the rain set in—and he wished he had caught the bus despite the vision of the freshly topped one that had disappeared from his memory by placing a street corner between it and him.

That evening, Mike returned to their home. It wasn't the top flat that some people dreamed about—with all those feelings of forbiddingness and sexual peccadilloes that shouldn't be entertained. It was the same flat, perhaps, as the one in the dreams—but now with redecoration apparent, nicer fillings and a slightly better position in the building, and a slightly better building itself.

"It's been a helluva day," said Mike. "Did you hear about the incident on the underground?"

Susan nodded as she placed his dinner on the table. He was red-faced from climbing the stairs from floor to floor (the lift being left unattended if not out of order)—and she was red-faced from the stove. They were apparently in their middle years, not yet having reached the bruised look that old age had in store for them, given a glimpse into the future. They had lost the youthful sparkle and any body-hair was tarnished with discolour or no colour at all. Mike was—and, probably, still is—a forthright man, but kept his distance and downplayed any passions. Susan, equally, but her eyes often sparked with anger for some, and anguish for others.

"Yes, terrible wasn't it?" she said as she sat down. The wireless played softly from the kitchen as she had forgotten to switch it off.

"That station that looks like an open market, round the corner from the office..."

She nodded, having previously heard Mike's description of it, although she never visited Mike in the area where he worked. Sometimes, she wondered if his description of it was the result of a dream, and it was merely a coincidence that it fitted in with the news report she had heard on the wireless.

"Well, when they started coming out the sides from under the roof... they were covered in blood. Even the walking wounded were terribly bloody, as if they should have been on stretchers. Soon, it was a whole army of them. We did what we could, till the ambulances arrived."

A crimson infantry, was not an expression that came easily.

"Did the air ambulance come?" Susan asked.

"At least one did but the roads are so narrow round there for landing. Its rotors were inches away from the office's back wall—and actually sliced through the open empty edges of the station itself."

Coincidentally, last night, he had had a dream of being flown in a helicopter. It was unclear now but he had not before been in one in real life, but it was just as he imagined it. He was normally afraid of flying and, in his dream, the dreamer vaguely recalled this fear from real life... as the helicopter slanted close to some trees, almost entering amongst their branches—and he fully expected it to crash, but it landed in the grounds of some Italian Villa.

The air ambulance, that day, near his office, had also looked precarious as it landed between the buildings and really huge compared to its air size.

"They took away some of the wounded but I couldn't see how they decided which patients would go by air and which by road."

"First come, first served," she suggested.

Later that night, Mike lay awake trying to imagine sleep away whilst sleep itself imagined him awake. He got up for a sluice; and saw that the floorboards in their living-room were bare. The floor itself was several floors up but, tonight, the instinct was different. They were very close to the ground without even space for ratruns or airflows. This was no dream. It was so real.

He wondered if a burglar had stolen the carpet. But why? All the furniture was still in place.

He found himself delving into the wood of the floor as if he had found an opening in human flesh—a natural vent, rather than one he had forced open with his fingers. That babies were to emerge, one by one, not twins, but multi-aged siblings, did not occur to him until he discovered himself delivering them... through the floor. The ground was speaking by giving birth. Thinking, too. And he felt its thoughts as if they were his own thoughts.

When Mike and Susan suddenly found themselves with children, they thought they had always had children... ones named Amy and Arthur... hauled to the surface from the coal-face of the world's creation.

Mike listened to their crying from the cots in another room. Susan was off working in Ogdon's pub. Mike had never visited the pub because he didn't really want to see the conditions of her work... he'd feel guilty. Working in an open-air market was far below his own original ambitions as a child. He had the ability to get a far higher paid job, even it were in an office. Once his creative abilities had almost allowed him to secure quite a high position in an Advertising Agency. His CV had let him down however and allowed someone else (similar to him) through the back door, leaving Mike with a destiny he would not normally have chosen.

Tears came to his eyes as he looked back at the various paths he could have picked on... chipping away at the cornerstones of Fate so he could make the turning towards the goal he had once set himself.

In the distance, he heard the lonely sound of a helicopter—vanes clacking lugubriously—followed by the equally lonely drone of an air-liner as it passed empty over the city. It was the deep echo that made it sound empty.

Air-liner? Hmmm. He laughed.

Susan wouldn't be home for some time. Pubs had funny hours these days. No licensing restrictions—and Susan mainly served the night people.

Arthur remembered his father, with tears, too. None of the families at this stage in their trees could recall the names of forebears, none of which were written down. Nobody cared to dig into the past to find their roots. That had grown deeply unfashionable with the genealogical obsessions fizzling out into inexplicable mass suicides. Such family research was now banned, naturally.

Arthur looked across at his wife Amy. A mere coincidence that it was his wife because having sisters was not a recognised relationship any more, following the genealogical obsessions. Arthur's hands were covered in his own tears as they had brought his fingers too carelessly near his streaming eyes. He felt utterly nemonymous.

Mike woke from a dream. This had been a real dream. Others had not been dreams. They had been visions thrust upon him by some narrative trickery with a wild weirdmonger trying to force him down byways which his destiny had no right to encompass.

Mike knew a real dream from a false dream. The former often contained words he'd never use, words he didn't understand. Or was it the other way? Distinction was clear, if not the terms of the distinction.

He straightened the direction-finder of his reality, although this was a subconscious act as he shrugged off any aberrant forces working on him. He was a worker, a drone. He worked in a hive. He laughed. He worked at an Advertising Agency, he had a lovely wife, two lovely kids and plenty of money—and lived on the ground floor of a palatial block of flats on the edge of the city. His wife was homemaker. This was the truth. All else was dream and subterfuge. The compass point pointed steadily at it.

Until the next time.

The ceiling was quite ordinary, plain white, with a central rose whence the electric flex dangled towards its own pendant lampshade and bulb. In ancient days, before ceilings were invented, they would have had strange beliefs about ceilings, no doubt. That they were ghosts in disguise would have been the strongest and strangest. Some even believe that today.

John Ogdon—landlord of the pub where Susan worked—was dreaming of over-flying his own pub in a helicopter, except the roof was hidden by the large overhanging buildings in the same street. Either warehouses or tall covered markets, the dream didn't allow him to remember. He did remember, however, another dream when he was at a family dinner, believing himself to be one of the adults, so it was quite a surprise to find himself placed with the children on a lower table adjacent to the main table. It was only later he had lost touch with himself and, after a period of being literally a down-and-out, had struck a patch of good luck and been given the job of managing a downtrodden pub in the city.

He thought he saw his old friend Crazy Lope, a tiny figure negotiating the ratruns and back doubles: and at this time of day it was not surprising that he was one of very few individuals en route between two ends of their own business... hardly a time to be *idly* wandering, Ogdon thought, as his dream helicopter banked and disappeared further into the dark horizon of his sleep.

There was some kind of race through the house, but it was unclear who was racing whom and whether it was me or him or her or us or you being chased—but certain was it that the house was a palatial one or rather a large stately house through the ornate rooms of which visitors would normally be guided. All I knew (if it *was* me) was that I seemed to possess far more stamina than I expected myself to possess at my age—*and* nimbleness. As the painting-hung walls sped past, I managed to keep well ahead of my pursuers, negotiating the various corridors and, even, the ups and downs of trapdoors, oubliettes and attics. Yet most of these areas were well lit and it remains unclear (even today) whether the race was in earnest, life and death, or merely a game.

The helicopter hovered about the country house, it seemed, for hours, hanging from the white ceiling that was the sunless sky. It was reconnoitring or spying for forces that remain mysterious until this very day. At points, one could even just discern the goggled pilot sitting stiffly in his bulb.

John Ogdon looked up from his paper, as Susan walked into the bar for her turn of night duty. Despite his down-to-earth occupation (*if* supplying processed alcohol via a pub was indeed down-to-earth rather than spiritual by intoxication), he had been day-dreaming about floating above the sparkling sea in the early morning, upside down in a helicopter or balloon (more likely the latter as there seemed to be no noise) where the scintillating waves' expanse between four identical wall-to-wall horizons was a ceiling or watery underside of some far firmer roof beyond it.

Day-dreaming was quite different from doing it during the night. Less control.

Ogdon shrugged. He needed to get back to the state of the bar's surface—preparing himself to get his own hands dirty. The pub's cleaner was missing—hauled off to attend to some personal morbidity, apparently. He laughed at his own turn of phrase. He would also need to persuade Susan (officially a barmaid) to get stuck in.

"How's Mike?" Ogdon's voice failed to disguise his own irritation at the happenings of the day. The inner laughter at the wordy surrealism of his mood was already wearing off. His face looked more like a policeman's than a pub landlord's. His stomach flatter than that of his own caricature.

"OK. But the roof's leaking. That's why I'm a bit late." Susan never questioned her own state. Life was to be accepted, whatever what. She was half attractive, half determined to accentuate the other half.

"Children?"

Susan had to think for a moment. Life sometimes took you by surprise, even with its own ingrained acceptance of fixtures and habits. How could one forget one's own children? It was their bedroom that was leaking.

"A bit damp." She laughed.

Without explaining her quip—but, depending on previous information she had given Ogdon, she looked out of the pub window before embarking on the cleaning which she didn't really need to be told to do.

She caught a glimpse of a figure of a caped man disappearing into the black backdrop of a huge liner in Dry Dock, as if he had nearly been caught ear-wigging their conversation. The cranes on the liner and its gantries reminded her more of an old-fashioned coal mine where chains hauled up and down the man lifts. She knew it wasn't that, but it seemed more appropriate that it should be. She heard the distant clanging of heavy-duty engineering—

and she wondered, perhaps for the first time, how the liner had been transported here (so far from the river or the sea) and for what reason. This area had, she knew, been the site of a Dry Dock for several generations.

Tonight, Susan's sister was coming in together with her husband, Susan's brother-in-law, but at the moment there was just one solitary pub regular talking about a dream he had had the previous night. He was talking to himself, in truth, but Susan pretended to listen to enable him to believe that he was not just talking to himself, although he was.

"I was part of a crowd coming into the pub—a special rough cider was being offered at cheap price from a wooden cask. I wasn't me in the dream but someone else. Good job as I don't usually like cider and even though it was just a dream, I could really feel the bits of real apple with my tongue…"

Susan nodded as she proceeded to polish the bar, ready for the 2 a.m. rush. Why there was always a rush at that time was mysterious. Probably because various parties threw out their guests roughly at that time.

The regular nodded, too, as in agreement. He was not invited to the parties in the first place.

It was at this point that Susan's brother-in-law swaggered into the bar.

"The road's hairy!" he shouted, as if his sister-in-law would understand.

"Where's Beth?" she asked anxiously.

"Oh, following on—she's got a loose hair to clip back into place," he announced sarcastically: his way of saying she had gone straight to the loo.

"Hairy road?" queried Ogdon from the other side of the bar, where he was emptying the fruit machine.

"You don't expect roads with uncut verges, edges with hedges—and pavements with long weeds—in the city," was the reply, as if this explained everything.

"No," said Ogdon... knowingly.

A few more customers had already arrived—without Susan noticing—in advance of the 2 a.m. busy period. She half-expected Mike, because a childless couple, as they were, could have a devilmaycare attitude with regard to the necessity of sitters or minders. Wishful thinking, perhaps, because another advantage of childlessness was quiet sleepful nights, but that was lost on Mike and Susan as they often spent most of the night awake in any event.

One of the new arrivals was Greg—an ex-office worker—who had been made redundant and often told of his experiences in trying to get back into that sort of work. But the longer it went, the harder it would be, particularly as his appearance was fast approaching the nature of the "hairy road" that seemed to be preoccupying her brother-in-law. Beth had not yet appeared from the loo.

Greg meandered on about a recurring dream: as if Susan was interested! But on he would meander: "I go back to the company I used to work for time and time again—and many of my ex-colleagues have been promoted—and I have to wander the corridors of a new office block... knowing it's also the *same* office block—looking for a previous colleague who I used to be in charge of... so that he of all people can show me the ropes of the slightly different procedures..."

He gave a sob as if the dream were real and it certainly was real when he was dreaming it—so not much of a logic there. Susan felt sorry for him but was soon re-preoccupied by the arrival of Beth. A blonde curvier version of herself, with all the mutual envy and recrimination that that implied: filtering both ways.

By the time Crazy Lope arrived, not long after Mike's own arrival, she knew all these people had not met in Ogdon's pub tonight by coincidence. It was exactly 2 a.m. and she was not surprised when Ogdon bolted the front door—and all of them left together by the back one in the shadow of the liner in Dry Dock—if shadows could be cast at this time of day when most of the lighting was at foot level, dim though such lighting was. So late even the night buses had stopped running, parties or not.

They became a search party. For two missing children.

If children suddenly realise they exist, they ask themselves whereto the rest of their past childhood. Were they brother and sister, they wonder, or completely unrelated and, thus, perhaps, childhood sweethearts incubating a future marriage when they would tell their own children of their erstwhile romance resulting in their children's own subsequent existence as children. But, for all they knew at this crosspoint of time, they may have common parentage, and they hugged in the cold darkness—in the vicinity of the open-walled market—one hug as childhood sweethearts, the next hug as siblings, believing they gambled on one hug being true, choosing, as it were, between a belief in God and a non-belief in God. Both equally comforting.

They had not *become* lost. They could hardly recognise themselves as lost, but lost they were. They realised that 'becoming' was not a necessary pre-cursor of 'being'. Only adults didn't understand that—and there were many years in the pipeline before Amy and Arthur would become non-understanding adults themselves. One pipeline, perhaps, leading to a more mature love affair, another pipeline to estrangement as argumentative siblings.

The late night bus passed in the distance, leaving a heavy silence. Although the darkness was cold, these two children were not cold at all. They had a carpet over them like a stiff blanket, having discovered it in a nearby dereliction, unpinned from the floorboards that it had once hugged as a soft underfoot surface—and, strange though it may sound, it was free of its floorboards because the floorboards had been stolen by a burglar for building a shed. Not that the children knew that history and only a dream could explain how the carpet's subsistence survived its lack of foundations. It had sagged towards a cobwebby heart where red-eyed rats lurked but spared the children knowledge of the true extent of their maggoty existence. The carpet, surprisingly, had well survived the damp hollowness beneath it... and now provided a very serviceable blanket as the children speculated on the basic story-telling that underpinned their wherewithal as "babes-in-the-wood". Better out here in the open city than in that ramshackle rat-den. A carpet was not as snugly body-hugging as a proper blanket would have been, but the sky seemed distant enough to hide the pin-pricks that were its perforations for heat absorption. The sky shaped itself to a larger body... and Arthur told Amy this was God's shape and the sky hid the top flat where He lived and where, one day, they'd seek Him out in His bed. Arthur knew he, Arthur, lied, because city flats (especially top floor ones) were always seedy and bent out of any sane shape of comfort. Yet the concoction or myth gave a believeable context (i.e. God living in a city flat) and, thus, comfort to both of them, even the liar.

At the centre of the earth, there is a face—pock-marked, pox-mouthed—in three dimensions as faces should be if they front the heads that wear them. There is blood seeping from every pore, from every pustule... and the nostrils dangle a rubbery blood that bloats bigger and bigger without ceasing to be rubbery—neither exploding or imploding. And the tongue speaks through bubbles of blood hawled from a chestful of hard core: "For once this is no dream—this is fucking real—so deal with it!"

Mike took Susan's hands. They had found each other yet again, destined, perhaps, to find each other time and time again. Each a romantic epiphany, but equally horrifically real in the implication of needing to find each other time and time again. This time they knew their children were lost and this accentuated the horror, coupled with a wondrous fruition and fulfilment if they could find them. While thinking of people—like John Ogdon, Crazy Lope, Greg the office-worker, Beth and Beth's husband—Mike had forgotten his name, forgotten indeed that Beth's husband was Susan's brother, if in fact that was true. However, it was a search party, although 'party' was certainly the wrong word, too.

Mike tried to drag logic from the illogic of his mind, tried to explain something to Susan that he couldn't really explain to himself properly—as they followed the others across the night landscape that lifted the city skyward.

"It's like that TV programme, Suse, isn't it—you know the one. Where they evict people from the house gradually. But this is the other way round, where people are voted into a scheme of reality which fits the reality as we see it…"

"Yes," said Susan, neither encouraging nor discouraging his blurted rambling tones that cut the night air.

"…like now, tonight, it's as if we're fine-tuning everything, looking for new housemates, even children to complete the picture. But also do we know who is acting true to themselves, not emotions so much as nemotions…" Mike's wordy speculations were his method to avoid the critical repercussions of the search itself. Like doodling with philosophy as he might have fiddled with prayer-beads. Susan nodded. She'd heard Mike's rambling thoughts before, very simply expressed on the whole but peppered with words she couldn't understand like nemonymous, weirdmonger and big brother, although she had heard of the book "1984" and some other things that were relevant, having known them as part of a tribe consciousness rather than as a product of her own personal learning. Mike, she knew, was a hawler but, in her mind, she spelt it as 'hauler' and she didn't know what it meant, but it seemed natural, nevertheless. The TV programme to which he referred was a mystery. He'd probably watched it when she was out working in Ogdon's pub, a pub, thankfully, without a TV or a juke box.

Near to the open-walled market or underground station, there was a tall building, access to which was by lift—indeed a very complex lift system which Greg often used before he was made redundant from his job in that building. He used to entertain business clients and had to help them negotiate the lift system—changing on specific floors for different lift shafts of higher reach. Some shafts were more palatial and business-orientated than others, some so narrow they could only be used for brooms or very thin utility workers. The highest shaft reached the open air area, leafed over like a wood. From there, once, Greg was sure he could see the distant sea through the unusually clear sky into which the wood penetrated. He imagined a finer, less definable surface barely above the sea but otherwise imitating its waves and swells—a double skin in perfect unison, but the lower one liquid, the upper spectral. Perhaps the second one was the ghost of a giant flying carpet taking invisible human vessels towards Arabian Adventure or towards the darker motives of 'suicide' rather than 'seaside'.

Greg had surreptitiously left the search party. If a maroon-party is an elongated picnic, then a search party is a day's hide-and-seek game which lasts endlessly into an equally everlasting twilight—except, in the city, twilight didn't exist, changing, as it did, from day to night with the flick of a seeming switch. Mike and Susan soon lost hope in the efficacy of their companions—and had not seen Greg sloping off to look at his old office block. Ogdon, Beth and her partner, together with Crazy Lope, were fiddling with dustbins and not really getting stuck into the search proper—their excuse being a lack of stamina. Only Mike and Susan themselves, the would-be parents of the lost children, maintained a hard workload of search. They did hide themselves, sometimes, to test out the others' search capacities and were continuously disappointed when they kept on being undiscovered in whatever easy hiding-place they found. So if not them, what chance the children? As yet, nobody even knew the names of the children.

In one test hiding-place, Mike and Susan had stayed a little longer. They had stared into each other's teary eyes and fondled their bodies between them... acting more like new sweethearts than seasoned spouses. They even believed, for an instant, they were themselves the children they sought! Meanwhile, time itself gradually dammed up against the tangible delay the two of them set up to test the other seekers' ability to undam it.

Dixon of Mason & Dixon was said to have been born in a coal mine. The two children had been forgotten somehow. Just silly worded day-dreams had intervened with certain members of the search party as they took a well-deserved rest at dawn beneath the shrinking shadow of the liner in its Dry Dock berth, floating upside down amid their clouded thoughts, as if the brightening sky were its sea. One word kept coming to Mike's mind and he couldn't fathom how he fully understood its meaning without actually understanding it at all—and why it kept returning to his mind unbidden or untranslated. He wasn't even sure it was a real word: *côté*. Looked French, but was it? This was the sort of effect of dreaming a word during a night's sleep rather than the flickering tail of a day-dream at dawn, whilst the party rested from what—he now remembered—was a desperate search for two children. He looked at Susan who also stared dreamily towards the towering Dry Dock—and her eyes later told him that they had forsaken their duty by not earlier informing the Authorities about the children's disappearance. Many others in the search party had by now wandered off in twos and threes. Greg was the last to leave, as he would soon be due at work in his office. He shuffled papers as he walked away quite quickly for fear of being late. The excuse for his night's wanderings was now lost on him. If it were children that were missing, surely the police would have been informed. On that evidence (or lack of it), he knew that no children were missing at all. A logic that seemed quite straightforward, as Greg entered the lift to take him to the top floor. Business-life always avoided any thought of crazy dreams and, for the next eight hours, he would not have the luxury of using his imagination.

Much of the building—including the lift that slowly lifted him between the walls of its inner space—represented a reality that could bear no imagination to be applied to it... although many of its constituents such as the walls that were towards its top, certain parts of the basement boiler room and rooftop garden, some of its I.T. (for example) yearned to be less real so that they could be imagined into existence for some satisfying or evocative fiction work. But the building was there, tangible, safe as houses in a scheme of actuality, and, therefore, it failed in its ambition to cease existing so as to become a shimmering fantasy fit for the wildest imaginings. Greg had the same feeling about himself. He was convinced he was less real than Mike and Susan (for whose lost children they had all been supposedly searching)—and these two were dozing at the moment near the open-air market and they did not know Greg had left them to go to work. The others in the search party were also more real than Greg himself, but that left him with the mystery of why he had forgotten their names. This begged the question—were things (living or dead) more real with names than without? If so, Greg knew his own name was Greg, which fact gave him a sense of well-being, although tinged with a subconscious regret at the loss of unreality that this entailed.

The power to imagine was perhaps the very Act of Creation in the first place.

Amy and Arthur slipped from beneath the carpet as the sun slowly lifted its upper edge above the market. Streams of office-workers emerged from the various wide entrances of the underground system—entrances so wide they almost blended into each other. They shaded their eyes as a shard of sunlight sharply sloped into a tall office block like a seaside aero-act. All grabbed their briefcases to their chests and hustled onward to their desks, fearful that, one day, they themselves would commit their own seaside act in some token of devastation... which was odd because, unless they dreamed it, they feared the devastation itself less than causing the devastation themselves.

Arthur helped Amy stand up—and they both shuffled upon the carpet, now using it as a lower surface rather than the upper one it had been when serving as a blanket against the night chill.

Instead of flying off on this carpet—as they would have done in a proper dream or an Arabian fantasy—they returned, as if by magic, to the room whence the carpet first emerged and where it had been downtrodden since time immemorial. Amy stretched and yawned, wondering how a carpet could ever have escaped from beneath the heavy legs of her bed. She had just been dreaming of the hawler—the first real image anyone had gained of such an entity, in dream or otherwise. It was as if each dream—each of everyone's dreams in the city and of the city—had been straining at the leash, forcing itself to depict—gradually and painfully—the hawler himself. A wide-faced creature masquerading as a man that lurked at the coalface of some underground powerhouse, whose only duty was to gather up all the material chipped away each night by several miners (Mine! Mine! Not yours!) and transported to the surface for processing. The full description—other than wide-faced—was still unclear. Additional dreams—not necessarily Amy's own—would be required before a fuller picture was obtained.

One irrelevant dream intervened, however, or it seemed irrelevant at the time—although the dream sickness as it developed and as it was better understood by dreamers and non-dreamers alike (and I think this was the first time it was pinpointed as a 'sickness' as such) did specialise, it seemed, in mock irrelevancy. This dream, then, was simply knowing—within the dreamer's mind—that it was a horror film and that all the people in the dream were really actors, but they were unaware, apparently, of this fact. So when the dreamer him- or herself saw the birth of a baby ape, it was simply known—without equivocation—that this would grow into a giant monster. Indeed, looking through to the hall (to where the "baby ape" had fled), there were seen various people treating a gigantic human figure with some respect and unsurprise, not knowing it was a monstrous creature quickly grown from the "baby ape" and that it was pretending to perform on the stage in the hall as part of some talent competition. It towered above all the normal people. The dreamer fled from the hall—where these things had been seen—to warn the rest of the town of what was happening under their noses. Was waking, however, before or after being caught by the monster relevant?

In a part of the city, there was a zoo. And it was known by the Authorities that any dream sickness affecting the rest of the city did not affect the zoo. There seemed to be individuals in charge of the city that the ordinary citizens failed to recognise—or ever to know they existed at all. These Authorisers, so-called, had some mandate to keep parts of the city as reservations of clear sense—where dream was clearly recognised as dream and real life as real life, and never the twain should overlap. Strangely, perhaps, the zoo grounds were one such reservation and those citizens suffering from the dream sickness often resorted there—on their holidays—just to be certain about themselves and about reality and, indeed, about the dreams that they still dreamed when at the zoo but they actually knew they were dreams, knew them for what they were. How they knew this fact was similar to going abroad to sunny climes for one's holiday—away from the cold, dank, often dark city—and believing it was for the sake of enjoyment and recreation, not the chore a holiday surely always was.

Here, at the zoo, the citizens knew similarly that they were free of deceiving dreams and what they saw—as they toured from cage to cage, enclosure to enclosure—were *real* animals and creatures. Only when the citizens were asleep, at the zoo hotel, did they know they would be in danger of dreaming—unlike in the surrounding city itself, where waking was no safeguard against surreptitious dreams taking over the minds: not day-dreams, but full-blooded dreams which one thought were real life when experiencing them. In the zoo grounds, however, such dreams were dreams, whilst waking was waking.

The entrance to the zoo was not at all imposing and it could have served as the gates of a small factory, where people came and went after spending the rest of their time in terraced back-to-back two-up-two-downs in the less desirable parts of the city. There was a turnstile—just a cover to indicate that this was a place for which you needed admission, as most zoos in other cities would need. No money changed hands and when people had time off from work they came here—all jolly and familified—and entered the place that was hidden by tall grey walls which made them feel they were indeed going to work all over again on their holiday! The turnstile was unimpeded and they emerged into an area around the first enclosure. In the distance could be seen the starts of corridors between lines of cages, the contents of which could not yet be seen, though their hubbub of loud meat could certainly be heard from this auditory vantage point just inside the turnstile. The first enclosure was empty, unlike the other enclosures beyond the cages, which, as visitors who had been here before could attest, were full of living exhibits yet to meet the gaze of greenhorn visitors. Why an empty enclosure was the first exhibit often mystified initial visitors, but this was soon explained as the various themes panned out in interlocking concertinas of myth and logic and as the total exhibition of the zoo revealed itself to the unpaying customers filing past.

The empty enclosure at the start of the tour—it was discovered—was a symbol of the loneliness of life and the even greater loneliness of death. Yet many claimed it was not a greater loneliness in death: for it was a greater loneliness in life. The paradox was not lost on the gaping citizens as they took their time off in the zoo. Many of them peered into the empty first enclosure, the children bawling in disappointment:

"Where are the animals, Mummy?" "You told me this was a zoo, Daddy!"

The parents tried to pacify their children by pointing to the corridors of cages where the zoo proper, apparently, would start—or so they promised. Meanwhile, it was their beholden duty to pause here a short time to view the empty enclosure in almost religious calm. Nobody, it was clear, took account of the insects that threaded the loose soil of this enclosure. Nobody realised this was an otherwise empty enclosure for insects. They wanted to see big things in a zoo. Life needed big things in the city.

Soon after by-passing the first enclosure, most visitors, in awed contemplation, would enter the first corridor of cages—a silence soon broken by the snorts, squeals and snickers of the first set of exhibits. Kept apart hardly at all by the cages, the exhibited could stretch limbs through the bars towards each other—and even uncomfortably close towards the visitors themselves. The latter cowered from the first cage only to find themselves backing towards another cage where something else was putting out feelers.

The remarkable fact—despite the circumstances—none of these caged creatures were as nightmarish as one might have assumed. Nothing could be nightmarish because this was one hundred per cent not a dream... and only dreams and their like could house nightmares.

Mike turned towards the others and said: "Quite sweet, aren't they?"

Nobody replied. They weren't so sure, because these initial cages seemed to house versions of the apes, a baby one of which had indeed featured in a dream dreamed by at least one of the party before entering the zoo grounds. Yet here, the apes could be clearly seen for what they were—apes with no potential to grow into man-mountains like Gulliver. That, Mike assumed, was what differentiated dreams from non-dreams. In the former, anything could grow into anything else. In the latter, things stood still ever as themselves. The status quo. They may be monsters in a non-dream, but they couldn't transmute into worse or different monsters.

They wandered further into the maze of cages, Mike in the lead. As a hawler, he could see things more clearly than the others, since he had travelled further underground in his consciousness and established fixtures and bases from which all else could be interpreted and evaluated: thus neutralising their ability to terrorize. Terror did not breed more terror, but less. Hence, Mike's justification in dredging more terror and horror into view, so as to neutralise it. He had not thought these things consciously—but when between bouts of dream sickness outside the zoo grounds, this had indeed been clearer, with the dreams themselves adding a needed logic of their own. Here, inside the zoo, Mike—although an instinctive leader—learned, from this prior in-built experience of dream negotiation outside the zoo, that, paradoxically, he felt himself to be at a loss in the uniform non-dream world of reality represented by the zoo around them.

The next set of cages was frightful and, if it hadn't been for the certainty of his logic, Mike would have been quite perturbed by the sights as they unfolded. It was as much as he could do to pacify the others in the face of a tentacular monstrosity that even the infinite star-fields (and what potential life they could conceivably hold) would not have been powerful enough to make possible.

Here they found Amy and Arthur whom they had been seeking all night throughout the city. They were pressed up to the cage bars as if in some desperate embrace with the monster that was contained by them.

Yet, nothing, surely, could be nightmarish outside a dream, a nightmare being merely a species of dream. Yet the two children—as Amy and Arthur still were inside the zoo—seemed actually tied outside the cage to its bars not by ropes and bindings but by the long locking claws of the beast that the cage contained. Mike and the rest of the search party quickly shuffled identities between them as none wanted to be responsible for leading a rescue mission towards this cage with a view to releasing the two children. Yet, this cowardly act could not be cowardly for long, because no sooner did one feel the cowardliness coursing through their veins than that same person felt an equal counterbalance of bravery... and they lurched forward to prise the children's fingers from the bars only quickly to realise that the fingers were not all the children's own—and cowardliness returned with redoubled force.

Meanwhile, Greg the office worker had rejoined the group unexpectedly—having followed the others after his lunch break into the zoo grounds—and had no time to be infected by the switching identities caused by an alternation of cowardliness and bravery. He had no second thoughts but to rush towards the cage and pulled the children away from whatever it was that kept them bound to the bars. Indeed, there was nothing in the cage... except a threadbare carpet lining the floor, a carpet peppered with indeterminate tiny droppings and sown with holes that needed darning.

The group were pleased to escape the zoo—via the back entrance which was not far from the underground market. They hadn't paid to get in but, somehow, they needed to pay to get out—as a man stood at a turnstile with his hand out. But the two children went free. All were pleased to escape without having their faith in the clear dream/reality dichotomy of the zoo undermined. They knew, however, once outside the zoo, each and everyone would be susceptible to the dream sickness. They needed a drink, so they sought Ogdon's pub—but the streets round the market had somehow changed from a negotiable pattern to one of mazy confusion. The two children were no longer children—and, having been rescued from their kidnapping, they returned to a more adult appearance and behaviour, treating Mike as if he were a child. Mike couldn't see Susan any more—but a certain loyalty to her memory forced him to stick by his promises to protect her against the onset of dreams, giving himself a more steadfast or statuesque image: a landmark around which the dreams revolved but which they could not affect. Susan would soon be able to return to this fixed point of Mikeness given the time and the inclination. He hoped against hope. He still loved her. This facility to be a fixed point amid the whirlpool of dreams that existed outside the zoo was akin to the ability of hawling: reaching to the core of the earth for one's bearings—and mining them for certainties and immutable compass points of direction.

He looked up into the sky. There was something lovely about a sky that was brightening with the arrival of day dream: dissipating the cloying nightmares that had just started to vanish from within themselves. A good hawler could plumb heights as well as depths for this brand of substance, sustenance and reassurance. Whilst it had been until now mostly land-locked, embedded with stone and grit, the sky (as he watched it) became the underbelly of a huge flying-carpet flowing diaphanously from horizon to horizon. Who flew upon it, he knew or at least he hoped he knew, were the nemonymous ones: angels and finer vessels of thought and spirituality. Beneath his feet, on the other hand, were weirdmongers and others of their name-driven ilk. A hawler, he knew or at least he hoped he knew, was a filter that worked in both directions of flow. But he only knew or at least hoped he knew for a while till he even forgot he was a hawler.

Susan woke beside her husband Mike in the bed she simply and unsurprisingly recalled falling asleep in. No better reassurance could there possibly be for getting one's waking feet on the ground. She wondered how—in her dream—she seemed to be named Amy. And Mike had been called Arthur. She wasn't sure how long the dream had lasted, but the actual reality within the dream had seemed to last a whole lifetime—until she awoke some time during the zoo sequence. Mike (or Arthur) had a role to play that nobody else could. As with most dreams, its sense of reality was fast fading as she continued to reach a full waking state—and the name given to this role tantalisingly escaped her.

She soon saw Mike standing at the open bedroom window watching a jet liner slowly cross from one side of the sky to the other. She left the bed and tip-toed along the carpet so as to give Mike a hug from behind. He would soon be off to the office and she to her barmaid's job. They had never made love other than at spontaneous moments. No pre-planning, and she reached round his body to see how hard he was. She nestled up to his buttocks, listening to him sigh, as they shuffled their feet deeper into the waking moment of the working day. The city was laid out in front of them like a map, the two of them being so high up as far as storeys were concerned. She yearned for the sea, where she had been brought up—yet the sight of the huge ship in Dry Dock on the city's horizon was more than just a little recompense. She listened to see if she could hear their daughter Sudra waking. This was her first day back at school. They had decided only to have one child—even though they both knew how difficult it was for 'only' children in later life. Mike and Susan both missed their brothers and sisters... almost as if they had once existed. Mike turned round—the sun etching his head like a black hole—and he took Susan in his arms, lifting high the bottom edge of her nightie so that she could snuggle up to him even closer. No fear of peeping toms—because the open window was a good Blackpool Tower or two above the now enlivening streets below. She felt him come inside like a huge welter of comfort—and the friction was just a side effect. It was at that moment Sudra had quietly opened their door—and she was old enough to laugh at her parents' predicament upon discovering they were being watched.

Sudra watched the city from the window, as if watching through the gaps left by her parents' clinging, cleaving to each other. It was her birthday today and she was expecting a welcome hug and a bountiful gift—yet all she saw were the bodies of the people she loved dissolving in the growth of sunlight... until even the bones themselves tingled slightly and then vanished. She rushed towards them over the carpet but only gathered curtains to her instead of parental love. Yet, love is invisible—even when the people "doing" the love are there. And Sudra could feel the love around her, even if there were no arms to gather her closer to that love. It would soon be time for school—and she walked off to the fridge to fetch milk and the kitchen cupboard to fetch cereal... yet her feet were becoming more and more draggy as she tried to reach the kitchen, as if the carpeted floor (several storeys up) had a magnetism greater than the earth's Core. Sudra could not even reach the body that was hers before it disappeared into the kitchen.

Mike turned round—forcing Susan also to swivel from the window in mid love-making embrace. He thought he'd heard a shuffle or a whisper—but there was nobody there. He picked up the freshly delivered newspaper from the table—as if shrugging off the extraordinary with the ordinary—and read the main headline:

MAD WRESTLING BY THE ANGEVIN KINGS

Without thought, he plunged it into his briefcase, and, waving a cursory backward greeting to Susan, he left for the office. Time had crept up on him and he was already dressed in his uniform of three-piece suit and bowler hat. This city lived in the Fifties and bowler hats were still evidently all the rage.

Mike had forgotten how he had been described in earlier parts so he assumed he'd always looked like this. Barely close-shaven hair in a crew cut before crew cuts were known by numbers for the respective choices of length. Bill Hayley and Elvis Presley were in the Hit Parade—milk bars full of pre-pubescent teenagers, because puberty was very late in those early days. The office—once he arrived—was full of massive desk-calculators (that, one day, could fit into the palm of your hand), surrounded by pipe-smoking jobsworths rattling at their numbered keys. Mike said a jolly good morning as he took his own seat in front of a calculator that was rare inasmuch as it had a ribbon of paper where his work was printed automatically for future posterity—churning out in endless ticketing spools as from an old-fashioned bus conductor's hand ratcheter. Still too early for his mind to be on the job—and he thought back to his walk to work, past the covered market, where many office-workers emerged as if they had been sleeping there all night—past the Dry Dock, the pub where Susan worked, the zoo gates—and before he managed to summon up sufficient concentration of will-power to face the calculator keys, he took a quick browse of the newspaper, the main headline being:

CHILDREN STILL MISSING

> An all night search of the innercity has produced no sign of the Angevin Twins—so further sweeps are soon to take place in the outer city towards the suburbs.

"They ought to try *under* the city," said Mike to himself. The Angevin Twins were the first-born of an important city family that had first grown rich over the generations by means of coal-mining on the Northern edge of the city. Mike had seen photographs of that area—big towers with turning wheels threaded by clunking chains, silhouetted against a sky that was more often as black as coal as it was ever blue. The prevailing weather thereabouts had made sure of that. Most citizens travelled south on their holidays and not even the weathermen could explain why it was generally brighter in that direction. Nothing concerning geography or science could justify such differences—almost as if the city seeped darkness towards its head... bearing in mind that its map was a direct representation of a human body: either purposefully or purposelessly reflected by the evolving architecture, town-planning and urban scrawl set in motion by the founding fathers all those centuries ago. On that symbolic template, Mike knew that before one reached the holiday areas surrounding the city's feet one needed to cross the standing water of a waste reservoir.

He looked into the mirror of the office toilet to remind himself of how he should have been described as a person—if anyone needed to describe him to any people who did not know him. He had just physically added to that standing water (of which he had just unaccountably pictured) and he smiled a smile which he decided was uncharacteristic of him when viewed in a mirror. He wiped his hands on a paper towel. Was this how hawlers were meant to look? A strong personal face with deep lines and searching brows. Black looks offset by sweet smiles? Only the nemonymous ones had tantamount to the blank expressions of those bodily projected ghosts on TV dramas—so he knew exactly what he was, down to the chipped toenails, even if he hadn't yet dared tell Susan and Sudra.

The office work had taken a backseat ever since the news broke about the Angevin twins. Nobody had given them a second or second's thought beforehand and maybe many of them knew nothing of their existence at all. The tea lady—pushing her steaming urn—had nothing else in her new gambits of conversation. Not long ago she had been on about the wayward progress of the latest evictions on 'Big Brother'. Now it was whether the Angevin twins had been kidnapped or simply run away like the Famous Five had to Kirrin Island.

None had been prepared for the startling information—and how important it would be for the city and its life—until the population had woken up to such breaking news: hearing of the twins' existence for the first time followed a few seconds later by more data upon their mysterious non-existence. The twins, before this extreme metamorphosis, had been surprisingly old for their age, so nothing was ruled in, nothing ruled out.

Mike tried to concentrate on his paperwork—without much enthusiasm—occasionally glancing up at his colleagues to whom he often remembered talking when times were more ordinary. It had indeed been a job where office politics often took sway—with alternating recriminations and reconciliations. Corporate entertaining of clients at sport and art arenas. Hitting the knuckle of the business with sensitive tweaking of figures and projections.

"How's your wife doing at The Third Floor?"

Mike's colleague—what was his name?—had actually spoken to him. The first attempt at conversation for several days.

"OK. Do you know her boss? Ogdon he is. He often serves behind the bar. Strange bloke."

Mike had answered, as if he had learned his lines parrot-fashion. Ogdon was known to most people. He used to run a pub near the office to where everyone had resorted at lunchtime for a boozy crush and exchange of business gossip. More was gathered at such gatherings... than gathering the proper statistics back at your desk. Life was human. Life could not be contained within restricted socks. Booze loosened the tongues and then facts flowed, too.

"Yes, Ogdon. I know him. In fact, I knew him before he was a pub landlord. He used to sit for days in a square between tower-blocks, by a fountain, writing novels…"

Mike's colleague might have continued, had not Mike himself brought the contrived conversation to an end with a throwaway line:

"Novels get you nowhere."

The bendy bus threaded the lower streets, having eschewed the mainstream for the back doubles. The windows were scratched by scores of cavalier vandals, who had tried to smash them just with their gaze until getting the milled edges of their shiny shillings to the glass in a pique of frustration that their lives were going nowhere fast. Arthur was behind the huge steering-wheel as the wheel tried to take him more than he was able to take the wheel. Much water had passed under the bridge since that time he and his sister Amy were sent missing: and even he couldn't remember the circumstances. He'd need a brainwright sooner. In a dream, he once believed he and Amy were some kind of Royalty with Franco-Anglo roots: and their disappearance had set the whole city into a quiver. Not at all like the true circumstances: just he and his grubby-faced sister taking their pluck in their hands to see if anyone really cared for them and escaping deliberately into the darkening streets rather than go home for tea. Just a test for their parents. To see if they had sufficient love to find them again. A crazy, mixed-up looking for nothing except for the goal of people looking for *them*. A quest for a quest.

The two children plodded the dawn. Then they saw other pairs of children plodding in from different streets—of similar ages, if quite various looks or breeds. Some were going in exactly the same direction as A&A, others more off-centre. Two were particularly smart, dressed in a material that could be described as brushed velvet in varied pastels. Most tried to discover each other's names.

"Hey, are you…? How long have you been…?" asked one child with a polished face and knobby knees. She failed to give any information about herself, however.

"Too long," said one of the posher kids. "There's a hole that goes to the other side of the world. But where?"

Indeed, whither the antipodal angst?

In the distance, one of the other children heard the hum of traffic—as if the city had started to re-ignite—and the odd flash of tall red metal as it wheeled between the distant openings of terraced streets was glimpsed by the children as they looked down the streets from their own end.

"But nobody will ever find it. It's only a way to make us hope," said a shrill voice from the now increased crowd of children as they crouched over a likely-looking manhole cover. Yet, some of these, in dribs and drabs, even single pairs, had often investigated such ground-level apertures assuming they were at the very least the top edges of oubliettes.

"There's a bigger hole in my Mum's carpet!" laughed a sarcastic rascal, one of the few children not part of his or her own pair. He remembered the high flat that most adults had told him existed somewhere—even if it were only in forgotten dreams; even the slightest infection of dream sickness itself could engender false imaginings of real things or real imaginings of false things. The flat was an archetype, especially with kids. A literally dreaded flat where an individual—who was once one's best friend—spent most of the day and night in bed. Nobody suspected this could be God Himself—as such seedy, tawdry dread could not possibly be any part of a divine iconography. Even the flat carpet had tantamount to melted into the grooves of the floorboards' ill-knotted and crumbly fibre.

The children shrugged off anything that should be beyond children. Their games were ones that only children could play—seeking the bomb-hole where some of them used to play when they were even smaller children on some (god)forsaken Recreation Ground beyond the back of the back of council estate terraced houses. The city had bomb-holes galore—having suffered many raids in the war during the blitz... but none deeper than the legendary bomb-hole which was the children's ultimate goal. No parents would understand it. The children themselves barely understood it—and why they had to find it... and to lose themselves in the process of finding it or merely seeking it without finding it, whichever turned out to be the case.

Mike was in the park with Susan and Sudra—feeding the swans. Sudra was not one of those children who ran away or even threatened to run away. A false threat, on most kids' parts, but some did run away although they didn't know why. But that's another story—as all endless quest stories (in an open-ended intaglio of triptyches or trilogies) ultimately become: in the same natural fashion that anything without an end eventually ceases to have a middle. Sudra skipped across the grass neatly lawndered in recent days: a bright shiny carpet of green that would have done a bowls match proud.

Mike pointed into the sky, drawing attention—for Susan's benefit as well as Sudra's—to where he saw a large kite being flown from outside the park by someone at the end of its tether. This looked like a huge chunky toy: a lego-brick device or even a model of a toy lorry the size of a real lorry—but then there was another kite appearing along the slant of another angle: a giant real model of a toy bus... followed by a complex Meccano contraption looking far too heavy to fly. Several other over-sized toys eventually floated above in delicate needlepoint: or a raggle-taggle armada... until Mike realised with a shock that they were not kites at all but real flying-craft in the guise of model toys... soon to be interspersed with the sounds of clattering vanes deeper and more threatening than a helicopter's... until that shock became real as he watched one of them accidentally clip another—with the result of both careering or cartwheeling from the sky, slowly crashing into parts of the city with sickening crunches that even his feet heard, bone to bone. Wisps of black smoke soon became billows. As if routed from an in-built rhythm of flight by the sight of the accident, others proceeded to fall from the sky—more likely however they had physically felt the previous ricochet—and Mike prayed that they would not crash anywhere near their own house... a strange priority as even just one of them crashing into the park itself would have threatened their lives, which were far more valuable than property. He also hoped that Ogdon's 'Third Floor' pub would remain intact. Then, quickly realising how vulnerable he, Susan and Sudra were in the open, Mike gathered Sudra up and told Susan to run alongside him—even though he didn't know if running away from danger was actually running into it.

The grass was scorched by their frantic escape.

He is dreaming. He knows it is him dreaming but, in retrospect, it could be just about anyone dreaming—Mike or Greg, even Ogdon. Hardly a woman, however, could have dreamed the dream—or a child like Arthur. Yet nothing is certain in such novel circumstances as dreaming a dream such as the dream he thought he was dreaming. He felt himself to be a man, not only within the dream context but also outside the dream as the person eventually to wake from it—and having already entered it via deep sleep, he seemed to mine even deeper. The dreamer had in his arms a girl and she was almost offering herself to him in skimpy night-clothes or an even skimpier evening dress. At first, he thought it was his daughter and, since then, within the dream, he has no reason to think it was not his daughter. She had shortish curly or bushy blonde hair and she was a bit plump so not at all like his daughter in what he later would consider to be waking or real life. But she was his daughter in the dream and it seemed they were both accustomed to these surreptitious flings and she was kissing him longingly, lengthily—eventually with her tongue. He felt a climax ensuing as he was now convinced it was one of those dreams that often end abruptly at good or bad bits of it, and the dreamer woke in a sick sweat. And that is all he can remember of the dream, and whether he is still trapped in such a dream is quite unknown to anyone capable of knowing there is such a thing *to* know.

The children arrived at the Dry Dock—but the ship had been moved back to the sea during the night. Each pair circled the area where it had stood for months between stanchions, breezeblocks, gantries and giant chocks. This was where they suspected the hole they sought would be found—a service tunnel bled from the ship's hull for off-loading unfiltered substances: leading into the intricacies of the earth's valves. Not that they possessed those words to describe it. They merely had dreamed them, beamed from elsewhere, during the returning onset of the dream sickness (a sickness that most people, even children, had forgotten).

One child thought of the maps that had been on board—in the maproom. A wall of maps overlapping each other. This child then told his other half about it: "They were wall-sized maps on hardboard, one on top of the other, hinged at the top where the ship's horizontal false ceiling ended in meeting the vertical—and you needed to lift one map to see the one underneath, lifting them again and again until you reached the wall itself. Some of the maps are blank, some very complicated with lots of wavy lines…" He tried to take a breath as he took a long run at describing everything that went through his mind. He had the word-power and the enthusiasm to match it. His listener was in awe.

Other children, with similar memories, could hardly describe them. "The walls were red," one of them said (a girl with bushy blonde hair), meaning to say they were read like a book.

"There was a map of a railway," answered another precocious child who held the hand of an older child with fuzz on his top lip, the latter not seeming quite so 'with it' as the younger one.

"On the wall?"

"Sort of *under* the wall. You had to lift the top wall up to see under it—and the first map under it was of a railway, not a map of rivers, roads or mountains—only tracks crawling all over it like centipedes."

"Funny map to have on board a ship!"

"Yes, but most people these days think about trains, rather than boats, planes or cars."

"Do they? What about helicopters? Do you count them as planes?"

Children crowded in to listen, whilst others searched the distraught area where the ship had once been stationed—still trying to locate the hole to the centre of the earth—and beyond.

"Some people remember the times when grown-ups used to travel to work."

"Commuting," chimed in a bright spark from the back of the crowd.

"Yes, something like that—but they say you remember the open platforms in the countryside and the platforms you used but now a bit changed, mixing up the direction or if you had changed to the right platform for the next train—going back in the same direction as you came, while you are mixed up because most of the other passengers are collecting themselves on the opposite platform to the one you are on—and you've forgotten whether you were travelling to work or travelling back home having already been to work..."

The chatter soon dissolved as the kids departed in dribs and drabs, having given up any chance of locating the pit entrance hereabouts. The chatter thus faded into the distance and, simultaneously, became more like chatter fitting for children to chat.

During their lunch-break from the office, Greg and Mike visited Ogdon's pub on the third floor of the New Trocadero. Mike was disturbed to catch Susan and Ogdon canoodling behind the bar when he and Greg arrived—but Susan quickly rectified herself with some careless excuse. Sympathies for all parties have been meticulously crafted by the implied omniscience of someone who stands behind all the characters. If only he or she were more up front with this task instead of keeping everything between the lines. And given these sympathies, one can try to imagine the sorrow in Mike's heart at this sign of seedy affection between Susan and Ogdon, plus the shame he felt at his colleague Greg also witnessing the tawdry scene and the further shame felt, indeed, by Susan herself. She quickly changed the subject, whilst serving Greg and Mike their lunchtime booze.

"The ship's gone, then."

Mike nodded. The huge funnelled monstrosity in Dry Dock—not unlike the famous Titanic, only slightly smaller with rather more complex ill-matched contraptions as if some little boy had got carried away with his Meccano kit—had long become a fixture on the city's skyline. Its abrupt overnight disappearance—presumably because all the work on its under-hull had been completed—was indeed the topic of conversation all over the city. This had coincided with the disappearance of many children who—despite the frantic searching by the Authorities—were still missing. Some had put two and two together and related the ship somehow to a vast metal Pied Piper…

"Nobody seemed to notice," said Greg. "It's not as if the sea is close by, but they must have re-cut the river to the sea overnight, too! Amazing what they can do."

"I heard the groaning of sheet metal throughout the night, but I couldn't wake up properly—to check," announced Ogdon.

Meanwhile Susan's sister Beth and Beth's husband had entered the pub. A childless couple, but they had great sympathy with those who had lost children overnight.

Crazy Lope was muttering to himself at the other end of the bar, but nobody listened.

"I went to his room—and he said he would show me his if I showed him mine. So I escaped back down the stairs, helter skelter. A long way from his flat to the ground. Heh heh! The sea, you say? It's not far to the coast from here, really. I once went..." He spat into his drink before he continued, oblivious that nobody was listening to his series of conversational non-sequiturs. "There was a plane doing a sort of air show near the pier. At first I thought it was an ordinary plane, but as it came nearer to us sight-seers on the prom, it turned more into a sort of model plane, with decorative fins, as if out of a cartoon manga—and I could see the pilot as a sort of Jules Verne character in ruffs and frills—and it skimmed off and grew bigger, amazingly, as it flew into the distance, and I could see a strange word: something like 'Angerfin' on its side. It almost clipped the edge of the pier and I was scared to see if it cartwheeled into the sea or, worse, into the prom where we were all standing...."

Nobody paid any attention to Crazy Lope's failure of communication, a failure even with himself. He didn't fill up the whole screen.

Greg and Mike soon left the pub, intent on returning to the office where the computers continued to work throughout their lunchbreak, like huge sensory calculators with amputated keys. Each man felt the other was a website, a blog city, a click on the right point bringing everything up in various stages of construction. Either that or they were slightly merry from imbibing on empty stomachs.

Beth was beautiful but she often seemed bitter... or strident... transferring furrows to the face that seemed out of place there. Her personality had changed the character of her face. Her sister Susan was less physically attractive, yet her nature was calmer, more amenable—not necessarily kinder or smarter than Beth, but less prone to have mind rage at the slightest setback. Patience was something Beth deeply lacked and her non-descript husband took the brunt of her short temper—to the extent of having any of his own personality stripped from him, like a gossamer upperskin peeling off and jettisoned: left just to cling on, for dear life, to the cast shadow in his wake.

When Beth's nephew and niece disappeared, Beth initially failed to react sufficiently: but as soon as she did take initiative on her sister's behalf, Susan stopped being simply bemused at losing two children she somehow hadn't realised she had. Beth had at first retained her habits, however—arriving in Ogdon's pub rather late and with cool nonchalance—yet later her inbuilt stridency took inevitable sway and she felt there was nothing to do but burn the candle at both ends, tussling insistently, if not violently, with the Authorities, whilst chivvying Susan and Mike into really believing that their children were missing and it was simply not good enough at all merely to reply: "What children?"

"Arthur and Amy, those kids you brought up…" Beth shouted, trying to get through to her sister somehow. The dream sickness was a factor that remained unsaid—unsayable. That such a sickness should have actually caused the children's disappearance and their parents' subsequent dead-eyed reaction to such a major event represented a complexity that such simple city folk could never envisage, let alone explain or even admit.

The dream sickness—like a 'flu pandemic—caused queues at doctors' surgeries for tablets intended for an illness from which they didn't know they suffered... but, unlike a 'flu pandemic, the dream sickness was inspired by an inference regarding an infernal mass-hysteria linked to a mass-suicide syndrome rather than to any individual's pain or conscious disability.

Many parents set up search parties—because Arthur and Amy were not the only ones believed to have inexplicably gone missing. Some search parties overlapped with other search parties. There were petty rivalries, even bitter disputes between them, believing their own children were being sought by other parties and vice versa.

Meanwhile, wells were dug all over the city towards the Northern coalfields. Separate queues were set up at these wells to reflect the medicine queues further south, as if some unknown synchronicity was sought to provide an explanation factor linking two imponderables and hopefully making them ponderable. Some children who hadn't yet run away from home played sandcastles around the wells—damming and river-construction games mocked-up from various substances abandoned by gardeners in allotment sheds previously rifled by unknown hands and given to the children. Weighing bucket against bucket was a common daily reality even though it sounds more like something they should have dreamed about... being tantamount to a *waking* sickness, assuming anyone could get their heads around such a concept.

Much further south, towards the holiday 'feet' of the city-shape, other queues formed near ranks of parked silver craft that had been earmarked and then advertised as vehicles for tours beyond the city toward the sea in pursuit of adventures of which Jules Verne would have been proud.

Crazy Lope and John Ogdon had booked for an undersea tour, but then decided against it. This would have been under the tutelage of a rather outlandishly garbed and dramatic Captain Nemo (or so it was blurbed in the brochure), cashing in on a vogue for such old-fashioned fantasy trips. Booking avoided queues but cost a lot more. Greg said he wanted to accompany them, but currently there wasn't a vacancy, unless a late cancellation arose. At that stage Crazy Lope and Ogdon had not yet cancelled. Greg wondered if he really shouldn't accompany Beth, Susan & Co. in search of Arthur and Amy. A holiday seemed a bit of a cop-out compared to participating in a pukka search party. Mike himself kept his own counsel.

Long ago, Mike (or others on his behalf) believed he was a hawler but, with a generally increasing number of inscrutable dreams, that concept had vanished into some forgotten sump of tribal consciousness. The only thing known about a hawler was that there was no fact to know about a hawler. A hawler being a wide-faced creature that sat at the centre of the earth was an earlier description—but whoever or whatever created that description had since disappeared and thus become unaccountable for it.

Greg, meanwhile, remembered the zoo visit with some clarity. His face was a bit effeminate—and one could easily imagine him performing a drag act as a hobby. A Danny La Rue manqué. He was a loner but people in the office where he worked thought he was a rather pleasant individual and they believed many of the stories he told about his non-existent life. His suits were immaculate. His jokes tasteful. His visits to the loo kept to the minimum as he hated mirrors. The zoo, too. Rather good at his administrative job, a whizz with the keyboard and could build websites at a flick of his wrist—or so it seemed. A pity he had such awful, guilt-ridden dreams about a daughter he'd never had. Nobody knew about this, of course.

He missed Mike. Mike had once worked in the same office, but with the domestic problems that later beset him, he had left and moved to the other side of the city with his wife and children. They seemed somehow distinct from the Mike and Susan with whom Greg had since become re-acquainted on the screen... in the era of televised search parties pre-occupying the 'Big Brother' reality-show mentalities of the gullible public. And Amy—one of the children—was later found grown-up and vacuuming carpets without even knowing Mike was her father. But that's an earlier story since abandoned for whatever reason. Or a later one yet to be told. Nobody was quite sure.

Crazy Lope was Ogdon's alter ego. And vice versa. The fact that one set of relationships between them could overlap another yet opposite set continued to make it possible that they remained separate people, despite the evidence otherwise. Writing fiction was his first love—often about a vampire called a Horla after a French writer's story of the same name—but this had soon fallen by the wayside. Nobody could earn money from writing such rarefied fiction—so he proceeded to put it on an antipodal back-burner whilst deciding to open a pub (his second love).

Ogdon gave himself an evening off from time to time, as pub life was generally very hard. But he spent most of this free time behind the other side of his bar, talking to regulars, if not to himself. Conversations on either side of the bar did differ, but it was all basically the same: 'pub talk': loosened tongues amid boozy brainstorming.

Ogdon: It's like fixing a painting with a special cold varnish, so it doesn't fade, or even change. Paintings can change, you know.

Crazy Lope: Change?

O: Yes—fixing dreams is one thing, like making sure we remember them a few hours after we wake up. But far harder is to fix reality itself—stopping it slipping or sliding into dream. That's the fixing I'm talking about.

CL: I didn't know you knew about such things. I've often had dreams which get confused and, sooner or later, lost forever. Does that happen to real things, too, then? I suppose you might be right.

O: Dream sickness—heard about that? Well, I've got a cure for it in a fixing-device... or a fixing-person, a new job that I think we need to fill. Government's not going to do anything about it.

CL: Dream sickness, yes, but nobody admits to it existing. Nobody actually says those words in public.

O: I know. I think it's better called dream spam than dream sickness!

CL: Hmmm. Junk dreams? Maybe your fixing idea's got legs, after all.

O: Changing the subject slightly, have you heard of the new holidays run by a firm that's organising trips based on Jules Verne?

CL: Yup. Don't like holidays myself. They seem like a chore half the time. I just enjoy staying in my flat and mouldering away. (Laughs)

O: Well, I know someone who went on one of those trips. They *do* exist, I'm sure, based on what he says.

CL: Who's that?

O: That friend of Mike from his office. Greg, is it? He comes in here often on his own now—Mike's gone north.

CL: Has he?

O: Yes, like all those others. Anyway, that trip Greg told me about—it was a submarine run by someone acting as Captain

Nemo. But not an ordinary submarine, that Nautilus sort of was, as I understand it. This submarine had huge vanes on top like a helicopter—and it churned down through the sea-water scattering fish and so forth in a great big stirpool!

CL: Sounds decidedly ungreen!

O: To say the least—but apparently the vanes were a protective system as much as they were propulsion. Deep down where Nemo took all the passengers and taught all those trippers about really deep things, quite beyond you and I. And green is the thing, indeed, in many ways, dark green, right down there... emerald scenes, with emerald beasts of the under-sea. Frondy. So Greg said.

CL: I thought it was all blue, the sea.

O: So did I. But at the deepest—down there—are giant green squid that have civil wars, it seems. Tribes of the same breed wrestling in mounds of black mud. Absolutely mad.

CL: Black as well as green?

O: Apparently so. Nemo called these squid vermin "ancient kings of besmirched sperm-banks." Greg remembered that as a line of old poetry.

CL: Whales? Sharks? They're in that same poem, I think.

O: Well, mutant versions, apparently. I didn't understand most of it. Greg seemed to know all about it, but he'd actually seen all these things. Seeing is believing, isn't it?

CL: Not so sure. Probably brings us back to your 'fixing' idea. Fictioning, similar, I dunno. You need a kiln for baking reality! (Laughs.)

Others who were listening laughed, too, as Ogdon bought another round of drinks, thus squandering his pub profits. Crazy Lope spat into his drink for luck.

O: By the way, I had a funny dream last night. I knew it was a dream, without having to fix any true waking life that came before and after.

CL: Oh yeh?

O: One part of the dream wasn't so clear—it was a pub that was a caravan-type thing that seemed high up on the side of a cliff, embedded into its rock. And you had to climb up to it—and it was much bigger inside than you could ever imagine from looking at its outside.

CL: Like Tardis? (Laughs.)

O: Maybe, but it had a Lounge bar as well as a Public one. I went into the Public and started chatting with someone, though I can't remember who that was. I seemed to know this person, however. I owed him money, it seemed.

CL: A him then?

O: Yes, I'm sure it was a man. Anyway, I repaid with loose change. (Laughs.) A series of one p and half p coins. It couldn't have been much or I would have used notes. Probably. Anyway, as I say, to the point, one of the coins was a quarter p! Smaller even than a half p—so tiny you could hardly handle it. I then knew it must be a dream, as everyone knows that a quarter p coin doesn't exist in England and never did exist.

CL: Exactly. Half p coins don't exist now, but they once did. But never a quarter p. You're right.

O: Ah well, there are *some* truths to life one cannot doubt!

All laughed and nodded as more drinks were purchased. A few of the regulars wore flat caps and they decided to have a game of darts. The pub talk was evidently fizzling out for a while amid much merriment, yet mingled with worried private asides and surreptitious glances.

If there were horror lurking somewhere—nobody would ever know for sure. Yet, deep down, this horror was aware of itself and, even without a mirror, it knew it had slobbery gums and long teeth and a face wider than its head. Not absurdly dreamlike but monstrously, nightmarishly real—just waiting for its time to come.

Beth's husband may not even have known his own name. He was nemonymous. Some of his friends recognised him and called him by a name they thought he was named. He was a working-class lad recently grown into manhood—slight fuzz on his upper lip—with the sole purpose it seemed of becoming Beth's husband. Beth could easily have hen-pecked him to death because she was a strong, impatient character who paid no heed to her own original beauty and feared no spoiling of that beauty with any hard-nosed actions. In fact her face had become more pointy and as if scorched by a cold cutting East wind—whilst all the time it was her personality that had given the features this unwelcome cast. Her husband eventually became her right-hand man who defended her and somehow complemented her with the backdrop of his near-absence accentuating her presence. Not that he was a pushover. He had pub-going pals and a career in waste management, driving one of the firm's largest lorries through the city and using his slippery guile to prevent the Authorities discovering what sort of waste he was transporting to the coalfields. It is reckoned that his intrinsic nemonymity helped with both aspects of logistics and surreptitiousness by making him able to drive skilfully under all radars, metaphorical or otherwise—and to dodge between the speed cameras... thus arriving in a timely fashion and in successful completion of the job. The envy of his colleagues. Thus, he was promoted—almost to Board level, but he still preferred to go AWOL and drive the lorries.

He met Arthur after Arthur grew up from being a child. They shared pints in The Third Floor—and not surprising since they both negotiated the city traffic in their own ways, one with a double-decker bus, the other with an articulated juggernaut. Arthur had a partner he called Amy and Beth's husband a wife he called Beth—but neither woman met each other so they never knew who the other one really was. This was strange as the two men were close friends and often talked about the old days that many had forgotten—and this forgetting was perhaps because either the dream sickness still prevailed but hiding its own history of pandemic or the dream sickness had abated allowing real memories to subsist instead.

Beth's husband, however, had secret vices. He didn't even recognise them himself, *if* that is the same thing as secrecy. He wove carpets. Many did this during the Nineteen Fifties in England—a hobby and a method of saving money. He had huge brush-stiffened grids of thread through which he leap-frogged a wooden paddle threaded with further thread—knitting tight each line of thread against another line of thread with his hard-padded fingers: as if tidying a rhythm of growing patterns of thick surface-veined underlay: except this underlay was a surface—but surfaces were meant to be 'on top' as that was where they always tended to go. An under-surface was a logical impossibility. He wanted one of his special carpets to be beige-coloured to match some future required necessity of appearance, one that fitted in with a retrospective destiny. There were mounds of these vexed textures of surface: each a fire-wall—or, rather, fire-floor—as if he were readying them to serve as an insulation device that even time couldn't penetrate. A cover for the hawler. Only Beth's husband knew how important his task was—masquerading as a rather effeminate hobby for one of such hard-bitten working-class background (or underground). Foregrounds were not even considered.

Edith Cole and Mr Clare controlled him from afar. But nobody now knew who they were or who they had once been.

Arthur, Amy and the other children had eventually reached the edge of the Northern Coalfields in search of the entrance to the vertical tunnel that would take them to…

It would take them nowhere. They knew this at heart, it is certain. The quest was for a quest, originally—yet now the quest had become this downward pit that led nowhere. An end in itself. The means to that end were just a subterfuge that contained their end like an insulation case around a live wire. "A fugue for a darkening city." Beyond the end, they knew there were no further ends. Otherwise they would have given up in sheer terror. Or they hoped so. It beggared belief to believe otherwise.

They were not old enough, thankfully, to realise they were too young to understand.

I stared at the screen wondering where I fitted into the schematic movements of the symphony. Not that I could hear any music at all. Silence.

The screen showed a clouded yellow surface, yet mottled with—if it were real—stains or signs of wear. Not yellow so much, I guess. Maybe beige. Not a uniform surface. Again, if it were real, it would bear perceptible bumps or lumps in its fibre. Fibre? Or weave. Or web. Or net.

It is as if I had created this site with a number of codes: codes that began with <hawl> and ended with </hawl>. I went to shut it down because I felt myself threatened by it, as if it were sucking me into it like a fly.

Now, I know deep down who I was. Or I was in the process of creating who I was. I was about to enter the intermittent and unsmooth flow of action. The yellowy web, hopefully, was to be the firewall or firefloor to protect me (or anyone else following me) from the dire horror that was a lurker on or within the threads of my discursive being.

Mike, Susan and Beth had reached the edge of the city's Northern Coalfields at West Wednesday. They were not far behind the children. As they entered each suburb, they heard talk of the children's prior passage through its streets, lifting manhole covers, peering into drainage/heating shafts, breaking into derelict houses to test the cellar floors and so forth.

Crazy Lope/Ogdon and Greg—calling themselves the Two and Half Musketeers—had reached the Left Foot of the city down south and were currently queuing up to buy tickets for the latest Jules Verne holiday-of-a-lifetime. *Journey to the Centre of the Earth—The Enjoyable Way.* Greg was to test it out for subsequent entertainment of his firm's clients. CL/O merely felt like a holiday.

Meanwhile, I tossed a quarter p coin to decide who I'd follow. I knew that Arthur and Amy would, at least, survive what was indeed to happen because it has already been reliably recorded that Arthur grew up to drive a bus and Amy to clean flats. As to the others—and myself—any survival was yet merely hearsay.

The coin dropped on its milled edge within a gutter's drainage slot.

Ogdon stared at the screen in his flat. He had started typing up his things here in this rather undeserving tawdriness, having spent the earlier evening writing afresh in the square by the fountain. "I am curious—yellow," he whispered at the screen, hardly daring to breathe. He scribbled in his bright red Silvine 'memo book'. He was more a dreamer than a pub landlord, but he needed a proper job to bring in the beef—and why not combine that with his second love (drinking and indulging in pub talk)? Dreaming never brought in much money, even when one could turn the dreams into words. He actually wore a long cape when he was the dreamer—and called himself Crazy Lope. He wore non-descript clothes when working behind the bar, as differentiation. These days, Ogdon hardly worked in his own pub, for various reasons, and had got in a locum as a manager.

He spent much of most nights exploring (wandering)—mainly the two disused airports on the eastern and western sides of the city—areas called the City Arms. They inspired with their direct emptiness and spent force. Bleak and windswept, he imagined the roaring of the jet engines, the clacking of old-fashioned propeller vanes, the residual sorrow and misused heroism of war veterans that still filled the air with poignant empathy. It was all good meat for his dreaming (he saw fiction as miraculously feeding the multitude) and these airports were much more efficacious in this regard than the large city-centre area of the covered market—now divorced from its secondary role as an Underground station. And more efficacious than the now disused Dry Dock where gargantuan ships and liners used to arrive for riveting.

The western airport area—now overgrown like a long-forgotten golf course—reminded him of another derelict airport he had seen on the web as part of his dream research. This one was in a place called Hawler—where was it?—in Kurdistan? Whether the city airports were connected with this middle eastern one in some way was uncertain, yet Ogdon believed in complementary ley-lines veining the whole surface of the earth, proud as inflamed swellings on a human body... invisible to most uncaring eyes as the eyes' owners conducted their selfish lives on a daily basis, lives only interspersed with sleep or with whatever sleep contained.

Ogdon reviewed his own dreams. The fiction could wait, as he shut down the sickly clouded crystal-ball of his yellow screen. He was quite aware that there was not enough detail, not enough provenance and not even enough providence in whatever had by-passed his mind. He recalled the city-centre zoo visit with some pleasure, but weighed down with equal displeasure bordering on dread. Had justice been done to this zoo? Mike was *still* not filled out as the real person he was. Some of the others had given a good shot at it and even gave a passing impression of having deep feelings and understandable impulses or intuitive intentions: mixed intentions, some logical, others paradoxical. All of them were like this, except, perhaps, for Beth's husband. Ogdon at first thought Beth's husband was the wild card. Little did Ogdon know, however, that he should keep a beadier eye on one of the children. A bewitched child. Yet nobody seemed to have put a finger on this. Give them time for nailing down.

Ogdon sighed. Despite the coin tossing, he was still undecided which of the two parties to follow. Either one of the audit trails could hold the crucial clue as to the rest of it. He prepared himself for dreaming about the huge man-made flying-craft down south. Next, he made a stab at dreaming of the dark striated horizon of the bleak north, its coal-towers and clanking works, all stitched skyward with the gigantic webby wings of real and living flying-craft.

First, he needed somehow to resolve the zoo visit. The much earlier clue as to Mike's "lorry-driver face" and his voracious approach to beefsteak were red herrings of the first water. Beth's husband was the lorry-driver (in waste management), after all. There was some confusion that Ogdon would never be able to resolve. Real people (as opposed to fictional ones) had real idiosyncracies and paradoxes that could never be conveyed by a dream or even by the near-photographic description of realities (because each description was imperfect by the nature of words): realities that were simply and inexorably realities, and nothing else. If people were such realities, then there was no way of imagining those realities—and this was because realities (by being real) were unimaginable. They kept avoiding Ogdon's flawed 'camera obscura' of a mind. And this applied to real things as well as to real people.

In the zoo, there had been a cage they all peered into with some trepidation. This scene had been left unreported, for whatever reason, but as things panned out, it gradually grew into view from a single atom of dread in one of the witnesses' minds. Poultry combined with beef in some complex miscegenation. In this cage was a truly massive pulsing amorphousness with feathers tufting in all directions from each suppurating pore. He first saw it as black but, in retrospect, he knew it was white. He wondered if further hindsight might make it later look red like skinned meat. But, no. It was unutterably white. No amount of retrospection could change that, he knew. A noticeboard attached to the cage had identification: "Infinite Cuckoo". That was when they all decided unanimously to leave the zoo grounds by the exit turnstile. They'd pay anything to leave, even if it were more than the normal ticket price of a few p.

Well, in further hindsight, the creature wasn't infinite at all, Ogdon thought. It couldn't be contained in a cage if it were. Unless it was a *bit* of an infinity. The implications were too wild to deal with today.

And he returned to his desk, across the littered carpet, and powered-up his screen ready for easier tasks. Fiction was always easier than truth, a generalisation with which he would need to come to terms... eventually.

There was a liar among them.

But what is a liar? If you tell lies without knowing they are lies, without any intention of lying, are you still a liar? Answer that question with care because it may land you in a lot of trouble when accounts are settled at the end of the day. I have told lies in dreams, for example, and the character I felt myself to be from within the dream knew full well that he was telling lies, i.e. that *I* was telling lies—yet all this as seen from outside the dream after waking was yet another lie in a way, an untruth, a falsehood, because I could hardly then remember the details of the dream and I am now making up what happened in the dream just for an exercise in fancification... making conversation as it were... stringing words together to create an interesting scenario which I can later work up as a story for the dinner party I was later due to attend in real life.

Someone stared across at me over the table, winking in tune with the candles, as if she knew that I knew that she knew she was telling lies. Her face was a cutting one when she was interrupted or gainsaid. I could tell she had once been very pretty, but now her character intervened and made the face carry the ingredients of an underface like a bird pecking for worms. I recognised her from the dream in which the lies had started their concertina domino-rally from unreality into reality—crossing some bridge that linked untruth with truth.

"What *is* a liar?" she suddenly and unexpectedly asked, thus causing such a non-sequitur to become an intrinsic constituent or continuation of the prandial conversation that was already taking place before she again so skilfully interrupted it.

"A liar?" I answer, after a long Pinteresque moment. Answering with a question is a knack I had learned as a useful ploy in the subtle manoeuvres of life. There is a darkness before life. There is a darkness after life. So one has to make the best of the light of life between those twin darknesses—and using questions as answers, I'd realised, was the easiest way to progress matters whilst avoiding responsibility for the progression.

I know that I am not a liar. I am perhaps *the* liar. I am in control of a dream in which everyone else is a participant within that dream's ambit—an ambit I've allowed the dream to have. The liar is the one who makes what he does absolutely true. This the knack that I now settle down with as a comforting prop, while sleep overwhelms the dream with its own brand of seeping darkness. It doesn't matter that I drown in death, because I am certain in my own way that I shall survive it by lying about its aftermath. After life. After death.

She lifts her skirt as she leaves the dinner table and wonders who had been due to sit in the chair opposite her partaking of bird soup ladled from a huge chipped tureen. A dinner guest who hadn't turned up—as the host had explained—because he had died suddenly that very afternoon.

Greg returned from the dinner party and stared at himself staring back at himself from the chipped wardrobe mirror. Wondering, extrapolating, brainstorming, lying—and none of it made the context obvious. The woman opposite at the dinner party he rather fancied, despite her aggressive nature. Beth was her name—introduced by the host in such a way as Greg suspected matchmaking. Another lie in the making.

Back in his flat, the face in the mirror began to talk. Greg's face—showing not a mixed race, but a mixed class. The barely sprouting fuzz on his upper lip belied his youth, but the eyes spoke a working-class directness and a raw but instinctively astute naivety together with mechanical awareness... whilst the moving lines of his lips forming the speaking mouth indicated a more academic or professional or at least clerical/administrative slant. The face spoke and he could not stop it speaking.

Pinnochio's nose grew longer when he told lies. Yet we have no easy way to judge lies in real life. There is a question whether a single lie, once told, creates other lies in its wake, then radiating, spawning more lies, new and different lies living off each other—like a butterfly theory of chaos—moving round the world like a disease till everyone tells lies, Russian Doll lies, until they return to the original liar himself who accepts them as truths—because he started them in the first place and he has persuaded himself, by being in denial, indeed has simply forgotten that he lied in the first place and that he had started the lies moving round the world. Yes, a lie sickness, a plague of lies…

Greg smiled as he realised that the face in the mirror had come to a halt... frozen like a sepia photograph of one of his Victorian ancestors... gradually growing yellowy, staining the surface with feathery fibres between the beige-ridden silver backing of the mirror and the front glass itself: spraying apricotty ice follicles across. He imagined, not a nose growing longer with each lie, but a small white feather beginning to sprout from every pore of the skin. One feather per lie. The originally bendy bone of each feather's spindle fused with the bones beneath the skin, all their flossy sprigs striving but failing to be animal fur. Everyone's blood is normally red, whatever the skin colour, yet the thickening plume-spindle bones of the werebird's new covering turned its blood into an utterly pure white consistency dripping to his flat's carpet...

The sun literally seemed to scream at the holiday party as they arrived in the tour coach at the edge of the Left Foot Plateau to the south of the city. Its rays gradually spread along the then empty horizon like orange marmalade—the bottom arc of its orb dripping something like thick liquid to the point on the horizon whence it had just fully risen. The holiday-makers were due to go from viewing one arc to another. They were to board an ark as it were and become participants in the latest Jules Verne expedition that had been advertised as going to the centre of the earth. Booked as a holiday, many now indeed saw this as a useful escape route from the unsaid dangers that had begun to beset the city.

Greg turned to look at his wife Beth and shrugged. They were in two minds about this whole trip because, clandestinely, they were not real holiday-makers or, even, escapees from a world that no longer welcomed them but, instead, they had a mission to find the Angevin children who had vanished from the city under the cover of rumours. Indeed, Greg and Beth both knew that other people (including Beth's sister) were trying different apertures to enter the earth further north in the Head Region of the city. There was more hanging on these events than just a jamboree or self-indulgent adventuring or, even, conscientious objection to what was going on in the city.

The horizon and, indeed, the upper sky, were now filling with huge kites upon slanting rope-tethers to the hands of as yet invisible kite-carers on the ground. The individual kites were—as a promotional vision for the Jules Verne Holiday Company—shaped like some of the craft the Company had used for previous jaunts and some, even, models of proposed future ones.

Lightening up, Greg laughed as he spotted one of the kites was a flying carpet prancing higher and higher from yet one more slanting tether. He was older and hopefully wiser than before with his bum-fluff moustache having by now matured into a full set of whiskers upon his pink chops. His eyes still betokened the rough and ready innocence of an artisan, but he now carried an instinctive articulative wisdom, even when not talking.

Beth remembered that Susan, her sister, was, even at this same moment, approaching the centre of the earth from a different terrestrial angle. She missed her. She missed her comparative softness and empathy. She was wasted on that Mike. Beth felt herself to be, on the other hand, too brittle, without the calming influence of her softer sibling—yet Beth tried to hide this by smiling at her husband. Often, however, a false smile is worse than a lie.

"Hey, some of those kites haven't got people flying them!" suddenly announced Greg, as he pointed to one in particular with no obvious tether in its wake.

Beth was more interested in viewing the craft that was due to take them to the centre of the earth. That was a far more important priority at the moment. At first, she was mistaken as to the correct craft in question, as she spotted a long queue of would-be holiday-makers near a large landcraft which multi-resembled a cross between various forms of transport (that was the only way she could describe it). She thought she and Greg must be on the wrong side of the platform as it were, in the wrong queue, because their own queue was much shorter, indeed depleted to just the two of them being led by an inscrutable Jules Verne official whose face they had not yet seen—but it was not long before they rounded a deceptive dune to witness the first sight of their own potential craft.

It was awe-inspiring. Strangely, from the distance at which they first viewed it, the craft struck them as simply more than gigantic. It was literally bigger than a mountain and, surely, would become clogged in the earth's throat, at such a size. Tilted at an angle, it was a wildly proportioned Drill… with a bit at its tip, pointing at the earth and tantalisingly only a few inches from the beachy surface. Even more strangely than before, the nearer they approached the Drill, the smaller it became, but still reasonably massive judging by mere human proportions. Beth could now actually pick out the pilot in the cockpit behind the bit-tip. He was dressed in a period costume with frills, ruffs and a feathered peaked cap. He smiled at Beth as he gave the Drill's ignition a quick trial grinding roar... and she watched the bit-tip spin, splinters of orange sun spraying in all directions from its sharp bright torque.

The most amazing item on the craft, however, which Greg was the first to notice, was an outlandishly protrusive set of slender rotor-blades or vanes upon the back of the Drill like that on the back of a helicopter. Insect-like. He could not imagine how the Drill could be able to dig its way through the earth with that as part of its propulsion system. He originally imagined the Drill sliding through the earth like a knife through butter, but that thought now went straight out of the window.

But the matter was soon forgotten when they were abruptly introduced to the Drill's 'Captain Nemo'—who appeared just as suddenly on a ladder that dangled from the boarding-hatch in the side of the Drill. He was a tall figure with a certain resemblance, as Greg recalled the people he had known in the city, to Ogdon or, even, Ogdon's sidekick Crazy Lope. The Captain was not however in any way related to these two people, as both he and Beth soon instinctively gathered.

"I'll take you in and show you the wallmaps in a minute," he crooned with a nut-brown voice.

Beth was entranced. Greg sceptical.

"Wall maps?"

"Yes, charts and so forth of our route."

Greg shrugged. Surely there was only one route to the centre of the earth. As the crow flew. A straight line. A slanting tether.

"I have books on board to keep us amused during the long journey," the Captain continued.

"Books!" interjected Beth. "I hate books. Ever since I gave one as a present—one I valued as if I'd written it myself—inscribed it lovingly to the recipient—and then I found myself eventually buying it back because I saw the same copy being sold on e-Bay!"

The Captain shrugged as if this was a silly reason to hate books. With only one backward glance at the shadow of the vertical sun above them amid the increasingly crowded sky, Greg and Beth excitedly followed the Captain on board the Drill. The name on its side had escaped them: "The Hawler".

Mike was a solid figure of a man. Not at all like Greg with Greg's slight figure despite the years that had thickened his facial growth. Not wide so much as bushy. But that was Greg, and attention must perforce spotlight Mike again for a while. And Mike was still doubtful about his own beginnings—barely remembering even the shadowy figures who had been his parents in the Fifties. He had compassion, however, having long forgotten the earlier years as a child when he played pretend games in the garden and up the bullace tree—sometimes masquerading as Davy Crockett in a long-tailed fur hat, sometimes as an even more distant memory: the creature he inscrutably called a hawler (although the spelling was doubtful). All that concerned him now were naturally the concerns of today—his middle years—as he and the party with which he had joined were trekking northward to what was loosely named the city's Head Region.

Until recently, he had been working in the city centre's covered-market, living a frugal existence—together with Susan, a pretty woman who, unlike her sister Beth, had failed to gather frown-lines during her middle years. When she and Mike had decided to live together, she already had a daughter called Sudra who was now herself growing into a pretty woman with pig-tails, a style that was too young for her. Sudra laughed often. Yet she had an aura of malevolence or, at best, bewitchment about her. She, too, was in Mike's party, together with her two similarly aged friends Amy and Arthur, friends of doubtful relationship with each other, with nobody questioning this because there were some lines drawn beneath which it was impolitic to delve. Amy worked as a domestic cleaner, Arthur a double-decker driver—both salt-of-the-earth citizens who would never have dreamed of travelling north... unless times were extraordinary.

How extraordinary the times had become only hindsight could know. The identities of Amy and Arthur—it was believed—had been stolen by lostlings or foundlings or changelings who had escaped with much of their victims' past cloying to them. These were apparent children masquerading as the children Amy and Arthur had once been in earlier perhaps less extraordinary times. This belief in such stolen identities opportunely gave an indication of how truly extraordinary the times actually now were, making it difficult to describe these events with any degree of seriousness. However, if they're not treated seriously at face value, then times have a tendency of coming back with a vengeance and biting the people who disowned them.

The five of them trekked because public transport had long since departed, having been earmarked for some important matters ordinary citizens like them were not considered suitable enough to know about. As he strode along, Arthur imagined the stuff underfoot—the party having finally left the pavemented area of the city streets—to be residue of his childhood 'experiment' games with household substances. This was probably his own version of a retributive past coming back to haunt him. Amy smiled as if she could read Arthur's thoughts. Arthur, however, soon became preoccupied by what evidently preoccupied Mike... and what gradually preoccupied all five of them.

The sky was slowly, surely and imperceptibly becoming more of a roof than a proper sky—as if they had entered a much larger version of the city's open-sided covered-market—which, incidentally, Arthur now recalled was where Sudra's stepfather worked as a waste manager. Having a roof—one might have thought—would have afforded protection from the weather, but they all still felt a soaking drizzle as though rain had been replaced by some variety of sprinkler-system.

Nobody mentioned the colour. Indeed, could darkness be any colour other than black or, at best, grey? A monochrome of darkness, gathering in around them more like mist than darkness proper. Yet, they could still see the even darker shapes hunching upon the distant terrain towards which they hiked. Nobody mentioned the colour, as it did not come up in conversation, bearing in mind the preoccupation caused by the difficulties underfoot.

"Hey! Look—are they volcanoes?"

Mike pointed at the rough cone-shapes each with an odd flame-like plume fitfully being spat by what he assumed to be some of earth's many apertures.

Sudra quaintly described them as "Redoubts"—but nobody seemed to understand, least of all, perhaps, Sudra herself, what she meant by this word. Amy and Arthur laughed, for the sole reason that they felt laughter still within themselves and they didn't want to waste it before it expired as one of their possible human reactions to events. "Redoubts" in itself was not a funny word. On the other hand, the word "Côté" was written on one broken brick wall that they were now passing—almost as if this were the last sign of the city proper. Not written so much as scrawled in a clumsy attempt to follow a trend that was already very fashionable in the city itself: graffiti, tags, pieces... all now lost in these initial stages of a thin-topped underground. A mine with the mere vestigial veneer of a break-even point between upper and lower.

Yet, what was that?

"What's that?" shouted Susan, flustered but retaining the studied innocence characteristic of her.

There was what appeared to be a pier on stilts—of the seaside pleasure variety—reaching into or across a very shallow inner sea—not a sea so much as a series of dark gleaming puddles creating the feel of an elfin archipelago that had gone to seed, made from patches of black sand. Near this pier was a stained-yellow block-building of inferior architectural qualities which once—they guessed—had housed an amusement arcade. They thought they could hear the ghostly whirrings, blurps and chortles of erstwhile jollification.

And nightsome gurgles of waves against the pier's stilts. "The pier's pillars are made of wood," said Amy, as if in a speech she'd learnt parrot-fashion. She was desperately trying to be herself, not someone else. She needed to be herself—otherwise nobody could sympathise with her as a potential human being. The once thick-thighed oaken hafts were slowly decaying into the brine, even as she watched them. Wilting as boniness would.

They soon passed this real or mocked-up (they weren't sure which) version of a seaside resort from Fifties England... not even something the city had *ever* boasted. But here it was. Seedy growing on seedy.

In the distance, beyond the puddly sea, they all saw two small figures—no bigger than match-stick marionettes—employing their own silhouettes to crouch and peer into or under—not a manhole cover but now, far from the city proper, the first of many under-underground oubliettes that peppered the northern night lands in an un-manmade state of existence.

"I can hear something," said Mike. He heard it as if his feet were ears. A distant downward noise—not of underground trains that were what such noises pertained in the city but, rather, underground dogfights by second world war spitfires that felt just as much at home within earth as air. Yet, Mike didn't put his description of these noises into words. He was more concerned with the others in his party running away from his own position near the puddly sea towards the matchstick silhouettes that were sinking slowly into a surface which once seemed solid enough to bear their slightest weight as well as for them to walk upon.

Edith and Clare were in the fort holding the city. They were twins and had spent most of their formative years living inside one of the city walls—the tallest part of wall that had become so tall the local residents called that bit of the wall a tower. The city was not completely surrounded by walls—otherwise that area of the city outside of the walls could not have been called a city at all. There were gaps in the wall for throughways to the two airports on both the eastern and western arms of the city—but the gaps were closing up with growth of brick as well as of foliage/ weeds, although common sense would indicate that it was only plant material growing because brick generally didn't grow. Brick is more prone to crumbling. The aerodromes were derelict so the throughways were moribund. Other gaps in the walls around the inner city were customarily found to the north and south—but these, too, seemed to have narrowed, but this time the narrowing was simply imagination, because everything using the gaps had widened.

Edith and Clare, when they fell asleep, the walls vanished as if they had never existed in the first place. And when they woke up—the walls were back where the two girls knew the walls had always been. One twin tried to stay awake while the other twin slept... so as to check out the walls, but they could not sleep or wake without the other one sleeping or waking. They dreamed each other alive.

Edith and Clare were once quite young. Now they were old. If one of them died, they wondered if the other one would also die. Identical twins were one thing, but mutual twins were twins even a step beyond mere identity.

Greg had two recurring dreams of characters that he called (from within each dream) Edith and Clare. In one dream, they were twin sisters and, in the other, complete strangers who meet up and conduct an even stranger relationship. In the latter dream, they did not live in a city wall but in a tied cottage near a tree with an enormous knotted girth of crusted bark—about twenty-five feet in circumference at its base but a normal amount of various branches emerging in a tangle from the tapering top of this oversized cone-topped trunk—making it seem like a normal tree from about eight feet high onwards. A bottom-heavy tree that was called a Canterbury Oak.

However, each time, before Greg could pin down any memory of the tree's identity or its significance to Edith and Clare, he woke up with a start into a situation he could not remember how he had reached in real life prior to sleeping, until a slow waking-up process reminded him. He was on board 'The Hawler', a vast Drill thing, with helicopter vanes, that was to take Beth and himself underground on a trip to the centre of the earth by means of a well-trodden route from the Left Foot region of the city... as the Captain had informed them—and if the vertical chimney-tunnel was already "well-trodden", they asked the Captain, why the need for it to be a Drill at all?

"Because the tunnel has closed up again, as it always does... the tectonic plates ensure we have to forge the route anew each time we make the trip from here."

The Captain's answer had an air of disinterest about it. But Greg and Beth nodded with full understanding. They had been astonished—when they first arrived on board—at the facilities of the Drill's interior. Very modern and high-tech but interspersed with antique or fine art accoutrements so as to make it feel more salubriously civilized than it actually was. They had to clamber through various tasteful 'floors' via attic-like spaces and even smaller passageways that one might have called open-ended oubliettes. In fact, the Captain teased them into a race from floor to floor so as to see which of them arrived first at their private cabin.

Imagine their disappointment, however, when they both breathlessly reached the highest floor in the Drill, at the furthest point from the Drill's leading edge of a bit-tip. Their cabin turned out to be a mock-up of a seedy city flat, with a damp smell, hung with stained and slightly bulging wallpaper... and a worn beige carpet or, dependent on the light, yellow carpet on the floor.

"There is always at least one thing that makes any event imperfect," had said the Captain with a wry smile, as if this explained the inferiority of the couple's quarters within the Drill.

It was here within the damp bed that Greg had awoken from his by now fully forgotten recurring dream—Beth beside him. And, indeed, the cabin itself had reverted to its original state of a sleek comfort-zone of tasteful décor. Not one single sign of seediness or mildewy carpets or peeling wallpaper anywhere.

Greg recalled, with still increasing wakefulness, that, the next day, the Drill (and them within it) would be setting forth on its big adventure. He smiled to himself as he listened to Beth contentedly dozing beside him in the cabin's plush double bed. Her snores could not disguise the trial revving noises of the Drill's bit-tip as the pilot rehearsed its re-ignition of spinning, even now at the dead of night. The Drill's launch would be quite well prepared by the time daylight appeared, Greg was sure—and a daylight firework display would be set off in celebration, with the sparks in cascades and their colours designed even to outshine the sun... colours that would include black as well the more usual brighter colours of fireworks.

Mike took one glance at Susan, Arthur and Amy, the three of them vanishing towards the point on the dark horizon where they had seen the two small match-thin figures sink down into it—and he loped after them, conserving his energy because distances looked further than they actually were in the north's night land.

A number of black seagulls flapped their wings inefficiently above him as he plugged on beneath their migrating cloud. One defecated on him. Gulls were traditionally prone to a sod's-law more than any other foulness of the sky—certainly as far as human targets were concerned. But this was no normal birdmuck. It was gull vomit that stung the top of his head, searing his scalp through the hair. Gull's vomit—a sign of bad luck. *Black* gull's vomit—worse than the worst bad luck. All the vomit was spotted with blood-flecks whatever the gull's own body colour. So one could never be certain which type of gull had splattered you unless you saw the gull itself. And the sky's roof camouflaged any of the stub-winged birds that managed to coast or skim along its under-surface.

Ogdon sat on the customer's side of his pub's bar, staring into the decorative mirror behind the gleaming shorts and their optics. The reflective glass had the word C – O – U – R – A – G – E etched in swirls of artistic lettering at the top of the mirror: an advert for one of the bitters that were sold there. Ogdon could see his own face lower down between a bottle of rum and a bottle of vodka. But it wasn't his face but that of a Spanish playwright by the name of Lope de Vega who, Odgon always thought, was the author of "La Vida Es Sueño", but he also thought William Congreve had written "She Stoops To Conquer", so whether Ogdon was correct about any literary matters was anybody's guess! In any event, he imagined a dialogue between himself and the reflection in the mirror. There was nobody else to whom he could talk—the barmaid (a replacement for Susan) being down the other end of the bar and not seeming to have anything much in common with Ogdon; and she freely admitted to being a fan of the 'Big Brother' TV show and other Soap Operas. And it was now that no-man's-land of time between popular drinking sessions: and next to no customers were present to listen to his pub small-talk.

Ogdon: There is one people carrier.

Reflection: A people carrier?

O: Yes, a human being who's infecting the birds with a virus, and not vice versa.

R: Now that sounds possible, but how do you know?

O: Well, the birds are becoming more like red meat than white poultry-flesh when you cut them open.

R: As if they've got an animal disease?

O: Turning them gradually, from a bird into an animal or half and half. And they've caught it from us humans. Or they have just started to catch it from us humans. That's why many of them can't fly any more and only hop about. Their whole essence is somehow corrupted.

R: So, they don't need roofs to aviary cages any more in the zoo? Makes you want to cry.

O: There is one single bird that is in charge of all the other birds. Did you know that? A sort of Bird God. This Bird God is set to wreak vengeance…

R: Really? What do they call it?

O: Like all gods in religion, the birds know it with different names or no name at all.

R: If it's got no name at all, what do the birds think of when they think of it?

Ogdon pulled a sheet of paper from his pocket, placed it on the damp drink-stained surface of the bar and started to write out a few of the possible names for the Bird God. He then folded it up and returned it to his pocket. He had by now forgotten about the conversation... until the reflection brought him back by asking a further question: "Can the Bird God, whatever its name, stop birds coming in contact with the people carrier?"

"It remains to be seen," answered Ogdon, now forgetting his own point or why he had started the topic or even the whole topic itself—as if he had simply been doodling with words and concepts... in the composition of an abstract poem. If he thought the destiny of the whole world depended on the outcome of his thoughts, he would have been more careful with those very thoughts or just tried to be less thoughtful altogether.

"It's the beer talking" was a saying that Ogdon's mother often said—usually about his father, her husband. His mother was very wise, he thought, as he called out to the barmaid: "Chalk up on the blackboard that drinks are on Happy Hour all night!"

He returned to his thoughts, desperately wanting the people who were caught up in these thoughts of his to be believeable, sympathisable figures: because, if not, there would be no way that the conflicts in store for them would be sustainable conflicts at all. These people were in danger, he thought, of becoming mere ciphers acting in a game, or a dream, or a lie. Little did he know, however, that the people themselves (Mike, Greg, Susan, Beth and so forth)—currently on the brink of enormous human significance—were essentially real: tangible bodies with flesh and blood, owning minds that could be hurt or filled with joy, thinking thoughts that could be clarified, confused or defused.

Meanwhile, by comparison, he, Ogdon, was the emptiest cipher of them all, less real even than his own reflections. Hence, the sheet of paper.

One viewpoint is that his dream is separate, insulated, uninfecting and uninfected.

An alternative viewpoint would be that the dream itself—this we read—was infected from outside.

Or, yet, as there always are three alternatives, the dream itself infected other dreams, other realities.

Reflection:

The daylight firework-display on the open plateau of the Left Foot Region was indeed a sight to behold. It was intended as environmental context for the Drill's 'lift-off'. The bright primary colours of each of the individual swellings or plumes of flame, their sprays, cascades and visible thunderous bangers were so sharp-etched, sharp-edged, they seared to the very optic fuse of one's retina. The wide shiny blue sky faded by comparison. Some of the colours were not colours as such but various shades of black, many being utterly black slices and slashes of display—accentuating how faded the sky's otherwise bright backdrop had become. Meanwhile, the revving throbs of the Drill's engine took sway as the sunlight sparked off the fast-revolving bit-tip at the Drill's lower leading-edge. The pilot could be seen grappling with the controls in his cockpit as the bit-tip finally met the beachy terrain beneath it with a sickening crunch—both the bit-tip's self-induced sparks and the crunching noise now outdoing the firework display which had previously outdone all else.

Ogdon turned from the mirror and busied himself with more pressing duties that the current Happy Hour in his pub had created.

Mike reached the area on the horizon (a horizon now turned into the hard-rippled ground beneath his feet) where the rest of his party seemed—at the previous distance from which he had viewed them—to have slowly sunk from sight. The others had, in their turn, been pursuing two stick-thin figures of child-size that, it was assumed, were the stolen or missing identities as children of Amy and Arthur who were also in the same party pursuing the same figures. Mike's wife Susan and her teenage daughter Sudra were also in the party, so Mike panicked when thinking that something evil had befallen them. He could not remember why he was so behindhand with his own pursuit.

Any possible quicksand needed to be respected by means of a slow approach to its suspected whereabouts. He had shouted out warnings to the others. However, there was no sign of quicksand at this headpoint in the northern coalfields. The sky had, by now, grown even darker and he wondered how dark any sky could possibly grow. Was there a black blacker than black? Despite this, there was a thin effulgence which picked out an untidy mound of what appeared to be old stiff and rumpled carpet in the vicinity of where the others had last been seen. That was the only way he could describe the sight before gingerly approaching the odd crumplings to investigate what it was and whether any blackness could exceed any other blackness. This and different rhetorical questions buzzed through his head, some relatively sensible, others completely crazy or off-the-wall—and he felt himself desperate in not being able to differentiate the crazy from the sensible.

He was a hawler, he knew, and, amid the current mishmash of his mind's thoughts and questions, the concept of 'hawler' seemed—against all the odds—to crystallise. A miner went down to gather fossil-fuel never expecting to return to the surface. The word 'miner' derived from 'mine'—as in 'belonging to me'. It all seemed so simple. That was why the Himalayas were so high. It made sense. And the *Mappa Mundi* in Hereford Cathedral seemed to set a varying context of clarification. And the Ewbank—a brand of non-electric carpet-cleaner. Hoover, too. Who? Bewhiched—Susan's Herstyle—much was unravelling as he tried to gather his thoughts… Hurler... Horla… hair-curler…

He looked down at his own hands. The nails were too long—the recent events preventing all manner of ablution or body-care. His tongue felt his teeth, teeth that now seemed too big for his mouth—a most uncomfortable feeling. He needed to sink them into something juicy... or creamy. He needed to reach the core of things and haul off its bone-caged heart. Feast off its pulsing meaty pith. Milk its weakening metabolism. And he knew, in this context, that filters could work both ways…

At that sudden point in his thoughts, all his teeth clamped and became (or felt like) a flickering hinge of two scooped out bones.

Soon, however, the storm of thoughts subsided and Mike became worried again about the others in his party. There was a gap in the blackness of the ground beneath his feet; he lowered his head to peer into the ragged aperture. He sensed it was merely an oubliette of vacant earth—so he was amazed to find a further sense that followed the first sense indicating it was the start of a shaft that reached beyond any conceivable depth possible within the context of earthen tunnel-able dimensions. When did depth become height? Another question that was soon forgotten when he saw, in the thin effulgence, that there was a spiky hedge filling the gap in the ground—and, at the back of his mind, he somehow recalled the time when he had first encountered such a hedge, needing to thread his own body through such a tangled mass of twigs and sharp leaves. But, then, it was a horizontal hedge which grew along and from the surface of the ground. This new hedge was a vertical one; he knew instinctively it would be relatively easy to push aside and penetrate its nettly growths in a downward path—but if he changed his mind and tried to come back up through the hedge, such growths would have closed ranks, changed points of direction, with each spike jagging against the matted grain, making any escape impossible.

He heard the other's voices below him from within the hedge's ambit but he could not judge whether they called for help or for him to join them in the renewed pursuit. Nor could he judge if they had fallen accidentally through the hedge that had opened up its scratchy spindly arms to welcome them into the undergrowth (in the true sense of that word) or if they had jumped with joyful shrieks into its enticing knots of wood-nymphs. His mind was evidently still trying to play tricks on itself. At least all this explained the stick-figures that had tempted them this far. Explanation, however, is not a two-way filter.

Reflection (talking to itself with alternating prurient relish and prim properness in a now empty pub):

It is hard to reconcile the earlier characters of Mike, Susan, Sudra, Amy and Arthur with their later madness in undertaking such a downward search. Mike had soon faced this conundrum even more starkly by investigating the so-called crumply mound of 'carpet' only to discover it was a pile of discarded clothes. All of them had indeed needed to take off their clothes to be able to slide with greater ease through the hedge-filled tunnel as the spikes would have otherwise snagged on the teased and worried material of even underwear. Therefore, they spent their first sleep-stop completely naked (it couldn't be called 'spending the night' as the thin effulgence that seeped through the tunnel was uniform, thus making it impossible to differentiate between seasons of time), but they had managed by then to re-establish their personalities, inhibitions and vulnerability to fear—just like the real people that they had been when first walking through the city zoo, certain then what was dream and what was not dream. This hedgy drop was another area—as with the zoo—where one could be oneself without fear of becoming other than oneself. Not confusing what was real and what was not real. What was and what was not.

Ogdon (returning out of the blue to his position opposite the mirror, cigarette glowing redly):

But don't forget when they were in the zoo, someone, for whatever reason, left quite unreported one of the sights they saw in a cage just before leaving the zoo!

Reflection nodded sagely.

Amy finished carpet-sweeping, turned over the Ewbank and emptied what it contained. Not only flies from a cabbage fell out.

Greg inside the Drill, just before its 'launch' and its now famous daylight firework-display, had dreamed of Amy in various inexplicable roles—which was a bit surprising as he didn't know Amy at all well. Amy was more Mike's acquaintance than Greg's. Yet, Greg had also dreamed that he, Greg, was not Beth's husband and equally Beth's husband was not Greg. A further dream, or rather, nightmare, made him live through an existence where he and Mike were the same person—which belied their quite distinct characters as men of the world. Perhaps Greg's dream had reflected that they—he and Mike—may indeed have been distinct characters, but also that nobody (other than Greg and Mike themselves) could distinguish one from the other. In another dream, Greg felt as if trapped within an outlandishly huge trunk of a Canterbury Oak—unable to budge up or down. He heard voices, familiar voices, but from within the nightmare he sensed that they were quite *un*familiar voices and that he failed to grasp that it was a Canterbury Oak at all—because in the dream he was simply trapped in a vertical body-hugging coffin.

He woke in a sweat—only to feel the Drill around him starting to throb, as its pilot made a few playful testing twirls of the bit-tip before making the final teasing approach towards earth encounter.

Beth, already up, having creamed her face with beauty unguents, was standing at their cabin window, eager for the start of their trip. Indeed, it was ironic that the best view of the trip would be the one currently from this window, because soon the window would be immersed or covered with earth's own crumbly curtains for the duration. Inner earth itself was—like the city zoo—a discrete dream-territory and any dreams they dreamed once they'd entered the earth would be clear-cut dreams, unconfused with waking life—so they would need to acclimatise in due course with the new conditions. Meanwhile, they could enjoy (if that was the correct word) the blurring of reality and dreams as a thought-provoking accompaniment to the start of their journey—against which backdrop they would soon be able to enjoy dreams for dreams' sake rather than the enforced dream-curdling of the rest of their waking life which prevailed above ground, in most places, other than designated areas such as the city zoo. Speaking of which, the city zoo had a lot to answer for, because it was too high-profile, too often trumpeted as the only discrete dream zone, a fact which created a situation where most people forgot that being underground was a better way of sorting dreams from non-dreams. There was far more underground available to explore and where to spend one's time than upon the finite surface of the overground.

Greg got up from the bed and joined Beth at the window. It was yet a few minutes before the final 'lift-off' and he knew there was to be a firework display as accompaniment—a display which had apparently now started. But it was a pretty pathetic affair—a few spluttering Roman Candles, a Catherine Wheel that refused to spin on its nail, a number of bangers that farted in a spinsterly fashion. One of the fireworks, however, wasn't too bad inasmuch as it quite successfully depicted a peacock with a fan of rainbow fire, pluming smoke in grey sculptures that reminded Greg of maps in the making. The traditional bonfire was ignited but spluttered to a dead heap since it was not doused enough in petrol... but the Drill's bit-tip at last struck the beachy terrain with a teeth-on-edge grinding... as the Drill began to delve towards its journey's path. The firework display thus soon became an irrelevancy.

Greg now sensed one of the helicopter vanes from the Drill's back flashing by their cabin window like a camera shutter strobing or a dose of rarefied migraine or a foreign flicker at the screen's edge as an old film was projected upon it.

Earlier, upon their first arrival in the Drill, Greg and Beth had met two unexpected additional paying-passengers on board. These were dowager ladies by the names of Edith and Clare—and nobody knew from the way they acted, whether they were just good friends, blood sisters or more than just good friends. If they were sisters, the family likeness was quite remarkable. The Drill's Captain seemed to know these two ladies already—but he retained a professional approach to any passengers and had promised them all to show and comment upon the various sights through the window of 'The Hawler' during the coming trip.

The two ladies were avid readers in the Drill's library, being particular fans of Marcel Proust's *Du Côté De Chez Swann*—and there was also much promise of them sharing their reading passions with Greg and Beth, should there be periods during the trip when there would be time for all of them to kill…

Ogdon held his head in his hands after he had looked round his empty pub. The headlines of the newspaper in his hands spoke of the mysteries of *Angevin* which had taken away most of his customers—and even those who remained in the city stayed in their houses these days dreaming of drinking Angel Wine... or even drinking it for real.

Nevertheless, there was still activity in the city and, in the distance, he could hear the sound of serious clanking—so hugely riveting—so vastly ear-splitting and ground-grinding—he guessed it was another huge broken ship or liner being forcibly dragged for mending to the Dry Dock nearby. A gigantic contingent of shift-workers and trained apes were involved in its transport to this its temporary berth... and no doubt many of this contingent would be visiting Ogdon's pub later... but with no bar staff left, he may as well lock the doors now.

However, before Ogdon could do so, he spotted a face in the bar mirror opposite, a face that wasn't his own. There were tears running liberally down its cheeks. The face spoke:

"Help me, I'm Greg. *Please* don't let me be Mike. I know it's easy to confuse us but I'm the one who's on board the Drill. I once worked in waste management as a lorry-driver. Mike was the office worker. I'm desperate to be real, but only if I can be me, me, Greg. Because I *am* Greg."

Ogdon's own eyes were also filling up, feeling helpless to help. There were too many people who needed to become their real selves. It was difficult enough for Ogdon to hold his own mind together.

"I'm Greg," continued the face opposite. "Help me, I'm Greg. Help me to be Greg. And not Mike."

It was a ghostly chant or intonation. And Ogdon threw his glass across the bar and it smashed itself before it smashed the mirror and all the mirror's contents.

But he still heard the plaintive, haunting voice: "I'm Greg. Please don't let me be Mike."

And now the face was scratched and freshly scarred as if it had been dragged through a hedge backwards.

Crazy Lope was settled in front of his drink of Angel Wine, surrounded by the customary sticks of furniture that populated the top flat of an inner city block. He had just switched off his wireless because, he guessed, the news was full of lies. His cape hung on the door-hook like a giant bird-of-prey at rest. He stared at the Angel Wine before daring to take a sip. It was sold like milk in the city these days, without fear or favour, to rich and poor, young and old, sane and insane alike. In fact, it looked like milk, but even whiter, creamier. The supplies had been freed up to prevent a black market emerging for it—yet a lot of money was still being made by those who *were* supplying it. From whatever source, nobody knew. Its original tradename was *Angevin*, but most customers in the city could only get their mouths round the English tongue—and soon Angel Wine (a very evocative name, as it turned out to be, from the mouth of whoever coined it) took over and now it was on all tongues.

Lope slowly raised the glass to his lips and allowed them to sip slowly, then sup noisily, lapping with a relish... not at all like milk to the tongue's feel or taste, but more a slimy consistency with a fabricated flavour of aniseed which could not really conceal its insipid chemical quality: he sensed a deeper undertaste or aftertaste even more insipid. He was savouring not so much the taste or drinkability for a deadened thirst but more the mental effects that sped to his brain in a direct socket-to-socket fashion from the tongue, or so it seemed. The relishing experience prevented him from spotting that he had accidentally spilled some of the Angel Wine—in a slow motion of the liquid's sluggish specific gravity—to his flat's carpet.

Somewhere, in a clouded mirror, appeared a wide face—wider even than the mirror itself so that one could not see the face's edges, howsoever they stretched beyond the mirror's frame. Slowly, but as quickly as the time passed, the wide face grew cloudier and yellowier—and a beak emerged as part of a narrow face from within the original wide one that faded from around the second face, with a pecking and sharp-nodding combined.

"I'm me. *Please* don't let me be other than me..." And tears runnelled down the face like Angel Wine. The words spoken, however, weren't from an English tongue.

Sudra squatted with her young nude body upon a narrow ledge in the thin effulgence of the hedgy tunnel. Her companions snored nearby—in equally precarious sleeping perches—no doubt dreaming. They had just undergone a long but relatively easy descent so far—and it didn't seem to matter that none of them truly appreciated the real purpose of their quest. A quest for a quest was the nearest they could come to it. In times of trial, solutions presented themselves in odd disguises and even created thoughts they would never have dreamt of thinking as thoughts in more ordinary times.

The hedge itself had almost *helped* their descent of passage: a far cry from hindering it as they originally expected—but woe betide if they should need to climb back up through it, whereupon it would surely turn upon them with a vengeance. The only real problem was the soot-like substance that clung to the hedge's twigs and branches, a damp consistency that Arthur seemed to recognise (but he kept his cards close to his chest) and that dampness tended to get down their chests causing coughs which they prayed were nothing to do with the more general sicknesses they'd heard rumoured in the city before embarking on this journey. The stickness (not sickness or even stickiness) of the two pursued creatures, suspected as substitutes for Amy and Arthur, was simply more than a dream away—despite their often hearing these creatures crackling (if not cackling) further down in the hedge towards even lower regions than anyone could imagine approaching without feeling the traditionally believed molten heat of earth's Core.

Soon enough, Sudra herself dozed off on her ledge and dreamed. She dreamed of being a small girl again and of the Christmas when she was due to receive a pair of new shoes as a present. She knew it was a real dream because she was dreaming it far beneath the surface of the earth—and it mattered little that the events in the dream took place above ground and in the past and upon her old bedroom carpet. She simply knew instinctively within (and, later, from outside) the dream that it was a real dream and not real life—although the dream was *about* real life, a real life from the past, filtered by both her dreaming and waking minds—so it was uncertain whether the dream was exactly how the real events once were—but they were surely close enough to reality to be called a reflection of reality in the future of the past, Sudra's past.

Those promised new shoes had been important to her as a very young girl that Christmas: more important than anything else before or since. Even the flies in the cabbage were forgotten when she turned her mind towards the prospect of the new shoes that she had been promised. The flies in the cabbage had been originally important because she'd been instructed to clean the cabbage ready for supper and the task had now taken on a frightful dimension when she discovered a nest of black stringy flies at its heart. All she needed to do, however, was to think of the new shoes (which she imagined as supple yellow leather with blue laces)—and then all the troubles that beset her young mind seemed to be assuaged, healed, removed to a new dimension where she did not exist and if she did not exist there why should she worry about anything that happened in that dimension? This was not exactly an out-of-body experience but more a projection of a troubled ghost from her body into areas where that ghost could be left to cope with problems by paradoxically escaping the same problems otherwise besetting her real self—here—today.

She dreamed about all that in the future but once upon a time she had lived through it all for real, indeed lived through all such thoughts as real thoughts. She tried not to recall who had told her to clean the cabbage. It was probably her late father (whose name she had since blotted from her mind). He had been a nasty man. She hated him and pitied her mother. She was later pleased when he died and Susan eventually remarried, and Mike became her stepfather. But in those old days Sudra pitied Susan having to live with such a nasty man as her real father. It had been Susan who had promised Sudra the new shoes—and, as the words 'new shoes' returned to Sudra's mind, the thoughts of her father, then and now, dispersed into forgotten memories, yet memories that lurked and silently threatened to return should she lower her guard. So as to prevent this eventuality, she kept repeating the words, 'New shoes, new shoes', time and time again, until the words 'New shoes'—more and more quickly said—took on a new meaning, almost a new sound, a new single word: 'Newshoes' and she could not even visualise its spelling, least of all fathom its meaning.

"Flies in the cabbage" became another expression or mantra which she tried to enchant with her chanting repetition of this phrase's syllables. "Flies in the cabbage, flies in the cabbage", trying to weld the words into unbroken letters and unbroken fragments or phonemes or morphemes. Yet, on this occasion, the spell didn't work and it brought her dead father to the bedroom door, staring at her, beady-eyed and smiling. Sometimes, smiles were evil. Indeed, smiles were always evil. People only smiled if they wanted to get something out of you, achieve something, delude someone. A smile was always a lie. Even her mother's smile, Susan's smile, hid something below it. And at that moment, the dream became a nightmare as a swarm of flies flew from her dead father's mouth and nose.

She woke with a start. Not from the dream she was dreaming but from the dream she was dreaming *about.*

"New shoes, New shoes, New shoes," she quickly chanted as she found herself in her dark bedroom—at the cusp of Christmas Eve and Christmas Day. She smiled to herself as she saw a shadowy figure with a prodding horizontal beard at the place where its chin should have been—with a long cape-like body silhouetted against an even darker backdrop, a backdrop that seemed to ooze the natural darkness into the room. She hoped she knew who this figure was. She convinced herself she knew the real colour of the cape-enveloped shape, because red wine often did look like black wine when Susan left a bottle of it in a dark corner. The figure placed a package on the bed, with a crinkly paper sound, together with its heavy weight upon her feet that were in the part of the bed where the package had been laid upon it. She sighed and fell asleep with a sense of satisfaction, submitting herself to dreams she was destined not to remember when she woke up on Christmas morning.

The Christmas bells woke her with a steady tolling—and the sun surprised her with its Winter power as it shafted through the ceiling-light and also surprised her how it had not woken her before the bells had woken her. "New shoes" were the first words she spoke—both an incantation and an expression of truth as she pounced out of bed intent on reaching the package left at the end of the same bed from which she had just pounced. The words doubled up on themselves in unnecessary repetitive patterns as if to delay the time before she opened the package, because, even if she herself didn't realise what was happening, everything-else-that-could-think thought that she would be devastated by the contents of the package and anyone describing these events needed to spend as much time describing these events as possible to delay the inevitable—describing aspects of the room, its carpet, the sunshine, the bells, all of which were quite untrue—in the increasing desperation of preventing the young girl from reaching the package in which she believed were lovingly wrapped new shoes of supple yellow leather and blue laces that she had been promised for Christmas, new shoes with feminine trimming, small studs on the soles to create sparks on the pavement, vestigial spurs on the heels to allow her to pretend she was an elf or fairy—and toecaps of silver beauty that would spark more naturally than the studs without any sharp friction, sparking in the sunlight that still shafted through the ceiling-light as she finally, inexorably reached the package, eager to unwrap it without caring whether the wrapping-paper was torn in the process because the all-important things were the package's contents, the new shoes, the new shoes, the new shoes, the new shoes, the new shoes, the new shoes, the new shoes that she would wear all day, that perfect Christmas Day—and Boxing Day, too. And, in the end, she reached the package without much help or hindrance from outside forces and she started to unpeel the various wrappings as if it were a pass-the-parcel game for one person. A cunning game for first thing on a Christmas morning. She could not hear her mother stirring—although she sensed the front room fire was already blazing. And, at last, there they were—the new shoes in all their glory. She whispered "new shoes" through her milk teeth, with awe and wonder and an intoxication beyond any angel's wine. She was past all possible excitement. This was now a tranquil moment, amid the hubbub of her busy childhood. A moment to cherish forever. If a moment could indeed last forever. The new shoes were no disappointment. Supple yellow leather, indeed, and black laces. Not blue laces, but that didn't matter. The colour of the laces was only a minor detail. These were perfect shoes. The new shoes to complete a childhood. All else could be forgotten.

She woke she knew not from which dream within which other dream. The nightmare was not the contents of any dream but not knowing how many dreams she had to travel as dreamer and dreamed to get back to her real self. "New shoes," she whispered through her milk teeth or through her old yellow teeth or through her toothless mouth. "New shoes," she repeated as she walked to her bed on bare floorboards, the carpet gone. All that she was sure about was that *the laces had tied themselves.*

Sudra woke on her shelf in the hedgy tunnel and smiled.

It is common knowledge, of course, that Beth's husband had in truth remained in the city—within a safe-house—whilst Greg was currently in the Drill masquerading either knowingly or unknowingly (it mattered little which of these) as Beth's husband... thus providing Beth's husband in the safe-house with an alias or, even, an alter-nemo (a more subtle form of alter-ego). *Notes to be clarified, scratched the stub of the pencil as it wrote out various repercussions regarding this knowledge.*

Beth's husband, in this way, was rather proud to have become Beth's *real* husband, there having been a rather complex arrangement between various parties—including Beth herself—for this situation to prevail. Beth had deliberately and voluntarily brainwashed herself—by a neat lie technique invented by a certain wing of the City Authorities, not a lie-detector as such but more a lie-fixer or a lie-fictioner—to believe that Greg was her real husband. Meanwhile, her really real husband—as yet nameless—arranged various factions back in the city to deal with the transport and distribution of the *Angevin* substance and its offcuts.

The only source for the raw materials that made up *Angevin* was the cream substance found to be cached at the earth's Core. As with all scarce resources cherished by certain factions of humanity, there was both a cost and a danger in harvesting it. Or mining it, if that's a better word.

(1) The logistics of travelling to the earth's Core,

(2) grappling with the 'Corekeeper' whose name needed to be fixed and thus neutered for prevention of its impeding the necessary work in the broadly difficult mechanics of the harvesting process itself (details of which will have to be left to kick in later, so that the full implications can hit home in full relevancy),

(3) the harvest process itself, and

(4) the hawling of the 'cream', i.e. transporting it back to the earth's surface where most of humanity lived and where it could be refined in the 'Dry Dock' facility (a mobile industrial complex that was used to fool the other wings of the City Authorities). *Meanwhile, barrels of the stuff are in impenetrable containers stockpiled within the covered market (the underground part of it for obvious reasons) and the purest form of it (worth millions of pounds) is now held, by all accounts, in certain enclosed areas of the city zoo.*

All these mechanics (some unspoken)—including the inevitable 'hawling' process which was more difficult than the earlier harvest process—aren't necessarily listed out as logically as it seems. Most of it is a mere summary of Beth's husband rehearsing the whole tangled process from beginning to end... rehearsing it in a rather fragmentary conversation that he was conducting with a new *Angevin* recruit who sat with Beth's husband in his flat housed at the top of the safe-house.

The recruit was evidently female behind a veil which she twitched from time to time giving her co-conversationalist tantalisingly sexy glimpses of her inscrutable face.

"Regarding point (3), has anyone got any nearer nailing the Corekeeper's real name?"

Her voice was lilting in a rather Welsh fashion. Her shoes intermittently were scrunching the carpet, rumpling it up towards the table where various official papers sat, papers instrumental to the conference that was still proceeding between the two of them.

On one wall was a series of large hinged maps on top of each other, maps which Beth's husband would later lift to show to the female recruit as part of revealing the Nemonymous Navigation intrinsic to the whole master plan for the contraband and its later distribution—including any financial interchange which, after all, remained the vital end result of everything that went before it.

On a second wall was a reproduction of Rubens' *Massacre of the Innocents*. On a third wall was another painting, by an unknown artist—depicting a naked man with a beard who had a large white swan sitting on his lap... and he was fondling the long neck in a rather salacious fashion.

The fourth wall was bare but sporting central curtains on a *Twin Peaks* trademarked silent runner, implying there was a window behind them. In the distance, a night bus could be heard faintly droning past. Helicopters weren't allowed over any part of the city these days.

The flat otherwise was quite neat, as if a cleaner and/or decorator had worked quite hard to spruce it up, but it still showed indelible signs of previous seediness.

The recruit nodded and briefly slipped aside the lower half of her veil to reveal the pique of a smile.

Beth was more impatient than her sister Susan—so she was eager for the Drill to reach its destination and their holiday proper to begin. She had been told to bring all manner of things in her luggage, including respectable swimwear and a high factor suncream. So her expectations were quite sufficiently filled with excitement. But, all in all, she didn't really know what to expect.

The mention of Susan in her mind reminded her for a moment that Susan had faded from her life in recent times. In fact, Susan had faded from many lives including anyone who was interested in her fate, along with her husband—what was his name?—Mike? Beth could hardly visualise them—and the excitement of each moment prevented memories from filling the less than momentary gaps between those very moments. *But they were all later symphonically saved by the portrait dreams (more of which later in this movement).*

The actual logistics of the Drill's journey itself, the means as it were to its ends, she would need to leave to her husband Greg to describe or rationalise or reconcile or extrapolate upon. All she herself could recall was that the Drill's first penetration of the earth's crusty rind was carried out with a tremendous amount of vibrating, as the helicopter-like vanes on its back took the strain of the task of industrially churning the excess waste from the downward path's terrestrial backflow... in fact those very vanes created that rubbly backflow, as the Captain had called it when warning them about it before the journey started. A wonderful invention this Drill, she assumed, but she failed to appreciate the scale and the complexity and exactly how the various interconnecting devices worked as a synergy of 'human coning', as the Captain called it.

Thoughts of the Captain again reminded Beth of Greg. She hadn't seen her husband for several days and she assumed he must indeed be with the Captain, in the secure cockpit ambit of the lower Drill... being shown better views (better than her own views) via windows nearer the bit-tip. All she could see through her own cabin window or the library windows was the passing sameness of crazy-paved slabs of lubricated earth—lubricated by a creamy oil that the Drill exuded from several 'pores' or 'gills' along its hull to ease the drag of friction or the danger of gouging by rogue rocks. After the initial teeth-grinding vibration, the Drill's journey so far had been relatively smooth, give or take the odd crunchy jolt.

Thoughts of Greg had in turn reminded her intermittently to connect herself to the 'lie-fixer'—although she didn't call it that. It was more like the need for beauty sleep or sunbed treatment. It was a contraption that looked indeed more like a sunbed than a science-fictional synapse adaptor with throbbing electronics (which it effectively was). She simply needed to lie on it and be reminded... literally.

It was a rather refreshing and feminine activity to have to do. Far better than those mud baths she took regularly for her complexion. The mud, actually, on board the Drill, derived from loess.

In the Drill's ornately leather-bound book-lined library, Beth often met up with the dowager ladies, Edith and Clare. It was akin to the coffee-mornings which Beth used to conduct in the City—when Greg was out at work. The turning over of gossip and the planting of metaphorical daggers. Edith and Clare were however more intellectually inclined than any of the previous members of Beth's hen parties. There was classical music going all day in the library at least as an undercurrent of sound—such as Philip Glass's *Akhnaten* or Wagner's *Parsifal.* The two ladies often knew the exact name of the music being played and details of the composers. They were also very well read, trying to get Beth into reading Marcel Proust's *In Search Of Lost Time.* Beth, however, soon gave up—without even finishing the first volume: *Swann's Way.* The sentences were far too long for her and too florid—and nothing much happened to the characters (whom she couldn't really visualise in any event) and what was all that about dunking a *petit madeleine* cake in a cup of tea?

Beth accidentally picked up a fantasy book entitled *Crazy Lope & Godspanker* by someone or other, but the first sentence put her off: "The carpet was quite ordinary." Surely, there were better ways to start a book, she thought. In any event, she didn't like Fantasy or Science Fiction—and certainly not Horror. The blurb on the back cover mentioned it was an 'alternate world' fiction treating of the rabbit plague in Fifties England where the rabbit's disease—myxomatosis—mutated and spread into a human-to-human disease, thus wiping out the population. Dreary stuff, she thought, slapping the book back on the table, next to Proust.

Edith finally found some classics for Beth such as the Brontës and Jane Austen, until Beth did manage to find some pleasure in this middle-of-the-road literature, even without fully understanding all the social undercurrents of the historical settings. She did however have a good laugh at the title *Wuthering Heights.* She thought of the Drill as wuthering depths! Dickens and Shakespeare could probably wait for the return journey, suggested Clare. If there *is* a return journey, thought Edith.

The two ladies were very touchy-feely and Beth finally decided that they were not her type of people, but beggars couldn't be choosers in such confined spaces. Like coach trips on the earth's surface, one tried to mix with the other passengers to help the time pass much more pleasantly. Polite standards and talking terms needed to be manicured.

All three of them shared the loess treatment in the form of white mud baths—to tone up their otherwise scrawny bodies. Beth cringed however one day when she spotted Edith eating a bit of it as she wallowed in it.

At night, after several weeks of these dreary waking hours between her bouts of sleep, Beth dreamed. She knew they were dreams because she was now so far underground, they couldn't be anything but dreams. She slept in the cabin meant for her and Greg, but by now she had almost forgotten she had come on holiday with Greg. There was not even any intercom to the cockpit, where she assumed, if she assumed anything at all, Greg was being guested by so-called Captain Nemo—hobnobbing as men of the world tended to do.

The dreams were almost literary, if not literal. Quite beyond her control. No doubt her mind had been affected by the middle-of-the-road fiction or literature she had been fed by the dowager ladies. Each dream was a short prose portrait of each person she had once known and thought she had forgotten.

At first, there was, of course, Susan. She saw Susan's pretty face, prettier than her own, but when they were younger, Beth had been the prettier. Susan spoke and hoped Beth was OK. This particular portrait approached the nature of a nightmare as Beth thought she saw Susan in near-darkness, naked, being scratched by a spiky hedge-like thing.

Mike, too. He, however, was more forthcoming with the circumstances of his scratched-face plight. He smiled at Beth, nevertheless. Beth tried to remember what Mike had done as a job in the city. Was he a warehouseman at the covered market or a lorry-driver in waste management or an office businessman or even a bus-driver? Mike answered but when she woke up from the portrait, she had forgotten what he had said.

Arthur reminded her of someone she once knew as a child, but she couldn't now place him as a grown-up. She dreamed of him—much thinner—mixing some foreign substance into her bath of loess treatment. Amy was a similar portrait, except Amy was with another girl called Sudra, and they both fought over a pair of yellow shoes (crazy stuff, dreams!) and Beth couldn't really differentiate one portrait from another.

Ogdon, the pub-keeper, was always a good friend to Beth. He was still this friend even from within his carefully constructed portrait. Like all the other portraits, it was described at great length with elegant words in a carefully crafted syntax of prose. The semantics were fluid, however. Delightfully so.

Beth woke from the Ogdon portrait with a start. The Drill had just jolted so violently all the light had been sucked from the cabin.

All those children who had earlier left the city along with Amy and Arthur—or along with the foreshortened versions of Amy and Arthur as they subsequently turned out to be—were evidently seeking apertures in the earth but carrying out this search without any known conscious reason for so doing.

They had, however, in hindsight, been 'lie-fixed' to seek apes for breeding—and these apes were said to live in caves. But that begs the question, how deep can a cave become before it loses its identity as a cave? Even Plato's Cave was above sea-level. Surely, the deeper a cave becomes the more it approximates a pot-hole. In its turn, the deeper a pot-hole becomes the more it approximates a terrestrial oubliette or unhawlable cache—especially as there is no access from the surface to reach such an oubliette or cache. On the other hand, the children themselves were, perhaps, apes in the making, having been force-fed some mutant form of *Angevin* to reverse the evolutionary process. History apparently was full of Angevin Apes and they played a large part at the Battle of Agincourt, but exegesis of primary sources (such as excision of any knowledge of the infections brought back to England by Henry The Fifth and his cohorts) has ensured that vital components of the *need* for apes today and what part they played throughout Toynbeean history are now largely forgotten.

Some children, as already hinted, did, however, remain in the city, either variably untouched by the 'lie-fixer' or simply too lame to travel far—and these children now ran wild, because many of their previous external authorisers as well as their own self-discipline were so badly dissipated by every attempt to corrupt all levels of society in age, wealth, creed and sanity.

These children often made visits to the now semi-derelict zoo, believing that its reputation remained as a rare area of surface land where dream-clarification and dream-justification were easiest to accomplish, as well as being a reputed seat for zoological learning, with or without implications to any history (alternate or not)... although the latter was not important to the children, even if they had understood it.

John Ogdon, now increasingly at a loose end as a result of his pub lacking customers for ordinary alcohol, also spent some time in the zoo for its dream qualities, but also masquerading, as an excuse for his presence, in the shape of the zoo-keeper, i.e. the Authorities' last redoubt against civil unrest amid their pretence it was still a proper zoo where law-abiding citizens could spend a relaxing afternoon as well as learn about Natural History or Zoological Biodiversity.

Ogdon had now 'come out' (to the surprise of every onlooker) as a cross-dresser, strutting as he now did amongst the cages and enclosures in high-heels and a beige frock. The children called him 'Hilda'.

Crazy Lope was now rarely seen, except, in Ogdon's absence, when it suited him to turn up in his cape and scare the children with his antics. It was believed that a few dark myths such as those depicted in old Nursery Rhymes were a vital factor in a child's upbringing, and Crazy Lope was pleased to fulfil such a role. All light and brightness make Jack a dull soul, as the saying goes.

One day, a clutch of these residual children (now much thinner because of various imposed dietary factors combined with the ill-sustenance that general scavenging in the city enforced) turned up at the zoo for a desultory kickaround. The first enclosure was, as ever, empty. The cages and enclosures further into the real meat of the zoo were still no doubt at least partially inhabited by exhibits because they were fed by certain nightly manoeuvres of metabolism and airfly—but very few grown-ups went to check and any such remaining exhibits had inevitably become hearsay, as the children said they didn't know or deliberately didn't say anything at all. It was rumoured that the zoo's many birds had died, claws-up on the cage floors... except for one giant creamy-white poultry-thing that gradually bloated as if its claw-ends had rooted themselves into the ground (via the riven cage-floor) like a massive feathered plant-thing feeding off some unfathomable nourishment. It deeply chirped, but eventually it was mostly silent, still pulsing with some form of dubious existence.

The children—for whatever reason—usually played football around the outside of the 'empty' enclosure which had once been assumed (at least in one of the interpretations) to exhibit barely visible insect-life. On the day in question, one child took his eye momentarily off the ball and pointed excitedly at the scrubby soil in the enclosure.

"What are those?"

The others peered over the enclosure's barrier and gasped. Scattered all over the ground, within the enclosure, were what seemed to be hundreds of discarded toys. Clockwork ones, some budging slightly as if they had been insufficiently wound up. At a closer scrutiny, some were actually trying to burrow into the ground, making a very bad job of covering themselves for dignity's sake—showing, perhaps, that they thought themselves to be little better than catmuck.

As Ogdon later determined (on his tour of duty as zoo-keeper), the contraptions had indeed been a multitude of mini-Drills complete with gossamer vanes on their backs, each attempting—with some difficulty—to penetrate the hardened zoo floor. Meanwhile, in real time, the children were about to climb over the barrier to double-check the nature of what they still thought to be toys, toys with what one of them described as 'cockpits', but another child interrupted with a shout:

"It's Lope! Scram!"

Crazy himself turned into the zoo, intent upon becoming the children's routine nightmare of the day.

They scattered and vanished into all corners of the zoo, before gathering together instinctively like a flock of migratory birds, only to escape screaming with fright (or joy) by means of the now untenanted exit turnstile.

Later, Ogdon, still in full female regalia, was tripping the light fantastic down one of the city streets. Even at these darkest times, people like him shaped up larger-than-life and became a bigger-hearted version of themselves simply to face out the creeping dangers that the world supplied in the form of night plagues, dream terrorists or simple lunatics.

He spotted an evidently off-duty double-decker bus trying to park neatly outside a block of flats and he admired the preservation of such civilised standards even in these outlandish times. The vehicle was having some difficulty because a mini-tipster dumper overlapped the bus's usual allotted white-lined space alongside the pavement. Suddenly diverted, Ogdon stooped toward the sidewalk where he had spotted some feathery fur sprouting like white mould through the cracks between the paving-slabs, threatening to ooze further up and carpet the world with warm tessellated under-precipitation. He stooped lower to stroke it as if he felt he was in touch with something of which he was fond but would never begin to understand. *Never eat yellow snow*, was an army expression. It meant more now than ever, as he saw the mould grow mouldier.

Meanwhile, the bus had managed to budge the mini-tipster from its clamped spiky plinth into the kerbside gutter like a clumsily sizeable unwound toy. But, at that moment, a large explosion sounded from the Moorish quarter of the city and Ogdon found himself running with several others to see if he could aid the maimed and the dead.

The real 'Beth's husband' was now late-labelled Dognahnyi: perhaps one denemonisation too far, but he was still interviewing the new recruit (following the revelation) in his pent-house, the log fire glistening off the Rubens like neutered indoor-fireworks.

Dognahnyi (an early worm in any conversation): Have you managed to fix your dreams yet?

Recruit (still veiled, speaking Welsh-prettily, if semi-nasally): Fixed them, yes—or so I thought—but last night someone told me or I dreamed that someone told me that they had a dream recently of a foreign body torpedoing itself into their tower office-block. You know the one—the block round the corner from here with a roof garden and a complicated lift system that books on architecture often write about.

D: Yes, I know the one you mean. Where our man once worked when he was still a 'sleeping' hawler. I presume the torpedo thing came from the dream terrorists.

R: I suppose so—but it wasn't the classic jet-liner attack—it was a replica of the tower-block itself coming in at an abrupt angle and sticking itself like a pig about two-thirds of the way up.

D: Hmmm…that's interesting. I think if you have dreams or dreams of dreams like that, we can certainly use your skills for furthering the hawling process everywhere.

R (smiling beneath the veil): Thank you.

D (walking over to the curtains on silent runners making as if to open them): Out there are many situations that need fixing.

R: I know.

D: Such as that tower block—as you've just suggested—being attacked from the sky by itself! A very good example, that one is.

R: I believe you.

At that point, she slowly removed her veil.

Mike sat upon a ledge in the downward tunnel—just beyond the point where the hedge petered out together with a tapering into horizontality of a new tunnel—or a *perceived* horizontality from the perspective of the in-built sextant in this underground world and its effect on the brain's balance.

The hedge itself had tended to prevent dangerous free-fall but, equally, had not hindered their nude scaling-down to this point in the earth's interior.

Mike was pleased that it was now slightly more 'civilised' at this juncture of his party's journey. The stick-like 'hares' or decoys were indeed now fully absorbed into the Amyness and Arthurness of two among them. The group had grown somewhat, but the main constituents were still the main constituents.

Furthermore, there was now a service tunnel parallel with their own tunnel of concourse—and this service tunnel was complete with pulleys and ropes, passing clanking buckets to the surface from the Core itself. He readily assumed all was part and parcel of some quite complicated hawling-process which he was due to oversee, once his training was complete. And, surprisingly (but, in hindsight, not surprisingly), there were warm clothes waiting for them at this crossover point in the tunnel systems. Indeed, this must be an official root-exchange, whereby Mike now realised that all other approaches or 'attacks' towards the centre (such as the many Drill companies he had heard about) were quite *unofficial* or simply subterfuges.

He had heard earlier rumours that the immediate surrounding area of the Core was populated by a set of creatures known as Carpet Apes who tended to the necessary ablutions of the Megazanthus (one of the names which Mike was aware had been given to the Corekeeper)—and that the marginal 'land' around the Core itself was the legendary Agra Aska... but the facts were still uncertain even if the non-facts were now clearer.

However, the Carpet Apes (so-called) were probably a false assumption or, at best, an unfixed dream. He looked down at the coat with which he (and the others) had been supplied: a stiffish, ankle-length carpetty thing with simple arm apertures. At first it was uncomfortable to walk about in but one soon grew accustomed to its combination of warmth and bodily support. He had not yet questioned the fact that the nearer the Core they travelled, the colder it was becoming, despite history saying such a process should mean that you were approaching a molten heat centre.

He looked at the others—Susan, Sudra, Amy, Arthur etc.—in their carpet coats and he somehow knew whence the legend of the Carpet Apes must have derived—and he laughed at the antics of the others. One of them was doing a puppet-like jig in his or her stiffened coat and it was terribly funny. Apeish. Mike felt cheered.

Yet Mike questioned himself. He realised he was a hawler—always realised this perhaps—but now he knew it wasn't because he had previously been a hawler, but because he was about to become one. Self-identification by an as yet unproved anticipation was a dream-fixing he needed to address. It all seemed a very unsteady grounding for a vocation or a raison-d'etre. Mike shrugged and peered at his step-daughter Sudra as she now began to practise walking in her carpet coat. She took delight to tease him with her imputed beautiful body hidden beneath the dumpy beige covering and the ungainly yellow clod-hoppers on her feet—clogs, in fact, that were on all their feet. The thin effulgence of the previous hedge tunnel had given Mike few glimpses of her nudity…

He shook his head to himself. He should not be having such thoughts about a step-daughter, should he? He was a hawler, he knew. Yet a flawed hawler. He suddenly stopped laughing. *Later: Stub of pencil writes: Amy complains that readers have lost sight of who she is!*

In the days before the sudden jolt had stolen the light from Beth's cabin in the Drill, Greg and a few other nebulous businessmen were entertained by Captain Nemo in the corporate lounge, a select area on board that boasted viewing-windows close to the leading-edge of the bit-tip. The proceedings were a combination of a scientific lecture upon what they were seeing and pure holiday entertainment, all laced with cocktails.

Meanwhile, over the years, many had debated why the city needed two airports instead of one... now both derelict sites on the left and right arms of the city proper. This hadn't come up in general conversations or newspaper reports for quite a while but one must be seen to address this issue nevertheless, even if it's just for the sake of chasing some noumenon.

These airports were always benighted even in their respective hey-days. One theory was that they only served each other, i.e. short-haul flights between them taking place for their own sake, because it was easier to travel across the city by other means, even if one wanted to travel across the city at all. These airflights were later assumed to be merely acting as cover for their real flights—beneath the ground, with the main runways leading steeply down tunnels into the earth from each airport.

That extrapolation, however, was often taken too far and was nipped in the bud before it could actually take off. However, in even more recent days of the *Angevin* conspiracies, there was a renewal of its hypothetical undercurrents regarding the internal workings of the earth. More, perhaps, of that, in due course. What one has to take into account, meanwhile, is that nobody at all has been in control of hypotheses for a long time now, and any crazy brainstorming has indeed eventually become the norm—with even written documents (where one should normally have inferred a responsible writer of such documents or, at least, an editorial chief/steering-committee) being considered just as bad as pub talk. Equally, the inverse may be true, i.e. when something is written down it lends credence even to pub talk. It depends on one's point of view.

The optimum, the fail-safe assumption, is to believe nobody is in control.

As a tangent, however, whilst these subjects are in the forefront of our minds, many documents since discovered have touched on ash clouds, dreams, lies, fictions (fixions), all of which seem to have become a form of sickness or disease, approximately in the same general time-zone as the bird plagues that killed off so many of us. Allied to the dreams etc. were ghosts (it has to be said), and many people actually began to believe in ghosts, to the extent that each person necessarily had to have his or her own ghost—implying that there were two of everyone. But, no. Not the person and that person's ghost as the pair in question, but two ghosts, each a ghost of the other (with no real person involved at all). Symbiotic haunting seems a good term for this.

Which brings us straight back to the question of why there were two airports in the city, where even just one airport would have been redundant. So, with further extrapolation, not only did people or living creatures become tangled up in this two-ghost hypothesis but supposed inanimate things, too, such as aeroplanes, helicopters, other craft. In fact, *all* things under the sun, not just means of transport, but even buildings, household artefacts etc. were subject to this hypothesis.

Such a supposition would pre-suppose much inadvisable loose-thinking, of course. However, it would serve to explain the eerie sightings (during the days even when people were more down-to-earth) of ghostly craft skimming across the city from airport to airport, complete with scary droning just upon the hearing threshold. Simply to call them 'scary', however, doesn't necessarily *make* them scary. You had to experience them to know how really scary they were.

As a boy, I used to wander around the Left Hand airport, the one that by then had become a disused golf-course. It was always dark there, it seemed, but I loved the den I built beneath a hedge where I and my friends played Cowboys and Indians or Doctors and Nurses. The Cowboys and Indians, Doctors and Nurses were delightfully, if sometimes chillingly, real—or, at least, seemed real because they were some of the ghosts that appeared to be attracted to the area as if it were a spectral magnet.

The slots in the turfy ground which had been passed off by the Authorities as stretched-mouth golf-holes gave some substance to the theory that history is bunk. But also gave substance to the possibility that under-flights took place from this erstwhile airport. At least, for me, they did. I often saw with my own eyes grey shapes skimming above my head, leaving for the other side of the city. But I also saw similar shapes entering the ground as if taking advantage of inverse vents.

Those days are now long over. I'm not sure even if *I* exist any more, let alone the two of us that were once the 'me' I can now only vaguely recall, if at all.

The Drill's corporate lounge windows—like the other windows where Beth, Edith and Clare had been left to have their mud baths and generally to while away the journey in feminine yellow-wallpapered cabins—revealed at first just the same boring panoplies of passing slabs of earth, glistening with the suppurations of oil from the Drill's gills. However, eventually, at the leading-edge of the Drill, where the lounge windows were situated, the vista became clearer as if the vanes were now managing better in clearing the forward (downward) thrust's waste further back towards the tail-fins.

There is no description that can do justice to what wonderful, awe-inspiring and sometimes scary sights they saw—but the inference is that the words of the Captain conjured more than he actually said.

Captain Nemo: Now what do you think of that?

Greg: Wow!

CN: Follow my finger—there are some of the things that exist down here. They are not what they seem—they are modelled on aircraft you've seen before, but these are their equivalents, better to call them earthcraft. They are crewed by some who've never been to the surface.

G: It's just like a real sky. There's even a sun.

CN: That's the Core itself, of course. You must have guessed that. But there's no real heat coming from it—as some have believed for centuries. That's simply its colour you can see, not a symptom of a heat source. Scatter-orange I call it. And that, my friend, is the brightest scatter-orange you are ever likely to see. That's why I made you wear those glasses. They've got a tint that makes the scatter-orange just about bearable. Makes it look more yellow or even beige, than orange doesn't it?

G: Well, it looks just like the real sun when you use smoked glass to look at an eclipse coming up.

CN: Yup yup. The glasses also protect you from its jagged iciness, although that iciness is in fact an optical illusion, but one can't be too careful.

G: The earthcraft seem to be wheeling around each other—oh, look, I'm sure they're using the blazing Corelight as a means of cover… sort of hiding from each other…

CN: Yup yup. Not exactly friendly with each other, it has to be said. They sometimes fight or feint a fight more like and we have to be careful ourselves but up to now they've left us alone on each trip. But that won't last forever, I fear.

G: It's all gone again. Back to the slabs.

CN: That often happens when our vanes get clogged up with our off-detritus. We'll probably see more later. You haven't seen half of it yet! (Laughs.)

Greg sipped at his cocktail thoughtfully. This was turning out to be a wonderful holiday. But, like all holidays, it had its moments of stress, no doubt.

Dognahnyi gasped when he saw who was behind the veil. Apparently, his new recruit had turned out to be none other than Amy herself, the woman who regularly cleaned his flat.

Dognahnyi: I thought you were with your brother on holiday... and those others from the pub you use.

Amy: How do you know Arthur is my brother? Everyone assumes that. I thought you were Beth's husband…

D: I am!

A: I've been pretending to be a domestic cleaner and Arthur's brother. I am really what you call a 'brainwright'. Heard of that? Anyway, one of the reasons was to get closer to you and clinch an interview. I've managed to shoot the rapids. I'm here …. *and* I'm there. (Laughs.)

D: You can't be in two places at once.

A: Can't I?

D: Well, if anybody can, you can, I suppose. I was very impressed how you just conducted the interview with me. You must be someone very special. Beautiful, too, if I may say so. Never realised before—in your cleaning overalls—quite how beautiful!

A: Thank you. I bet, before tonight, you wouldn't have been able to describe me at all. You always seemed to ignore me. Now this context, this setting, only proves what I am capable of. I am sick to the teeth of that Sudra taking the sexy role in all this. I am going to show how a real female ticks. Just let me show you what I can do. We'll have all Angel Wine going through your processors and no other processors. Just trust me.

D: You don't like Sudra?

A: (Chuckles.) I've got her favourite shoes. She's not missed them yet.

D: Well, enough of that. I do trust you. But how do we deal with the Megazanthus?

A: Well, when I arrive at the Core, along with Mike & Co.... oh yes, he thinks he's going to be the hawler (laughs)—they'll all be like putty in my hands. It's easier now that the genealogical strictures are in place. It was all rather gimmicky when everyone wanted to trace their family trees. But it put a lot of spanners in the works, when folk realised they weren't who they thought they were! Now that sort of thing's gone out the window, it leaves so many loopholes for someone like me to exploit. And what's that? The Megazanthus? It is only an assumption that there is any Corekeeper at all, even if that is its name. Let's address problems as they arise. Amy will be able to deal with them. Rest assured.

D: I'm impressed.

Dognahnyi opened the curtains upon their silent runners and watched the gulls flopping from the sky like body snow.

It is difficult to imagine the world being better or worse than it actually is. However, without humanity to stain its pages, who knows what will then become imaginable or even real? There is a theory—to which I subscribe—that humanity "strobes" in and out of existence, selective collective-memory then forcing the 'alight' stage to forget the previous 'switched-off' one... time and time again. Mass consciousness flickering in and out of existence like a faulty lighthouse... or, indeed, a fully working lighthouse.

The Drill's corporate lounge is empty and silent, except for the odd eerie shaking of the wall maps as its relentless path—through the ribbons of reality that is Inner Earth—continues towards the Core. There is now nobody, even Nemo, to watch the vista through the windows, as the vanes once more struggle to clear the Drill's off-detritus to the rear from the leading-edge. There is what seems to be an old-style caravan stuck on a crag—above a deceptively real sea—and (in the Core's scatter-orange light), a sign can just be discerned saying 'The Angerfin Public House' planted clumsily on its roof—but then it is gone. Must be a crazy dream. But whose?

The jolt has finally finished, if one can actually imagine a jolt (by definition) that endures for more than just a few seconds. The rearward cabin is empty—as can be seen when the light slowly wells back into it. The window still simply shows the passing crazy-paved slabs of earth. So, at least, that vista was not just the inhabitant's imagination. A tortoiseshell hairbrush falls to the carpet, having sat as an object ill-becalmed for a while on the edge of the dressing-table following the initial jolt. Then silence again. And a mirror merely reflecting yellow wallpaper.

The city pub was empty. Merely that. The optics of the shorts gleamed as time threatened to begin another diurnal round with unforgiving dawnlight. The city started to thrum, but thrummed with what? It may never be known. A barstool clattered to the pub carpet (clattered, despite the carpet) and remained there, unlifted and artistically sacrosanct like a Turner prize. What caused it to topple was a short sharp jolt that nobody felt.

The top flat still retained its open curtain policy on silent runners. The empty Dry Dock could be seen, even in the dark. A tall tower-block in the distance winked like a gigantically based but underwhelming lighthouse light. A computer screen in the room blinked blankly in curious yellow. An empty veil fluttered on the carpet like a butterfly.

The covered market was at rest, no commuters changing for even the wrong routes, let alone the right ones. A route exchange, a root filling... and the container lorries neatly parked alongside—perhaps forever, until they dropped an inch or two upon tired wheels.

In the service tunnel—where the hawler and his party (now unknown, unnamed, forgotten or even nemonymous people) had been training for further encroachment towards the Core itself—there was still the rattle of buckets as if in automatic fire-drill climbing towards the surface on pulleys. There were a few discarded carpet coats and yellow clogs. One pair of clogs had spurs and silver toecaps, the spurs still slightly jingle-jangling as if someone had just taken them off in a pique of feminine tantrum.

The city zoo echoed with snorting squawks. After all, it was only humanity gone missing for the nonce. And a few (very few) residual clockwork toys in the insect enclosure were still pitifully trying to bury themselves.

"Dreams leak, books leak..."

Rachel Mildeyes

(from MY CULINARY AFFAIR WITH *BIRDS WHITE SAUCE)*

NEMONYMOUS NIGHT

Perhaps the carpet was not quite so ordinary, after all.

I shall remain nameless, as is fitting. And at that time, nobody, not even me, was around to act as an expert on carpets, so, now in hindsight, all that *could* be said about it was some reference to ordinariness. Yet, had we all known, we would have *indeed* known that the stains were signs of some incipient endgame. They were stains worthy of the word stains, not just years of wine and grime or mishandled vacuuming or the once careless knees of Amy and her brother's friends as they scorched their shameful toys through the rough of tufts. And the less said about the odd tread of strangers, the better.

One could hardly tell that the carpet had once been yellow. Only Amy knew that.

The carpet's companion accoutrements were rather down-market sticks of furniture in spite of the dusting and polishing by Amy who rather enjoyed the varnished gleam of knotted wood more than the clean lines of a carpet's cleanliness. She needed dusting herself, even at her moderately young age.

"How are you today?" I ask.

Amy (who spent her childhood in this room) follows me about, as far as she can follow anyone in such a small room. Not surprisingly, she appears as if owned or, rather, controlled by the room while—with rather more panache than the situation demands—she keeps adjusting ornaments... also brushing dust into a pan.

"Not so bad," she answers. "News on the radio is bad again."

"You mean about the…?"

"Yes. We're not allowed to eat anything that comes from eggs. Not even…"

"I know, I heard it from Beth this morning."

Amy has a pretty face, but when she speaks—even lightly, thoughtlessly—there's a frown that appears and a deep divot within the frown's area. Hair a fashionable matted brown, so very 'her' it's only noticeable if it suddenly isn't there. Apron fails to hide her sexuality and high-heels seem out of kilter with the dustpan.

"Best not to think of it," I say. "How's…?"

"Dognahnyi?"

"No, not him. I mean the girl... you... you know... you kick about with. You've been very happy I know with... what's her name?"

I am delicately pretending to forget her name.

"You mean Sudra? No, that's gone a bit sour. We had an argument... something very trivial... but she was so petty... I couldn't handle it any more."

"Sorry to hear that, Amy. What was it about?"

"Oh, something or nothing. A pair of shoes. See! You're laughing!"

"Life turns on trivialities," I say, knowing already about Sudra's side of the story.

I am a comfortable pair of ears, I guess, although some may have different words and put capital letters where only small ones belong, laced with swearing! What's the word? Counsellor, hmmm, Interferer, Meddler... someone who drags things from your soul to let it breathe more easily. I haul on your guy-ropes and see your tent rise again. I have some silly concepts about it but I'm sure my radio phone-ins do achieve quite a lot of good.

I've come a long way since my ancestors worked in the coal-mines. I've just discovered that one of them was a 'hawler'. In the old days, he would have been involved in moving coal from the coalface, coal that had already been worked by others. I think the 'w' is a misprint in the 1901 census records I got off the Internet. Anyway, hawling is an art form in itself and one fraught with many logistical problems. Today, however, there are no coal-mines and therefore haulers have died out. Now, with the plagues, I reckon that butchering of meat may be within a hawler's brief. Just a whimsical thought on my part. But I try to keep my mind busy, as there is so much to worry about otherwise. Perhaps, in fact, thinking about it, a brief for meat and poultry, especially as—God forbid!—the two seem to be blending in a very disturbing fashion. Cutting prime complex cuts from now badly understood novelties of meat that combine all sorts of animal and bird in one. But I hope it's not what I fear. I love pure beefsteak so much—isn't there a saying, almost a proverb, that everyone once knew but I never understood—that I, and others like me, are "so voracious we eat beef till it's raw"?

A far cry from radio counselling! Then, I need to be precise and careful. No brainstorming allowed. I still have to think quickly on the hoof, however.

Today, I intend to visit John Ogdon in his pub but I doubt if anyone I know will be there and I hate drinking alone. John will be too busy to talk to me. The park is second best: a good place for thinking. Susan's on my mind and Susan may indeed be in the park with her grown-up daughter Sudra. I still can't believe in the coincidence that Amy has been close, if not intimate, friends with Sudra. I only knew Amy because, well, I was a sort of Uncle figure to her in the old days. Still am, I guess. I originally knew her mum before she gave birth to Amy. But that's a long story. I met Susan (Sudra's mum) quite independently, and Sudra already knew Amy quite well even at that stage. A sort of secret between me and Sudra that we both separately knew Amy.

I have usually steered clear of married women, but life's never simple. I didn't admit to myself then that I really fancied Sudra (more than fancying her mother probably), but that's taking us into an even longer story. I thought both of them were a case for a hawler... and I even began to use that terminology on my local radio counselling programme. It even caught on as a name for a sort of modern-day shrink. It was worth a few shillings too in the bank account. Still is.

Much is inexplicable, yet it will become explicable when put into practice and seen for what it is. I suspect that there is more to Sudra than meets the eye. She often tells me about her dreams and they are CRAZEE!

I now gingerly walk across the park ground. I wonder what stage of the housework Amy will by now have reached in her top flat. Amy is always doing housework, these days, as if it takes her mind off other things. Ewbanking the 'yellow' carpet is only attempted by Amy once in a while. I glimpse Susan and Sudra. Neither of them are particularly friendly to anyone, but I guess they have a soft spot for me. Fame opens doors, in many way.

I am a hawler, after all, and most people instinctively treat hawlers with respect even if I haven't any real qualifications for this line of business. I feel tears prick out at the thought of Amy. I wish I had been kinder to her when she was a girl. Her Mum Edith always turned a blind eye.

I imagine a plate of sizzling beef. My stomach tells me something that words can never explain. An empty nagging pain. I look up into the sky. Not even a flying pig! But, no, I am wrong. There is a flying pig, of sorts, that day. And a hot air balloon with people on board who surely have an enduring love for flying, even with any mechanical aircraft whatsoever now grounded (perhaps meaninglessly grounded—and do keep listening to the news on the radio and all may be explained). As ever these days, there are a few outlandish kites (including the flying pig) that citizens have taken to flying from the ground in some subconscious grief, no doubt, at the disappearance of anything else in the sky. But, first, I need to pluck up enough courage to approach Susan and Sudra, leaving any residual thought of Amy to the vacuum.

Amy talked to herself. She imagined knives and saws and axes, with blood along the tips of their edges. But that was part of herself she had ignored or not even known so as to be *able* to ignore it. The talking revealed more. She expected a role that she hadn't yet been given. The as yet missing part of herself meanwhile visualised me carving joints of unrecognisable meat. The ribbing thicker than most poultry but with a vague appearance of a fish's backbone, whilst with the floppy feel of sirloin as it slid too easily off the T-spine.

"What to do," she asked or stated. The vacuum churned noisily, cutting out such thoughts before they hit the fuse with a deafening spark of the earth wire failing. Her missing part viewed a vista of a dull pinky yellow sun smoked over with clouds of birdlife as seen from a distance. A craggy sea and a giant submarine with rotors just nosing into view from the creamy waves. A cruise liner was halfway up the steep side of a cliff, dry-berthed if not literally shipwrecked. This was a concoction of several dreams, if she had but realised or known she was effectively (at some unconscious level) sharing in a vast communal vision just below the threshold of knowledge or even belief.

Her actual conscious self meanwhile brooded on the real past. I had not quite come into her life as yet. She was still living as a child at home with her mother and brother. Her brother Arthur had always been a bit of a loner, non-expressive and wild. He concocted experiments with household goods, mixing them into a chemical syrup by means of adding garden mud to substances like washing-powder, disinfectant, flyspray. Symbolic, in hindsight, of mixing dreams, too, just like those to which we have all needed to grow accustomed in recent years because of the world's difficulties. Fixing dreams, too.

These misalchemies were alive—at least in her brother's eyes—and Amy laughed as she remembered their mother's remonstrations of despair while she tried to talk sense into her son but merely ended up communicating with the "cowpats" of mixture he had left in his wake. At least he did the experiments outside. And indoor fireworks only came out of Christmas Crackers in those days, so they were not an all-year problem: those sizzling wormcasts on the seasonal carpet. That was a Godsend. One day, they'd invent daylight fireworks for the outside! She laughed to herself. Why had nobody thought of daylight fireworks before, so potentially au fait with the way the world was now going, with street riots meaning there was always a strict curfew during any dark hours.

Amy was scared to recall the past because, by dragging it onward through time, trawling it through the coarse-grained muslin of memory's filter, she could too easily tug or tussle through into the present's more dangerous element of the past, undoing, in the process, everything I had since done up for her. Untying the nemonymous knot would release a booby-trap—and she continued scraping the lower surface of the vacuum across the grit in the carpet that had collected there like any dust collects there... from wherever dust and grit and, indeed, stains come from—a mysterious source only hawlers are able to fathom.

Dreams came from below, not above. She shrugged, turning over the vacuum and emptying it of what it had collected. Her missing part now viewed a scene in a park, a park so cultivated its grass was more like a plush lawn for the toes of effete royalty or fairies. She saw it in her mind's eye, but failed to recognise the fey walkers that positively languished in its heady Proustian delights. A man she knew instinctively (yet still unconsciously) was named Swann walked past with a girl, her sleek *fin de siècle* dress buttonholed with cattleyas.

In the past, Amy's mother, Edith, having finished with adjusting the oven, reached the apartment window again and eagerly scanned the inner square between the walls of the four blocks that formed it. There was a solitary fountain at its centre—and a few all-weather seats surrounding. Not much for children to do in the square but it was certainly better than the city streets amid which this square was a relatively safe oasis. She saw a huddled figure on one of the seats: a man writing. She grew suspicious.

Clare, a schoolteacher, had just announced her visit by the officious knock on the apartment door. She'd come up in the lift. No doubt there was some problem with Amy or Arthur. Or even both... at once.

"What can I do for you? Would you like a cup of tea?" At this moment, Arthur arrived, Amy in tow. They must have spotted their teacher arrive from wherever they had been in the building. Arthur's hands were covered in some sort of heavy-duty grease, as if he had been oil-changing a large ship in Dry Dock. Amy dragged a tiny toy trailer behind her, in which was seated one of her dolls. A large ugly one, more in keeping with a punch-and-judy show than one in a little girl's keeping: it almost looked knowing enough to be alive. Yet she loved it despite its plastic and mock synthetic hair and badly painted rosebud lips. Amy had rescued it one day when she found it in the garden trying to bury itself in the ground, i.e. soil which Arthur had just loosened as part of one of his 'mixing' projects, when looking for new ingredients below the surface of top earth.

Hawling is not dissimilar to being a liftman, pressing the buttons, allowing beings to board or disembark as each floor light flashes and results in the lift-doors sliding aside... new strangers coming in, old strangers leaving, but there is more to hawling than that—it's running a butcher's shop, listening to the carcasses crack as you lay in bed at night. I was also transporting fossil fuel from the depths of the earth (where the earth's soul was most attentive) to the surface for the fires of life to be lit and smoulder on... and eventually extinguish with a dying wink... which meant more fossil fuel was needed to be fetched from my mine.

I watch Susan and Sudra running through an unkempt, shaggy park, among stub-winged birds flapping from bush to bush, hardly using the air at all. I glimpse a figure in a cape watching them.

I woke in a cold sweat. I put one foot outside the bed to ensure at least the bedroom floor was still there. Nobody snored beside me, mercifully, it seemed, because anyone sleeping next to me would have been infected by the same dreams that had just beset me... or were still besetting me.

My body was the most mysterious thing about me. I could easily fathom my own mind—but my body felt like impersonal meat on a base of bones: somehow disconnected from the ground that

I—my mind—walked upon. Self-cannibalism did not occur to me, obviously, because, if it had, I would certainly have considered myself mad. Bad enough even to *skirt* such touchy subjects amid the other thoughts, let alone delving into them.

One nemonymous creature of applause—with the merged thought that each member of the audience in the concert hall remained (to themselves at least) single entities—sounded from the radio after Brahms' Double Concerto drew to its close. And I dozed off again.

At the centre of the earth there exists the strongest power in the Universe. All life radiated from this centre, gradually becoming fossilier, bonier, meatier, livelier, airier in various stages of animation from dead to aethereal. At a certain stage between meat and life sat the people that revolved around and radiated from each other in a dance of fiction or friction. Only the real was excluded because nothing real could be imagined and, in turn, that was because imagination could only possibly imagine things that were unreal. Only hawlers knew of the various layers through which anything or anyone could travel.

And to my reasonable knowledge, I am a hawler, but at earlier stages I myself didn't realise this at all. I so wish I had. Things might have turned out differently. However, still not knowing *for certain* whether I am a force for good or a force for evil makes me draw back from fully exercising the creative strength I know I possess. I even deign to compete with that Ogdon person—who, one day, started writing his own novel in a city's fountain square between four apartment blocks one of which, as it happened, housed the young Amy. As history once battled with different history to become real history, so one novel battles with another novel for domination in the right to fix fiction forever as the ultimate truth.

Meanwhile, I need to introduce Greg. My alter-nemo. This is a more nebulous form of alter-ego. The late John Fowles invented the 'nemo' in contradistinction to the 'ego' or 'id' in his book *The Aristos*. But such information inevitably interrupts the narrative flow. And narrative flow is the reason we are all here. One ambition that we all share, both as writer and reader.

Greg was at his golf course, during those heady days when he was a businessman. His wife was at home faithfully caring for the two kids whilst Greg surveyed the dips and dunes—almost *feeling* them with his golf mind—as he took stance for his first tee shot of the day. Golf was instinctive, knowing the contours, assessing the relief map between him and the hole... and as his arm swung back, he trawled the air with his club head for the invisible creatures that would eventually guide his tiny hard white ball above the alchemically magnetic layers of ley-line, currency crisis and geomantic quirk that only these creatures could fathom.

Arthur—despite all his damming games with the sand, earth, household chemicals etc.—became a bus driver. His sister, Amy, used to stand by his side, all the other passengers assuming this to be a flirtatious bus-driver groupie girl who often stood by the steering-wheel chatting about this, that and the other, i.e. fancying anyone in trousers especially if his control of a huge vehicle like a bus gave his manliness an edge it wouldn't otherwise have had. But in this case, it was the driver's sister disguised as a bus driver groupie, telling him surreptitiously when to turn left and right amid the maze of rat runs and back-doubles that the city had become in recent years. She was his 'brainwright': an old word for someone who acted as a brain for someone else.

It had been a miracle that Arthur managed to find a job at all, let alone such a responsible one as a bus-driver in the city. The fact that his sister was always at his side dressed as a flirtatious bus-driver groupie had been missed by the bus company's inspectors. Arthur was a good instinctive driver—despite all his driving documents being forgeries.

Arthur believed, in his childish fashion, that all meat was going off, but not simply growing mouldy, but *literally* going off (eloping?) with other meats from different animals, fishes and fowls, mixing, blending, into new concoctions of meat with arcane bone maps—all because of global warming and the banking bubble.

These were big things. Global things. Symbolised by Arthur knowing instinctively that he could control big things just with the flick of his finger. Like the bus.

Amy, before she had met Sudra, had lived with Arthur—and their neighbours must have assumed they were husband and wife or (more likely these days) boy friend and girl friend, rather than brother and sister.

Still, then, the horrors hadn't yet started. Various strange words start to build up—as if against the dam of sanity: connections and misconnections which fracture and fragment dream and mix it with real life: an impending doom that gradually increases in sickly strength. In fact, little did Amy and Arthur know, but the impending part of the doom was worse than the eventual doom itself. And worse still was having already lived through half of it via the creative medium of someone other than myself. Fixed for the wrong fiction, cross-grained against the truth, forming a diseased Canterbury Oak in my head. Or so it felt.

The area of the city where the covered market found itself was not at all English in atmosphere but had a dark magical realism more akin to Eastern Europe. It had open sides but did have a robust roof, so it was not *strictly* open-air or covered. On some days—when the rain clouded in with untimely gloom—it looked more like a warehouse, especially after the market attendants closed down the sides with temporary wind-breaks: the entrances between these 'walls' looking more like the beginnings of downward spirals to underground railway stations where the peasants under-crossed the city between the various farms and smallholdings which employed them on the perimeter of the city. I dreaded going near that place, in case I was dragged down and became mixed up with these transit groups who didn't belong to the city at all.

Susan worked in Ogdon's pub in an even more unsalubrious section of the city. It was the pub that many continually sought in dreams but forgot about seeking when they woke up. Well, it certainly fitted the bill, but she enjoyed working for the landlord called Ogdon. Anyone dreaming about this pub—unlike Susan who worked as a barmaid within its walls in real life—would be drawn towards it against their will, believing its regular drinkers to be rather low down in the scale of humanity. Both forbidding and attractive at the same time, but mainly forbidding most of the time; it was paradoxical that the attraction won when the forbiddingness was stronger than the attraction. But like all dreams, one couldn't quite get to the bottom of it. Susan, meanwhile worked there—a real place she couldn't avoid as she needed the money.

I lived in a top floor flat in the city centre. Anyone dreaming of this top floor flat would have the same feeling about it as the other dreamers felt about the pub where Susan worked and the same feeling that yet more dreamers dreamed of the covered/open-air market. A certain dread mixed with attraction: imagining the flat to be dirty, with threadbare carpets, rickety beds, greasy cookers, dubious bed-covers. And a feeling that you really did need to visit me there (although this was a dream and you weren't really visiting me at all).

My carpet was much older than any building that ever contained it; I didn't know exactly how old or who had once trod its threads.

When life is tough, most things take the backseat, everything except survival of oneself. If buildings carried dreams (or, for that matter, if dreams carried buildings), it didn't matter because all one was concerned with was those buildings giving shelter or giving work.

I could not shake off another dream. A dream of a hawler but, this time, in its misshapen form as Guy de Maupassant's Horla (or vampire).

A bus doesn't touch the earth with its metal body but has a layer of toughened rubber-around-air between it and the road it treads. As it floats round the city as only dreams can allow such a large mechanical thing *to* float, two passengers on the top-deck chat of something people on buses would leave well alone. Death. Just past the stop for the covered market.

"We're trapped on this bus."

"You can get off at the next stop. It's not like a plane."

"Yup yup. But a human body, like my own body, is something you can't get off. I'm trapped inside it and there is nothing I can do to escape it.

"To escape it is certain death. I wonder how we ended up like this in such a nightmare. Knowing it's all going to end with a blank while incapable of waking up from the nightmare.

"I remember many dreams I thought were real at the time I was dreaming them, terrifying situations I thought I could never escape—until, with great relief, I wake up and leave it all behind in a quickly forgotten dream. Life's problems, by comparison, are as nothing compared to those one sometimes meets in dreams. But this waking nightmare of the bodytrap, all our bodytraps, is not a dream you can wake up from. It's relentlessly and terrifyingly inescapable. "Who the devil landed me in this body? They have a lot to answer for. And I can't really imagine the devastating effect of complete and utter non-existence when this consciousness within my body finally vanishes.

"A paradox—that I hate being trapped in my body but I'd give anything to stay trapped there forever, because I can't face the outright blankness…"

"Yes, a paradox," answered the other man-on-the-bus in just one more of those typical conversations that wheel through the city like stories with no baggage to weigh them down.

I watched the bus turn the corner, its top blown off like a sardine can containing explosive sardines.

Captain Nemo took the controls himself as the Drill docked at Klaxon City. Their first stop-over on their journey to the Core via Inner Earth itself.

Just before this manoeuvre, the leading windows in the Corporate Lounge had sufficiently cleared to afford a view of another inner sea lit lugubriously by a now unprotected Core 'sun'. Their naked eyes had now been able to grow acclimatised to its combination of brightly icy scatter-orange and the contrastively wan effulgence actually given off from it (increasingly wan the nearer they approached it). The city of Klaxon was a vast collection of arabesque turrets peppering an out-of-place complex similar to a *fin de siècle* Paris on the banks of the Seine. And as the Drill burrowed nearer in a circling motion not unlike that of planes stacking up over an airport, Greg (invited into the cockpit itself) watched Nemo grapple with the joystick which was on a hair-trigger relationship with the Drill's vanes, vanes that were currently working overload on vast amounts of mixed off-detritus. Greg feared that Beth and the two dowagers would be seeing even less than before from their rearward cabins. But that didn't worry him for long while he grew fascinated with the docking pinion (on one of the turrets) that seemed to snatch the Drill in the same manner as old-fashioned catch-nets on the ancient railways collected letters and parcels without the train stopping.

A jolt—and then, even through the sides of the Drill, the relentless sound of a multi-tannoy system on permanent klaxon that gave the city its name. Greg could hardly imagine living a whole life in such a place with that noise echoing in your ears all over the city. Always with you. Accompanying work, love and play.

"Much like living trapped within one's own body and its everpresent frightful tinnitus of antipodal angst," said Nemo, as if having read Greg's mind.

Greg shrugged. He wasn't sure what Nemo was driving at.

I lay awake trying to imagine sleep away whilst sleep itself imagined me awake. I got up for a sluice; and saw that the floorboards in my room were bare. The floor itself was several floors up but, tonight, the instinct was different. It was very close to the ground without even space for rat runs or airflows. This was no dream. It was so real.

I wondered if a burglar had stolen the carpet. But why?

All the furniture was still in place.

I found myself delving into the wood of the floor as if I had found an opening in human flesh—a natural vent, rather than one I had forced open with my fingers.

That babies were to emerge, one by one, not twins, but multi-aged siblings, did not occur to me until I discovered myself delivering them... through the floor. The ground was speaking by giving birth. Thinking, too. And I felt its thoughts as if they were my own thoughts.

All this had been in Ogdon's novel, too. I could not shake it off sufficiently to warrant excluding it in my competing novel. I sensed Ogdon was intent on an unhappy ending for the world by means of the 'truths' he hoped to sculpt from his own version of those "synchronised shards of random fiction and truth". By contrast, I myself was keen on everything turning out happily, with the world having learnt the lessons that my own novel created and then, having created them, constructively destroyed for the good of all of us. You can't destroy evils without having set them up in the first place. Or so I believed. And still do. True paradoxes are sometimes very difficult to deliver.

Tears came to my eyes as I looked back at the various paths I could have picked on... chipping away at the cornerstones of Fate so I could make the turning towards the goal I had once set myself.

In the distance, I heard the lonely sound of a helicopter—vanes clacking lugubriously—followed by the equally lonely drone of an air-liner as it passed empty over the city. It was the deep echo that made it sound empty.

I returned to my sleep.

I woke from a dream. This had been a real dream. A dream that I had once published a series of fiction magazines called 'Nemonymous'. Now simply a dream that could not be believed. Other dreams had not even been dreams. They had been visions thrust upon me by some narrative trickery with which a mad Ogdon was trying to force me down byways that my destiny had no right to encompass. I knew a real dream from a false dream. The former often contained words I'd never use, words I didn't understand.

Or was it the other way? Distinction was clear, if not the terms of the distinction.

The ceiling was quite ordinary, plain white, with a central rose whence the electric flex dangled towards its own pendant lampshade and dull yellow-glowing bulb. In ancient days, before ceilings were invented, they would have had strange beliefs about ceilings, no doubt. That they were ghosts in disguise would have been the strongest and strangest. Some even believe that today. Sheets of whitened surfaces marching through the city at the dead of night, like frozen wafers or thin slabs of *Angevin*. Much like Charles Dickens' walking coffins in *A Tale of Two Cities*. Far more believable, I believe, than the spontaneous combustion of Krook in *Bleak House*. Floors paradoxically seemed far more dependable. If not the ground itself.

John Ogdon was dreaming of over-flying his own pub in a helicopter, except the roof was hidden by the large overhanging buildings in the same street. Either warehouses or tall covered markets, the dream didn't allow him to remember. He did remember, however, another dream when he was at a family dinner, believing himself to be one of the adults, so that it was quite a surprise to find himself placed with the children on a lower table adjacent to the main table. He dreamed, too, of Klaxon City where the inhabitants spent their whole lives in ear-muffs, dodging around the backstreets eager to find sound-proof specialist clinics where they could remove their muffs and clean out their ears once in a while. They all looked dogged but cowed. Come morning, the dull yellow Core in their sky would bring no relief from the klaxon. At least there was never any wind, in fact not much weather at all. He then dreamed of his alter-nemo Crazy Lope, a tiny figure negotiating the rat runs and back doubles... hardly a time to be *idly* wandering, Ogdon thought, as his dream helicopter banked and disappeared further into the dark horizon of his sleep. I'll leave him to his dreams. They are now redundant, as are the rest of his machinations with the pen. He only wanted unhappiness for us all. I at least seek a happy ending. Not just a quest for a quest, as he did.

History, however, often needs to rear its head.

The helicopter hovered about the Drill as it sat ready upon the plateau of Left Foot. The helicopter, it seemed, spent hours hanging from the white ceiling that was the sunless sky. It was reconnoitring or spying for forces that remain mysterious until this very day. At points, one could even just discern the goggled pilot sitting stiffly in his bulb. He must have imagined the climbing race then going on between the attics and oubliettes of that very Drill's interior until two as then unknown protagonists reached the top cabin at the Drill's tailfin. He also watched many workers scaling the sides of the Drill filling the gills with vast barrels of a creamy lubrication. And then the helicopter ratcheted into a sleeker beast than a helicopter and soared even higher—to view the whole city 'body' striding like a pseudo-Dickensian imagining into some geographical future towards a point of the compass that was not actually any of the normal ones.

Today, I have been dreaming about floating above the sparkling sea in the early morning, upside down in a helicopter or balloon (more likely the latter as there seemed to be no noise) where the scintillating waves' expanse between four identical wall-to-wall horizons was a ceiling or watery underside of some far firmer roof beyond it. I woke as soon as I approached land with the appearance through fresh mist of an ungainly pleasure pier.

We soon left far behind the hedgy tunnel entrance (now our only known exit to the above world, although an impractical one)—then followed the hawling-system for a while, running its pulley-rope through our hands as a sort of guide and confidence-booster in the increasing darkness. I could hear Amy and Sudra bickering over trivialities. Yet this was a strange comfort as it brought worldly concerns to a very unworldly situation.

If there is such a thing as global warming, then it's not inside outwards, it's outside inward, as the 'atmosphere' became colder and colder—until, just for a nonce, we were slightly warmed by a clearing of the darkness and a sudden thrilling vista of the Core: it was like a sun in the roof, a roof that was, in hindsight, below us as a floor. But then the spherical light vanished just as quickly, with the re-onset of darkness. I knew we would catch glimpses of this from time to time on the journey, the disc-light growing bigger each time, but equally less warm.

How we survived and conducted ablutions (a euphemism for many things) and provided ourselves with comestibles I cannot now recall. Not recalling such things actually gives more credence to the events than recalling them clearly. It simply proves that whatever we did, we did successfully, because I am here now to tell you about the important matters: the journey and its eventual repercussions for us and the rest of the world. That's why I cannot recall what Amy and Sudra were bickering about. Meanwhile, Arthur kept his own counsel, although his mixing skills did come in handy (and this I do recall with relative clarity) with the preparation of comestibles from waste material.

Meanwhile, I have to admit I'd lost sight of Susan.

There was a glimpse of a figure of a caped man disappearing into the black backdrop of a huge liner in Dry Dock, as if he had nearly been caught spying on my dreams. The cranes on the liner and its gantries reminded me more of an old-fashioned coal mine where chains hauled up and down the man lifts. I heard the distant clanging of heavy-duty engineering—and I wondered, perhaps for the first time, how the liner had been transported here (so far from the river or the sea) and for what reason. This area had, I knew, been the site of a Dry Dock for several generations. Dreams are often too late to throw any light on more important matters that have already arisen.

Beth Dognahnyi came into the pub together with her husband but at the moment there was just one solitary pub regular talking about a dream he had had the previous night. He was talking to himself, in truth, but Beth pretended to listen so as to enable him to believe that he was not just talking to himself, although he was.

"I was dreaming I was part of a crowd coming into the pub—a special rough cider was being offered at cheap price from a wooden cask. It was white cider. I wasn't me in the dream but someone else. Good job as I don't usually like cider and even though it was just a dream, I could really feel the bits of real apple with my tongue… You don't expect roads with uncut verges, edges with hedges—and pavements with long weeds—in the city."

It seemed he was remembering two separate dreams at once.

If children suddenly realise they exist, they ask themselves where their past childhood has gone. Were they brother and sister, they wonder, or completely unrelated and, thus, perhaps, childhood sweethearts incubating a future marriage when they would tell their own children of their erstwhile romance resulting in their children's own subsequent existence as children. But, for all they knew at this crosspoint of time, they may have common parentage, and they hugged in the cold darkness—in the vicinity of the open-walled market—one hug as childhood sweethearts, the next hug as siblings, believing they gambled on one hug being true, choosing, as it were, between a belief in God and a non-belief in God. Both equally comforting.

The late night bus passed in the distance, leaving a heavy silence. Although the darkness was cold, these two children were not cold at all. They had a carpet over them like a hard blanket. Their arms through rough-cut holes in its stiff weave. And the sound of rattly pulleys from the Dry Dock kept them company.

"Yes?" said Edith and Clare almost together.

Beth at last mustered the words to her mouth: "I've just realised... we haven't seen my husband or the Captain for weeks."

They had been allowed off the Drill for a short break, whilst the stay at Klaxon City delayed the holiday for a time.

The other two had not heard exactly what Beth had said, as they were still preoccupied with the loathsome insects they had discovered beneath a stone.

It was almost midday by Corelight, a lightsource that the inhabitants seemed to call the Sunne (spelt out in their noticeboards and shop-window cards).

As the three women entered a derelict building for increased shelter from the klaxon, they were surprised to find its carpet covered in stones and lumps of larger rubble. A painting on the wall was the only decoration, depicting a ship in a storm; Clare, as she peered closer at it, saw that the ship was called 'The ReynBouwe' and was evidently sinking. She spelt out its name for the benefit of the others.

"Who's the painter?" queried Beth, half-heartedly.

She thought that the ship's name was strange... strangely familiar.

"Can't make out the signature."

Edith was decked out in a soft-horn hat and heavily made up with turquoise under-eyes, a Proustian parasol hanging from her limp arm.

"What a mess!" said Clare, turning to view the despicable floor. Beth was admiring the marigold-window, in the wall opposite to the painting, which cast slanting lines of light through the dusty air.

"Edith, come here, though," urged Clare, who was now turning over stones in the corner furthest from the window. Clare, like Edith, seemed in her mid-fifties and, although not as smartly dressed, was more attractive than her. Her hair was fastened with a butterfly clip, but wayward wisps seeped out like smoke.

The stone she had turned revealed a wriggling knot of unrecognisable insects buzzing somewhat at the disturbance.

"Ugh!" Edith flinched off, waving her parasol like a sword. Beth turned from the window—a little white flake clinging to her lip like a remnant of food—and stared uncomfortably at her two companions. She needed to speak but evidently she was finding it difficult to make her mouth formulate the words; she just made embarrassing sucking noises.

Today was Sunne-Stead. A ceremony for which the Drill had delayed its journey.

Many had gathered on the quays to view, through optic-scopes, the temporary fixity of the city's light source. The various craft had moored to their turret-pylons for the duration, well out of the way; the Holy Stone had been cleared of tourists to allow the scientists to set out their telescopes and sextants at its topmost tower. Their other contraptions hung like intricate scaffolding from each cornerstone and gave the three women, who viewed the scene from their room, an impression of a clock-house that had been turned inside out. They adjusted their ear-muffs as the klaxon wailed on.

They had indeed intended to view Sunne-Stead from the marigold-window. The moment came and went. The Sunne, rising from West to East, shuddered to a halt, poised in the white hell of the 'sky' for what seemed almost a minute and, then, returned East to West.

The three women held hands in serenity for interminable hours, drawing as much spiritual significance as was possible into their communion. It was a frozen tableau, a mistress-piece and, as the heat gradually went out of the day, as 'dusk' met 'dawn' in the same quarter of the 'sky', their alabaster skin crumbled to the floor; and, if darkness came then the room would echo with the initial clumps of falling stones followed by the increasing clatter and final crescendo of collapsing masonry.

The black roof-sky was a Queen Catherine Wheel of the Inner Earth's traffic, dodging in and out of the aperture-speckled wastes.

One man in particular climbed the tow-path of the city's central turret-pylon from which several craft dangled like dead horses, He found the one he had been seeking—'The Reyn-Bouwe'—the name was painted in all-weather gloss on its side. He inserted his limbs into the contour-seat and launched himself towards the inner circles of earth. Pulling and pushing at various levers and gloating over just as many dials, he found himself spinning like a dying fly towards an under-sky where the Sunne was about to lift its cool rim. But, as a result of his not being able to control the machine, the fuel burst and flew up into his face... like being sick on a funfair ride. The over-sky had turned turtle below him and he was diving, nose down, towards the last zenith, desperately struggling with the release harness in his seat. Fumbling for the mercy-ejection device, he lurched between what he believed to be two Sunnes in violent love with each other. He was surely dead.

The last fragment crumbled to the floor; and the marigold-window had been shattered by a shooting star-crag... or at least a crumb of one.

It was almost Midnight, almost Moon, and a slick of slime slowly slewed across the surface of the painting from a cake of wrigglers nesting in its frame.

From Stone to Sunne and back again, there were other lives and lovers dodging death and damnation, but in the utter solid darkness of Inner Earth, who knows whether there is a vast wide face between the two giant imaginary eyelights. And where's the mouth... or beak... for eating... for breathing... for speaking ...for kissing? Megazanthus Rampant.

I took Susan's hands. We had found each other yet again, destined, perhaps, to find each other time and time again. Each a romantic epiphany, but equally horrifically real in the implication of *needing* to find each other time and time again. All thought of my step-daughter's charms abandoned my mind when, within the darkness, I could no longer reconcile Sudra's ugly sharp tongue with the beautiful body that I knew she wielded beneath the carpet coat. I belonged to her mother. I was Susan's. And Susan was mine. My wonderful mine.

We had all encountered—on our downward trek—some increasingly common oases of light where the Core dispersed the Inner Earth's darkness like the sun above ground often would disperse stormclouds—or even like such normal sun would take advantage of a riven nightsky to reveal an untimely evidence of its reflected antipodal earth-warming presence.

I tried to drag logic from the illogic of my mind, tried to explain something to Susan that I couldn't really explain to myself properly—as we followed the others across the ground-housed landscape of Inner Earth.

Meanwhile, elsewhere in the tunnel:

Sudra: I suppose we ought to make it up.

Amy: It wasn't me who got so touchy about a pair of shoes!

Sudra: I know, but with it all changing—and my step-dad so 'funny' with me... I now need someone in this darkness to hold my hand and *mean* it.

Amy: OK, Suds. I've not been myself these days. I'm sorry, too. I feel something creeping around me.

Sudra: What do you mean?

Amy: A sort of... another me. Another me I don't want me to be. As if removing a veil inside my head. I can't put it into words, Suds.

Sudra: I think I know, Ame. What's it trying to make you do? Making you imagine we're walking in a tunnel heading for the centre of the earth or something? (Laughs.)

Amy: Well, surely it *is* a sort of nightmare. But it can't be, can it? You're there. I can feel you in the darkness like in the old days before things started going strange. And Arthur he's still my brother, but on the other hand he's changed, I reckon. I know he has always been a bit queer, since a baby... but him now mixing up things from nothing in his ear!

Sudra: Has he always had such a big left ear? (Laughs.) Its lower gutter seems to contain all manner of substances!

Amy: Well, it's always been bigger than his right, with a flap that allows storage at the bottom. The doctors said it was a birth aberration and, short of serious surgery, they thought he would need to live with it. It wasn't so noticeable then.

Sudra: It's huge now! Still, would we be able to survive without him?

Amy: By the way, did you watch the latest light period when the Earth's Core came out like a sun?

Sudra: It was longer than usual. Yes. It was more stripey, with dark and light together, sort of.

Amy: I thought the shape of the uncleared dark bits that formed together around the Core looked like a giant black bird, its wings stretched as if there were things trying to tear it apart.

Sudra: I see what you mean. Imagination can play all sorts of tricks.

Amy: *Or* it really was what I saw.

Both girls had a bout of the *shyfryngs* as they settled in each other's arms to sleep; now silent as both suspected—without telling the other—that their conversation was being earwigged.

Near to the open-walled market or underground station, there was a tall building, access to which was by lift—indeed a very complex lift system which Greg often used before he was made redundant from his job in that building. He used to entertain business clients and had to help them negotiate the lift system—changing on specific floors for different lift shafts of higher reach. Some shafts were more palatial and business-orientated than others, some so narrow they could only be used for brooms or very thin utility workers. The highest shaft reached the open air area, leafed over like a wood. From there, once, Greg was sure he could see the distant sea through the unusually clear sky into which the wood penetrated. He imagined a finer, less definable surface barely above the sea but otherwise imitating its waves and swells—a double skin in perfect unison, but the lower one liquid, the upper spectral. Perhaps the second one was the ghost of a giant flying carpet taking invisible human vessels towards Arabian Adventure or towards the darker motives of suicide rather than seaside. And then the same building in duplicate appeared from the clouds and speared *itself* about two-thirds of the way up. The ultimate suicide by architecture. But that is deja-vu history of sorts and only has bearing on itself. History of history. History hugging the same history, without reality to come between their embrace. His story. My story. Nostory.

The power to imagine was perhaps the very Act of Creation in the first place.

In these hard, awkward days in your distant future when a Horla cannot even get a decent drink, my plight brings tears of a pink cast to my eyes and a faint quiver of the upper lip upon my toothsome fangs.

It was known by the Megazanthus that any dream sickness affecting the rest of Reality did not affect the Core. Anywhere else on or in the earth that claimed such a distinction would necessarily be a perpetrator of an inanimate lie

The Coreseekers who approached the Core via drilling, burial-by-another-party, exploratory pot-holing, self-interment-by-shame or simply merciful immolation knew similarly that, there at the Core, they would be free of deceiving dreams... and what they would see—as they toured from cage to cage, enclosure to enclosure within the Core—were *real* animals and creatures, one of which was the Megazanthus itself, the 'zookeeper' who also occupied a cage of its own to disguise not only its identity but its capacity for infinity.

Only when the Coreseekers were asleep, at the Core's very own core, did they know they would be deliberately exposing themselves to dreams—unlike in any surrounding Reality where sleep was not a prerequisite for dreams.

The entrance to the Core was not at all imposing and it could have served as the gates of a small factory, where people came and went after spending the rest of their time in the less desirable parts of Outer and Inner Earth. There was a turnstile—just a cover to indicate that this was a place for which you needed admission, as most Cores in any planet would need. The turnstile was unimpeded and the Coreseekers emerged into an area around the first enclosure. In the distance could be seen the starts of corridors between lines of cages, the contents of which could not yet be seen, though their hubbub of loud meat could certainly be heard from this auditory vantage point just inside the turnstile. The first enclosure was empty, unlike the other enclosures beyond the cages. Why an empty enclosure was the first display often mystified Coreseekers, but this was soon explained as the various themes panned out in interlocking concertinas of myth.

The empty enclosure at the start of the tour—it was discovered—was a symbol of the loneliness of life and the even greater loneliness of death. Yet many claimed it was not a greater loneliness in death: for it was a greater loneliness in life. The paradox was not lost on the gaping Coreseekers. Many of them peered into the empty first enclosure, their own vestigial ghosts bawling in disappointment.

The Coreseekers tried to pacify their own ghosts by pointing to the corridors of cages where the Coregrounds proper, apparently, would start—or so they promised. Meanwhile, it was their beholden duty to pause here a short time to view the empty enclosure in almost religious calm. Nobody, it was clear, took account of the beaked plankton that threaded the loose soil of this enclosure. Nobody realised this was an otherwise empty enclosure for such creatures. They wanted to see *big* things at the Core. Like the Megazanthus itself.

Soon after by-passing the first enclosure, most Coreseekers, in awed contemplation, would enter the first corridor of cages—the silence soon broken by the snorts, squeals and snickers of the first set of Megazanthus-imitators, many just small apes. Further on, however, kept apart hardly at all by the cages, the exhibited creatures could stretch limbs through the bars towards each other—and even uncomfortably close towards the Coreseekers themselves. The latter cowered from the first cage only to find themselves backing towards another cage where something else was putting out feelers.

The remarkable fact—despite the circumstances—none of these caged creatures were as nightmarish as one might have assumed. Nothing could be nightmarish because this was not a dream... and only dreams and their like could house nightmares.

Greg, stopping over at Klaxon City, looked up into the 'sky'. There was something lovely about an overhead expanse that was brightening with the arrival of day dream: dissipating the cloying nightmares that had just started to vanish from his mind. He had dreamed of the Core as a zoo, where the Corekeeper was in one of the cages.

A good hawler, he guessed, could plumb heights as well as depths for substance, sustenance and reassurance. Whilst it had been until now mostly land-locked, embedded with stone and grit, Klaxon's 'sky' (as he watched it) became the underbelly of a huge flying-carpet flowing diaphonously from inner horizon to inner horizon. Who flew upon it, he knew or at least he hoped he knew, were the nemonymous ones: angels and finer vessels of thought and spirituality. Beneath his feet, on the other hand, were others of a more name-driven ilk. A hawler, he knew, was a filter that worked in both directions of flow. But he only knew this for a while till he realised he was not a hawler at all. Because *I* was the hawler, here in the tunnel much nearer the Core than Klaxon City! I laughed. But Susan didn't wake. I always kept my laughter to myself.

The woman soon saw the man standing at the open bedroom window watching a huge black vulture-moth slowly cross from one side of the sky to the other. She left the bed and tip-toed along the carpet so as to give him a hug from behind. They had never made love other than at spontaneous moments. No pre-planning, and she reached round his body to see how hard he was. She nestled up to his buttocks, listening to him sigh, as they shuffled their feet deeper into the waking moment of the working day. The city was laid out in front of them like a map, the two of them being so high up as far as storeys were concerned. All they could hear was the incessant klaxon that no longer warned them as all warnings should, but now simply thrummed at levels of the hearing to which thresholds of sound had accustomed themselves.

He turned round—forcing her also to swivel from the window in mid love-making embrace. He thought he'd heard a shuffle or a whisper—but there was nobody there. He picked up the freshly delivered Daily Klaxon from the table—as if shrugging off the extraordinary with the ordinary—and read the main headline:

MUD WRESTLING BY THE ANGEVIN KINGS

Unaccountably, he thought of King Arthur and the Knights of the Round Table.

Then of some other history nearer to home, a World War that affected England like a dream once slept through... despite all the evidence that it had been all too real.

I have forgotten how I described myself earlier: and I now try to find the essential Mikeness of me.

"I ought to try looking *under* the earth," I said to myself.

Whatever the case, I would try more than anything now to shake off those encroachments of doctored repetition that were from Ogdon's original wordings in his novel and, thus, give more rope to my own words and concepts. Otherwise, there would be some danger of his novel becoming the victorious prevailing reality: a fact which would be a vast disappointment to us all, as my own novel was the only novel that contained a happy ending.

Hawling, after all, is dragging positive from negative and crystallising it. A novel is shorthand for a novelty trying to find its permanent fixture or berth as a well-established truth. And my scatter-brained extrapolations from all manner of different truths and fictions were—and still are—trying desperately to fit their novel jigsaws of shard into the ultimate picture of probability and, from probability, learning to summon the sinews of certainty... carving the perfect dimensions (inner and outer) of the sphere where we can live forever happy and content, having defeated those who wanted to smash it to smithereens even before it was formed.

There, the definition of hawling... at last!

Yet, meanwhile, I had to face one problem. It was Ogdon who first created Mike as a character and, therefore, by syllogism, myself! It was like trying to unclog the throat of my existence from the choking flying-threads in the air I involuntarily breathed to maintain that existence in the first place.

The children plodded the dawn. Then they saw other pairs of children plodding in from different streets—of similar ages, if quite various looks or breeds. Some were going in exactly the same direction, others more off-centre. Two were particularly smart, dressed in a material that could be described as brushed velvet in varied pastels. Some in little better than makeshift carpets fashioned into coats. Most tried to discover each other's names.

In the distance, one of the other children heard the thrum of traffic—as if the city had started to re-ignite—and the odd flash of tall red metal as it wheeled between the distant openings of terraced streets was glimpsed by the children as they looked down the streets from their own end.

Things were evidently coming back to life after the strobe systems of reality had jolted out of kilter for a short few moments.

"But nobody will ever find it again. It's only a way to make us hope," said a shrill voice from the now increased crowd of children as they crouched over a likely-looking manhole cover. Yet, some of these, in dribs and drabs, even single pairs, had often investigated such ground-level apertures assuming they were at the very least the top edges of oubliettes.

The children shrugged off anything that should be beyond children. Their games were ones that only children could play—seeking the Second World War bomb-hole where some of them used to play when they were even smaller children on some (god) forsaken Recreation Ground beyond the back of the back of council estate terraced houses. The city had bomb-holes galore—having suffered many raids in the war during the blitz... but none deeper than the legendary bomb-hole which was the children's ultimate goal. No parents would understand it. The children themselves barely understood it—and why they had to find it... and to lose themselves in the process of finding it or merely seeking it without finding it, whichever turned out to be the case.

The city of Klaxon had gathered to bid farewell to the Drill on its renewal of burrowing towards the earth's Core. Greg shaded his eyes from the Corelight, like a salute, as he gazed towards a deceptive hill, a hill that had grown from two vast encroaching earthworks shifting together towards the variable cavity-space that housed Klaxon—shifting together during the Drill's stopover. A huge Canterbury Oak seemed to be standing proud upon this hill above the city turrets and 'Parisian' quarters, bellowing out its wild, tortured wailing within the echoing hollow that was Klaxon. The multi-tannoy system that was used to imitate its wailing had been switched off, whilst the real thing reclaimed its ability to fill the city with its siren.

There would be no fireworks to mark the Drill's departure because no fires and resultant smoke were allowed in Klaxon. For obvious reasons.

Beth and the two dowagers boarded in advance of the businessmen class's own ceremonial boarding—especially as the women had further to go. Right up to the top for the rear cabin, where the Captain—it has to be said—had arranged for some redecorating by Klaxon workers—so as to make the journey more comfortable and easier on the eye. Adjustments had also been made to the huge insectoid vanes on the Drill's outside so as to help improve the views from the rear cabin's windows once en route via renewed intra-uterine burrowing.

Beth recalled the vision of two huge eyes in the Klaxon 'sky' and she shuddered, having now forgotten whether the ceremony of Sunne Stead had been a dream or real life. She had forgotten, too, self-evidently, that there were no such things as unrecognised dreams within Inner Earth. So it must have been real. Clare and Edith were too preoccupied with their next choice of books from the Drill's library to care either way.

Greg took one last backward look at Klaxon, wondering if he would ever be able to relive his adventures there. They would make a small book all by themselves.

He also recalled the multi-manhandling of the mighty Drill from its pylon-turret's pinion, with some difficulty, by the Klaxon workforce. But, eventually, the Drill was pitched upon the banks of the river near Klaxon's own Notre Dame Cathedral, the bit-tip once more poised over burrowable terrain. He imagined that the bit-tip's whirring and eventual screeching as it met the under-surface would out-noise even the city's wailing sirens. Meanwhile, the Canterbury Oak, with gigantic bole, but sparse branches aloft, was still etched against the wan Corelight. Now silent. Hence the renewed man-made sirens opening up their avant-garde threnody à la Ligeti or Penderecki.

The other businessmen whom Greg had hardly examined during the first part of the journey were still nebulous figures or an undercurrent of company rather than specific hard-drawn faces of mutual communication—but they were no doubt due to share the Corporate Lounge's facilities with him again. Hogging cocktails and anchovy munches and canapés. This time he thought he recognised one of them. At first a waft of Ogdon's smell. But, without the cape, Crazy Lope looked quite different. He didn't seem to be out of place. So *in* place, therefore, so basically unnoticeable that, in the end, Greg didn't notice him at all.

He just day-dreamed of their overground City following them on, digging with its airport arms.

Dognahnyi had returned to his pent-flat and stared at a flatter day that welcomed him back from a short unexpected strobe-holiday: stared, too, upon an even flatter threadbare carpet, which he had not bothered to replace for years, despite being otherwise surrounded by hi-tech equipment together with what he boasted to be an original Rubens on the wall opposite to the other wall where glowed the closed drapes-on-silent-runners.

Amy, the new recruit to his level of narration, had also disappeared with the initial abrupt reality strobe-out, but, unlike Dognahnyi, she had not returned here to continue the interview. Perhaps she thought she had already passed the necessary tests, before being strobed out. However, he feared she might have been caught up in last night's explosion in the Moorish quarter of the city—near the Bridge. However, it was more likely (he hoped) that she had already joined her alter-nemo in the tunnel's level of narration, i.e. two levels below Dognahnyi's own.

He laughed. The day was suddenly becoming less flat. He knew there were two main narrative levels below his head-lease narration—i.e. John Ogdon (aka 'Hilda') and myself (Mike). Both in intense rivalry to produce the 'truth' of the event-conspiracies, dream sicknesses, contaminations etc., although Dognahnyi sensed the narrator he knew as Mike was too sentimental for such machinations since Mike had already admitted he was intent on a happy ending. Little did Dognahnyi *actually* know, however. *He* was not the head-lease narrator at all. There was one level above him which pulled all the strings, including his.

However, Dognahnyi actually *suspected* that he might not be in complete control. He would not have been strobed out (albeit momentarily) if he were in *complete* control. But this suspicion was little more than sub-conscious, a synaptic undercurrent that hardly vibrated his thought cortices. However, the suspicion was subtly symbolised by his own tingle of fantastical belief that the city around him was also underground to other cities—just like Klaxon and Whofage and Agra Aska were, in turn, underground to his own city. The sky in Dognahnyi's city was indeed filled with stars, yes, but these were perhaps pinprick apertures to a further upper world where people were as yet preparing to travel to explore Dognahnyi's city in Drills and pot-holing expeditions. He loved fantasising. The real City itself, the one around him with covered market, Dry Dock, derelict zoo etc., was perhaps itself a living creature preparing to lift its airport arms and follow its own corpuscles' flightpaths to the essential Core of things. But then fantasising was a thing you could take to the Nth degree and still allow the brain to survive to deal with more down-to-earth concerns such as his imminent supper…

…and such as the contaminations. Dream spam. Riots in real life between dreamers from different nightmares. Dream terrorism—where no cause was too slight to warrant dream-suicide in its pursuance. Day-dream junk of confused waking. Contaminations where animal meat and bird meat welded together, even dead bits of each shuffling together in various fridges: yearning to weave threads of sinew together into the weft and woof of new palpitating substances. Dognahnyi even speculated on giant insects. If you cut them up, would their 'meat' be meat as he understood the term? There was a theory that insects when blown up out of proportion were the instigators of meat-off-the-insect-bone that resembled an interpenetrative mixture of poultry and beef, interleaved with yellow insect fat.

He returned to making his supper. Fantasy, even the dream-concerns of narrative level, must take a backseat to survival, he thought, as the blue flame bloomed from his cooker-hob beneath the frying-pan.

As he cooked, he speculated on his own definition of 'hawling', viz. dragging truths through various levels of competing narrations towards crystallisation.

In the past, Sudra skipped across the grass neatly lawndered in recent days: a bright shiny carpet of green that would have done a bowls match proud.

I pointed into the sky, drawing attention—for Susan's benefit as well as Sudra's—where I saw a large kite being flown from outside the park by someone at the end of its tether. This looked like a huge chunky toy: a Black & Decker drill the size of a real lorry—but then there was another kite appearing along the slant of another angle: a giant real model of a toy bus... followed by a complex Meccano contraption looking far too heavy to fly. Several other over-sized toys eventually floated above in delicate needlepoint: or a raggle-taggle armada... until I realised with a shock that they were not kites at all but real flying-craft in the guise of model toys... soon to be interspersed with the sounds of clattering vanes deeper and more threatening than a helicopter's... until that shock became real as I watched one of them accidentally clip another—with the result of both careering or cartwheeling from the sky, slowly crashing into parts of the city with sickening crunches that even my feet heard, bone to bone. Wisps of black smoke soon became billows. As if routed from an in-built rhythm of flight by the sight of the accident, others proceeded to fall from the sky—more likely however they had physically felt the previous ricochet—and I prayed that they would not crash anywhere near our own house... a strange priority as even just one of them crashing into the park itself would have threatened our lives which were far more valuable than property.

"The walls were red," one of the children said, a girl with bushy blonde hair, meaning to say they were read like a book. Or perhaps she did. The Yellow Book, however, blended into the wallpaper and remained unread.

I nodded. I did not wish to approach her, because, these days, touching was not allowed, even by teachers. I pointed to a huge funnelled monstrosity in Dry Dock—not unlike the famous Titanic, only slightly smaller with rather more complex ill-matched contraptions as if some little boy had got carried away with his Meccano kit—which had long since become a fixture on the city's skyline. Its abrupt overnight disappearance—presumably because all the work on its under-hull had been completed—was indeed the topic of conversation all over the city. This had coincided with the disappearance of many children who—despite the frantic searching by the Authorities—were still missing. Some had put two and two together and related the ship somehow to a vast metal Pied Piper…

I suspected that there was more to this trade in Angel Wine than met the eye. The girl looked as if her veins were full of it. Bulging all over like raised contours on a wall-map of a soft Antartica.

Crazy Lope was muttering to himself at the other end of the bar, but nobody listened then and nobody listened now, especially as he wasn't there... but someone or something was still there with the same speech on tape-loop. Or, rather, was it a flesh-corrupted ghost... or was it a spirit-diluted body? The voice *sounded* like his own, despite the lack of mouth muscles or any possible throat/chest resonation. But the voice was clear, nevertheless.

Voice reflection: "There was a plane doing a sort of air show near the pier. At first I thought it was an ordinary plane, but as it came nearer to us sight-seers on the prom, it turned more into a sort of model plane, with decorative fins, as if out of a cartoon manga—and I could see the pilot as a sort of Jules Verne character in ruffs and frills—and it skimmed off and grew bigger, amazingly, as it flew into the distance, and I could see a strange word: something like 'Angerfin' on its side. It almost clipped the edge of the pier and I was scared to see if it cartwheeled into the sea or, worse, into the prom where we were all standing...."

Tapeworm-loop: Want another drink, Craze?

Susan:

My sister Beth is beautiful but she often seems bitter... or loud. I'm right ugly by comparison—but perhaps calmer. I don't go into rages, like Beth does with Greg. Still, she's still getting over Dog. That was a relationship and a half, if ever there was one! Anyway, when we thought the children had disappeared, Beth was a tower of strength. Just shows you. I hope she's enjoying her weekend break with those *Jules Verne* tour holidays. I hope she and Greg are managing to patch things up. I have dreams myself. I could do with my own break. Mike is a blighter sometimes—he just leaves me alone—and when we sleep at night, I hear him snoring peacefully whilst I return to those dim dream-caverns that I can't escape—where I dream he's staring at Amy and Sudra cuddling each other. Dreams don't make it untrue, I say. Just because I sense his nature by means of dreams, doesn't mean I can't function properly when I finally wake up. There are words I don't understand that keep coming into my dreams. Jules Verne things—like Musketeers. Mistaken, perhaps, who knows? I was never one in waking life to know anything at all about such things. Who wrote what and whether I love music beyond the normal run-of-the-mill, but the dream thinks I love listening to quite strange things—because the caverns echo with opera and that noisy philharmonic stuff. I'm sure I'm at least dreaming *that*. I just love me old television, back home. Back home? *Big Brother, Coronation Street, Neighbours*—that's what I really enjoy. I can't be doing with anything like these nightmares that I can't get out of. Mosquitos, more like—not Musketeers at all. And Minizanthi (I don't know if that's spelt correctly but it doesn't matter as I'm saying these words not writing them down), things that peer round boulders, real ghosts in unreal dreams, with wide faces, having a break from hauling on the bucket-pulleys, their faces all smeared with white as if they've been naughtily at the cream cakes from my old Mum's larder. I love Mike. I wish he could see that. I try to make him love me in the dream. Because I know there is no real hope when I wake up. We both seem to be covered in a stiff coat, just with armholes, and I try to share his armholes with mine, taking his mind off the two girls. Amy's been a bit strange lately. She's been insufferable since she made it up with Sudra. I don't think I can trust Amy any more. Sudra has always been a worry to me, ever since her real Dad was so nasty to her. Flies, more like—not mosquitos. He stuffed her mouth to keep her quiet. I called the police, but he was little more than a cabbage when they came to take him away. I bet not many women have got their husbands put away. Most women put themselves away, I guess. I wish Sudra would not be so... innocent. But we're all in strange times down here. All bets are off, as they say. Just recently we had a whole long period of light from that shining thing in the dream. Arthur's ear is now growing again. No wonder he walks lopsided. But now it's near to darkness as darkness can be without being truly dark. I give Mike a kiss. He kisses me back. And at last we snatch some sleep, *together* for once, rather than him sleeping and me waking, or vice versa. And we're back in what I can only call real life—just for a short while at least. The sun is shining. The traffic has started up in the city. And I get up to switch on the TV. But before I can do that, I wake up again (or return to sleep?), and I'm here. I kiss Mike as he snores. He smiles in his sleep. Only his smile is there. Arthur's earwigging us, no doubt, hoping we may give a clue as to why we're all here and not at home in front of the TV. He never talks to his sister any more. Amy's real strange, you see, as if it isn't her any more. But she loved Sudra before, and she still loves Sudra, so I guess there is some thread of truth somewhere between the first Amy and the second one. People never stand still. They are always changing. I need something myself. I need Mike to come to me at the window where I look out at the city and the sun, then for him to put his arms round me… This coat is so difficult to wear. I can't even get it off, even if I tried. I need something more than all this. I need… I thought that there were some places where it was clear if you was dreaming or not dreaming. I'm not sure I believe that any more. But perhaps I'm mixed up and I'll soon wake up again and be less mixed up…

A waft of musky Angevin in its raw state interrupts her reverie... and eventually, having thought about it first, Susan snores peacefully for once, with no dreaming. That begs the question, however, where exactly are you when you are asleep and not dreaming? I listen to her snores which keep me awake.

Beth:
My Susan's soft! I always knew she was softer than me. Twin sisters come in pairs of 'hard' and 'soft', generally, and I was always the hard one, Edith. No, Clare, stop shaking you head... Oh, I see it's the Drill shaking it! But nothing to see out there at all except

damn rubble-storms, so you may as well listen to me as stare out there, ladies. And put your snobby books away. They're full of words I don't understand, and I'm pretty sure you don't understand them either. Edith, stop staring at that photo of your kids. They're grown up now and can look after themselves, I'm sure. Amy included. She wanted to be someone different. Now she has the chance. Not many of us get that chance in life. *Big Eared Arthur once drove a Big Bus.* Isn't that an old Music Hall song? He can now drive a whole world to its centre given the chance, I reckon. Private Planet, Vehicle Earth, Private Person takes the World on holiday. See, I've still got some gumption, even words that *I* don't understand I still use for some reason, despite being put away by men into this yellow cabin. Greg's as bad as Dog, I reckon. Greg and that Captain are hand in glove to keep us quiet up here in this top flat berth, while *they* see the Corelight rise above the new cities of Inner Earth through their own windows cleared by the vanes… They little realise, at the end of the day, that the Core is just like another Full Moon above the earth, casting silken curtains of light across the black waves of night's chilly sea (what poem, did *that* come from?). Men! They think they're heroes at every glimpse of a new adventure. I suspect the Core is really little more than a cake, baked hard like a lump of solid carpet, a misshapen lump of tufts to gag upon. Eating that cake opens a whole vista of lost time, they say. Let them eat cake. Hope it chokes them! Susan, you ask? Well, she always used to look after wounded birds she found in our garden. In fact, I think Our Father up in Heaven meant for her to stumble on every poor creature under the sun so that she could exercise her nursing skills as a potential earth mother. I remember her once sitting in the parlour, a lump of feather-filled blood on her lap and she cooed at this lump expecting it to coo back at her. And it did. She brought it back to life. But I say—what's the point of bringing such shipwrecks of nature back to life once they've been left high and dry on a crag by an egg vandal who broke its shell and left the innards to wilt stinkily in the salt winds? But Susan always rescued them. Even as a child. I scolded her for being so bloody soft. Therefore, how, dear Edith, have I allowed myself to be relegated to a backseat in this Drill? How, dear Clare, are we all so cowed by a world slipping by within men's hands? If everything is to have a happy ending, then we need to tell someone that it is we instinctive women (soft and hard alike) who must win—who must reach out to the Core where there are no dreams at all, no confusions of truth and lie, we women who must reach out to the Core where (when we are within it) we'll know what is true and what is false—finally and clearly and undeniably. We are just biding our time, Ladies. Don't let submission fool you. Submission is for Susan, not me. And even Susan, I reckon will be waking up to her strengths the nearer she gets to the centre of things.

I may not even have known my own name. I was nemonymous. Some of my friends recognised me and called me by a name they thought I was named. I was a working-class lad grown into manhood with the sole purpose it seemed of becoming nemonymous. I worked as a radio phone-in 'agony uncle'. Although that may not have been me at all. I met Arthur after he noticed his ear was getting even bigger. I tried to ignore it by staring at his other ear. We shared pints in Ogdon's pub—and then he worked behind the bar mixing cocktails. He simply loved mixing things... sometimes mixing allotments of time together with events to make plots.

I had secret vices. I didn't even recognise them myself, *if* that is the same thing as secrecy. I wove carpets. Many did this during the Nineteen Fifties in England—a hobby and a method of saving money. I had huge brush-stiffened grids of thread through which I leap-frogged a wooden paddle threaded with further thread—knitting tight each line of thread against another line of thread with my hard-padded fingers: as if tidying a rhythm of growing patterns of thick surface-veined underlay: except this underlay was a surface—but surfaces were meant to be 'on top' as that was where they always tended to go. An under-surface was a logical impossibility. Arthur admired them when I brought samples into the pub. He was still not old enough, thankfully, to realise he was too young to understand.

I stared at the screen wondering where I fitted into the schematic movements of the symphony. Not that I could hear any music at all. Silence.

The screen showed a clouded yellow surface, yet mottled with—if it were real—stains or signs of wear. Not yellow so much, I guess. Maybe beige. Not a uniform surface. Again, if it were real, it would bear perceptible bumps or lumps in its fibre. Fibre? Or weave. Or web. Or net.

It is as if I had created this site with a number of codes: codes that began with <hawl> and ended with </hawl>. I went to shut it down because I felt myself threatened by it, as if it were sucking me into it like a fly.

Now, I know deep down who I was. Or I was in the process of creating who I was. I was about to enter the intermittent and unsmooth flow of action. The yellowy web, hopefully, was to be the firewall or firefloor to protect me (or anyone else following me) from the dire horror that was a lurker on or within the threads of my discursive being. I was the head-lease narrator, the one from where they all had their essence and being.

Except they had escaped!

They were soon to reach the Core where truths would shine out and dreams dissipate. I shuddered. I was losing control. Mike and his party were, I suddenly discovered, on the point of reaching some mountain cutaway within the largest cavity that Inner Earth possessed—and Corelight would skim through like *real* sunshine to reveal the sorrows of mankind, but also illuminating a way to heal them. Mike would gain all the credit. Not me!

I punched away at the keys (having failed to shut down the screen) to prevent his party from ever reaching that Core or its Nirvana. Meanwhile, with my eye momentarily off the ball, I saw from the corner of my head that 'The Hawler', the lubricated Drill that threaded the rubble-storms, equally nearing the same Core, was about to crash-land on the outskirts of the Core itself—near Agra Aska—where they would rescue young love from the dreaded *shyfryngs*... and using the powerhouse of this love, they, too, i.e. Captain Nemo and his party, would reach Nirvana—without me!

I was aghast and I re-punched the keys, creating codes and tags for a new site of my dominion and power. A new blog city. It would be a battle of wills. And I was sure to win. I was determined to seek the information I needed, information that someone was hiding from me. *I* was the head-lease narrator. How could *anyone* be hiding anything from *me*?

Meanwhile, I tossed a quarter p coin to decide which party I'd follow. The coin dropped on its milled edge within a hole in my carpet.

Later, I stared at the screen in my flat. I had started typing up my things here in this rather undeserving tawdriness, having spent the earlier evening writing afresh in the square by the fountain. "I am curious—yellow," I whispered at the screen, hardly daring to breathe. I scribbled in my bright red *Silvine* 'Nemo Book'. I spent much of most nights exploring (wandering)—mainly the two disused airports on the eastern and western sides of the city—areas called the City Arms. They inspired with their direct emptiness and spent force. Bleak and windswept, I imagined the roaring of the jet engines, the clacking of old-fashioned propeller vanes, the residual sorrow and misused heroism of war veterans that still filled the air with poignant empathy.

I believed in complementary ley-lines veining the whole surface of the earth, proud as inflamed swellings on a human body... invisible to most uncaring eyes as the eyes' owners conducted their selfish lives on a daily basis, lives only interspersed with sleep or with whatever sleep contained.

I reviewed my own dreams. The fiction could wait, as I shut down the sickly clouded crystal-ball of my yellow screen and turned to the Nemo Book with a long stub of pencil grasped like I used to grab it as a child: in the fist like a dagger.

Notes:

Dream viruses. They are mutating, I fear, becoming more able to fly from dream to dream without culpability. This allows the contents of each dream to swill in and out of each dreamskin, and they can even penetrate the skin of life itself and enter the mainstream. These viruses are similar to birds with revolving beaks like drillbits, each a little pesky explorer. They multiply by ease of dreams being soaked into the birds' lubrication-pores. Filters can and do work both ways. Each 'bird' burrows from, say, my dream into, say, your dream. It takes a bit of me to you, and a bit of you to me—mixing reality and dream, *as well as* you and me. Then extrapolate that at a geometric progression. Each 'bird' (or dream virus) has its own consciousness but that also multiplies as its mutation increases, not changing its Drill's body so much, but changing the clouded specifics of its mind, each specific mind becoming a human mind that thinks it has got a human body—plus interaction with other 'human beings' of their own kind as if it is real life on the surface of our world, but really they are self-imagined figments within the bird's cockpit as it lays waste the skins of dream throughout a mass Jungian consciousness. I know it is difficult to grasp these concepts. I have faced the situation in my own mind that I myself may be one such dream virus (or, at best, a harmless dream spam): and I'm easing the skins to open up to the manifold plankton of dream-interstitialists. Birds of Plague riding their luck as they multi-dream—'multi-' because there are a lot of them in themselves but also 'multi-' because each Drillbit carrier has more than one mind (and often several) within its very cockpit, minds *believing* they are real human beings and not interactors in a fabricated drama or fiction. There are also human minds who have fallen off their own perch and 'walk' independently (or so they think) within Plato's Cave. But that's too deep for a notebook. But whilst we are on intellectual matters, I do now realise that *La Vida Es Sueño* was written by Pedro Calderón De La Barca, not by Lope de Vega. Meanwhile, the interaction of civil riots and religious troubles and suicide bombs (bombs that explode without fear for their own cockpits of self-assumed multi-mind) and global warmings/global warnings feed off each other back and forth. That list of possible Corekeepers: Megazanthus, Godspanker, Dognahnyi, Weirdmonger, Etepsed-Egnis, Azathoth. Dreams leak, books leak...

I tore up the page I had been scribbling on. And I returned to my desk, across the littered carpet, and powered-up my screen ready for easier tasks. Fiction was always easier than truth, a generalisation with which I would need to come to terms... eventually.

He called her Tho, as a gratuitously eccentric shortening for Thora. He was Hataz. Always had been. In full.

Hataz was more oriental than he looked. He and Tho were not necessarily a match made in Heaven, yet fair enough for two lonely strangers who both admitted they needed somebody. Their single attempt at love-making proper had been a clumsy exercise, neither of the participants earning flying colours for their efforts. They didn't really get near enough to each other. They were probably scared of the final penetration: a fact left unsaid.

After that, by tacit mutual consent, they never indulged in a blatantly physical approach again. Going to the only cinema left open in the city, making big talk and small kisses, the ritual holding of hands, walking in derelict parks... these activities were surely sufficient for people like them, because (as Tho thought) "spirit rode the flesh like aura".

They also played childish games unchildishly in Hataz's place, such as Ludo and Draughts—and, even, despite the size of the flat, hide-and-seek.

Inevitably, affairs of innocent convenience wind down and, today, Tho was bluntly determined to cut Hataz from her life before she became too enmeshed—not because the relationship was particularly claustrophobic, but simply because she was scared of a dream.

"A dream you've dreamed?" asked Hataz, genuinely puzzled at the sudden mention of dreaming. They had just returned from a concert in one of the riot areas of the city near the old Dry Dock—where a little known jazz combo called Erich Zann had given a desultory performance on vibes, flute and zither in an obscure unlabelled nightclub. Now, she had chosen this moment in Hataz's flat to make a prepared statement, one she had seemingly rehearsed in front of her wardrobe mirror.

"It's not a dream I've really dreamed, as such—it's strange, I can't explain it."

Hataz had started the evening hating the music. Now he was more generally confused than irritated—an uncommon feeling with him. Usually confident about life in general (if not with girls in the shape of Tho), tonight's disorientation was difficult to fathom. He had already felt vague indications of being unbalanced on previous dates, but nothing quite like now. Surely she was not going a roundabout way to ditching him. His pride, as far as the opposite sex was concerned, seemed fragile enough, already. For one peculiar moment, he felt these thoughts were not his, but Tho's. Osmosis? A twinning of auras?

"It was the edge of a dream, Hataz. I could see the dream in my bedroom, as if it had a transparent cover. Not really a bubble nor a balloon. Just a shapeless watery skin. Inside were all the nightmares I knew should have been in my sleep. I was awake, watching an independent dream that nobody was dreaming. There were glowing things that walked about. One of them I later saw was you, Hataz. Or someone who looked like you."

Tho coughed. She had tried to make it all sound natural, but Hataz was fully aware that she was reciting something she had learned parrot fashion. It almost felt as if he were dreaming. And the recital was silent.

"One looked like me? What are you trying to say?"

He had the uncanny sense that he was also reciting something, learned without his having remembered learning it.

"It was you, Hataz. You were inside the body of somebody else, trying, I think, to yank yourself out, using the shoulders as a lever."

There was a silence, broken by more silence, only this time it was a silence deeper and more frightening. Hataz's flat was always a quiet place at the top of a tall building. Tonight, there were no lonely aeroplanes droning over the sky from a forgotten airport.

In many ways, she didn't need to say the words. Hataz's newfound faith in the phenomenon of osmosis was nurtured by the silence, as she sprayed further implications and he allowed his inferences to burgeon. But, then, of course, her words would spill out autonomously, more visible than audible.

"I could see the host body's neck tightening," she continued, "bursting at the seams, as you tried to clamber out, except the seams were knotted veins rather than rows of stitches. Other creatures gathered at your feet—things I couldn't recognise, let alone describe. Some just a mass of wriggling tentacles. Others with more head than body. Tails and teeth. All chanting bits from an invented religion. To describe things in a dream makes remembering them more easy. The words and the names of the things seemed the most natural parts although, afterwards, they were the strangest. God knows how they were spelt. A good job, perhaps, that one can't remember every dream. But this dream was different, being one I was viewing from the bed, whilst still awake. It was growing in size, too. The dream's wobbly skin getting nearer and nearer, as it filled with more and more nightmares. Can't you see, Hataz, how I've been worried? I didn't know how to tell you. Nor if I should tell you at all."

"Do you want a drink?" Hataz asked, thinking that a psychologist would probably call this a nervous breakdown. She needed humouring, not scolding. He still couldn't shake off, however, the suspicion of a sting in the tail. Tho wanted to chuck him. That was bloody obvious, if nothing else was. In the meantime, though, she needed help.

"A drink? Yes, why not? A coffee, perhaps. Make it with milk if you've got plenty."

She heard him pottering about in the kitchen, as men did. Hataz imagined her hearing him—the chink of cups easing the silence more efficiently than the earlier exchange of words had done. Words were not really sounds, when they meant so much. Meanings were there whether one said them out loud or not. She shook her head. Or so Hataz inferred. How could she be thinking such thoughts? Thoughts were words injected straight into the vein. Surely she had intended to tell him of his host body in the dream with its skull splitting, tilting sideways from his own skull which was inside it. Bone within bone. The brain slid down his face like porridge, hair brylcreemed with blood. It was strange she could describe things better aloud, than describing them silently to herself. Osmosis was telling him too much of what she thought.

He returned with the cups of coffee and placed them upon the small table between Tho and himself.

"Are you feeling any better?"

He bit his tongue, without knowing why.

"All depends from what standard you are judging 'better'. I've never felt better, Hataz. It's as if I've never really been myself before. I was once a girl living in a dream. Now, I'm awake and I can see myself for what I am. No illusions. Just a dead-end girl who'll never be 'better' than average. You see, I was in that dream, too—eventually. Not one of the creatures slithering on their backsides. I was a finned figure that emerged from the shadows, soon after the body you once inhabited had disappeared. We didn't recognise each other, since we were both somewhat different than in real life. Then, I saw myself in bed, peering through the skin of the dream, from the outside of the dream, yes, peering at me in the dream."

"Tho, it was just a nightmare. You shouldn't take it so seriously. Everybody has at least one godawful dream in their lives—one that sticks with them."

He smiled. Was he on the point of ditching her?

"No, I told you, Hataz, I was not dreaming. I was awake. I was that girl in the bed. Fully conscious. Knowing exactly what I was seeing. And then you put one of your hands through the skin."

She screamed. A short sharp laugh that she had intended to come out as a full-blooded scream.

"Then your whole arm poked through," she continued, "reaching out for me with fingers that were webbed with some backward evolution. It was as if each fingernail were a tiny spinning drill. I screamed in real life, then—dreading that a dream without a dreamer could actually hurt more than just mentally."

Hataz sipped his coffee, sorry that he could not hear one of those droning aeroplanes. It must have been the fog that had cut them off from the sound of the thrumming traffic down below, interspersed with the odd clatter of overhead vanes or a fitful bomb-blast in another quarter of the city. He decided to let her have her head. No further point in interrupting or even commenting at natural breaks.

"Hataz, believe me, when I tell you, I was scared. So rotten scared, I closed my eyes, to blot out the dream."

"I bet you still saw the dream, though."

This time Hataz bit his tongue with the full foreknowledge of so doing. He had contravened his own rules of engagement.

"No, it was black inside my head. Not even a glimmer showing through the eyelids. The dream was not throwing out any light of its own. My bedroom was indeed as dark as it should have been, with the lamp off. That seemed to prove beyond all shadow of doubt it was a dream I'd been watching, not a dream I'd been dreaming. This must all sound so incredibly crazy to you—but when I felt the kiss upon my cheek and the strange words in my ear..."

"You became a Sleeping Beauty reversed, never to wake again!"

Hataz laughed at his own non sequitur. Humouring Tho had got him nowhere, so mockery had to be his next ploy. She reddened and simply stared through him into space. Having finished his coffee, he got up to look outside through the window. Not a glint. Not even a hint of anything beyond his gaze. Silence met silence through the glass. Eventually, with his neck aching, he turned back to face out Tho. It was about time she came to the point. And if she didn't, he would. At least one of them would have to cut the other from his or her life. But the vibes were all wrong. What he saw was the most horrific creature in the whole of the cosmos.

Nobody.

The Nobody who was ever the essence of loneliness.

The milky coffee he'd prepared for Tho was untouched, left stirlessly to a look of barely lukewarm and growing a meniscus skin.

Near to bursting with a passion he had never previously experienced, Hataz headed for the kitchen. He sought the bread knife or, preferably, something slightly more surgical than culinary—simply to lance the boil that his whole body had become. Playing hide-and-seek didn't allow the hidden one to squat, thumb-plugged, inside the searcher, did it?

Hataz returned with emptiness in his grasp, planted his face in the grail of his own webbed fingers, shaking with the *shyfryngs*. He later sipped the piping hot coffee to the sound of droning skycraft. Eventually, he heard a needle enter the deepest groove of all—and to the silence of Zann's zany zithers playing 'Nethermost Blight', he felt abysmally sad for someone he'd never find because it was himself. Azathoth's eyes poured out their sorrow. A thick cuckoo-spit bubbling from the centre of Infinity.

'Backward girl' doesn't mean backward in the sense of having a few slates loose on her dolls-house, but backward in an inverted *Remembrance of Things Past* or *In Search of Lost Time* way, the girl's past already bewitched by the future she had yet to live. Hawling is another word for such a process, a process that was just about to begin that day many years ago when Sudra's Mum asked her this question:

"Sudra, what do you want for Christmas?"

Her mother Susan stared as the small girl played with her single toy—a log lorry that she moved across the carpet between the legs of the armchair. She pretended that the darkness under the seat was a secluded area where the driver could get out and stretch his legs. It didn't seem to matter to her that the driver in the cab was firmly glued to his own seat, with his plastic legs and face all the same colour as the rest of him.

Whilst Sudra was imagining the procedure she had set in motion under the armchair, she looked up at Susan. Her father (Susan's husband) was away long-term at the present time—and this fact lightened Sudra's heart somewhat but she wasn't old enough to gauge exactly the magnitude of the relief that this same absence also afforded Susan's own spirits. Uncle Mike was due to visit before Christmas—and Sudra ever enjoyed his visits, if only because it put a smile on Susan's face. And Christmas was a time for smiles. Even smiles of disguise.

Sudra trundled the log lorry from under the seat's shadow—and parked it between two frayed lines in the carpet's growth of pattern. She undid the mighty hawsers that kept the logs in place and proceeded, gradually, to reposition the load close to the roaring coal fire in the grate. Sudra basked in the pink heat. She felt that teasing the logs with the proximity of fire was rather a funny joke and she laughed before answering her Mum's original question.

"Can I have a real doll, please... or a pet dog… Or some new shoes?"

Susan smiled. Not the broad Uncle Mike-induced sort of smile, but a smile nevertheless. Sudra guessed that Susan guessed that Uncle Mike was, in fact, at that very moment, shopping for just such a doll to lighten Sudra's Christmas morning. Far more fun to play with on that special day than clothes—even new shoes. Sudra, however, deep down felt that she deserved clothes as well as a doll, as well as a dog. Her clothes, for example, were more threadbare than the carpet. And her only pet was one she herself imagined. "If it's a doll, Mummy, can I have new shoes, too?"

"You have enough shoes, Sudra!" Susan frowned. Susan's own shoes were little more than moccasins made from remnant squares of flooring—even more worn than the ill-tufted patches where Sudra kneeled as she listened to a crack or splinter in some quirk of coaldust subsidence around a larger chunk... as the December wind moaned in the chimney.

"I only have one pair, one ugly pair," piped up the plaintive face by the fire.

"Your Dad may get you some new shoes."

"Where is Dad?"

"He's visiting someone on business."

Sudra wasn't sure what the word 'business' meant. "Is he going to the centre of the earth, again, for us?"

Susan laughed, despite herself—as she realised that Sudra hadn't forgotten some of the white lies her husband used to tell them as an excuse for his regular absences. She also had her own armoury of excuses that she issued on his behalf, like "He's off with Bunting hunting for rabbitskin" or "He's carving stars for the night sky" or "He's singing songs with Bobby Shaftoe and Little Tommy Tucker" or, indeed, "He's on a journey to the centre of the earth, he really is."

"How do you get to the centre of the earth, Mummy?"

"Well, you *can* dig straight down but also you could choose to go overland."

Susan spoke the customary words as this was a well-rehearsed home-made Nursery Rhyme in the form of conversation. Customary words—whatever the words—often give young children comfort.

"Overland, Mummy?"

"Yes, overland to the centre of the earth."

This part always broadened the smile on Sudra's face. And the next bit of the exchange always brought the broadest smile of all.

"How can you go overland to the centre of the earth, Mummy?"

"By tricking, my dear... by tricking the Above and the Below and the Across."

Sudra's smile soon turned into a full-blooded laugh but, quickly, both the laugh and then the smile faded as she returned her attention to the log lorry—reloading the logs from in front of the fire. A coal spat and then settled as a flame bloomed then doused itself.

A loose thread in a garment or carpet or quilt is traditionally known as a 'roving'—and as Sudra decided spontaneously to scorch her log lorry's wheels fast across the carpet away from the fire, one of its back wheels got tangled in one such roving. She imagined her imaginary dog that moment snaffling into the living-room with a tangle of meat in its long teeth (it often ate disused meat till it was raw) and forthwith snaffling out of the room again. Dogs were meant to be affectionate, loyal... but all this imaginary version did was suck meat off bones, then it ground the bones...

Sudra looked at the roving in the carpet. The carpet was her version of 'overland'—but here was a snag. She tried to lower her face so that she could bite out the roving thinking for one instinctive moment that her own teeth were the imaginary dog's teeth. She found a sinewy roving of meat between two of her own teeth, which made her wince at the gums' pang when she removed it with a yank.

Yes, a doll for Christmas would be lovely. Uncle Mike was probably buying it at this very moment. Travelling overland to fetch for her a doll from the very centre of the earth.

"Stop dreaming, Sudra," said Susan, as she stroked her daughter's hair. The girl was now sound asleep coiled in front of the fire, log lorry forgotten. Uncle Mike would eventually arrive at the door and Sudra would skip fast to greet him, before Susan had a chance for her own pre-emptive cuddle and kiss.

Uncle Mike, if it turned out to be Uncle Mike, would not say what was in the package he put beneath the Christmas Tree. He did not tell them it was a real cabbagepatch doll with long doggy teeth and its own new shoes. But, of course, he would not arrive till nearer Christmas itself.

He had been roving overland for days, he would eventually claim, but now, by the warmth of their coal fire, he had reached the true centre of his world, here with Susan and Sudra.

The Drill broke through a fossil-bank close to Agra Aska, cartwheeling free from rubble-traction into the relatively clear space of a huge cavity close to the Core itself.

The city was laid out like a map, until Captain Nemo released the Drill's parachutes, which worked jerkily in the unusual air consistency of Inner Earth. The map turned turtle but eventually approached more steadily, and Greg could see at last the famous Balsam River and its mighty Straddling Cathedral, whilst the Drill's bit-tip intermittently scribbled over it like a biro nib in the soft putty-like effulgence of the Corelight.

Pinnochio's nose grew longer when he told lies. Longer wooden teeth, too. Yet we have no easy way to judge lies in real life. There is a question whether a single lie, once told, creates other lies in its wake, then radiating, spawning more lies, new and different lies living off each other—like a butterfly theory of chaos—roving round the world like a disease till everyone tells lies, Russian Doll lies, until they return to the original liar himself who accepts them as truths—because he started them in the first place and he has persuaded himself, by being in denial, indeed has simply forgotten that he lied in the first place and that he had started the lies moving round the world. Yes, a lie sickness, a plague of lies…

As the Drill landed with a hefty banking towards the Straddling Cathedral, Greg laughed upon spotting a kite being flown by an Agra Askan citizen, a kite identical to a flying carpet... prancing higher and higher from its slanting tether. Greg was older and hopefully wiser than before with his bum-fluff moustache having by now matured into a full set of whiskers upon his pink chops. His eyes still betokened the rough and ready innocence of an artisan, but he now carried an instinctive articulative wisdom, even when not talking.

Beth Dognahnyi remembered that Susan, her sister, was, even at this same moment, approaching Agra Aska from a different terrestrial angle, i.e via the hawling-tunnels of man-city. She missed her. She missed her comparative softness and empathy. She was wasted on that Mike. Beth felt herself to be, on the other hand, too brittle, without the calming influence of her softer sibling—yet Beth tried to hide this by smiling at Greg. Often, however, a false smile is worse than a lie

"Hey, some of those kites haven't got people flying them!" suddenly announced Greg, as he pointed to one in particular with no obvious tether in its wake.

Agra Aska was indeed now alive with kites. Beth and Greg had left the ill-tilted Drill. Captain Nemo, the businessmen and the dowagers were nowhere to be seen. Probably still preening themselves prior to disembarking. Beth and Greg had made reunion soon after the Drill's crash-landing by parachute. Beth was still wondering where Greg had been for the whole journey but didn't question why she hadn't questioned this before now. She however did complain about the dowagers and their over-eager book recommendations and the dreary yellow wallpaper in their rearward cabin. Beth and Greg knew perhaps that they were a template for love (albeit a forged or fabricated one) so they needed to act up their affection for each other at all times now that they had arrived in Agra Aska—and they wondered if their mission in Agra Aska was indeed a predetermined one for stamping this very template upon a younger couple who even at that moment were being touched by a bout of the *shyfryngs* at the well-demarcated edge of an enormous Coremoon—a vast glowing pale yellow 'half-sky' that even at this moment reared its arc through a mountain cutaway towards the south end of Agra Aska.

By now, in this renewed light, the bustle of barges upon the Balsam River was beginning a noisy trade of richly woven carpets and Angevin spices. Yet there was far more description to be endured before Beth and Greg would be able to do full justice to their vantage point, viz. the interlocking sights and clandestine intricacies and heady implications of such a place as Agra Aska and its near neighbour: the Megazanthine Core.

As our tunnelling party approached—at last—the mountain cutaway of South Agra Aska, I am sad to report a death. I am devastated—to the extent that I am not sure I am still the Mike I think I am or the Mike I think I have always been.

The whole incident has taken a lot out of me. But rest assured there is a consistency of viewpoint, a conviction that what I am reporting is the unvarnished truth, however poignant or indeed tragic for me (or for Mike if he is still me) that it happened to be. It is difficult to be certain about anything after such a long downward trek, interspersed with hawl training that was imposed on us by the intermittent appearance of service-tunnels alongside our main journey shaft. Both the girls, Amy and Sudra, were very game. They took all in their stride, despite the unfashionable carpet-coats and yellow clogs that any other young modern misses would no doubt spurn. Arthur has been a bit morose, weighed down to starboard as he is by a vast elephant ear. He has however acted as provender source, and there are no complaints on that score. Susan has been a real dream. I still love her.

Well, I can't delay the incident's telling, however long I dwell on trivialities to avoid addressing its terrible vision or loss. Sudra slipped in a momentary mess of darkness that smeared her vision, if not the vision of us others. We could see she was blinded by a mixture of darkness and a scalding flash of Corelight that was a freakish occurrence within her eyes alone: a combination far worse than the confusion of pure darkness itself. She hung over a mini-cutaway (one that was as nothing to some of the much bigger cutaways we had already experienced in our journey, but sufficient to waylay Sudra's steps). Amy rushed to her assistance, grabbing her wrists: and then for an eternity of anguish, there Sudra hung. I, too, rushed, from a nearby tunnel where I was silver-plating pulley-hooks. A goodly task for an evening's Corelight. But I mustn't delay. I was there soon enough to see Amy kissing Sudra's brow—as if in abandonment. Surrendering to an inevitable. Tears streamed down both girls' faces in pangs of lost love and despair. I grabbed Amy's ankles in an attempt to tug Sudra, via Amy, from the reaching abyss. I then managed to claw my way up Amy's legs and hugged her thighs within her carpet coat, tears now streaming down my own face.

"We should have gone overland."

These were Sudra's words as Amy finally let go. And echoing through the abyss: Sudra's screams of "New shoes, new shoes, new shoes, new shoes…" until even these strident sirens of hope faded into silence.

Sudra quaintly described them as "Redoubts"—but nobody seemed to understand, least of all, perhaps, Sudra herself, what she meant by this word. Amy and Arthur laughed, simply for the sole reason that they felt laughter still within themselves and they didn't want to waste it before it expired as one of their possible human reactions to events. "Redoubts" in itself was not a funny word. On the other hand, the word "Côté" was written on one broken brick wall that they were now passing—almost as if this were the last sign of the city proper. Not written so much as scrawled in a clumsy attempt to follow a trend that was already very fashionable in the city itself: graffiti, tags, pieces... all now lost in these initial stages of a thin-topped underground. A mine with the mere vestigial veneer of a break-even point between upper and lower.

I cannot now remember to what Sudra once referred when using the word "Redoubts", but it does cause me to wonder yet again who let go of whom on the edge of death's cutaway when Sudra plummetted to her own abrupt cutaway. Who saw what in whose eyes? They both held each other's wrists. Did Amy let go... or did Sudra let go when she looked into Amy's eyes—flimsily disguised by tears of fateful surrender—only to see someone other than Amy behind those same eyes?

Amy was distraught. I could hardly comfort her, as she wailed and wailed into the sleep period. Susan, surprisingly, for a bereaved mother, was quite calm, as if she had been released from a burden of bewitchment—as if what Amy had carried behind her eyes had been passed off to Sudra in that critical moment of broken wrist-links. Or Sudra's own shadow—which I had never noticed—was a stronger shadow than even Amy's shadow. Indeed, once that Amy had recovered from the initial shock, she seemed to enter a new strobe period, without the necessity of us others having to strobe in tune with her own strobes. She became distant, detached, finally re-attached, but calmer. I felt as if a suicide bomb must have exploded inside Amy's head and she had survived it by simple virtue of being strobed-out of existence at the instantaneous moment the bomb ignited itself.

It is difficult to dwell on the repercussions of Sudra's death. Indeed, I can't recall Arthur's reaction in any way whatsoever, but it did inevitably mean Amy spending more time with him in alternations of sibling rivalry and sibling bonding. Susan was stoic and—if I say so myself—so was I. And we now need to address the circumstances of our arrival in Agra Aska. "Ever look to the future", my Dad always said when he was alive. I always replied, in boyish pique, to his great astonishment, that such a tenet was a veiled threat, because futures often blighted pasts. That's perhaps why I was destined to become mixed up with 'hawling', but then of course that word had not yet channelled its way down the generations to me in that period of my childhood (as it was later to do).

Agra Aska is now not at all what it was like in the distant strobe-era spoken of elsewhere, when John Bello and Joan Turner became young lovers to the backdrop of Ervin's shriving—and of the political war-machinations that surrounded David Binns, Dictor Wilson, Robert Orwell, Chesterton and The Archer-Vicar. Today Agra Aska is blander, albeit still maintaining the now famous Straddling Cathedral and the Balsam River trading business. It substantially thrives on the *Angevin* cream that it mines from the Core—an export hawling business that will play a large part in the future of our campaign. So, yes, this *is* a mining city that has settled within its own strobe-history as near to the earth's Core as it is possible for any civilisation to be positioned in such a city-shaped formation, i.e. in the manner of the more distant cities of Whofage, Klaxon and London—but, despite this infrastructure, still maintaining a conveniently short direct two-way filter to the Corecombs of the Megazanthus itself. By the way, I've just mentioned London and this city (established at sea level directly above the man-shaped man-city whence I and my party derived) is rumoured to harbour the domed cathedral of St Paul's that was the original template for Agra Aska's straddling version which, in its turn, is a vast structure that possesses the ornate and iconographised religious thoroughfare (aisle?) along the roofed bridge between two Babelline towers. The Balsam River torrents below this 'bridge', its relentless current leading to the tributaries of Abrundy and Tiddle.

The under-surface or floor-division between London and its strobe-twin city beneath it (i.e. man-city with Dry Dock and covered market) is a mere lightweight ceiling or carpet... or, rather, mere symbols of these things, in gossamer arcades of nothingness, barely differentiating between the two cavities or air-spaces that harboured each city. However, I assure you, the sea 'unlevels' do also help to maintain this division.

Having said that, I am minded to give my own personal impressions of Agra Aska as we emerged from the last earthen cutaway and viewed the 'half-sky' Coremoon settling above its silver pinnacles. We all heard a distant lonely flute. And a dog yapping. I hate dogs. Sudra would have been delighted. We knew it was a city, and indeed Arthur, with his over-extended left ear, could hear more than us—as city-life surely thrummed beneath us. Oh, by the way, I also spotted the 'shipwrecked' Drill lodged on a crag escarpment that bloated unnaturally from one of the Cathedral's Babelline towers. But more of that later.

What I wanted to say, really, was that, for me, Agra Aska is the sea. It's strobing in and out of existence so fast, beyond the scope of flickering eyelids, that it appears to be a swaying creature of waves.

Even the buildings are waves and the river just another channel of current, criss-crossing other such channels at the culmination of forces that make me believe in a ghost of a pier which I watch shimmer more slowly in and out of existence. Of course, all this might have been just my imagination.

Edith and Clare were in the fort holding the city. They were dowager twins and had spent most of their formative years living inside one of the city walls—the tallest part of wall that had become so tall the local residents called that bit of the wall a tower. The city was not completely surrounded by walls—otherwise that area of the city outside of the walls could not have been called a city at all. There were gaps in the wall for throughways to the two airports on both the eastern and western arms of the city—but the gaps were closing up with growth of brick as well as of foliage/weeds, although common sense would indicate that it was only plant material growing because brick generally didn't grow. Brick is more prone to crumbling. The aerodromes were derelict so the throughways were moribund. Other gaps in the walls around the inner city were customarily found to the north and south—but these, too, seemed to have narrowed, but this time the narrowing was simply imagination, because everything using the gaps had widened.

When the dowagers eventually disembarked at Agra Aska—faced with an undignified long-skirted clamber down one of the Babelline towers of the Straddling Cathedral—they certainly felt suspicious they hadn't actually travelled *anywhere* but had been confidence-tricked by means of a 'U Turn' within Inner Earth or some sleight of compass prestidigitation regarding the tricking of the Above, the Below and the Across. The compensation, however, was that Agra Aska represented an oblique, if opaque, home from home—where all gaps went missing. Indeed, the whole of Agra Aska seemed to have landed within a blind spot so that they had to keep turning their heads to avoid not seeing it at all: and in the process saw only the legs of Clare (if you were Edith) or of Edith (if you were Clare) rather than any breathtaking views of their new home city that the descent of disembarkation would otherwise have entailed. It was rather like going into a bare room with bare floorboards, then imagining that if you took up the floorboards nail by nail you'd discover a carpet laid neatly *underneath* them.

What they did particularly notice was the temperature, the feel of the air, the Aska Agran ambiance. It was not as cold as they feared from what they had been told of the increasing cold the further Coreward one travelled. The legends circulating among the surface cities represented the other extreme, i.e. that the Core was red hot. Captain Nemo had indeed explained to them when they first signed up for the holiday that an effective blend of two legends prevailed. One legend that it was molten *Angevin*. The other that it was frozen *Angevin*. With the benefit of mixed myths, therefore, one could survive anything. He had laughed leaving the dowagers to fathom out what he had just explained. But it all seemed to make sense now. The Core itself could be seen spreading with a creamy consistency (outward from their fast diminishing blind spots) across half the sky, here more moon-like than sun-like, the quirk of refraction making it more yellow than white, followed by a blend of both colours when proto-incidence kicked in later during the natural diurnal process of Agra Askan sky systems.

Edith and Clare were the only Drill travellers who enjoyed an official welcoming party. A young couple, hand in hand—an emblem or living symbol of the love and affection that depicted the Agran Askan optimum ideal of existence, an ideal celebrating the beneficial hindsight effect of the curatively legendary times when the original young lovers in this city had had to endure one hellishly onerous quest as well as the religious shriving of their private parts in the process. Edith and Clare had arrived—partly in ignorance but partly knowing they would be using their trained counselling skills to further this ideal, and Mike (who had often acted as a radio phone-in agony uncle on the surface) would be supplementing their skills with his own special skills wrung from a mixture of hawling experience mingled with a semi-conscious self-condemnation for his own wicked thoughts and desires. The mixing of myths was the optimum, good and evil alike, used in the war against evil. The dowagers wondered if Mike's stony path to his own *Road to Damascus* (or Road to Agra Aska!) had by now reached culmination. They could not yet see any sign of him or his party—expecting them, as they did, to appear duly shriven by the underfoot dangers of Inner Earth's deepest pot-holing together with the hair-carpets on their backs. But they remained confident that they would soon arrive and bolster the dowagers' own efforts to gather themselves to the tasks in hand. Any *Angevin* smuggling could be left to the others. That was merely a by-product of the mock-holiday, one the dowagers could safely ignore—although they wouldn't decline any of the profits once they returned to the surface!

The young Agra Askan lovers (now called Hataz and Tho) led them by the hands towards the Core, lit from behind by a now wildly yellow innersky exploding into a balloon shape not dissimilar to the Augusthog icon or flying-pig kite glimpsed before in their travels. Followed by the quickly fading ghost of the Megazanthus itself with wings stretched between two infinitely distant horizons. The ladies would need their own brainwrights, to be sure, as they continued to fathom the real reasons for this their increasingly complex presence in an increasingly complex Agra Aska—all lies and dreams forgotten... at least forever.

The intense primary colours of each of the individual swellings or plumes of flame, their sprays, cascades and visible thunderous suicide-bombs were so sharp-etched, sharp-edged, they seared to the very optic fuse of one's eye. The wide shiny blue sky faded by comparison. Some of the colours were not colours as such but various shades of black, many being utterly black slices or slashes or sheets of black fire—accentuating how bright the daylight's backdrop of sky had become.

Dognahnyi turned from his window and, after sweeping his curtains together upon their silent runners, he felt relieved that his room had become relatively subdued: protected against the outside's sharp relief: now a room with an atmosphere more fitting for the conference he was conducting with John Ogdon—sitting, as Ogdon was, in full feminine regalia, beneath the painting of the man with the salacious swan.

Dognahnyi: Celebration, but celebration for what, Hilda? Tell me that.

Ogdon: That the man-city is at last united?

D: (barking) Excuse the cough. It's my way of laughing. Well, the city is certainly stirring.

Even as he spoke, the building trembled, moving the waxen blooms of flame to and fro in their holders.

O: Man-city is something we've lived with. We thought the Ancient Father built it that way in the shape of a figure, but have you noticed?

D: I know what you're going to say. Something about me being a Barker?

O: Sort of. The man-city is gradually burying itself like that legend of watery Venice. You recall? Rubens painted it. But what I was going to say is that few have ever noticed (and I think *I* failed to notice it till recently) that our city, our man-city, is all there is. There is nothing beyond the airport arms.

D: Or beyond its other extremities? No geography except itself. You would have thought with helicopters we could have sussed that out before now. Doh!

O: You can feel it in the feet. We are sinking. The city is sinking. It wants to join some cosmic battle within Inner Earth.

D: That's a bit romantic. By the way, is your—what do you call it?—your alter-nemo on board the Drill? That Drill they called 'The Hawler'?

O: Yes, disguised as a shy businessman. Even the Captain's been kept in the dark about that.

D: Are there such things as shy businessman?

O: (Laughs, then barks in mockery of the other.)

D: Well, what about the other party? My beyoootiful recruit got rid of the bewitched Sudra. That creature—if she hadn't fallen—would certainly have queered our pitch. There would have been confusion galore of alter-nemo and alter-alter-nemo otherwise! Yet, I'm unsure if the shriving is complete. We need full penitence of all party-goers before we can set in motion the plan for widening (by strength of love) the sluice-gates of *Angevin* towards the huge mouth that yearns for the white slimy flow down its twitching throat.

O: That's a strange way to describe shortening the supply-line!! (Barks loudly).

D: There's only one possible fly in the ointment.

O: The Megazanthus?

D: Hmmm. The Megazanthus is a loose cannon, true. We don't know whether it yet has its own alter-nemos. Like Godspanker or Azathoth. No, Og, what I was really referring to is the *simple* need for an unhappy ending. That should clinch everything. The ultimate paradox. It's not easy to bring off such a required tension, a tension from the tension of identical opposites... especially with Mike Wassisname working in another direction completely. So, yes, without our own version of tension, the whole *Angevin* mine will spectacularly implode and, *even* with the help of man-city, we'll all end up in Queer Street!

O: I'm working on it, Dog. *I* am providing the ending.

Not Mike Smartarse!

Amy, once she had finished carpet-sweeping, turned over the vacuum and emptied what it contained. Not only flies fell out but hairs from a cabbage.

Amy was now hoovering the carpet of our Quarantine Quarters in Agra Aska. The Askan authorities had decided—a bit late in the day—that both visiting parties should be held together *in camera*, to ensure no leakage of disease or, indeed, of dream from the surface. Hataz and Tho, the emblematic pair of young lovers from Agra Aska (and young lovers *in actual fact*) were also necessarily quarantined in the same room as us—bearing in mind that they had already come into skin-to-skin contact with the dowagers, Edith and Clare.

The room was an ornate one—and windowless—decidedly stuffy compared to the startlingly panoramic vistas that had first met us in Agra Aska. The room was eerie, too, in a nice atmospheric way, but an atmosphere soon to turn jaundiced, when anything haunting the room turned out to be more insidious than it was cosy, as any hauntings of that room were soon to do in all connotations of that thought. Yet, none of us (the room's inhabitants) had suspected what fear truly was until the hauntings of that room made themselves plain... making themselves plain, but not without losing their dubiously inherent quality of mysterious eeriness.

Still, none of us would yet know true fear until the later endgame was upon us, an endgame which hung above us like a slowly eroding cliff or impending cutaway of Inner Earth. That would diminish the Quarantine room's hauntings to a handleable perspective, by comparison.

As we were earlier trooped—in Indian file—within the portals of the room's entrance, many of us gave a wistful look at the crippled Drill squatting like a giant's disused toy upon one of the Straddling Cathedral's craggy towers. Many Agra Askan sightseers were staring moon-eyed up at it, shaking their heads. The members of my own pot-holing party gave versions of their own shriven glances at the Drill, equally as bemused by its sight as the locals were.

But, once inside the room, the wide-screen sights of Agra Aska themselves diminished to a fast-receding full-stop in the same way as an ancient TV would once disperse its black-and-white picture... upon someone switching the set off.

Captain Nemo seemed strangely diminished, too, outside the jurisdiction of his Drill. He slouched into a corner seat and sat there staring mindlessly at whatever transpired.

There had been no mutual welcoming between the two parties when we all started to interact within the room. Our meeting up in such strange circumstances was taken for granted and we started conversations as if we were finishing them.

Edith had initially been tearstruck by the sight of her two offspring, Amy and Arthur. They had been lost as small children and, despite much searching by the authorities, never found... eventually assumed to have wandered off into the Northern coalfields of the city's Head region, from where few ever returned. She hugged them, made a low-breathing comment into her son's ever-fattening earlobe cavity—and then withdrew, taking matters for granted, as the others seemed to do. This was part of the beginning of the room's hauntings: i.e. low-key reactions to high-key events.

Amy had grown into a fine physical woman, but Edith left unsaid her own suspicions of what or whom actually lived inside her head. Amy meanwhile cleaned the carpet with an automatic sweeping motion—a tangled tussle of an affair, as the carpet was mostly long-shanked with what looked like human hair. Some patches had been crew-cut which made the sweeping easier.

She later started polishing one of the paintings. One had a gilded frame but not much to speak of within its margins. A haunting of an image that was as faded as the flock wallpaper around it. However, the aura of the room's general ornateness maintained itself despite the tawdriness of individual furnishings.

Clare retained a hands-on affection for Edith. Neither Amy or Arthur recognised Clare from childhood days as their headteacher.

"What's your name?" asked Clare, suddenly turning to one of the two young Agra Askans in love with each other.

"Tho," replied the girl.

"Hataz," replied the boy, simultaneously, even though he hadn't been addressed.

"Quaint names," said Clare, almost for Clare's own ears, if not Edith's.

The two lovers seemed just as subdued as the rest of us. Perhaps we knew the exact nature of the room's hauntings before such hauntings made themselves plain.

Greg and I were seen talking in a desultory fashion. We knew we were mutual alter-nemos—and when such individuals met, they often had empty conversations, and this was no exception. A shadowy businessman from the Drill's Corporate Lounge took no heed of what we said, because he knew he would learn nothing new by so doing. The other businessmen were busy disappearing into their own shadows, by sidling towards corners of the room that were not any of the more usual four corners of the standard cube-space that the room apparently was. Human-coning was another expression which brought back memories to some of them, but not to others.

Susan was the least subdued. She now found Beth rather unsatisfactory as a sister, the latter having lost much of her grit. Susan had always depended on Beth's get-up-and-go when they were younger and here, suddenly, Susan was (uncharacteristically) the only one in the room with any vestige of creative impulse. Even I felt jaded. What was more, Beth hardly reacted to the news of Sudra's death. To Susan, it felt like pummelling a large slime punchball that was too heavy to swing.

The hauntings perhaps were that there were no hauntings in the room. Meanwhile, one of the gilt-framed paintings started to emit a whiney pathetic klaxon, of which nobody, including me, showed awareness.

The two dowagers—in undercurrents of recitation—spoke aloud parrot-learnt excerpts from Marcel Proust's *Du Côté De Chez Swann*—and there was also much promise of them sharing their literary passions with the others, should there be periods during the Quarantine when there would be time for all of us to kill.

As to food, there were 'cold numbers' in bowls, numerical shapes of indeterminate flaccid cooked-meats in an unwarmed reconstituted form.

Once Amy had finished the housework, we all started looking for beds.

Ogdon spotted a face in the bar mirror opposite, a face that wasn't his own. There were tears running liberally down its cheeks. The face spoke:

"Help me, I'm Greg. *Please* don't let me be Mike. I know it's easy to confuse us but I'm the one who's on board the Drill. I once worked in waste management as a lorry-driver. Mike was the office worker. I'm desperate to be real, but only if I can be me, me, Greg. Because I *am* Greg."

Ogdon's own eyes were also filling up, feeling helpless to help. There were too many people who needed to become their real selves. It was difficult enough for Ogdon to hold his own mind together.

"I'm Greg," continued the face opposite. "Help me, I'm Greg. Help me to be Greg. And not Mike."

It was a ghostly chant or intonation. And Ogdon threw his glass across the bar and it smashed itself before it smashed the mirror and all the mirror's contents.

But he still heard the plaintive, haunting voice: "I'm Greg. Please don't let me be Mike."

And now the face was scratched and freshly scarred as if it had been dragged through a hedge backwards.

In times of trial, solutions presented themselves in odd disguises and even created thoughts many would never have dreamt of thinking as thoughts in more ordinary times. The hedge itself had almost *helped* their descent of passage: a far cry from hindering it as they originally expected—but woe betide if they should need to climb back up through it, whereupon it would surely turn upon them with a vengeance.

Being inside that Quarantine room was worse than any hedge-shriving—but we were eventually evicted one by one, having proved our 'purity' through dream-detector games and obstacle courses controlled by klaxon or tannoy. We also had to kill the 'mole', before the last one could emerge from the room. And this was by a daily vote. Hardly a game. More life and death, I'd say. I was sure the 'mole' was Amy—for obvious reasons. But, by some quirk of semi-alliances or double-bluffs, it turned out to be Captain Nemo who was the 'mole'—Captain Nemo (aka Dognahnyi, according to Beth) whose blood was eventually on all our hands. In fact, he and I were the last ones quarantined in the room whilst all outside surveillance had been withdrawn (we'd been assured)—so it's just between him and me what actually happened.

Nemo's blood may have been *metaphorically* on the others' hands, but I had his blood—literally. But I'm not admitting to that. I quickly draw a veil of denial over such matters. I effectively retract my own overblown omniscience on that score. I even clip the wings of my omnipotence simply to avoid a Horla's shame. And I trust Ogdon turns a blind eye, too—wherever Ogdon now is, if he exists at all. It's probably just him against me, now. Ogdon against 'Mike'. Or possibly just me. Endgame impends.

In the covered market area of man-city, Ogdon remained alone amongst those known to the authorities by actual name. The rest of the citizens were at best nameless or, more likely, nemonymous. Ghosts, if they exist at all, don't exist as such: but float in inexplicably verifiable shades of non-existence barely beyond the threshold of sound or feeling. Other than Ogdon, any residual souls left in man-city—who felt the vague sinking feeling that often accompanies the beginnings of anxiety, later fear and finally terror—were such ghosts bordering on lies or dreams.

And the stirrings of clockwork driving will-powered machinations beneath the Dry Dock and covered market gave the impression that the city's airport arms were beginning to whirr, almost spin, like sluggish propellers. And huge angel-shaped wings of earth flew upward in mountainous slab-cascades on each flank of the body politic or body civil, as the city's cantilevered sous-centipedes of diggers started to delve a far more awesome shaft than a million Drills (in the shape of 'The Hawler') could or would ever have ever been able to excavate so as to make room for their communal passage downward toward Inner Earth.

Ogdon sat in his deserted pub—surrounded by smashed glasses and toppled barstools. His teary face was in his hands. He couldn't actually believe what he was doing. Yet, relentlessly, automatically, he was man-handling a huge key in the pub floor, ensuring the massive tessellations of clockwork remained taut, on a hair-trigger of sprung power—to drive the city ever downward. It seemed appropriate that a pub turned out to be the powerhouse, not only of drunken small talk or wild boozy brainstorming, but also of the more momentous or eschatological concerns of mankind—put into ratchetting motion by this morally-neutral hawling process of unbelievably gigantic proportions. Yet Ogdon sobbed, as he began to stroke the ape in his lap.

Endgame rampant.

As we emerged into Agra Aska, the relief from claustrophobia was tangible.

The sky was still halved by a scimitar of Corelight, like an overripe sun that had bloated beyond its capacity to shine through clouds like a yellowmanker custard.

A vast winged angel-icon on splints floated overhead and we guessed this was just a tethered kite-symbol or a free-agent balloon-emblem that pre-figured the real angel-thing itself—when the doors of the Core eventually opened to reveal the Megazanthus swagged in its mucus strands of rancid cream. But like telling lies, guessing was only one minor stage further along the spectrum of truth.

Amy put her hands over her ears. I couldn't understand how the silent image we all watched could have caused such a reaction. Perhaps she heard something that we didn't. A metaphorical Sunne

Stead within her own brain? Or, as she told me later, the sound of a robotic machine cranking into ignition but so well-oiled it tip-toed, just as she tip-toed herself in the shoes she had managed to salvage from Sudra's stowaway mini-wardrobe that Sudra herself had secretly carried all the time, as it turned out, during her rite of passage with us through Inner Earth.

Beth slouched to a distant seat by the Balsam River to watch the trading-barges in their resplendent flag finery and drape-carpets. She remained confused by the incriminating nature of Captain Nemo's identity as the 'mole' or 'burrower'. Yet, confusion *was* at least a stage further on the truth spectrum most of us had not even approached!

Edith, Clare, Greg & Arthur were taking holiday snapshots (with the help of Tho and Hataz) of the Straddling Cathedral. They took each other in smiling poses. Arthur even stretched his ear to its fullest extent, as he stood saying 'cheese' in front of a statue of a former Agran by the name of Chesterton III.

But where was Amy now?

Endgame not quite so rampant, after all... yet.

I had deliberately and voluntarily brainwashed myself—by a neat lie technique invented by a certain wing of the man-city Authorities, not a lie-detector as such but more a lie-fixer or a lie-fictioner—to believe that Mike was my real name.

In our eventual hotel room in Agra Aska, on one wall was a series of large hinged maps on top of each other, maps which I lifted to show Greg (my alter-nemo)—as a demonstration of Nemonymous Navigation leading to Nemonymous Night then Nemonymous Numinousness (Numinosity)—including any financial interchange which, after all, remained the vital end result of everything that went with the *Angevin* trade.

On a second wall was a reproduction of Rubens' *Massacre of the Innocents*. On a third wall was another painting, by an unknown artist—depicting an unknown youth (not dissimilar to Hataz) who had a large white swan sitting on his lap... a foundling fondling the long neck as the swan itself acted rather salaciously.

The fourth wall was bare but sporting central curtains on a silent runner, mis-implying there was a window behind them. In the distance, I could hear some of our Agra Askan fans chanting. Since the shenanigans in Quarantine House, we'd literally become hotel-bound celebrities, a fact which was more than most of us could bear, even though, paradoxically, we'd been trying all our lives to seek out such celebrity for ourselves!

Amy did a spot of cleaning now and again to keep her hand in. She yearned after the state of her prior ordinariness more than any of us.

Eventually, there came the day when we all made our first close encounter with the Core itself. Or what we had before loosely named the Core, later-labelled as... well we've not reached that point yet.

I say all of us, but we left Greg behind as ceremonial rearguard. He said goodbye to Hataz and Tho because, as part of the first encounter with the Core, we were due to deal with their carefully-nurtured symbolic young love and—not so much 'sacrifice' them but rather tender them to the 'caring arms' of the Core itself, a ceremony only such initiated celebrities as us could carry out every generation or so. Human Coning to the Nth degree. We'd been given a very instructive and well-crafted black-skinned book entitled *The Nemonicon* about it all—much to the delight of Edith and Clare. The prose was Proust perfect.

The Core was at the top of a peak within a neighbouring lightly-valed cavity to that of Agra Aska itself, and you could see the Core (from Agra Aska) as almost a rounded half-sky of beige- or yellow-coloured light, but then the nearer you approached the more it became the whole-sky and an unknown colour... by contrast, however, strangely diminished (yet still relatively huge) when we were right up close to it at the highest point of the peak. The veiling effect of proto-incidence, perhaps. Or so our book hinted.

I was the first gingerly to touch the shimmering skin of the Core. I saw within a giant sleeping form of an angel, breathing in tune with some strobe rhythm that was relative to the reality of the 'angel' rather than our own reality. It was half bird, half beast, I guess. Its mane was an underlay or weave of feathers vestigially carpeted by patches of yellow fur and an archipelago of raw underskins or red meat. Yet this vision of its nature was unclear through the Coreskin. Its vast furled wings were lifted from time to time—in its evidently dreamful slumber—to reveal millions (I say millions, but there may have been more or there may have been less) of naked human beings in eternal carnal embrace (I guess eternal, judging by the book's further hints). An interwoven slobbery population of white, brown and black limbs and torsos of flesh, but their heads (and thus identities) mercifully hidden by the nesting techniques of the 'angel'. *Stub of pencil: The produce of this Arthurian mix of human substances within the Core was dependent on the incubation/chemical process of the 'angel' itself.*

We all kissed Hataz and Tho farewell before passing them through a breach in the Coreskin.

And distantly we heard the voices of Agra Askans in a chorus of: "Wonderful, Counsellor!"

It was awe-inspiring.

Before leaving the site of our first encounter with the Core, I looked down towards the lower nipples of the Core sac, where the Letting Agents (again mentioned in the book) were siphoning unrefined wads of *Angevin* cream into wide-mouthed pipes—and onward, via arcane hawling procedures based on creative gravity, I guess, to the earth's surface. Except, as I wasn't to know at that stage, there was nobody then on the surface. The game was surely up, even before we knew about it. But confusion often brings the most unexpected clarity. I did not cross bridges before I came to them whilst I kept my own cards close to my chest. The others seemed to be quite out of their depth.

I took the hands of Susan and Amy as we proceeded to descend from the Core, our first job done. *Stub of pencil: Beth and Greg may have had to be the next couple 'sacrificed', when the time came, even though, when compared to Hataz and Tho, they were rather too long in the tooth to be called young lovers! Edith and the rather gender-indeterminate Clare, even more so.*

As we reached the lower slopes of Corepeak, I even wondered if what we had just seen was the *real* earth's Core. Or was there a core within a core? Or even a series of 'Russian Doll' cores? Bizarre thoughts, maybe. *Stub of pencil: Mere untrammelled corespeak.*

The dreams were almost literary, if not literal. Quite beyond Beth's control. No doubt her mind had been affected by the middle-of-the-road fiction or literature she had been fed by the dowager ladies. Each dream was a short prose portrait of each person she had once known and thought she had forgotten.

At first, there was, of course, Susan. She saw Susan's pretty face, prettier than her own, though when they were younger, Beth had been the prettier. Susan spoke and hoped Beth was OK. This particular portrait approached the nature of a nightmare as Beth thought she saw Susan in near-darkness, naked, being scratched by a spiky hedge-like thing.

Mike, too. He, however, was more forthcoming with the circumstances of his scratched-face plight. He smiled at Beth, nevertheless. Beth tried to remember what Mike had done as a job in the city. Was he a warehouseman at the covered market or a lorry-driver in waste management or an office businessman or a bus-driver or a radio phone-in counsellor? Mike answered but when she woke up from the portrait, she had forgotten what he had said.

Arthur reminded her of someone she once knew as a child, but she couldn't now place him as a grown-up. The big ear seemed out of place. She dreamed of him mixing some foreign substances or murky mythologies into a huge tin bath. Amy was a similar dream portrait, except Amy was with another girl called Sudra, and they both fought tooth-and-nail over a pair of yellow shoes (crazy stuff, dreams!) and Beth couldn't really differentiate one portrait from another.

Ogdon, the pub-keeper, was always a good friend to Beth. He was still this friend even from within his carefully constructed portrait. Like all the other portraits, it was described at great length with elegant words in a carefully crafted syntax of prose. The semantics were fluid, however. Delightfully so. She feared he was now dead. The portrait dream showed him alive, however.

The various Cores were not 'Russian Doll' within each other, as it turned out—but, rather, side-by-side cores in different geographies of lateral time. The strobe theory of history was now debunked and many scholars questioned its validity as a basis for much of what had happened and what was about to happen.

Let me baldly state that my credentials are impeccable and I can't be blamed for any misinformation as to what level of narration I actually work within. I am—to myself at least—all-knowing. If others know more than me, then, self-evidently, I do not know them.

Beth and Greg—whilst Mike and his party were still present in the vicinity of the one *known* Core—took advantage of their historic potential and eventually entered a rent in the Coreskin themselves... disguised as young lovers. Consequently, they are now—like Sudra and Nemo/Dognahnyi—as good as dead within the known transpirals. Greg and Mike did not say much to each other in advance of this event, because alter-nemos are notoriously anti-social among themselves. Beth did say goodbye to Susan with a hug, however.

Edith and Clare prepared themselves for a similar 'sacrifice'. They continued to absorb much fine literature on the assumption that whatever their brains carried outside the Core would be carried within it, too. This was 'sacrifice', not 'self-sacrifice', after all. Perhaps they depended on some form of osmosis.

The pair-of-young-lovers permutations of 'sacrifice' among the residual members were still undecided. Mike argued the case for himself and Amy being one pair, whilst Susan would bring up the rear accompanied by Arthur. We may never know the outcome of that, although we could guess. I simply don't know.

Meantime, man-city further stirred downward, the fly in fate's ointment. Clockwork without clockwork was the easiest and clearest way to explain its method of propulsion, now that Ogdon was no longer available to wind it up.

Ogdon was tripping the light fantastic down one of the city streets. Even at these darkest times, people like him shaped up larger-than-life and became a bigger-hearted version of themselves simply to face out the creeping dangers that the world supplied in the form of night plagues, dream terrorists or simple lunatics.

He spotted an evidently off-duty double-decker bus trying to park neatly outside a block of flats and he admired the preservation of such civilised standards even in these outlandish times. The vehicle was having some difficulty because a mini-tipster dumper overlapped the bus's usual allotted white-lined space alongside the pavement. Suddenly diverted, Ogdon stooped toward the sidewalk where he had spotted some feathery fur sprouting like white mould through the cracks between the paving-slabs, threatening to ooze further up and carpet the world with warm tessellated under-precipitation. He stooped lower to stroke it as if he felt he was in touch with something of which he was fond but would never begin to understand. *Never eat yellow snow*, was an army expression. It meant more now than ever, as he saw the mould grow mouldier.

Meanwhile, the bus had managed to budge the mini-tipster from its clamped spiky plinth into the kerbside gutter like a clumsily sizeable unwound toy. But, at that moment, a large explosion sounded from the Moorish quarter of the city and Ogdon found himself running with several others to see if he could add to the maimed and the dead.

Later he would indeed be found dead in a state of *Rigor Mortis* or *Shyfryngs*… leaning at his body's slope upon the large still-turning clockwork-key in his back.

It was not exactly a TV interview. It was more Candid Camera. The four remaining Drillmates were left de-briefing the whole affair in advance of what they expected to be a grand climax, the exact nature of which was still unclear. The interpolations of any interviewer are left untranscribed.

SCENE: A disused Agra Askan grocery, lit inexplicably with arc-lights. A painting of The Archer from the old days is on the wall near some droopy turnips on shelves, looking remarkably like Thatcher.

Mike: It was wonderful to see the peacefully happy look on those youngsters' faces as they slipped through the coreskin. It made everything seem worthwhile.

Susan: I have a funny feeling, that it's not all over. Surely, Sudra is coming back. That was a dream—that part—wasn't it? I was told it was a dream.

Mike: Who by? No, that was not a dream, I'm sorry to say. Nothing is a dream when underground. Although, I suspect the zoo was not all it was cracked up to be when we were told it was dreamless. We should have guessed. The zoo is not underground. (Mike nods to the unseen interviewer.)

Amy: Since my change, I've taken nothing for granted. I don't even take myself for granted. At times, I think the city itself is coming after us—a suicide-bomb strapped to its waist, ready to blow the Megazanthus and its coreskin to smithereens.

Mike: A suicide-bomb? That must be the covered-market, then?

Amy: Yes, one must assume so. And I once dreamed I operated a car bomb near the bridge. It was terrible.

Arthur: We must get back to the Drill. I know Nemo had many muskets stowed in a cabin somewhere. I heard him tell that to one of the businessmen when he thought I was too far away to hear what was being said.

Susan: Surely muskets will be like flea-bites on an elephant when the city arrives!

Mike: There's no telling. Sometimes things are more symbolic than physical. I learnt at least that during my tour of narrative duty.

Amy: (smiling) You mean you *know* things? I'm sure I don't, even though I've been programmed to know everything.

Mike: I don't think any of us even approach knowing anything.

Amy: But you know you were meant to be a hawler, if everything had gone to plan?

Mike: Hasn't everything gone to plan, then? I don't even know what a Horla is, after all this time. Something to do with time and memory and dragging things from deep inside one?

Amy: A hawler is many things. It also means dragging things from inside other people as well as from yourself.

Mike (Remembering the incident with Captain Nemo): Well, I think I'm beginning to understand. It's like loving rare beef... as a sort of symbol. Hmmm.

Susan: Don't forget the birds. That angel in the core reminded me of a huge diseased bird. Despite the good it was doing to its nestlings.

Arthur: But there's no doing good simply for the sake of doing good. At the end of the day, the whole thing is being driven by the milking of Angel Wine from the Core, and selling it up the line. (Nodding to the interviewer) ... Yes, I know that's unproven, but it makes common sense.

The interviewer then left the grocery, someone who had been hidden by the TV cameras rather than revealed. Even as he left, his cape concealed his real configuration as truth or fiction. The four Drillmates' conversation continued after the arc-lights were switched off, but we have no means to continue our surveillance of what they said.

Mike questioned himself. He realised he was a hawler—had always realised this perhaps—but now he knew it wasn't because he had previously been a hawler, but because he was about to become one. Self-identification by an as yet unproved anticipation was a dream-fixing he needed to address. It all seemed a very unsteady grounding for a vocation or a raison-d'etre. Mike remembered his step-daughter Sudra as she began to practise walking in her carpet coat. She took delight to tease him with her imputed beautiful body hidden beneath the dumpy beige covering and the ungainly yellow clod-hoppers on her feet—clogs, in fact, that were on all their feet.

Now Sudra was gone. All of them were now on the point of going, also. One thing that had been established: the earlier belief in 'carpet apes' in attendance upon the Angel Megazanthus was wide of the mark. The whole setting of the Core had turned out to be more angelic, more spiritual than any of the surviving visitors had ever hoped. Either the scurrying apes that catered for the ablutions of the Angel had never existed in the first place or—if they had once existed albeit in a mere state of nemonymity—they had since grown into Agra Askans (like Lilliputian Yahoos into giant Brobdignagians). If the latter version, any history books in Agra Aska had been expunged of such evidence. A textual exegesis or, if not, perhaps the strobe theory of history was a true one, after all. As it turned out, the primary-source evidence pointed to the Angel effectively caring for its own ablutions as well as for the ablutions of its wing-wrapped nestlings within the Coreskin, as part of the incubatory process involved in the constant orgasm of angevinisation. It even nursed its own wounds of disease as they intermittently grew scabs and subsequently ruptured with blurts of depressurised pus. A self-sufficient *moto perpetuo* state of parthenogenesis. A recurrent dream of mutual self-healing made real by retrospective hawling.

Today, as they sat by the Balsam River on their last day together, Mike was trying to persuade Susan that he should enter the Coreskin paired with Amy as 'young lovers' rather than with his wife (i.e. Susan herself) of many years' standing:

Mike: Who would go in with Arthur, if not you? Amy is his sister, after all. That would not be right, I'm sure you would agree, Susan, love. I think we lose all consciousness once we're in there, anyway, and so you won't know it's not me that you're paired with. I love you, I have always loved you, Susan, but now is the time to crystallise our love at the precise moment of separating. Our love would be diminished by continuing to conduct it as just a tawdry echo within the Core under the surveillance of the Angel…

Susan: (Tears in her eyes) It's meant to be more than just an echo. Did you actually say echo? It's supposed to be more than just sex. It's a culmination of all we've been together. (She has a musket on her lap and she fiddles absentmindedly with its trigger.)

Mike: But it's a bit of a cheat, anyway, Suse. We're meant to be young lovers when we go in and we're—what are we?—fifty or so? It's not as if we're taking the whole thing seriously. It's just for show. Amy will need my protection once inside…

Susan: I thought you said we lose consciousness of who we are…

Mike: I know, but we remain who we are even if we don't continue to know who we are. (Mike's own eyes are suddenly glassy with tears, as he pretends to watch a Riverboat moor in the distance.)

Susan: I don't understand, Mike, I really don't understand. If we don't know what we know when in there, it won't matter if Amy and Arthur go in together paired as brother and sister, will it? They won't know that they're sister and brother. I would really be happier going in with you, even if I don't know it's you afterwards. I'd feel safer. More able to return the love given to me by whatever you turn out to be within the Core.

Mike: I think I really must... go in with Amy. And we ought to go in soon, before... you know… (Looking at the musket on his own lap).

Susan reaches out to give Mike a kiss, but he turns his head away. But, eventually, he cannot help himself—as he and Susan hug farewell… forever.

Amy looked at her brother's ear—and laughed. He may not even be able to get into the Core at all with such a wide obstacle as an appendage. She kissed him farewell. A little prematurely, as it turned out.

They both now looked at the long queues of Agra Askans leading up to the Core—and they couldn't understand why they themselves were in a shorter queue, so short it was just the two of them. Perhaps they were in a more important queue, albeit one leading to a different part of the Core. They wondered if they were doing something wrong or had been misdirected. They couldn't see Mike or Susan. They expected the older couple to have been in the queue already. Amy wasn't sure why but she *already* knew she wasn't the Amy she thought herself to be—even before entering the Core. Otherwise she wouldn't have earlier consented to going in with an older man like Mike, leaving Susan with no choice but the mixed blessing of Arthur and his big ear. Earthur, she called him, as a joke.

The other queues were now tailing off in a different direction with much ruckus, like the contents of a zoo on holiday release.

In the days before the sudden jolt had stolen the light from Beth's cabin in the Drill, Greg and a few other nebulous businessmen were entertained by Captain Nemo in the corporate lounge, a select area on board that boasted viewing-windows close to the leading-edge of the bit-tip—allowing vistas when the storms of the Drill's off-detritus didn't obscure them with the moving rubble of confusions or lies. A bit like this book where I've invited you to stand at its own viewing-windows in its select, very select, Corporate Lounge of plot and counterplot.

The proceedings were a combination of a scientific lecture upon what they were seeing through the windows and pure holiday entertainment, all laced with cocktails. But that was the past. If any of these characters still existed, they didn't even stir like ghosts in the calm latency of spiritual birth-pangs let alone in full-blooded existence as ghosts proper.

Dream Sickness: is this being sick *of* dreams or sick *with* dreams? Perhaps, both, but one can only be certain about the existence of the former state. And as I approach the end of the book, I am quite aware that I am sick of dreams, as you are, no doubt, also sick of dreams as well as lies, ghosts and so forth... having endured, although voluntarily, such rituals of passage from surface to core.

My own worst dream or nightmare is quite mild. I worked hard to gain the qualifications for University entrance—much to the pride of my working-class parents whose son was beginning to embark on something quite beyond their understanding or ambition. Such humility prevailed in those days—forty years ago. People like me simply didn't go to University. Once there, I ended up doing reasonably well, despite going through a potentially bad middle period during the three-year course when I began to sleep long into the mornings, skipped lectures/ seminars/tutorials—and only managed (with the help of my then future wife) to salvage the situation by the skin of my teeth. Upon this bare survival of academic growth I managed to consolidate my studies towards the endgame of Final Exams. In my worst nightmare, by contrast, I do not manage to salvage the situation: a long-term recurring dream where I didn't bother to look at the various noticeboards to establish what essays I should be writing for the course seminars etc.—whilst everybody in authority seemed to remain silent, failing to alert me to my missing gaps. I sat back and occasionally wondered how easy it was to keep up at University, together with experiencing a nagging doubt that things were slipping away from me. A recurring dream, a recurring denial, but I always woke up—to realise that I eventually did get a good University Degree and the dream was quite false, perhaps not a real dream at all, but merely me dreaming a dream, although what this 'dream' left with me was a feeling that it had been very nearly correct in its interpretation of a past reality, hawled forward for me to suffer unduly by a process of Proustian logistics.

This book is in honour of that recurring dream, in the hope that it gratefully *remains* a dream, and that, as a dream configuring new dreams, doesn't mutate into a worse dream, perhaps forever, to become a dream threaded with the surfaces of reality.

Amy's doll was an ugly one. It buried itself in the garden amid the discarded remains of her brother's latest 'experiment'. This memory was in complete denial of the fact that inanimate objects could not even be *imagined* to be capable of carrying out this act on their own.

The beings who chased themselves and each other through the Italian Villa (which once belonged to the famous writer Lope de Calderón)—to the sound of a clockwork helicopter—were involved in an eager game of creative hide-and-seek, where hiding was tantamount to a complete revelation of concealment by even outshining the shiniest scatter-orange cushions upon a Proustian verandah.

The mud-bath was empty of finely-sieved loess—empty even of crude mud—revealing a frighteningly naked middle-aged lady lolling in its emptiness... looking up into the Agra Askan half-sky and expecting her Matinee Idol to arrive from its wide-screen scree.

Vacuums strobed. Carpet-bombs flowed in a sootstorm or blitz upon the unsuspecting pinnacles of the Straddling Cathedral—an advance guard for man-city itself. The Core rose above itself, flinching in half-defence, half-attack towards the half-sky's scree—as the last few pairs of young-lovers boarded its ark of exquisition. That was the Core itself. The odd tread of strangers. The final Happy Hour. Half price *Angevin* in plastic mugs.

Crippled kites still managed to fly erratically upon tenuous tethers across the flank of the Core, often blindly crashing into its shimmering yellow-white surface, finally stuck like thinning long-pigs within its dull beige under-surface, becoming miscoloured broken needles in search of empty stitches.

The Power to Imagine is the first Act of Creation.

Mike pointed his musket into the yellowing scree of the half-sky—as if he simply knew the approach of downward doom. His bullets crackled pathetically—weakening, strobe by strobe, into a shuddering shadow that massively man-stained the lightning-lit roof that arched physically between inner horizons.

Photo-negative Sunne Stead possessed a swivelling pair of deep penetration-eyelights of darkness.

The River ran with spillage or simply seepage from the straining Core, white-ribboning its surface currents—whilst redness ribboned along any competing under-surfaces.

Mike had just handed Amy in towards the inner sanctum of the Core where Angel Megazanthus lifted its welcoming wing to each sacrifice to which it, in turn, sacrificed itself. Mike was still holding her hand, while still brandishing the musket with his other hand, ready to embark himself upon the encroaching Drill-hallucination that the Core was fast becoming, complete with internal spinning bit-tip nipples or sousipedes instead of feathers.

The shapes of Susan hand-in-hand with the now one-eared Arthur are already dissolving towards the translucent folds they pass between... out of reach of Amy whose hand Susan also held before fingers could no longer cling between the two expressions of farewell. Indeed, they had been trying to enter as a foursome, not as a pair of pairs, after firing off more pathetic musket-shots into the increasingly man-stained half-sky of scree. But the Core sorts pair from pair whatever the pitiful plans of prior pairing. It simply seems to know.

Mike cracks one last musket-shot helplessly into upper Agra Aska—while entering the Core himself, watching Amy's wattled back vanish by thinning-out into a realm he cannot seem to reach... it is as if, effectively, he is entering the Core alone. Amy is no more. She has never been. Or she has joined Sudra elsewhere in nothingness. Susan and Arthur were already in the wings. Mike, in two minds, tried to escape the Core. He knew he could not have entered it alone. A pig's breakfast of an entry. But he *had* entered alone. And thus he, too, never was—and became his own alter-nemo. And a ghost of a ghost hardly exists as much as even a ghost proper.

And the massive man-stain emerging like tangibly multi-dimensional dry-rot through the scree sky faded, too. Its job done.

The Angel Bird crew long, crew loud in final anger. It tussled into existence through its own skin, becoming a crude bifurcated core itself, moving in exquisite hope and joy through the solid clouds towards Heaven—but its matted hide was infested with crawling human-life in every interstice of its creatinous body, so weighed down by human vermin filling vacuums of uncleanliness that it eventually didn't rise towards its just rewards in Heaven but toppled into the thick white ocean of Hawling-Hell (a core within a core within how many other cores it is impossible to determine) where stains spread like islands of rancid top-flat grease, before it was engulfed completely with a belch like a tufted two-legged cathedral of pain.

The book was its own suicide bomb.

The lift systems were too complicated to understand. They went up and down the vestigial service-shafts of the book, unattended and in vague orders of priority for ciphers to embark and disembark in the precise matching rhythms that allowed all the gaps to be filled at all possible permutations of history.

A ceiling of time and space, stitched with neat insect-ranks of long-pig right through a stick of holiday-rock, became a woven fire-wall or fire-floor of meaning via textures of text unfathomable to man, bird and beast alike.

It is difficult to imagine the world being better or worse than it actually is. However, without humanity to stain its pages, who knows what will then become imaginable or even real? There is a theory—to which I subscribe—that humanity "strobes" in and out of existence, selective collective-memory then forcing the 'alight' stage to forget the previous 'switched-off' one... time and time again. Mass consciousness flickering in and out of existence like a faulty lighthouse... or, indeed, a fully working lighthouse. The Drill's corporate lounge is empty and silent, except for the odd eerie shaking of the wall maps as its relentless path—through the ribbons of reality that is Inner Earth—continues towards the Core.

The jolt has finally finished, if one can actually imagine a jolt (by definition) that endures for more than just a few seconds. The rearward cabin is empty—as can be seen when the light slowly wells back into it. The window still simply shows the passing crazy-paved slabs of earth. A tortoiseshell hairbrush falls to the carpet, and becomes a yellow pig lung.

The city pub was empty. Merely that. The optics of the shorts gleamed as time threatened to begin another diurnal round with unforgiving dawnlight. The city started to thrum, but thrummed with what?

The top flat still retained its open curtain policy on silent runners. The empty Dry Dock could be seen, even in the dark. A tall tower-block in the distance winked like a gigantically based but underwhelming lighthouse light. A computer screen in the room blinked blankly in curious yellow. An empty veil fluttered on the carpet like a butterfly.

The covered market was at rest, its bomb simply being a pair of clogs with spurs and silver toecaps, the spurs still slightly jingle-jangling as if someone had just taken them off in a pique of feminine tantrum.

The city zoo echoed with utter silence. And a large human ear in the insect enclosure was still pitifully trying to bury itself.

Apocryphal Coda

My first glimpse was the hill where stood the Canterbury Oak, if standing and growing could be reconciled. That was not the tree's real name; nothing bore its real name in my book. Nothing bore its real name, I dare suggest, in Klaxon City itself. If Klaxon City called itself Klaxon City, then it lied.

I had crossed the Inner Plains from a life I preferred to forget so, having tried to forget it, there would be a certain counter-productiveness in rehearsing a re-living of it merely to fill in the wavy area of my past with childish colouring.

I knew beyond the hill would be Klaxon City; the Canterbury Oak was responsible for this name, a name given as a means towards an easy fantasy: a convenient digestibility of facts that make up any fantasy, even if, for me, this particular fantasy was not a fantasy at all.

Klaxon City, therefore. A city full of noise, a noise like klaxons or sirens. So a name like Klaxon City makes things straightforward. I shall not bother with its real name, a name which means nothing or, if it means anything, is lost in some mire of esoteric history or legend. The Canterbury Oak, too, is named thus because it is similar to a tree I once saw in Canterbury. A bottom-heavy tree with warped bark, almost a diseased bark, I guess, with a girth—shall I say of a million miles in circumference? I may as well. I should never be able to convey the *impression* of its irregular wrinkled girth (that lower end of its bole that met the earth) by any claim to know its measurements or any *standard* of measurement common to all who would like to know its measurements. Scales are quite out of the question. The trunk—as it tapered towards the top where sparse branches started to claw at the sky—had a wind-chewed roughness (I knew it was rough even from the distance I saw it but remained unsure of the wind), growing like a giant serpent whereby all its inner wooden fat had sapped towards its rooted tail, leaving it so dissimilar in bulk when bottom was compared to top. The branches were images of its relentless pain that had once been conveyed by its own internal sirens.

Now, with its sirens quiet for at least a generation, I was soon to learn that the citizens, having long been inured to its ancient noise (now dead or deaf to itself), needed to customise their own background of audible pain: thus building a city-wide tannoy-system to act as temporary coverage of such sirens. So, given the Oak's recent bouts of cyclic silence, their own homegrown versions of siren-sound in the city seemed to take sway, as if the Oak had decided to remain silent now more often, in face of such unrivalled clamour. However, the citizens themselves—perhaps because they had grown irritated by mock sirens as opposed to the real thing—had started to hire surreptitious ear-muffs to assuage the skewering edges of sound. Some even trod a highly secret route of sound-proofing their houses. Once seen, however, the difficulty of such a task would become apparent.

Meanwhile, I crossed the brow of another hill as I completed my trek—from across the Inner Plains with just a portable tent and meagre rations—which started when an untold past had ceased unfolding and ending as I approached an as yet unknown future. I witnessed the scattered pylons of Klaxon City bearing their tethered skycraft. I knew to expect these. However, I had not been forearmed with any knowledge concerning the vastness of the city—occupying a space within a cavity of truth that housed a whole dynasty, not just one tranche of civilisation. However, that as yet unappreciated fact abandoned my mind when I suddenly became appalled by what hit me with the force of a tangible soundwave—the tannoy-system kicking in with a hair-trigger difference between silence (on one side of the brow) and cacophony (on the other).

Greg lived with Beth in London, but they also had a beach hut at Clacton on the coast about 90 minutes' train-ride from Liverpool Street station. They were an ordinary couple, unmarried and childless. Yet nobody made that judgement of ordinariness about them, because nobody knew enough about them to warrant such a view. Greg thought he was ordinary. He worked in Waste Management as a lorry-driver. Beth thought she wasn't ordinary at all. She was indeed ordinary, if in that thought alone. Both were malleable, but one of them fought against being malleable, and each thought the other to be the one fighting that particular fight. One of them was right.

If they thought about it at all.

Beth worked in Klaxon City—an amusement arcade near Soho—a sight better-class than the arcades in Clacton, where saucy hats and bingo were more the rage. In Beth's arcade of work, there were high-prize jackpot fruit machines as well as mock-casino games with real tellers. Robot croupiers were not too far-fetched in the sort of computerised world that amusement arcades had now entered, following the miniaturization of machines everywhere—even in Clacton. So there were tellers who handed out chips and made masquerade of gambles being unforethought... mingling with robots who smiled wickedly, giving the punters confidence that all was random, because how could thinking machines not deliver the chance one always seeks in life: the pure chance? Only humanity snags the wheels of chance, with their intentions and misintentions of subconscious thought.

Many fought against thought.

Beth was one who fought against thought. She just dreamed of that ultimate chance where she could safely say that she was full of unmixed happiness. A dream she forgot immediately she woke up from it, although sleep was not the necessary prerequisite for thus dreaming. Not a sought happiness, because that always failed. But a found happiness. One that simply enveloped one, given the lack of forethought or ambition that the very act of seeking it would have entailed, given self-consciousness: a self-consciousness that women of Beth's ilk luckily lacked. Meanwhile, she simply plugged on. A pretty face neatly sunk on skullbone.

ⵔ

A plug makes things work. An electric plug. A bath plug. A rawl-plug. Even an advertising plug. The latter made a name into a catchword and the circling businessmen would cause manufacture of anything to match the catchword and made it work in tune with the catchword's neatly fitting its round peg in a round hole whilst making square holes of us all, without us noticing.

In modern screen drama there are swishes of sound to alleviate the changes of scene, large noisy tractions of vision that overwhelm the quiet reflective scene with an abruptness that life never really has on reflection: all misery is gradual, just as lives are gradual, never fast-changing, even if one can destroy a marriage with one simple act, but it takes days, often, to percolate and reveal its repercussions. Never in drama. Never in fiction. We need the swish of the curtain. A single alert. A sudden siren set off to indicate a change of scene, a change of dream. A false plug. Where amusement is taken from not knowing where things were or who people thought they were.

ⵔ

The sirens were strangely in advance of the emergency.

The Death entered Klaxon City. The real Klaxon City, where pylons in a terrestrial metal garb were like vertical gantries or simple lamp standards with outspread feet, of various heights, from the top of which stretched out in the wind (the wind?) many skycraft with each one's make, build, substance, inflatability, non-inflatability, traction, torque etc. mere seeing from 'ground'-level could not fathom. You had to climb up to them to discover if they were, say, flyable. Having flown to their perches there was no guarantee of future flyability. A few weren't sufficiently rendered from the flesh and bone that some (not always the few in question) once were. Not render*able*, let alone non-friable enough to safeguard against weathering. But weather was a dubious topic in Klaxon. It depended on the nature or mood of the city's geographical cavity at any one time in the vertical cross-section of its dynasty as opposed to in the more usual horizontal considerations of surface cities.

I had died more than once, and, then, it was at least once on the surface that I had died, but several times below the surface. I had suffered a fatal knife-wound in a casino when the gambling laws were relaxed, because I questioned whether the silver ball was in the right hole when the robots visibly tilted the roulette-wheel with their hands, and the tellers later blamed it on an earth tremor. There was no disembowelling of their rules. Even Henry Fifth would have been given short shrift. Unto the breach…

But I was trying to forget my past. I even imagined the deaths. How else can deaths be imagined other than by imagining them, because if real... well the rest is common sense.

As I wandered into the city streets from the brow of the hill I last left our readers watching my progress: I took one last glimpse at the Canterbury Oak, which visibly moved at its thin spacious upper levels, giving the uncanny impression that its large trunk below moved in unison. It was soon stolid, however, etched like a giant black hold-all that God had dropped there in disgust because there wasn't enough room in it for as many effects as even magic could have managed, let alone a full-blooded religion.

I turned to the abodes. Solid rock-caves that had been built like houses out in the open, where a few scrawny children played hide-and-seek. I knew things would become more palatial the more towards its centre I approached. And at least there I would also find grown-ups grown-up enough to interact like real characters. Not just children acting as human scenery.

One skycraft tethered to one of the few pylons stationed this far into the city's outskirts was a strange seemingly solid rocket-ship that, like the Canterbury Oak, was misshapen where you thought misshapen would be out of the question. Its business end seemed at the bottom where a single pin glinted in the light of the Sunne#: a pin often twirling lightly in a whimsical nostalgia for its former firedrill##. Nobody would be on board, I knew, and thus the whimsicality of its lower pin's twirling only gave tiny shadows of doubt. Like speckled ants on my skin. It was not a balloon. It seemed solid enough, with several storeys, sieved by sightholes. It just hung there as if its specific gravity was too hard to match with rhythmic gravities elsewhere. Unlike some of the other pyloned skycraft that were like proud pennants in stiff winds, it almost sagged, and visibly bloated. But that was the effect of the incessant klaxon noise, something to which I had already grown accustomed without even mentioning that I was trying all the time to forget it, relegating it, as I did, to some wishful-thinking 'white noise'. Yet this klaxon noise (whether oak-or tannoy-derived), I suspected, was indeed the 'wind' I had earlier doubted existed as such. Noise as air movement.

#The Sunne acted like the sun but was not the sun. This does not represent a fantastical or imaginary approach to cosmology, merely a shorthand for something that will eventually become quite reconcilable given the circumstances of intertextual reality. For the moment, please treat Sunne and Sun as blood brothers (i.e. crude synonyms), if you currently lack confidence to revel in their essence and truth as spiritual brothers (mutual metanyms, if not alter-nemos). *Stub of pencil: Sunne = Sunnemo?*

##'Firedrill' was a difficult concept to grasp in this context. This made me think that The Death would have indeed been preferable after all, rather than now (alive) having to explain what is meant by this or that word or concept. I hope they will clarify themselves naturally in the course of events, with the description needed for such events hopefully allowing collateral construction of clue-semantics *vis a vis* many words or concepts otherwise ungraspable.

Stub of pencil: However close you get to someone, you are never more than just a couple of entities separated by the skulls of the head.

Greg suffered from an unbearable tinnitus of the Inner Ear. The only way—in his desperation—to cure himself of this incessant cricketing was to deafen himself. Whilst it would be relatively easy—given the will—to blind the eyes, ie with spikes, it is far more difficult to bring such instruments to bear on the hearing, short of bringing the deafness of death itself to one's aid. Slicing off the ears themselves would surely be counter-productive as this very act itself harbours the possibility of even more tinnitus that is allowed greater access—via the creatures of noise—permanently to attack an Inner Ear thus denuded of the mysteriously effective protection of the Exterior Ear. Doctors and Ear Specialists would probably disagree with this prognosis, but Greg wondered how they could know for certain. Only doing things to oneself and feeling the effect in oneself directly gives the ultimate certainty of one's own senses, i.e. the evidence of the self 's senses at whatever level of felt reality one is working through. So, Death seems the only exit from the noise. Sleep does not dull it as dreams often increase the efficiency of the noise or change its very nature into a series of new home-grown noises, a gestalt of noises being dreamed as louder and more relentless. Klaxon City was one such dream. The Inner Earth. The Inner Ear.

As they scaled the pylon from their earthcraft, Greg and Beth began to stretch their legs in yawning downward strides. They had been cooped up in a serial cabin-fever for several months of travel in individual body-hugging room spaces. The dream of a Corporate Lounge on board the earthcraft—where an urbane Captain dished out cocktails and scintillating sights of Inner Earth—proved to be a dream even deeper than a dream being dreamed by merely one other single dream. Indeed, a single such cause-and-effect dream in the concertina of dreams proved to be even less reliable: whereby two dowager ladies known as Edith and Clare were not such ladies at all but chivvying dream-stewards ensuring that dreams were correctly threaded in the correct order on any particular ribbon of reality or strobe-strand... presumably also to ensure that believability was not unduly affected by crossing any threshold of disbelief. These two stewards—when failing to maintain their 'lady' disguises—often became, by involuntary default, large bird-headed individuals who employed the otherwise human nature of their own residual-'lady' bodies in the seeming behaviour of insect-articulated ratchet-limbs that became (in their minds at least) spiny or spiky appendages that the large beaks of their heads actively tried (but failed) to snap up self-cannibalistically as tasty buggish morsels.

Greg, as he neared the pylon's base, turned to take a closer look at the misshapen tree on the hill overlooking Klaxon City—knowing instinctively that it was the perpetrator of the inner sky's wall-to-wall wailing: a series of echoes that bounced around the bowl of the city's cavity. Several separate ribbons of spatial reality—mixed with tangible strobes of time—fluttered in the air-movement of noise: a wind of striated history... a vertical cross-section of which Greg traversed. The earthcraft tethered to the top of the pylon seemed, for him, to become a religious vision that curdled gradually into a huge plume of black smoke from a global-warming turning inward on itself with a heat so over-bearing several incremental levels of dream were needed to intervene as a combined firewall to guard against its ferocity. Dream-fighting on a superhuman scale. And, indeed, as each dream kicked in one by one, Greg was able to ignore the noise and the heat as he ruminatively considered the panoply of Klaxon's geography... while he continued to scale himself down. The vista of its configuration was like a huge human ear—a canyon, a ridge, a lobe, all constituents of the city's mingled God-given nature and subsequent fabrication.

Greg grabbed Beth by the hand as they left the environs of their earthcraft's pylon—without bothering to think that the meter needed inserting with an unknown currency of coinage.

"That's for others," said Greg, eventually, to himself, vaguely recalling the duty of parking fees on or within the scarce resources of a finite earth but also that he and Beth were simply crew members, not owners of the earthcraft.

The streets radiated as streets (i.e. as gaps between) from the area sparsely planted with pylons to other areas where more cavernous buildings clustered around thicker clumps of variously-sized pylons—some pylons with craft tethered, others empty, and a few currently being roosted by kite-shaped birds with large black plumages. In the distance, the ambiance of a city built as a patchwork of overlapping quaint village-scenarios was disrupted as the rims of giant *Angevin* tanks were spotted in an apparently camouflaged industrial estate unglinting in the bright directionlessness of Sunnemo Cathedral's broken shafts through stained glass.

Greg and Beth, however, were window-shopping on a much lower level, as they passed through a precinct where some earth-stripped caves were neatly thin-roofed and glass-fronted. These contained the hardly static wares of a thriving chamber of commerce even if the gaps between these 'shops' were deserted... window-shown to any chance passers-by breaking this empty pattern. One labelled *Sudra's Shoes* brought a wry smile to their lips as they inspected the various jingle-toed items of footwear.

They dodged into something labelled Cavé for some refreshment, hoping that any necessary payment by unknown coinage would be subsumed by serendipity.

Inside were two non-descript locals of short standing whose conversation Greg and Beth began to overhear—during which they decided to intervene with convenient questions, convenient to real visitors such as Greg and Beth themselves and to any possible vicarious visitors coiled on their backs like old-men-of-the-sea. Convenient if the conversation made any sense beyond its semi-conscious ability to refine sense into nonsense, or vice versa.

Beth was described in an unreported part of this exchange as middle-aged, buxom, pretty face scarred with frown-lines, still perky enough to lift her head above the narrative parapet. Greg remained naïve despite a mature aura of be-whiskered pink chops. He still tried to maintain his own identity in face of all attack to divert it elsewhere, but all descriptive resources remained counter-productive in this direction, whatever or whoever took up responsibility for them.

Crazy Lope: Where's the air from, then?

Go'spank: Sea air—it's sort of caught by the melting tectonics, you know, internal tsunamis carried within caches of air-movement made from noise.

Crazy Lope: Don't understand. Words don't do much for me. Any words. But specially those words. Where do words come from?

Go'spank: The words are like moving air, too, or fingered sound. Words are what drift through it. Tricking the above, the below and the across… (Laughs.)

Greg: Been here long?

(Crazy Lope seems perturbed at the interruption.)

Crazy Lope: We've been here longer than you two.

We've been taking the washing in.

Greg: Taking the washing in? Is that a sort of password?

Crazy Lope: If you don't know it's a password, then it's not a password.

Go'spank: Or if you think it's a password what's it a password for? The whole background of black noise is just one never-ending password, perhaps. (Laughs.)

Beth: (Frowning) How *do* they put up with all that here?

Crazy Lope: I block it out. Or rather the blocks block it out.

Go'spank: Dream blocks, yes.

Greg: Ah, but I was brought up to believe dreams were a sickness. They are perhaps defence systems, I see. Rather necessary evils. Yet so much depends on the gaps or streets between the dreams. Are we in a dream now or a gap?

Go'spank: Wish we knew. And if we did know how would you know we knew?

Crazy Lope: Wish You Were Here. Shine on Crazy Diamond.

Beth: It seems you can't talk properly without, you know…

Go'spank: I know… It's difficult. Conversations are obstacle courses rather than proper communication. And to say all those words "*I know… It's difficult. Conversations are obstacle courses rather than proper communication*" has taken a lot of effort and concentration. I've never been able to say anything sensible for this length of time before, or perhaps this exact length is my personal best so far.

(The noise of a distant explosion is carried further than it would otherwise have been by sound atmospherics of the moment, as the other Cavé customers do runners.)

Greg: What's that?

Crazy Lope: What Go'spank just said.

Go'spank: Yes, an air cushion, even an air tsunami perhaps.

Beth: (Flicking a speck of dried mud from her eyelid) There's no noise now.

Crazy Lope: Probably the next few minutes' of noise has turned into silence because it was crowded into those earlier few seconds when the jolt came.

Greg: Sounded like a bomb.

Go'spank: No, I think it was condensed background noise of the sirens in time-shift from a period to a moment. Lope was sort of right, for once!

(Beth sniffed at the drink she had been brought by an attractive waitress who turned all heads.)

Greg: What *are* you two characters up to here?

Crazy Lope: Bringing the washing in. Told you. (Laughs.)

Greg: Yes, but…

Go'spank: (Squeaking like a grey mouse and pointing at Beth in the waitress's wake) I like your wife, Mister. She's nice.

(Beth frowns deeply but her eyes receive the information of such admiration with a glinting smile.)

Go'spank: Can we show you round?

Greg: (suspiciously) If you like. We shouldn't leave our pylon too far behind in case it, you know, can't be found again.

They left into the relative outside using strung hawl-pulley hooks as direction-finders (the cost of the Cavé bill blandly settled during a gap between two intersecting dream-streets) and they all looked up at the newly blackened sky-cavity, with Sunnemo Cathedral's fantasy light-source as a fairy castle nesting in a violet cloudscape now just a dull beige disc not unlike the coin just exchanged in the Cavé for a packed lunch.

Greg and Beth wondered why their two benighted companions now kept calling each other Edith or Clare in some new game of nemonymous passwords.

Stub of pencil:

My head's led from the diseased wood of the Canterbury Oak that wraps me. And there is much for me to think about. Can a planet from which I am able to be thus created, i.e. one called Earth, be more than just the head of the person who first imagined it? An Earth from the Ear to the Ground

Who first imagined this Earth? Meanwhile, who imagined the head that imagined another head like the Earth? The thought extends both ex-ends of the dynastic ribbon of reality from first cause to last effect and realises (with both ends now missing or sharpened away) that imagination is not the best tool for imagining reality because reality is unimaginable being already there in an unimagined state. To imagine an unimagined reality would be to corrupt it or create it as a new imaginary thread through a headless head. Then this single thread, by an uncontrollable volition, would stiffen its sinews to masquerade as an imaginary weave of many threads bearing the tread of a head-leased, heavily head-led reality... the only sort of reality that causes the bodies of its inhabitants to grow cancerous.

I find that, without the Earth on which to be born with a head and to fill that head with learning and to experience or express life via its means, the same head creating the Earth needed another head to create it. Or have I already said that?

Klaxon City being a dynasty rather than a single city on a plain, Greg and Beth—our Essex couple, our salt of the earth—now are indeed (through the imagination of imagination that in turn can summon a new strength to dream novel-ly without the use of fiction) invested with the background noise of spirit needed to reconfigure their existence as new visitors to the Megazanthine Core whilst having already visited it once before—a fact which, effectively, was imaginable because they had ceased to exist as real people having once entered it as a by-product of producing the creamy Angevin or Angel Wine and thus became their own seed without having created the seed in the first place. It takes two to retro-tango.

As Greg and Beth left the environs of the Cavé, they decided they were being escorted by two child-sized stick-figures who used Sunnemo's closure as a light source (with silent drapes) to feed their own emptiness from anything but manipulative bone... to feed it with charcoal drawings from another pencil stub that had a point of incipient darkness for any shading. Like a lost cartoon by Leonardo da Vinci combined with one by Walt Disney who now lived (from death) in such cross-hatches foreign to the smooth technicolor he once so relished. Yet these creatures maintained the dulcet tones of Edith and Clare—which gave a sense of comfort, especially as in their prior Lope and Go'spank modes their voices had been far too shrill.

Greg could just discern the tannoy-system strung with wires that had emerged from the earlier hawl-pulleys as part of one giant soundweb of communication—and the tannoy's loudspeakers themselves were shaped like large human ears rather than the more normally acoustically-efficient cones. A decorative system that didn't lose its irony in the transit from symbol to reality. One clockwork-type of tannoy (it needed to be kept wound up to keep its emissions of noise at full swell) was so violent in these emissions that it was fast burying itself into the ground... as if extreme sound was a downward motive force of drilling within Inner Earth, as well as being a wind-source, even a tornado torque.

The wailing was now deafening—now several blocks away from any possible firewall of dreams. Greg often witnessed

Klaxonites passing by along the paving-slabs with huge muffs on their own ears—and others were clambering on the thinned-out roofs of some newly externalised cavities or chambers to restore any sound-proofing lost in the thinning process. Large coats of a glue-like substance were being 'painted' over all visible tectonic cracks that pavy-crazed this their growing 'internet' of homesteads. Yet, Greg felt that Sunnemo's intermittent emissions of daylight—if that was what it was called—would later give a better view of these customary tasks of the natives amid all the daily wear-and-tear caused by both automatic and clockwork tannoys, which would be useful since he later intended to write a semi-scientific, semi-autobiographical book about his time in Klaxon City as well as his childhood elsewhere, attempting to fill in any gaps later.

As if the thought had transgressed some stewardship of dream that Edith was currently nurturing, the word 'book' in Greg's thought evoked some literary talk on her part:

"Marcel Proust's book treats of separate selves of one individual through a cross-section of time. Sometimes the selves interact, without understanding they were selves (or cells) of the same person. Nothing strange in that. Though we owe Proust a lot for his fiction and such ground-breaking concepts."

"Pessoa, too," added Clare.

"Yes, and Joseph Conrad had a feeling that there were so many layers of intention…"

Greg wondered how he could hear them talking—not that he was terribly interested in the content of the dowagers' literary musings—if the wailing tannoys were so deafening. It was as if noise not only produced air movement or downward proclivities of twisters, but also a means to transfer thoughts inside such air movement without the use of speech, but retaining a disguise of speech. He tried it out:

"What are those chambers?"

He pointed to some unusually constructed areas uplifted into a huge portholed lobe of swollen earth membrane.

"They're the Healing Chambers."

Greg and Beth were taken into one. There they found creatures that evidently had once been human like them—but now suffering from Bird Flew. Each body (including face) was currently being cream mudbathed with *Angevin* (this being a new discovery of its curative qualities in addition to its known dream-masking) to remove feathers at their root so they would not return. Each patient—to have been admitted to this particular chamber and its specialist healing process—had been forced to show the depth of their illness by actually proving they could fly: hence the name of their disease. One of them was in such a state of desperation that, having once flown, he or she needed to show, so as to be treated, they couldn't fly any more: a method that necessitated the painful process of plucking. Those that were incurable and more intrinsically (indelibly) Bird Flown or still-Bird-Flying (albeit only in dreams) were forced from their beds and frog-marched next door to what was called a Lethal Chamber.

One patient was jerking in his or her bed—as if pitifully trying to fly from within the heavy quilt. The nurses—who themselves were not dissimilar to human-like ostriches—continued, undeterred, the painful process of plucking that did not seem out of place amid all the wailing noises.

As Greg and Beth left—after their tour as tourists—they spotted a long winding queue of hopping creatures leading to one of the notorious Lethal Chambers. Some hopped a few feet into the air and then flopped back. Greg averted his eyes. None of this would go in the book.

Stub of pencil:

The word 'indelibly' was added in brackets. It may be rubbed out later. I hope not. Despite the culling that followed the plucking, I shall ignore this topic for the moment. I shall instead treat of other matters. Greg and Beth had earlier visited the Megazanthine Core so couldn't really visit again. Yet there is a theory, as I may have mentioned already, that having produced their seed for the Angevin-bank when in company with the Hawler they were accidentally born again from that seed in re-transit—logically entailing that they never went to the Core in the first place: or that they never existed at that time to warrant their later existence beyond the fiction of their original creation. Only fiction, indeed, is able to cope with such concepts. Thanks to fiction, we are able to address the possibility—which may have never been addressed otherwise—that they could revisit the Core and thus bring back the rarer forms of Angevin needed to counter Bird Flew here in Klaxon but also in the surface cities of London, New York etc. Only an overtly illogical possibility of such a revisit could be the catalyst for the aforesaid rarefication of refinement in the Angevin process, one necessary for the ultimate virus-buster of them all. It was like a scientific process of Parthenogenesis (coincidentally the first book in the Bible)—whereby creation's re-ignition is possible by means of creative imagination rather than by years of empirical scientific study—with cells revisiting their earlier carcinogenic selves to restore them to health. A shorthand for much else. I cannot be clearer at this stage. And I hope nobody rubs this out, simply because they don't currently comprehend it.

Greg and Beth were offered a chance to view more specialist operations upon Klaxonites who were suffering from a version of Bird Flew deeper than their own bodies, with diseased feather-spindles spreading their cancerous spike-ends unto the soul itself. Beth, even with her hard-nosed Essex-girl image, was reluctant to accompany Greg on this part of the tour. So Greg—putting himself in the hands of a masked surgeon—was taken on his own to not a Lethal Chamber as such, but something far worse. Lethal Chambers would at least staunch the pain eventually.

Here Greg saw a patient—etherised upon a table—presenting a pink wasteland of body surface tussocked with Bird Flew. Apparently, this patient had earlier indeed managed flight as high as the highest pylon of the city, only flopping to earth with a wing-stressed bounce—because, otherwise, a mercifully heavy fall from flight would have ended his illness there and then. Illnesses tended to die with their patients. Except in the most diseased cases.

The surgeon was wielding a instrument like a pen-torch that emitted a beam of siren-sound more intense than any hearing could bear if that hearing had insufficient dream protection—which, luckily, had been provided for Greg by one of the dream stewards from Klaxon itself. Edith and Clare had washed their hands of the matter, pretending that it was impossible to offer such protection, but, if the truth were known, they simply didn't know how to do so. The dream steward who actually took over from the dowagers, in this respect, was a character by the name of Blasphemy Fitzworth, once cat's meat salesman in Victorian London, who was so full of makeshift dreams he was able to find one perfectly suitable for concocting a particular madness that produced impossibilities such as engendering Greg's immunity to the shrieking 'pen-torch' surgical instrument.

The patient himself was resistant to any application of *Angevin* ointment to help with humane plucking. So, the surgeon (equally protected by one of Blasphemy Fitzworth's dreams) aimed the 'pen-torch' beam of sound towards the most obtrusive of the rooted feathers and seared hard at its clawhold for some hours, as Greg watched the surrounding flesh sizzle and then melt away from the column of healing key-hole sound. Eventually, the surgeon could yank the feather-spindle from its tenacious grip on the patient's bony soul-matter. Only the patient's resultant wild screaming at the top of his voice was the final danger of sound-deafening proportions to any onlookers. But, with that withstood, the surgeon and Greg left the patient to recover for a while—before they returned to attack the next feather's root in a long line of such feathers carpetting the patient's flesh.

Greg learned a lot from being allowed to watch the urgent Chamber Surgery that was required in view of the advancing Bird Flew throughout Upper and Inner Earth. He was told, however, there were equivalent physico-psychological operations which in fact could benefit himself. Greg was aware that the purpose of his visit to Klaxon was indeed twofold—or even threefold—i.e. to have a holiday break, to record events regarding the spread of Bird Flew for posterity and to cure himself of unGregness (or Greg Flew). Klaxon, with all its bespoke chambers of good medical practice, comprised the only symbolic literary clinic/health retreat in the Magic Mountains of Inner Earth. And his illness was not being Greg. And he wanted to be who he was by right of identity and body recognition, i.e. to be Greg, and not anyone else. To rid himself of this disease of the slipped liver.

Firstly, dreams were a sickness in themselves, because if you suffer from too many dreams, this adversely affects any residual waking life (if any), and can be classed as a sickness, till one is cured by losing any ability to have a waking life to *be* diseased... or by ridding oneself of the cancerous growth of such dreams altogether through treatment in the Klaxon Chambers of Body/ Mind Commerce. It made sense at the time, i.e. at that stage of raw dreams that Greg was suffering precisely when the disease was defined or diagnosed in his case. Any diagnosis essentially depended on the dreams prevalent at the precise astrological epoch of the diagnosis itself. And other considerations of planetary transits and mind/body interaction. So it was an art rather than a science.

Secondly, dream sickness featured dreams *about* sickness—such as dreaming of bodily nightmares that—given just a single stretch of imagination—could even beset the dreamer whether the dreamer had this dream or not.

Thirdly, there were dreams created by tablets that were prescribed for any mind's debility during waking (non-dream) life, i.e. tablets that changed the patient's personality, changed the you you were or were ever likely to be or have been.

Greg was sick of all such dreams. They kept recurring like bad pennies of the mind—until that night in Klaxon when the doctors chose to use some of their skills on curing Greg instead of those dreaming patients spiked from outside the dream by the feathered arrows of a real disease spread by birds in waking life.

Even Man needed a retort.

Greg smiled at the latest inexplicable non-sequitur. "I'm sure I can live without dreams," he said as he self-hypnotised an attempt at persuasion that he had fully woken up—at the same time as he found himself emerging from a particularly numbing dream that had eased some of his pain. However, even more painful were the dreams that meant nothing or, worse, were filled up with nonsense or, worse still, created plugs for products such as Death—thus creating the need for yet other dreams to neutralise them, i.e. spamicidal dreams or dream redoubts.

The doctors had given him a sound-torch similar to those employed in gouging out patients' feathers, but this one had to be self-operated on his own body, by stroking it up and down like an electric razor—applying the focussed sound on the flesh, starting with the face, as he began to delineate a full limned-out Gregness of Greg with the help of a magnifying shaving-mirror which he had earlier used in the daily ablutions of attacking his own bewhiskered pink chops.

Greg: What next?

Greg-in-the-mirror: You could try the left ear. It's far too large or cauliflowery for real Greg... yes, that's it, ah, that's nice. Spread the torch up and down. Do I look more like you now? It helps with the noise of the sirens, too, the earhole closing up with a web that dissolves the sound before it hits the inner drum. Pre-empting the kick-in…

Greg: I didn't know I had such a big ear. I felt I loved Beth but she surely couldn't have loved me with an ear like that. (Laughs.)

Greg-in-the-mirror: Don't delay with such things. You now quickly have to rub out the Mikeness from Greg's mouth and then the I-ness of I from each eye.

Greg: (Waving the sound-torch up and down over his face) Good as done. But it hurts the eyes…

Greg-in-the-mirror: But you can see us better now and we can see *you* better through them.

Greg: Windows of the soul.

Greg-in-the-mirror: That's a bit trite! More a two-way filter than a window, I'd say.

Greg: What next?

Greg-in-the-mirror: The whole body needs to be done eventually. A nip and tuck to bring back the sleek English lorry-driver that you truly were. Get rid of all the irrelevancies of flesh and identity. Bring in the washing to untense the washing-line of your true being.

Greg: As each minute passes, I feel the real Greg is becoming me again.

Greg-in-the-mirror: Or vice versa.

Greg: But *who* are you?

Greg-in-the-mirror: Just a reflective sounding-board. Don't worry about me. I have no axe to grind.

Greg: (Turning away from the mirror) I hope so. I really hope so. I'm no longer Mike. No longer the false I that I never wanted to be in the first place, despite the sense of security being an I made me feel.

Greg-in-the-mirror: (From behind Greg) A *false* sense of security. But, thinking about it, you are still not talking like a lorry-driver, are you. Argghh! (Glass crazes over as if in a psychological road crash.)

When Greg had finished the sound-shaving process, he relaxed back into the newly undisguised welters of Chamber Music, waiting for the doctor to return following a set period of mind-confinement... to test whether any of the process had actually 'taken' and Greg was satisfied with the plug of his own recovered Gregness.

Shattered mirror: Do you know what the first sign of madness is? Being told you have hairs growing in the palm of your hand... and then looking for them!

Greg stared at his smooth inner-hand and saw a tiny hard knot in one pore which he feared might pre-figure the future tenacity of a feather.

o

Beth had been going through a feminine version of this process in a neighbouring Chamber but the facts are far more inaccessible since the various methods were privy only to the women themselves and to their beauty-sleep mentors. It is to be hoped, however, that she had removed any restricting characteristics concerned with any mutual identity-envy between her and her sister Susan.

A low-key end to what was a crucial soundfest.

When Greg and Beth emerged from their respective chambers of re-asserted identity, they immediately fell into each other's arms, with a renewed love surging through their veins—not so much reminding them of their old love as it once was but showing them the potential of their new love as a cathartic transformation of their old love... as a crystallised plug of wisdom to replace the angst that used to fill the growing hole of disappointment gradually and ineluctably encroaching upon them in recent years, to blot out what was once possible between them by revealing what was now possible again in the enhanced wonders of sheer togetherness and love for each other as well as for life itself.

The sirens had momentarily ceased their wailing, whilst the citizens were singing a Bach Cantata. Not stage-managed so much as the natural spontaneity of a flashmob.

Many gazed up into Klaxon's undersky, shading their eyes from a newly radiant Sunnemo, in fact two Sunnemos as one had emerged from a blindspot to become each other's ghost and symbolic of the love between Greg and Beth. Within the glowing skin of the master Sunnemo could be glimpsed the silhouette of the Angel Megazanthus itself slowly and repeatedly folding and unfolding its wraparound wings, a vast king in yellow, or a nesting mother-bird, or a token of a horror vision now made divine.

A scattering of hot-powdered *Angevin* fell from the two cores like Christmas snow.

Bach's Cantata draws to an end and the sirens resume, as Greg and Beth, hand in hand, continue their adventures of self-discovery within Inner Earth. He would need to visit Klaxon's cleansing chambers regularly for the Gregness of Greg to prevail. And to tussle with the Tenacity of Feathers.

Beth stared up at Sunnemo—and she wondered whether the Angel Megazanthus within its eggskin owned a sensory capacity equivalent to her own selfhood. Beth was the salt of the earth, full of natural Essex feistiness. She was so deeply in tune with things that she didn't understand she was in tune with, even her wondering about this fact took place without it touching the sides of her own selfhood's intellect (or lack of). A process that could only be addressed by the arts of fiction or fantasising. Imagining imagination that could not exist without multiple imaginations plugging in socket to socket. A power of imagination (a strength to dream) that could only be possible following contact with the Flew. Flown the next nest. Brain with new wings. Mind with old ones. Beth Flew. Greg Flew. All flocking together towards or from the Klaxon chambers as a positive migratory force of flight.

So, in short, did the Angel Megazanthus have its own 'consciousness'? Or did it manoeuvre its wings as part of some parthenogenetic spontaneity... or of a mysteriously insidious instinct of twitching or tweaking parts of itself to prove to any observers (such as Beth and Greg) that there was indeed a real creature lurking within its shape: pulling its own strings from within itself. Beth thought about one of her friends from school.

Rachel Mildeyes (as she was known to peers and teachers alike). Everyone loved Rachel. She had a self-creative gloss that girls like Beth could never aspire to. Nevertheless, Beth was one of Rachel's best friends... sharing those secret feminine moments that remain an enigma to most men.

Beth wondered if everyone's special friend—someone they recall with deep affection (remarkably without appreciating quite how deep)—populated the shape that was Angel Megazanthus. She imagined Rachel looking down upon her now—in Klaxon—as she and Greg wandered aimlessly from chamber to chamber, yet learning cumulatively the lessons of imagination whilst living within imagination's creation (fiction, fantasy or dream) as real people. Most fictions contained fictional characters... or once real people—now ceased to be real people (if retaining their real names)—fictionalised as fiction characters. Yet, strangely, Beth and Greg retained their hard-won, hard-worn identities as real minds and bodies while living and dreaming—unfictionalised—within a full-blooded fiction. A fiction shot through with reminders of itself via fluctuating volumes (from silent to strident) of Klaxon's noise.

Stub of Pencil:

Rachel Mildeyes peered through a slit in Sunneskin, feeling her huge wrinkled, webby wings on the outside of her body (joined to her but not strictly hers to use) lift slowly like imperfect flaps of her own skin merging (like shuffling cards with cards) into the sinewy membranes (half-cooked, but de-blooded, meat and/or poultry) of Sunne's last underlayer of surface skin. She felt herself to be a core but also a core's innards—but could a core have anything within it without the innards becoming a new core?

Beth laughed at the whimsy of such imaginings in the air about Rachel spotting her from aloft. It was bad enough living within imaginings without adding to them with one's own imaginings!

Greg asked why Beth was laughing—giving her a peck on the cheek in honour of their lately rediscovered love of and for each other—and as he did so, they happened to pass a lobe or dune near to new chambers about to be on their list of visits whilst here in Klaxon—to learn about preparations for war and other hand-to-hand conspiracies.

"Nothing really. Just an old schoolfriend. She was funny and I just remembered an old joke we had together."

"Rachel, you mean? You've even forgotten to send her Christmas cards in recent years. Life by-passes friendships sometimes."

Rachel shrugged, reading 'time' for 'life' in what he had just said. Greg smiled. Indeed, meanwhile, Klaxon was soon to be at war with itself—a fact that had been lost sight of, one that needed addressing because, as visitors, they owed it to themselves to get their loyalties sorted out like coloured threads in the eventual textured pattern of carpet pre-destined for their feet to walk. Captain Nemo had not briefed them about these dangerous inter-tribal machinations before leaving the now pyloned earthcraft. And here was Beth talking about an old schoolfriend! "Women!" he thought—and laughed at and against his own instincts.

Beth: Now we've rediscovered our love for each other, I get the feeling that they're splitting us up again by forcing us to be on different sides in a war.

Greg: I didn't understand all this about a war, until someone mentioned it in a cavé the other day... off the cuff almost. Klaxon seemed so peaceful when we first arrived.

Beth: (Laughs) Peaceful!

Greg: Well, you know what I mean. Citizens at peace with each other, at least, if not with this flipping racket of air signals! (Laughs, too.)

Edith: The war was second thoughts, I gather. Things were getting too boring... and tension *is* required for anything creative to work properly. Even Proust realised that as he created friction as well as fiction between levels of time.

Clare: And of sexual acceptability. Between levels of it, that is. Grinding levels sparking off further frictions... and spinning.

Greg: How do you ladies cope with seeing everything as if it's in a book? It's enough for me to get my head round reality! Isn't this place bizarre enough already without fictionalising it? This war, for example. I hear it's where a person becomes a Flew person and those who are not Flew are still themselves—and they open veins in their bodies to see if they can merge the meats between them—coming together in hugs that blend as genuinely as hugs of love always tried to be.

Beth: Or sex. Not love. Yet, it's a war. That's what I don't understand. It's not a love-in.

Edith: A love-between?

Clare: That's a better expression—a love-between, but the meats weren't meant to merge, because some people have become poultry—some even giant insects—leaving some other people as genuine human meat. And when they try this love-blending business, the meats reject each other. Like transplants in the old days.

Beth: Captain Nemo always spoke about something called Human Coning when we were all getting here on the earthcraft. Perhaps that was a misprint—I mean a mispronouncement for what you're talking about. War because the cones or clones don't 'take'. I'm talking beyond myself, now. But do you know what I mean?

Clare: I think so. It is only possible to understand rarefications like that if you fictionalise them—which brings us back to where we started.

Edith: So, what are we saying? As in Proust we need really long sentences to manage the concepts properly—whilst conversation is inevitably staccato. Like this.

Greg: All I know—is that the citizens are in two warring groups—yet simultaneously paired off as love-partners *between* each group. And they want us to nail our colours to one mast or the other. In fact, Crazy Lope and Go'spank are already involved. Up to their necks.

Beth: Not only warring, Greg, but *viciously* warring. The combatants are tooth and nail. Almost tearing each other apart—sinew by sinew. Both sexes, each sex with a different sex, or both the same sex together. It does not seem to matter to birds or insects. I could never tell their genders, in any event.

Edith: Proust hinted at all this in *Swann's Way*.

Clare: Needs careful exegesis, though, Edith.

Beth: Do they have any weapons—others than their bodies, I mean?

Greg: I saw a skirmish outside one of the Lethal Chambers. The sirens sort of joined in, increasing their pitch—as a cover for the weapons. Or to imitate the weapons, perhaps.

Beth: Old-fashioned muskets.

Edith: More than just muskets. The muskets, if they *are* muskets, had mouths—when they were popping. Muskets that were insect-like whatever the meat they grew from.

Greg: I'm sure there is more to the shape of the words themselves, if not to their meanings. Mask, Masque, Mosque, Mosquito, Musketeers, Mousquetaires. I seem to have lived with these horrible words every night when I dream. In fact, I've not really thought about all this before *outside* of a dream.

Beth: Old-fashioned dreams. There are no such thing as old-fashioned dreams any more. Fictionalised dreams are—well,

I'm beginning to think that fictionalised things are actually more real—more tenable—than non-fictionalised things.

Greg: Hmmm. I always preferred reading non-fiction because I thought it was real.

Beth: We are alone. This is frightening. True horror.

Edith: Don't worry, Beth. We are all in this together. We have been from the start. We visited you in your flat all those years ago, when Arthur and Amy were playing in the garden.

Clare: That's when we knew we had to protect you and each other.

Beth: But now we have to fight a war. Nobody warned us about that, when we signed up for the trip.

Greg: We could get back to the Drillcraft. And persuade Nemo to leave early for Agraska. Which pylon? I've forgotten.

Edith: (Turning to Clare) Sunnemo is a place in Sweden—Hawler is a place in Kurdistan. The surface is alive with places like that. Proust lived on the surface once. Many poets flew in his wake. Fin de Siècle.

Clare: Yes, Dumas' *Black Tulip*, too. Characters without depth. Silhouettes. I think to use the word 'cardboard' about fiction characters is demeaning.

Edith: Indeed.

Sunnemo released its demonised shafts of rainlight along the Inner Earth gutters surrounding the City of Klaxon. The sirens whined out their customary warning to earthcraft sailors—as the war was about to enter a cyclic moment of intensest victory or defeat. Consequently, the Canterbury Oak became as silent as the deadened or unwound stridency of buried toys—as it no longer needed to summon up the soundchecks that, given a slightly altered scenario, would indicate the impending challenge-and-response already in full bitter sway before the chance to record it was given.

I stood again beneath the very gravity-logged Oak, from where I had first viewed Klaxon all those clockwork ratchet-clicks ago. The ear shape of the City had, by now, become a mass of new dunes or lobes, some inflamed as with a disease from further inward to where even Inner Earth itself failed to reach. Millions of citizens in various stages of Name Flew were currently in individual hand-to-hand combat, comprising two armies both with their lethal plugs in the pylons... and, by dint of the power vacuum provided by the resonating echoes, it was difficult to judge which inter-combatant belonged to which army of ready-opened body-gaps bearded with feathered veins.

All the catacombed or labyrinthine out-buildings had retained their vulnerable chimneystacks despite the sideways weapon-like sound-torch gravities gushing along every channel of combat between shuffling individuals of volitional war-strength—and the organic structures built into or around these chimney-flues were remarkably still intact but many now had growths of coxcomb or wattle. From each roof, they crew long, they crew wildly at the fast denemonising of Sunnemo into Mount Core. Its Megazanthine flames like wings half-lit the embracing sky around me.

Edith and Clare had resorted to the same building where—cutaway or not—they had, together with Beth, originally watched Klaxon's ritual of Sunne Stead all those years before—watched it via the transparent offices of the building's marigold-window (since repaired).

The room itself had since been cleared of any rubble or off-detritus, although the oil-painting—depicting the 'Reyn-Bouwe' earthfly—still decked the wall, its frame now cleaned of its infestation by an insect-nest.

The war was clearly visible to the two dowagers—as they smoothed off the mist from the marigold's glass. Being battened down in here had been the only option left them short of joining in the war itself by means of their own lady-bodies. A sight of the warring millions seen from the Canterbury Oak's hilltop was one thing—but viewing the same millions from *amongst* them was quite another. The hand-to-hand battles were literally a few inches from the dowagers' window vantage-point, with the depth of combat beyond that only a guess. A guess or a dream.

"Look, Clare!" screamed Edith—uncharacteristically because being bookish she normally avoided any necessity of resort to hysteria.

She pointed at the room's empty fireplace where its chimney-flue was in the process of dangling down a pair of large bird-legs accompanied by the growth of groping as well as squawking.

Clare quickly thrust large amounts of scrunched-up newspaper into the grate and lit them with a Swan Vesta, causing the legs temporarily to withdraw upwards from the tall thin flames—while she looked round for more solid fuel.

Greg and Beth had meanwhile taken refuge in a Lethal Chamber—this being the only means of protection from the ricochet damage created by the warring millions. This was a collateral or lateral irony because, normally, such places were intended to deal out death to those who found themselves there via various stages of imperviousness to sound-torch surgery.

As described in The Yellow Book, those Lethal Chambers were not to be lightly entered—but, luckily, Greg and Beth happened to be together when the war first ignited and they had the combined nous to take the path of least resistance (albeit the most unlikely for safety) where the interior of this particular Lethal Chamber, by dint of a lateral irony (an expression that bears repeating), turned out to afford a relative immunity.

Unlike Edith and Clare, they could not view the war by sight since these chambers did not boast such vantage-points as marigold-windows. However, despite the blast of renewed klaxoning by tannoy of air alerts, they could also hear the rushing frictions of combatant bodies as they barely crossed the outside like a freak weather-storm.

To hear but not see was frightening.

Greg: I love you.

Beth: I know. You've always loved me. Most women complain that men don't tell them enough times that they love them. And it does need to be said once. But more than once—I wonder why they need to say it more than once, as if each time they have to say it, is because they feel themselves to have become a different person.

Greg: I am desperate to remain myself this time. Now that I've finally reached who I am. (He is visibly weeping.)

Beth: (reaching out to him) I know. I know, Greg. I know it's you now. Hold on to that.

They listened to things climbing on top of the chamber, just above the roof of their heads. The chamber's resident patients gurgled lightly in their sleep praying within their dreams for homelier hospices to host them than this one. Greg and Beth looked at them—knowing that such patients were safer in here than Greg and Beth themselves, by some further ratchet of lateral irony regarding ruffled feathers.

Sudra's sure that tiny people were involved. How can big ones have threaded through the pigeon flap? Or the trail of crumbs which she discovers along their erstwhile route almost indicates fairy story characters, if not actual fairies. Whatever the case, the perpetrators are definitely not animals. Whilst animals are tiny enough and, at a push, may be capable of creating random music, they do not have the aesthetic nous of real folk. Indeed, although the music Sudra heard admittedly possessed an atonal quality, it was underlaid with a nagging harmony which, surely, excluded full-blooded haphazardness. Yes, she thinks, only real people can wield the refinement of soul sufficient to strum the air so hauntingly. By the widest stretch of the imagination, crude animal instinct fails even as a spare spear-carrier. On the other hand, the truth stares Sudra in the top of her head, if not the face. Angels, as is commonly the case, disguise themselves as ceilings, albeit, in Sudra's chamber, crumbly ones.

Crazy Lope and Go'spank were ensconced in *Sudra's Shoe Shop* during the course of the war which—by some accounts—lasted at least two decades of bitter in-and-out fighting. Other accounts gave a shorter period, by virtue of a time angle not dissimilar to Proust's method of self-dissection with 'selves' sometimes overlapping but then becoming separate people with thus longer to live. Yet other accounts put the war as stretching even further into the future, where memories piled up to become tail-to-tail history books.

It is clear from other accounts that Greg and Beth eventually reached Agra Aska on an earthfly (disguised as a drill)—one called 'The Hawler'—in company with Captain Nemo (aka Doghnahnyi), the pair of dowagers plus the nameless shadowy businessmen from the earthfly's corporate lounge... there, as a select number of accounts attest, to meet up with Mike, Susan, Amy, Arthur and two Agraskans called Tho and Hataz.

Sudra had been left in Klaxon to set up a shoe shop as a business venture, since her alter-nemo had died in the hawling-shafts further towards the surface. And that business spread—in time—beyond both ends of its actual start and finish, because she failed keeping her own accounts in order. Sudra enjoyed selling shoes and the war meant plenty of unshod people, even soldiers who were served ill by the authorities regarding their need for these basic essentials. As such, there was no demarcation between civilians and military, even to the extent of there being a common uniform for everyone—even the same uniform for both sides in the war.

There was a third side in the war but the constituents of its army were invisible, if not completely non-existent (non-existence being a stage further towards disbelief than invisibility or nudity). Wars are difficult to conduct from three different angles of attack, especially without benefit of conspiracies, side-treaties, bluffs, feints and counterfeints—and so this third force of participants was kept shadowy on purpose (merely being referred to as Ogdonites in mysterious underbreaths).

The two main 'known' armies were simply known as Them or Us, depending on which side you were on or thought you were on.

Sudra had, by now, developed into a most beautiful woman and much of the remainder of our time in Klaxon will be concerned with her story, with little, if any, reflected taint from her earlier self or rumoured childhood as Mike's step-daughter or her nightly dreams of a wicked blood-father who made her eat flesh-infested cabbages in the hope of keeping Name Flew at bay (or that was the excuse).

The war was her backdrop. Equally, Sudra's story was the reason for the war because without her own story as *its* backdrop it would have lacked the forefront to give itself reflected point or focus.

The Weirdmonger, careless of the plots, meandered through park after park of scorched earth. He trod down tannoys to rid himself of their sirens—but not on purpose—simply making a bee-line for the shop that he knew was just beyond the last park of all. So he trod on concrete and sward just as readily as dune or lobe. Not even eschewing the mudpatches that prevailed in every single park. Dispersing children in their play. Elbowing bikes into untidy skids. Brusquely brushing aside attendant mothers and trainee nannies, as their prams escaped down some unlikely slopes towards where the war was still prevailing.

Each park merged with the next; some children's playgrounds seemed to straddle two parks at once, with railings cross-sectioning ride from ride and, in some cases, splitting single rides in half. Boating-lakes, too, had paddle-boats that couldn't land on certain banks, whilst others, of a different livery, could ply any part of the lake and put off on any towpath. The Weirdmonger could not fathom any of the rules and customs as he negotiated various rights of way and weaved between interlocking and overlapping mazes of bye-law and respective Klaxon-reclaimed or war-scorched jurisdiction. The further he travelled, the more he noticed the parks becoming shabbier and ill-kempt, railings battered down by winds and left unmended, pools allowed to seep at the edges, mud encroaching flower-beds and rockeries alike—even walkways sticky with a substance somewhat more akin to congealed cuckoo-spit than common-or-garden soil deposits. Or that was what the Weirdmonger wondered about in his crazy fashion, with or without the help of onlookers.

As the shop's curved runnel or lobe (as his destination) grew taller upon the edge of his sight, he was finding his rite of passage through the parks more and more problematic. The natural onset of war-scorched areas was slowly impinging upon the parks. There was one children's slide, for example, the silver sluice of which was inches deep with a texture of varying degrees of brownness and burnt yellow. Only a few individuals—of youthful persuasion—could be seen making merry... twirling on over-oily roundabouts and croaking swings, releasing fitful ochreous spillages from their central hubs or hinges. One boy with precocious chin hair called foul messages from the top of the slide. The Weirdmonger shrugged, as if to claim fellow-feeling with any who were left by parents to play in this godawful park... not like the neatly manicured bowling-greens and shiny primary colours of children's rides boasted by the earlier paths and parks he'd crossed... crossed in dream with a good measure of foreboding.

He knew that the shop towards which he travelled on foot housed not only itself but also the one he was destined to love. The Weirdmonger had endured his own fair share of past times... and he predicted that there would also be many wax figures of historical humanity in the shop, depicting ancient customs or educational themes. Tableaux of timely remembrance. One word from him and such fabrications would take on new tones, if not a life of their own. The words the Weirdmonger spoke flew from his mouth with the garb of essential truth, words like butterfly-birds and poisonous insects, words like flowers in free flow and historical primary sources, words like dragon-scales forming, eventually, into real dragons. Dragons with wings even bigger than the flames their mouths spewed.

He laughed. There was the shop. Sudra's shop. That'd bring the Weirdmonger's pretensions down a peg or two. He felt as if he were a child again, entering his first museum, harness held tightly by leather leads as he toddled in front of his mother on tenter hooks.

The Weirdmonger had indeed been a normal child before he'd thrown youth away like a crumpled sweet-bag. That was the day he realised that the words which he believed were true actually became true. Faith was everything. Faith dictated reality. And he had been his own father was all that he recalled—a strange fate for an even stranger sire—and he as the older Weirdmonger had taught the younger Weirdmonger how to throw words like balls in a game of Catch. Popping boiled humbugs or acid drops or aromatic crystallised figs from mouth to mouth. Perhaps his father was the true Weirdmonger, and the true Weirdmonger (so-called) was the true impostor. Words became impossibly tangled as soon as the concentration dropped and the years passed by, consigning his father to merely an oil painting of himself stippled with misdirected pellets—and the Weirdmonger (now the true one) went out into the world, park by park. But the world was hot and dry—and the parks were deserts of Inner Earth. But now they were global-cooling, artistically speaking. Today, the parks were wet and soggy—terribly muddy, denying the flowers' plots any ambition other than the extrapolated brown blooms upon wilting stalks, each one weeping yellow tears for a poet called Charles Baudelaire. Even the park-keepers had given up their watering-cans... and you know how officious they once were when school caretakers.

The Weirdmonger nodded as if he heard his father in his head. The shop stood there, now, tall and stately—with the waxen exhibits he expected staring through the windows, wielding axes like ancient Northumberland Reivers or French Angevin Kings, denoting the precise historical moments, bringing *then* to *now* with all the force of precariousness. History made real—whilst any students of his would become part of some fantasy world which learned the lessons head on. These wax figures, he was aghast to see, however, were simply shaped like shoes in odds and not pairs.

The Weirdmonger nodded again. He was his own son as well as his own father and now as the former he had returned to the turning pages and the juggling words as he did as a student—with the words sprinkling the air above the print like hover-flies, depleting the print by their very presence or, rather, the print had left the page and become the hover-flies themselves. He paid for his museum ticket at the kiosk—a guide-book to shoeboxes from Crazy Lope for a round tour, complete with ear-muffs and learning devices that were stuck straight into the body's veins. Go'spank smiled as he passed over the long spool of tickets, saying: "Enjoy the trip."

As if (the Weirdmonger thought) the parks hadn't already been enough. He looked back wistfully to see over-sized birds, with stubby wings, failing to fly from the last park. This was the first time he'd noticed how the mud had stopped all Nature in its tracks... as if mud was an effluent with which Nature had tried to oil itself but, in the process, had over-egged the cake that had been left out in the rain.

The Weirdmonger toured the Shop on the Borderland with torchbright eyes—or that was how he was subsequently described by an unseen onlooker. There were many oil paintings of shoes... and a whole host of nemonymous figures wearing them... their names queueing along the wainscotting beneath their wildly daubed likenesses, making the museum more of a modern gallery of ultramodern pretension than a potentially tedious array of educational wax figures, speaking in misalignments of recorded voice or reported speech.

He wondered why Go'spank traipsed in his wake, half-staggering, half-shambling back and forth in tides of indecision.

"Mr..."

"Yes?" he boomed.

"The shop shuts in half a trice."

Go'spank was evidently concerned that the Weirdmonger would be angry at not previously being warned *before* he had the tickets unravelled for him at such great cost. Go'spank seemed to hold a stub of a ticket for dear life in his mitt-end, as the Weirdmonger's booming voice belied the nervousness he shared with Go'spank.

Truth, sometimes, on a good day, can be felt as well as told. The Weirdmonger did not shrug, did not laugh, did not utter anything approaching the suspicion of a word... yet there were sounds of tongue clucks and palate cleaving, igniting a whole string of horror images: spilling from his mouth like regatta flags towards Go'spank. The only thing that could be said for the Weirdmonger was the free-flow of tears from his remorseful eyes, as Go'spank twisted amid the entanglements and coils of designer rudery. Rudery (a collective noun for rude things) was better, however, than, say, sweaty bird-heads: this being the giggly observation of an unseen onlooker. Better than the mounds of crusty scabs and curds of gangrenous pus from a million childhood accidental abrasions failing to heal. Better than corrupt organs that rotted because they had no owners to wield them. No more giggles. Only side-swipes at the absurdity of the situation from now a rather cool, detached onlooker. There was indeed a harvest of *healthy* rudery wrapped around Go'spank, a harvest of rudery, indeed, wielded by spectral athletes, gymnasts, body-builders and hawlers in yellow jingle-jangly shoes and invisible carpet-coats. Despite their already swollen appendages, the ghostly figures lovingly meted out more and more of their body-ends from the modelling clay of ectoplasm to form the ridged winding-sheets... swaddling poor Go'spank. Killed by kindness.

With his ultimate cliché thus uttered (tested for truth as well as timbre) the Weirdmonger left the environs of the shop for the purlieus of the nearest park. It was just one minute before the shop was due to close. Not that it really mattered now. The saddest part, if the truth were told, was that Go'spank's whole life heretofore had been as preparation to be a spear-carrier in an onlooker's scenario he would never understand, even given the chance.

But if Go'spank had been merely created for his own death, then what, if not who, was I? I, the onlooker, stared from the attic's own attic of Sudra's shop barely concealed among the ridges or narrower lobes of the roof. I gazed over the mudparks as they fitfully vanished towards the middle distance, even to a point where the war had re-started—as evidenced by the sight of new tannoys being built by combatants for sirens.

Like a geomantic zodiac, the mudparks formed the face of the man I'd known as the Weirdmonger, with brown eyes and even browner tears: above which hovered a creature with stubby wings: either a child bobbing upon a playground ride# (a ride so burnished it shone with pure invisibility) or an Angel that had been stripped to the bottom bone of meaning.

"Fly!" I shouted.

And it was.

#Stub of pencil: A third party claimed this was clearly a see saw.

Sudra was in her bedroom in the shoe museum listening to the newly prepared armies march-running towards war through the cutaways of Klaxon—measuring the pavy-crazed sluices between the lobes with the rhythmic onward march of their medium-pace limbs in running mode as opposed to any standard patterned walk. March-running is a forgotten art. Neat ranks of soldiers (mostly female) these were, keeping perfect pace with each other at the run, rather than the lift-and-separate of slow-motion goose-step or slightly quicker frog-march or general English slow marchpast for Trooping the Colour or Remembrance Sunday. Memories of Things Past—a hypnotic echoing march-run as the various sections of army proceeded—half in and half out of Sudra's dreamtime perception of them from her bedroom window—towards their billets in the various establishments of darkening Klaxon.

This was during the early stages of the war before sides had been picked, like children in the classroom exchanging bright coins of choice for the best runner on their team, leaving the solitary turnips to be the final choices. Sudra had earlier watched a strange individual visit her shoe museum—despite Crazy Lope (her doorkeeper) and his good offices to keep unpaying customers at bay—and she wondered if war was something that had come accompanying the visitor, rather than a genuine interest in viewing the shoes on mannequins' feet. Ulterior motives... led to a neat withdrawal of the visitor back to the mudparks whence he'd first arrived (Go'spank's dead body upon his back like a cancerous growth).

One of the march-running woman officers was to billet in the shoe museum. She was introduced to Sudra by Edith who was now in temporary charge of billeting arrangements in the city prior to full-out war. Armies needed their sleep, and armies were made up of individuals who thought sleep would help later as acclimatisation to death.

The woman soldier who had splintered off from the synchronisation of her fellow march-runners when she'd reached her appointed billet (in this case, the shoe museum) was shown to a bunk bed in the attic's attic.

"Rest here," said Sudra with a smile. A fine figure of a woman who had loosened her tie on first sighting the equally attractive soldier. "If you need anything in the night…"

"I shall be fine," said the soldier, listening to other sections of march-runners still rhythmically passing in the night, eager for their own billets elsewhere. The soldier slowly withdrew from her uniform while simultaneously covering herself with the carpet-blanket that Crazy Lope had earlier provided for the bunk, thus revealing nothing of her eager body.

It was like imagining one was in a dream simply for the sake of haunting oneself with it. A means to extend life. Wars often caused similar mentalities of false dreaming.

Sudra smiled, determined to bide her time. March-runners were now passing with the perceived sound of much smaller groups, silhouetted by sirens. Until only an odd pair of billetless march-runners echoed down the sluice-alleys that Sunnemo's withdrawal into its nightmask had created from the once wide esplanades of a finer siècle.

As Sudra settled into a feather-mattress, she heard the war crackle into existence on a far ridge of Klaxon with mere Muskets of Mass Destruction.

"Wagger Market, Wagger Market, Come to Wagger Market!"

The Weirdmonger once had a stall of his own at torrid Wagger Market (a suburb of Klaxon)—but today at the fun-at-the-fair, stuff seemed as tawdry as the sun now seemed cool. The brown canvases, once pulled taut by hooks on ancient tenter-frames appeared soggy, threadbare, frayed... even worm-holed. The wares as chipped and crocked as the costermongers' faces that tried to sell them from deeply-veined marble slabs, slabs so stained, the Weirdmonger knew that dead fish had once sat on them eyeing the customers... with imperceptible flicks of their tails…

No sign of the healthy human rudery that once hung from the tenter frames... much sought after by the mountain nomads as ornaments as well as carnifications. Nor were there now displayed those rolls and rolls of partly piled carpets and mats, with rough-sewn inner cylinders of space being home for numbers of creatures that had since become as legendary as they were once so far-fetched, despite their inarguable existence as forces for dream.

It was then the Weirdmonger was delighted to find a stall with a bit more get-up-and-go than the other downtrodden trestles of junk. It bore a sign with yellow lettering saying 'Olden Days' and a beautiful attendant who wore a name badge saying WAR. The

Weirdmonger lowered his eyes from her buxom comeliness to the stall's comestibles and purveyances of provender. These were all varieties of syrup, it seemed—ranging from some Happy Shopper stuff through branded Tate & Lyle—until eyes reached the more exotic end of the syrup market that stemmed from Far Samarkand and Ancient Cathay—flecks of spice generously lacing the aromatic glue-syrups and treacles, the slimy tentacles of which curled and coiled within the substance they themselves constituted, in and out of each other like tubular sinews of bee-honey.

More marmalady substances squatted like set jellies without the help of containers to hold them up. Thick cut & thin cut. Peppered with peels. Peels like orange ones. Or peels like lumps of hairy hide. All sitting incoherently within clear syrup as well as cloudy... like pickles or foreign bodies or sizeable splinters of rind or hardened skin. The top-notch syrup was not from the deepest, strangest Orient but from the Pacific Islands. Petals floating in silken tides. Tiny nugget-sown lagoons of amber wreathed with garlands... teased back and forth by weltering waterfalls.

Some syrups actually moved by their own volition—seething, gurgling, even burping—as bubbles broke towards the meniscus of more turgid marmaladery (at the lower end of the range). A single syrup was effervescent, as a series of prickling sensations cascaded into existence—microscopic air-pockets tingling to the Weirdmonger's imaginary touch. Then, he spotted letters floating about in it. Making words. Unmaking words. Poems being slurped and sloughed between the walls of the transparent jug. The words 'Olden Days' abruptly ratcheted into view, locking into some serendipitous significance beyond any semantic meaning. Telling, perhaps, of the particular stall that sold these sinuosities of syrup. Then—just like an ugly duckling—a lonely letter 'g' floated into view through the undulating avenues of aspic—and joined up just as the Weirdmonger's attention returned to the stallholder. Syrup, as well as silence, was golden. He felt dazed, as he momentarily bent his head under an impending emotion. This emotion was strong, more golden than anything. But then he was startled by the thought that came into his head—unannounced. He knew the game was up. His sluices of logic had been blocked by plaits of gooey love.

WAR smiled meltingly.

"Would you like to buy some syrup, Weirdmonger?"

"Yes, but can I ask why you call yourself WAR, WAR? I recall wars as men all mouth and trousers who fought till they found that fighting was harder than drinking."

"My father died of a broken heart over a botched result at his own World War."

WAR seemed even more pretty when she spoke serious. The Weirdmonger wondered what heights of passion she might engender if she actually talked dirty. He nodded as if he understood without the necessity of her continuing. Apparently, her father had lived his whole life upon the hope of winning the World War.

WAR said that she was continuing the investigation at the behest of some paternal beyond-the-grave power which could not be defied. When a corpse got its claws into an issue, there was the devil to pay.

WAR herself turned as white as a ghost, gaunt and stare-eyed... as she fiddled with the jars of syrup. A haunted woman. Prettiness draining from her by the second. The bitterness of something that wouldn't let go even in death. She sighed. Her eyes glazed as her father's eyesight spun from them like wasps. She wielded long cultivated fingernails which she scratched along the nearest trestle—as if playing noughts and crosses for real and in earnest. From the middle of her head there sounded two voices clicking like miniature wooden dolls—foully swearing. Then WAR slumped forward...

The Weirdmonger now heard the voices inside his own head. He shook his head to free these poor creatures of his thoughts.

Wagger Market resumed its business, oblivious of the tragedy. Nobody even bothered to clear up the huge mound of slime till the various corpses that had formed within muscley folds of it had disfigured.

The Weirdmonger had stayed away too long. The blanched thistles crouched like forgotten cruel love affairs—and he whistled with delight as he recalled the games of Catch he'd played here during those hotter days of youth. Not that he'd grown any older. Weirdmongers never did. And he was the only one left. Perhaps the only one that there ever was.

The landscape had changed. Cooler. Wetter. Strangely brighter. Or was it whiter? Paler. He tried to juggle the words. Despite the dankness, things looked shrivelled, burnt, desiccated... even more so than when Sunnemo had shone strong and high, during those endless days of his... youth. Yes, why not say the word? Even if it meant little, if not nothing. Agelessness was a burden that many carried, but the Weirdmonger carried it with some style and panache. Why use two words when none would do?

He shrugged. He had returned to the Klaxon Keys to renew acquaintanceships, if not with the original contacts of his "youth", but with their progeny. He had recently travelled—further than anyone could imagine—towards lobes and poles of Inner Earth where few appreciated his art-with-words, an art of uttering a word or phrase or saying which then immediately became a self-evident truth. The Weirdmonger's watchword was 'one word, one truth' for generations—but sometimes he needed to visit people able to have faith in this facility, thus to regain his self-confidence. Some, for example—in (god)forsaken clans of siren-driven wastes shadowed by Canterbury's gravity-logged Oak—had merely stared at the Weirdmonger, open-mouthed, expecting their own words to issue forth as true as his. And they never did. Others had not even bothered trying, especially amid the coming war, failing, as they did, to understand anything the Weirdmonger said. Yet, here, back in Klaxon, he hoped at least the people retained a modicum of empathy with 'one word, one truth', not that anyone could *truly* empathise. If they did, they'd be Weirdmongers, too.

He shrugged again. He watched two boys throwing a ball to each other, with, between them, a puddle that the relatively weaker Sunnemo had failed to dry up... although, judging by the hover-flies sprinkling about above it, there was steam rising…

The Weirdmonger could hear the nagging voice of the two boys' mother: a descendant, no doubt, of the woman he had known on his earlier sojourn in these parts... and for the likes of the Weirdmonger, knowing was not knowing nearly enough, there being far more about people than the people themselves or others could possibly imagine. The Weirdmonger recognised that knowing was tantamount to not-knowing, until he spoke the word, and *then* he'd know someone to the bottom bone of the soul. One word, that was all it took. One word from the Weirdmonger.

And today the voice scorched each Inner Ear... to *their* bottom bones. She was screeching for her boys to come in and not speak to strangers... and she stared across at the Weirdmonger, as if daring him to speak first. The boys, indeed, scampered to either side of her wide skirt.

"Git! We don't need you here."

The Weirdmonger touched his chimney hat with the tip of two fingers, fingers that had grown webbed since he'd been known in these parts. Even Weirdmongers can change. Even plural can become singular.

The woman's ancient great-grandmother Sudra had, if the truth were told, accused the Weirdmonger, in a dim past now beyond any torching out, of turning everything red. You've made bread red, she'd shrieked, YOU'VE TURNED BREAD INTO MEAT!

That was the day he had uttered the word which meant just one more gear up from breeding—where love was more a feast than anything else (if comparisons can be made so loosely). The word—even he had forgotten now... but it still seemed, from today's evidence, to run free in this present woman's blood. She had spoken instinctively…

"Don't worry thyself," the Weirdmonger said, with such simplicity, the woman immediately calmed down, held out her hand to him and smiled so generously, he wondered if laughter could possibly be as fulsome as her slicing grin.

"Welcome, Weirdmonger," she said. "A stranger like you cannot be strange for long." And she pushed her two boys towards him, uncaring whether they were being sacrficed to a demon or merely being introduced to a kind uncle.

The Weirdmonger offered to catch their ball. He held up one of his hands which was swollen like a huge keeper's mitt or oven glove.

"Thou, throw," he said.

And the ball, as if of its own volition, left the boy's right hand straight into the safety of his finger cage which the Weirdmonger's other hand had seemed to have become as his hands switched responsibility of catching.

There was always a catch. Even blind ones.

The room into which the Weirdmonger was shown was certainly not a showroom. Cramped, cluttered, yet beautifully cloisonné. The tassel on the blind clicked irritatedly against the window as a damp, then dry breeze absconded. A dry sound like a moth in a paper bag. A broken siren-breeze.

The woman frowned her two boys into the corner. They sank back into the shadows as if they were learning to swim or, at least, float... but silently failed to do so, smiles frozen on their faces like disguises for disgrace.

The kitchen, too, was nothing to write home about. There was meat stretched in strands from sink to worktop... like Christmas decorations. Sinews and threads of dripping muscle.

The Weirdmonger blinked. And the vision vanished. He dared not speak it... for obvious reasons. However, during the next few days, as soon as the boys had recovered from shyness, the Weirdmonger played trifling word games with them, like saying something along the lines of 'bubble' and a huge sooty one expanded from his mouth and—once complete—floated off. He'd say: a colour and, momentarily, the place where they were dallying—be it sitting-room or backyard—would blush to its roots with the colour chosen. Purple—and the trees swagging over the fence or window sill were like richly Royal garments or ecclesiastical vestments. Grey—and the boys laughed to think they'd returned to the days when films had a grey monochrome consistency; TV, too; black and white versions of Big Brother. Not that screens even existed at all now, even in colour. Screens had been kicked in ages ago, for all the right reasons. Visual image overdose had caused all manner of aberrations. Including no need for shoes as feet had become webbed and weather-proof like birds'.

He made as if to play catch with an imaginary tongue-tied ball of tumours, threaded throughout with veins and almost living morsels themselves. The boys cringed when they saw the Weirdmonger being so uncouth with his game. And the mother would cluck with distaste, despite being duped by phrases such as "Never you mind, my dear" or "Give me the benefit of the doubt" which flapped from the Weirdmonger's mouth like platitudes with a demon's wings disguised as an angel's.

One day, the Weirdmonger uttered some words which didn't quite take off. Whether it was a catch in the throat, a tickle caused by some misbehaving phlegm or a more serious seizure of bodily function, the words wormed out warped and wayward. He had meant to say, "Where is your father?" (and to himself, "Where is me?")—the optimum of a love he was beginning to feel for these boys, his new-found foundlings or changelings or lostlings now found. One of them had the biggest ear he had ever seen. All the better to hear you with, perhaps. Instead the sense shifted... in a language so foreign-looking it represented the outset of a civilisation that had never existed—until now. The words' exit was wrapped in cross purposes.

The mother wept. For she didn't know who the boys' real father was—having been taken in her sleep between one dream and the next. She had felt for some time that there was some deeper meaning to the Weirdmonger's words. She examined her own right hand. For as long as she could recall, it had been swollen like an oven-glove and the left one articulated like a cage with a trapped pellet of dry dung rattling in it like a ball valve.

The Weirdmonger was sad and deep kissed her. And she vanished like a fast shrinking red balloon into the fundaments of his being. The boys laughed and laughed till they died of it—or the Weirdmonger dropped the ball, whichever came first.

The Weirdmonger was then free to leave the Klaxon Keys—his feet crunching thistles like hollow bones. He held his chimney hat on against the dry wafts of air. Sunnemo never seemed to set any more, or it became a volcano called Mount Core. "Grey!" he shouted at it, with as much feeling to the word as he could muster. And he smiled at the black and white movie upon which he lived and had his being... before the screen blew its circuits, vanishing—as old-fashioned TV sets used to do—into a fast diminishing white dot.

Except he was never to know it wasn't white, but red.

It was a May war. Perhaps earlier, perhaps later, but May maybe was the best guess. Klaxon seasons were as slavishly followed as their months, despite the weather-mad waywardness of Sunnemo itself. Sudra watched her billeted soldier guest with beady, if not steely, eyes. Eyes both looking and looked at. She suspected the soldier (often now glimpsed intimately and seen to bear a body fit for all sorts of use and not only for cruelties entailed by war) of being someone else. Too much of a coincidence to believe it was Amy or a May-masqued Amynemo returned for a further bite at the cherry of Sudra's doom. Thus singled out from those thousands, if not millions, of march-runners—ceremonially making the relentless churn-churn rhythms of footwork by-passing the Klaxon sluices in pursuit of military glory—why would it be Amy herself snatched from these very churning ranks as chosen by higher authorities to billet in the shoe museum during the course of the war?

Sudra also watched the watcher—the man who had mysteriously visited the museum in past months, both as regular customer and as an inspector of museums. Dealt with by Lope, following the unexplained abscondment of Go'spank. This man stood outside staring up at the imaginary salacious silhouettes that were not silhouettes at all but shadows of the window-blind itself rattling in noise-breezes rather than at any sights that the blind itself concealed. Sudra watched a watcher outside in the city sluice thinking he was looking up at an attic's attic-window watching Sudra but really watching the empty spaces she left behind so as to darken in her wake like stains of deceptive movement—as she later surreptitiously sought her soldier guest in places where they had not yet darkened sufficiently to tease with the nipply buttons of military undervest or see-through camisole that dressed the fleshy spaces below the eyes that looked and the eyes that were looked at.

Lope could be heard floors away straightening the mannequins in their demonstration shoes. Much of the museum depicted earlier periods when shoes were more in keeping with not squashing the toes, but after toes had gradually pointened with layers of white poultry flesh—eventually hardening into horns or curlicues that no chiropodist could possibly cut—mannequins had taken on the role of stolid lifelessness more in keeping with hand-puppets that had lost the hands that worked them from within as if the puppet-skins were soft body-hugging chambers and the hands coxcomb flamingos shrunk to the size of gristle-flags. If mannequins could walk at the dead of night—with the cracking of bone that once typified derelict butcher-shops in hawling-days—then they surely no longer walked there now. Any footstep heard on the breath of night was Sudra's own or Lope's slow lope (so slow it had become rather a slouch or shamble) or, in recent times, the soldier's boots deadened by the thicker carpets she had insisted upon for step-comfort as well as insulation against the gullible spaces between floorboards and the cavity-rock.

Lope told Sudra of the man who visited the museum being someone he once knew as a younger man (both of them, he and Lope, often, it seemed, the *same* young man). Indeed, the watcher wore a cape similar to Lope's. Rumoured to be in league with the Ogdonites—but nobody in the know or otherwise was meant to be aware of this the war's third force or whether Ogdonite officers wore capes sufficient to hide themselves against the chameleon backdrops of Klaxon's lobes and dunes cresting the upper profiles of the city's more habitable chambers.

Sudra: I had a dream last night.

Lope: The Weirdmonger again?

Sudra: No, it was just that our guest was showing me out of the window the leading-edge of a vast surface city passing slowly through Klaxon's cavity as it worked its way towards the Core.

Lope: There have often been rumours of a man-city.

Sudra: It was difficult to see it all in one go to define its shape. It was just a vast city—with buildings, and streets, and people clinging on to what they could to help themselves stay with their homes—and I did see a long area or runway that must have been an airport oozing through Klaxon brick like knife through butter. It must have been a dream. How otherwise did it avoid coming through here? (She pointed to the long corridor of shod dummies that made part of her museum.)

Lope: And the carpet is untouched. It would have ripped it to shreds if a city had passed through it, surely.

Sudra: Yes. However, the soldier took off the top of her uniform and I could see shapes sliding through her flesh, like bones on the move…

Lope: Must be a dream. Like that married couple from Clacton.

Sudra: Yes, that was a dream definitely. But sometimes I think the city dream passing through here is still going on even though I've now woken up. Look out the window. Its walls in silhouette marching like staircases or collective chimney-stacks—all taking their slow-motion march-past—to war, via war, from war. One bit, the other day, like a vast model of a ship, got stuck in a chamber, and is still lodged there as if it's landed itself on a cliff ledge—a cliff ledge to it but part of Klaxon to us. Guess it depends on the perspective, rather than on whether it's a dream or not.

Lope: Yes, I wonder whether dream is a relevant term any more. If all is dream, it does come down to perspectives rather than an easy excuse of dreaming. Turkey-halting, I call it.

Sudra: Why?

Lope: Well Turkey is both a bird and a country.

Sudra: Yes, but how many times is the globe melting—making all countries one?

The conversation itself was being dreamed by Amy as she rested in her bed between battles. Between perspectives.

Arthur as a child enjoyed mixing experiments in the back garden—often watched by his younger sister Amy. He'd requisition household substances—Fairy liquid, white powdery Surf, Dettol disinfectant, creamy-white cleaning-fluids, soaps of all sorts and consistencies, dishwasher tablets, table salt, left-over food and so forth—then proceed to imagine he was a top scientist, plying thick pastes of such concoctions to looser fluids and hardened surfaces of impacted sponge or crystalline solids. 'Requisition' was a posh word for creatively transfer from one place to another. His mother Edith failed to notice much of her stock of kitchen lubrications had gone missing over time or she turned a blind eye to the 'messes' that Amy tried to tell her about if only she'd go down the garden to see.

Arthur saw himself as a top scientist. His experiments led to much global good. Even Amy was astonished when watching Arthur flick the tail of his Davy Crockett hat from his eyes as yet another steam creature erupted into the sky like a wet version of a firework display.

Sometimes, Arthur was also a top surveyor or geographer. Indeed, he often made dams from his 'messes' mixed with earth—and a moat of suspiciously multicoloured ditchwater around an island whereby his toy soldiers had a field day training amidst a sticky alien landscape of Tide and Toilet Frog.

He laughed as Amy turned up with a watering-can and flowerpot.

"I don't need those."

And she went off sobbing her heart out. Brothers weren't easy monsters in her world of blurred growth and incipient humanity.

Arthur continued shaping swill into barely erect castle-battlements on his island, fostering insect-nests to take root to give some semblance of unpredictable inhabitants threading in and out of the maze of half-frozen messes that the winter weather had brought about.

Often, he'd put his larger ear to the ground to see if any larger inhabitants were about to emerge, and being larger, noisier, too. The insects, if insects they were as opposed to chemically-induced mites of impossible lifeforms, merely created a relentlessly mild buzz barely above his young hearing-threshold.

He stared back at the tower-block where he saw Edith waving at him. Apparently this was the day for his schoolteacher's visit, someone who was most definitely not on Arthur's side in the race for Natural Selection amid a competitive world where children were no longer offered flying-starts. Amy turned on her heels, dropping the watering-can, but managing to keep grip on her flowerpot for dear life.

Arthur could also see—through the gap between two of the four tower-blocks—the square where a fountain played at its middle amongst four cast-iron benches where both residents and strangers could sit, given clement weather. Today, it was deserted, and the fountain frozen into the shape of the creature that had once been its free-flowing water-sculpture.

The teacher could wait. Arthur picked up the abandoned watering-can and peered inside. Nothing except a residue of some mossy paste that had been one of his now forgotten experiments from before the time he had managed to forge a memory of the past. Any past. Children only knew the future as and when it was crystallised as a memorable past—and today Arthur, for the first time, realised he had a past he could remember. Amy, by contrast, was still lost in a fog with which stunted growth did besmirch the infant mind even if it was on the point of emerging as a butterfly of Amyness from the dank turnip-egg embedded in the mulch of creation where she had wallowed, disguised as a human baby. Arthur laughed. No such thoughts had gone through his mind.

Yet nagging at him were further thoughts. Amy had left the watering-can because it was evidently not important to her. She still had the flowerpot as she left for the meeting with their schoolteacher. There was evidently something about the flowerpot or what was in the flowerpot or what haunted the flowerpot or a combination of all these things which had caused Amy not to leave it in his possession. And he took a last glance at his moated island of now bubbling earth-erosion, and followed in the wake of his sister, even if that brought forward the dreaded repercussions of the schoolteacher's visit. The flowerpot had become magnified in his new-found memory and would remain embedded there forever, even when he gradually became an old man with many more memories to harbour than just this single one about his sister's haunted flowerpot. A haunted memory, if indeed not a haunted flowerpot.

There was now a caped figure sitting on one of the square's benches, busy writing, oblivious of the weather-proof fountain that cracked like bones in a steady wintry wind. Arthur knew that was himself—a visitant from the future to seal or mint or rubber-stamp the memory that this sight would eventually become. A second memory to join that of the haunted flowerpot. This was a day rich with memories—because, a child's memories once begun and once adept in the art of storing themselves, multiply with a feeding frenzy.

That day's meeting with the schoolteacher would be a third memory that was destined to last for as long as memories remained. Including Amy's reaction to many confused instructions and recriminations regarding the shoes that belonged to a friend of hers. Thankfully, the meeting did not concern Arthur at all. For once.

Later, he returned to the garden—the family's own allotted plot amongst many other fenced subsections of agriculture or flower-display—and found his latest island of earth had subsided into a stinking compost of known and unknown colours. Despite the frozen weather, it gave off a warm steamy putrescence which was almost pleasant to his untutored nostrils. He could also still hear the relentlessly mild buzz of whatever lifeforms had evolved deeper down below his mis-mechanisation of stones, earth-deposits and man-made chemicals. Now more like gabbled talk than sirens. He poked a finger in and felt a large soft fleshiness that created the loudest screech imaginable.

He ran and ran, if only to escape the memory. Thankfully, he succeeded. The screech simply became the echo of a dream he no longer believed as a real dream let alone as waking reality itself.

His sister Amy squatted on the backstep of the lift shaft—tears streaming down her face—flowerpot clasped to her chest, as if she had kept it as a receptacle for any vomit she was about to let rip from the bottom of her lungs.

Arthur shrugged. Sisters. Strange creatures. Sisters were of that same group of creatures he would never understand, a group that also harboured his mother as well as schoolteacher. He looked into the square to see if that man was still there. He assumed it had been a man. It had the shape of a man, despite the concealing cape. Shapes could be imagined as well as seen for real.

He turned back to his sister. She had gone—leaving the flowerpot on the step. With his Davy Crockett hat's fur tail swinging, he went over. He needed some more swill for his moat.

The Weirdmonger—upon his now legendary rite of passage through Klaxon's peripheral mudparks—came across a dreamcatcher hanging in the sky. Feathers and netting upon a singular swinging frame of irregular shape—or, rather, of both regular and irregular shape. A collapsible frame when not in use, the Weirdmonger guessed. He wondered from where it was thus suspended swinging in the siren-breezes that played fitfully around it at this distance from the city proper. He looked into the cavity's half-sky and only the light of Sunnemo gave any clue: itself. But the same light glared into his eyes—thus making it difficult to ascertain the dreamcatcher's root.

He touched it tentatively and watched it swing more vigorously. Dreams flocked around it like moths or mosquitos into the netting, some stuck there as burrs would on fly-paper. One dream caught Weirdmonger in the eye: and he saw (ahead of time) his arrival in a war-ravaged city, his close scrutiny of Sudra's shoe museum where the smoke from the chimney was like a huge stilleto-wedge rather than a plume or umbrella-shape, and the hasty departure of 'The Hawler' flopping from its pylon towards the gravity-logging of its pull only for the Drill's bit-tip to grind uselessly against the beach terrain which was apparently harder within Inner Earth than it had been on the surface.

Captain Nemo had to alight himself to sharpen the bit-tip whilst it was still spinning. And away the Drill went, faces mooning at the portholes near its back set of vanes. The Weirdmonger knew—from the dreamcatcher—that the faces' names were Greg, Beth, Edith and Clare. The Captain was left stranded as the Drill proceeded to push on into the under-surface without him. Fears for his passengers blackened his face. Nemo and Dognahnyi parted company at that moment of violent alter-nemo dispute... a symbiosis in reverse decorated with a flare of more mosquito dreams caught by feathers. With Nemo's head yanked apart by a pair of its four limbs, the creature emerged from the red-sea gap in the skull with a smirk and a wave towards the Weirdmonger's future in the city. It was Weirdmonger himself (aka Dognahnyi).

The dreamcatcher had saved him the rest of his journey across the mudparks, so stub-of-pencil now needs to return that way itself so as to erase the relevant bit from the vexed texture of text with a renewed head of rubber, if not steam.

The Weirdmonger scratched his head. Identity was a very strange burden to bear. To take his mind off the momentary discursiveness, he wondered how Sudra's museum was allowed to smoke in a smokeless zone. Fire was not allowed within Inner Earth—for obvious reasons. And, shrugging, he went towards a cavé to give the locals a piece of his mind.

As well as Klaxon and Agraska, there is another known or tenable conclave within Inner Earth to which the name most often offered as label is Whofage. The derivations, even aptnesses, of these names are unknown whilst, paradoxically, the names have readily fallen into usage without any question of demur. Their real names remain unknown, whilst that named name of Klaxon still resonates, however, with an actual meaning that effectively entailed the tannoy siren-system to be created, not vice versa, i.e. character from proffered name, a phenomenon which is, when fully considered in the light of cause-and-effect rather than synchronicity, not surprising.

Whofage, in fact, was once named Synchronicity by some historic Inner Earth travellers during the days of Jules Verne, a fact now forgotten amidst repercussions of Klaxon's war spreading by strength of the battle echoes and air-alerts firstly ricocheting from chamber to chamber on a tight regional basis, then cavity to cavity between city-margins. Whofage (now named *against* the normal channels of sane semantics) was a place where Synchronicity began to be deemed as evil, thus giving Synchronicity a bad name at the same time as giving Randomness a haphazard boost by the strength of the craziness of war itself. Whofage seemed random enough (more random than using the name Randomness itself), and this even seemed eminently logical to the top brainwrights of Whofage's Inner City Council who were concerned to prolong the unpredictabilities of war (imported, by echo, from Klaxon) amid their various pragmatic uses of its collateral damage and bad karma... i.e. politics.

It is an unrecorded fact that THE HAWLER (with its index-number of H5N1 now visible for the first time from the direction of any observers) stayed over at Whofage on route between Klaxon and, eventually, one hoped, the Megazanthine Core near Agraska. Greg and the others alighted simply to stretch their legs and to discuss the disappearance of the Drill's Captain. Should they return to Klaxon to rescue him or forge on without him, both options impossible to carry out without his presence in the first place? They had crash-landed in Whofage having traversed random cavities in a rather spin-easy fashion of free-fall that did not entail any drilling whatsoever or any off-detritus clearance by the rubble-vanes. Even now, the Drill squatted on the craggy sides of Whofage's cathedral, having demolished half of the Gothic architecture in the process—making it look more like a bridge than Notre Dame. A bridge from and to nowhere. And over nothing. Greg had put such problems towards the back of his mind—as he wandered the back-streets of Whofage looking for souvenirs. There were feathery models of the Angel Megazanthus in many of the antique shops, but, at that stage, none of the party recognised these knick-knacks for what they were. They assumed they were dreamcatchers or frames of varying complexity or simplicity. The Core, to Greg and his party, was still a mystery and no rumours as to the Core's incubatory nature had back-tracked along the sound-veins from Agraska to shed any light on this mystery. Echo-filters, unlike some other filters, were never two-way. Beth did buy one 'dreamcatcher' to hang in her cabin in the Drill.

Another excursion—one not programmed in their original holiday itinerary—was to watch larger models of 'Megazanthus' dreamcatchers actually working. The party sat in a row of canvas deck-chairs—hired for the purpose to them from the rather business-like brainwrights of Whofage—at the edge of a cracked meadow. And they listened to a commentary from the city's own tannoy-system describing the various aspects of the air-show. One craft that slowly took off—by the use of a rather slow-motion lifting by spluttering fireworks—was a gigantic kite or glider that seemed a cross between a crop-sprayer and horizontal radio-transmitter. Bearing in mind its motive power, it was rather difficult to control at ground level and it soon diverted from its original advertised course towards a random one that entailed much collateral damage in the city itself.

Whofage, unlike the other conclaves within the cavities of Inner Earth, was prone to funnel forces—which, on the surface, were commonly recognised as whirlwinds or tornados. Often, Whofagers would glimpse a sparely nourished coil of discoloured sky, then slowly but ineluctably deepening and spinning into wilder, larger shadows of shape (whilst simultaneously trying to hone its integrity as a funnel)—finally, not spinning away into nothing as tornados manage to do on the earth's surface, but spinning into the underground, maintaining its force-fed maelstroms (now of rubble as well as of black-clouded air-space) as it wreaked further courses of crazy-paving via many under-surfaces, even via otherwise impacted areas of solid earth.

Before Greg and his party had managed to salvage the Drill from its open-plan sectioning of Whofage's cathedral, one such funnel-force had managed to accomplish this feat quite freakishly, almost balancing the Drill's form within the inner meshments of its visibly darkening torque until landing it lightly near the cracked meadow where the party were already watching an air show. All seemed highly appropriate, if essentially accidental—in keeping with Whofage's reputation for the syncromesh of randomness.

Also, with some panache, Captain Nemo arrived hotfoot from Klaxon—or someone remarkably carrying off this persona with skilful replication—claiming that he had utilised a number of short-cut back-doubles intrinsic to the hawling-shaft system of Inner Earth, comprising mostly rat-runs privy only to Drill captains. Nevertheless, it had been quite a journey. The other members of the Drill's party welcomed him with mixed feelings. Soon after, all of them left for Agraska in a quickly repaired Drill and for what was already to have transpired there *vis a vis* Mount Core (or Sunnemo) and the Angel Megazanthus. (Beyond the scope of this Apocryphal Coda).

Scene: Sudra's Shoe Shop in Klaxon City. Sudra is sitting in one of the stockrooms, surrounded by shoeboxes from ceiling to floor, having just received a surprise visit from Amy clutching a rather large flowerpot. They embrace and are now in close conversation.

Sudra: The last time I saw you was when you were holding me from falling in the hawling-shaft…

Amy: Yes, I'm delighted to see you survived.

S: I didn't! At least for a while. Until I woke up here in charge of this shop. Placed into business by some benefactor who stays unknown, even today. I still felt it was me that was me, but I suspect sometimes that I woke up as someone else. At first it was disconcerting…

A: Very! But you learn to live with yourself eventually as I did. I still have memories of a childhood, my brother Arthur and all that—and Mum—and Miss Clare our teacher. But then, I'm not sure I'm the same person who grew out of that child.

S: When I last saw you we were both hanging on to dear life, or at least I was! It was my life hanging in the balance, after all. I looked up into your eyes and I saw something or someone behind them which wasn't quite right. And then you let go!

A: No, you let go! I felt your hands ungrip around mine. I wasn't perhaps completely myself, true, but I wanted to save you—I really did. I had been recruited by Dognahnyi for something but I'm sure it wasn't to kill you. It was to do with the Angevin traffic…

S: All these years I believe you killed me. But life has to go on without recrimination. Since things went strange, I'm sure there's no possible blame. Even shame's gone out of the window. Dognahnyi—wasn't he also known as Captain Nemo?... *the one who travels overland to the centre of the earth* as they put in the 'Jules Verne Tours' blurb…

A: Yes, and I've since found out, he's also known as the Weirdmonger…

S: The Weirdmonger? Someone of that name has been lurking round here for a while—but I've not seen him for ages.

A: They said you had John Ogdon working for you here in the shop?

S: Who said? Has someone sent you here to spy on me?

A: No, no, Suds, it's just that—I can't explain it—or I can explain it. You probably know John Ogdon as Crazy Lope… You nod. Well, he's also known as Blasphemy Fitzworth or Padgett Weggs… A proper spy disguised as a dosser or cat's meat man or…

S: Well, I've not seen Lope for days, either. They say there's war afoot. Many have already left Klaxon. Most visitors have gone. You're probably the only visitor at the moment.

A: Not a war so much, Suds, as head-on collisions of bird-sickness plague, body to body… blending…

S: I don't understand. I don't think I ever will.

A: It's the Drill. Dognahnyi's Drill. It was originally intended by its designer (DF Lewis) as a plug to prevent the flow of Angevin back to the surface, as he believed it was not so much a recreational drug as a carrier of the bird-sickness in a more virulent form, encouraging people-to-people contamination instead of mere bird-to-people contamination. The latter can be controlled. The former can't be.

S: That's the first time I've heard mention of this Lewis bloke.

A: He's a rather shadowy figure. Arthur once told me about him. Anyway, getting back to the Drill or Plug—it has worsened the situation because of what happened at the Core when it got there. It just provided more fuel for the Angevin from the pairs of people who visited it—and then the hawling-process took it back with it, so not a plug to prevent carrying but the carrier itself. The sickness has now reached the surface via man-city—Viet Nam, Rumania, Turkey, later London, even Clacton—then New York, the whole globe infected not from the sky but by things that masquerade as birds within the globe itself and then come out as real birds having stowed away on the Drill 'plug' or, more likely, flowing like feathered torpedos with the Angevin hawling-flow. It's still rather confusing. But it can be stopped.

S: How?

A: It's something so oblique, so damn opaque, it needs conversations like this to approach from various brainstorming angles to reach some semblance of its basics. Something to do with the word 'firedrill' I believe. And that's just the beginning of the wild guesses.

S: Firedrill?

A: Let's relax for a moment. Talk about other things. Solutions only come when you don't try to think of them. How's the shoe business going?

S: Not bad. With the war coming, the armies needed shodding for a start.

A: I don't know how you put up with all those sirens all the time.

S: Well, they are only going when there are visitors in Klaxon. Otherwise, the tannoys play Classical Music all day. It's rather a blessing.

A: Classical Music! I think I'd prefer the sirens!

S: It's quite restful most of the time—Chamber Music by Debussy or Beethoven, Schubert—loads of Bach—but yes, they sometimes play some more modern Classical Music more related to the siren sound so we don't miss it too much! Ligeti, Bartok, Penderecki's *Threnody for the Victims of Hiroshima*, you know the sort of thing… But if there is at least one visitor in Klaxon, back to the sirens proper!

A: Rather you than me. I'll be pleased to get out of this place.

S: What's in that flowerpot, Amy, by the way?

A: Guess.

S: Can't guess.

A: OK, let me guess first what that thing is that is in the corner over there—it looks to be a cross between a shoebox and a proper shoe.

S: That's a shoe for a Grandfather Clock.

A: I wish I hadn't asked! Anyway guess what's in my flowerpot. It may help.

S: Arthur's ear?

A: Nope

S: My shoes that you once stole from me?

A: Nope. And I didn't!

S: A clockwork toy—a model of the Drill—an Angel Megazanthus brooch—a cabbage full of dead flies—a toy log-lorry?

A: Nope, Nope, Nope, Nope, Nope.

Amy puts her hand in the flowerpot and brings out her own childhood doll strapped into a doll-sized deck-chair and clasping a doll-sized flowerpot. And Sudra is alone again with her shoeboxes and bespoke shoes. Even the tannoys are silent for once. Just barely perceptible jingling from some of the shoeboxes.

Klaxon City was the name of an amusement arcade in London's Soho—sufficiently sophisticated to be considered a casino, or certainly abiding by the same rules and providing comparable opportunities for the punters. It was simply more open-fronted with looser membership conditions and lower grade jackpots, but otherwise it had all the trimmings: just on the corner from Leicester Square underground station.

A husband and wife team by the name of Greg and Beth were managers and the owner was Sudra Incorporated, the whereabouts of whose shadowy head office was even unknown to the managers, other than as a Registered Address which could not easily be checked out, short of a long journey to the ends of the earth, it seemed, or at least beyond Zone Six on London Transport. Greg and Beth were recruited via an agent by the name of Mr Dognahnyi who had a flat in Mayfair, but even he had indirect contact with Sudra Inc. Emails and cash transfers by PayPal. Only the odd visit from Authorities, most of which prying was kept at bay by mysterious paperwork behind the scenes in bent accountants' and solicitors' offices. There being no food involved, only the broadest Health & Safety Regulators were given the slightest excuse to pay heed to Klaxon City's methods, without any recourse to Cleansing Agents or Culinary Inspections. And even these turned blind eyes as well as deaf ears to some of the outlandish noises and migraine-inducing strobes.

Mr D's flat had original oils sporting walls to hang on that were so thickly chintzed one did not need to wonder how the thrum of London outside was sound-proofed for the benefit of the subtle Chamber Music playing from the tiniest speakers, but ones with the greatest dynamic range that Greg and Beth had ever heard. The walls of Klaxon City itself likewise did indeed have oils to set off the hi-tech walls of digitalised games and spinning mantras that constituted some of the 'amusements' and insidious temptations to gamble. Oil portraits of fantasy vistas which—when one became accustomed to the types of game on offer—were seen to accompany the risk-and-ride boxes-of-tricks as a pianist would accompany a singer.

Only a few were privy to Klaxon City's 'amusement' services because—from the outside—it looked quite seedy with a threat of muggings by scarred street-sleepers rather than promise of coddlings by bosomy croupiers. This was a way to keep the place select—a topsy-turvy method of restricting the clientele by aversion therapy with regard to the unwanted narrow-minded types of punter who only judged things by surface appearances. The games needed far-sighted specialisms of humanity to make them work at their optimum—and these prize customers were encouraged by winning large sums of money rather against the odds of most other casinos. It was creative payola for turning imagination into actuality—a method in a madness of which even Greg and Beth had hardly scratched the surface. The punters simply needed to get past the obvious signs of criminal danger that associated itself with most arcades and then they would find beyond such frontage the most benevolent form of creative gambling imaginable—and once imagined, the world was their oyster.

Greg and Beth used to run an arcade in Clacton. That was useful experience. In Clacton, one can be trained for all manner of deeper occupations which seaside resorts alone know how to harbour. A Dry Dock for the re-fitting of genius prior to its re-launch. And even for Greg and Beth, it was simply a short journey by train to Liverpool Street, then underground to Leicester Square followed by a warm welcome by Mr Dognahnyi on behalf of Sudra Inc. At first, rather troubled by the frontage of Klaxon City, they were—once inside, once through that initial burst of dismay at the grim-faced bouncers—soon glistened upon by every conceivable spinning-table of landlocked luck teetering towards the benefit of all who played them—and even the toilets boasted original oils.

The underground trains made the place shake with low-throated rumbles from time to time. Luckily, imagination drew short of imagining them to be bombs or quakes or even life going on elsewhere beyond surface after surface of surface appearance towards a recognition of the madness intrinsic to an existence still not fully in the know.

One wall-game was to shoot the birds. A spinning-vista of a lake sanctuary where you needed to aim at any feathers once glimpsed. And the more you shot off, the more you won. It was called 'The Tenacity of Feathers'. And a siren sounded out at every direct hit.

I wonder myself if there was a deeper symbolism in that phrase—'The Tenacity of Feathers'. And whether it was just another misleading frontage within the first misleading frontage. A meaning that we were all feathers in an eternal lifetime of identities, each identity a single feather that we wore throughout this time-line of crossed-feathers or ruffled ones, being indeed a single feather that we fought to preserve tenaciously, only to fail when one became the next feather (or identity) ripe for plucking. It takes more than one feather to make the bird. And somewhere a creature stretches its still sparsely feathered wings—but with gradually more tufts just starting to sprout on its huge balloon of a belly.

One day, I fear sound-fire will be drilled real deep by a dead-eyed punter towards my own feather's root. Crazy Lope—dead Red Indian. Null Immortalis.

"It's a need for immortality—whilst before in pre mass-communication eras very few people went down in history books and therefore religion provided the 'immortality' because there was no feasible ambition of 'immortality' in any other way—today, one can imagine one is in the public eye, and the public eye immortalises in a very insidious but also a believably crystalline fashion. Notoriety or self-crucifixion are two possible paths towards this crystallisation within the 'public eye' as well as more straightforward forms of fame—all as provided by the mutual reflections from the unreality/reality syndrome of mass communication-mirrors (and I would include the internet as well as TV as examples of these)."

The speaker in Earth Towers Hall paused. The audience could only wonder if they had correctly placed the quote-marks around words or phrases within his speech. How could they do otherwise? Speeches—like any other sounds or items of music—are interpreted and filtered by the listeners, sometimes quite differently from each other but all 'correct' for themselves. They are often dependent not only on mental capacities (prejudices, proclivities etc.) but also on physical ones actually to receive the sounds and translate them into 'meaning' via, for example, both Inner Ears. Likewise: visions, dreams, lies, ghosts, fictions, performances, poems-on-the-page, morality fables—all 'seen' (mentally and physically) as 'correct' by each and every one, but in a slant or shade that is peculiar to each of them one by one... often affecting (or not) the 'reality' within which the sounds or visions are placed or contextualised. And this contemplation of mine—words that you have just read as commentary on the speaker's speech and his audience's potentiality to 'listen'—was effectively another speech within my own mind as I waited for the audible speaker (compared to my silent 'speech' to myself) to resume his own speech, as he did:

"Here in Earth Towers Hall, it seems appropriate to digress upon the meaning of fiction in the context of what I've just said."

Earth Towers Hall was a new purpose-built building on the banks of the Thames quite close to the City of London. The tip of St Paul's dome could just be seen through the window that backed on to the hi-tech podium. Mock-architecture mixed with real paintings of Thamesian scenes. This was the inaugural event. An important slant on things real and unreal by a purpose-born Professor of Philosophy who was downgrading his thoughts by posing as a famous author of fiction.

"And one can believe that fiction and non-fiction share the same jigsaw, the same rattle-bag of broken shards of ancient pottery of thought all leading—potentially—to a pattern that we can examine, then use to solve problems (or to create them). An example would be useful. '*Nemonymous Night*' ostensibly deals with many current matters (as they happen) and today bird sickness has fallen lower in the sky—and we can only hope that the fiction itself is helping to lower influenza's temperature and eventually eradicate it. Fiction is that powerful. A happy ending (yes, skip to the end of the book, go on)—it's bound to be a happy ending or the author would never have finished it. He needs to be thanked for all his good work in harnessing the power of fiction to solve this single pressing problem by setting himself the goal of a happy ending, despite all the horror images he necessarily conjures up *in order to* reach that happy ending…"

I smiled. This speech made no logical sense to me. I did have some sympathy with the speaker's views on the blurring of reality/unreality, as exemplified by TV Reality Shows like Big Brother and the fact that audiences, these days, actually 'create' the event with their reactions (such as pop concerts)—but to extrapolate, i.e. to manufacture an audit trail between fiction (art) and the malleability of reality itself to the same fiction (art), was certainly something very difficult for me to swallow. I held the very book in question within my hands as I sat in the audience—skipped to the end and everything vanished, including myself. Earth Towers Hall echoed with the silence of bird droppings.

Stub of pencil: Many people each holding one large word and, if they found the right order, the words would tell a significant story. They shuffled places in an arc, until a consensus as to an optimum order. A camera swivelled taking a panoramic photo of the story... but broke before the end.

The millions of warmongers in Klaxon-under-the-Ground swarmed from pillar to post, ready to stone even stones as well as each other—displaying a mob hatred simply engendered to stem the tide of love's infections. A vital mutation or misalignment of possibilities.

Quite close to Clacton in Essex, there is Britain's oldest recorded town, Colchester, its tall Town Hall pointing at the sky like a stretched wonder of the world—so attenuated you wonder if you're in a surreal dream rather than a proper lifetime. The Water Tower is another land-locked kite of brick. The Castle an impacted rattle-bag of Norman stone, weathered to the gills. Yet a tree grows from its topmost tower. The Colchester Tree. Wet-weather fireworks of green. A ground-based kite-display beneath the empty sky.

I was brought up in Colchester from the age of eight.

"There is too much concentration on false endings. References to death. Half-hearted attempts to progress some semblance of a story-line—meandering like a blunt drill between the images—or like a Proustian discursiveness without Swann's long-feathered perfections of prose or poetry. Not even managing to convey the believable, truly-felt astringency of human failings. Just attenuations of mock-philosophy or many wild side-glances from a big Bird Brother with a desperately flirtatious squawk or tail-flutter. Then role-playing a kitten so that its own feathers would be squashed under its own immediate paw."

I listened to the speaker as he continued from the podium in Earth Tower Halls. His own lecture itself was indeed meandering like a blunt drill within already carved tunnels—also thrashing about in crazy dismay like a dying creature trying to reach some sense-bait at the end of its longest sentence. But he was reading from an invisible memory-aid that the technological advances of the new building supplied. Like a politician, he probably had not written the words—and was reciting them parrot-fashion. Even this my own interpolation was dragged kicking into the residual cavities or chambers of his very speech thus masquerading as his own words as dependant upon the hypothetical font used within the aforementioned memory-aid.

"My long-term hobby or labour-of-love: literary experiments in depersonalisation and seeking a unified morality from among the Synchronised Shards of Random Truth & Fiction: 'difficult' extrapolative empathy in the art of fiction writing: and creating/

distributing the acclaimed but non-profit series of multi-authored anthologies entitled *Nemonymous...* "

The platforms were being queued haphazardly (and often over-vigorously) by those waiting for their turn to take the long trains that had now been shuffling steamingly within sidings for some hours of impending preparation. The hawling-tunnels had by now been freshly railtracked to furnish easier journeys to the Earth's Core without having to travel overland. And most were eager to take advantage of these technological advances. The first public trips had been well-advertised and the demand was great. Ticket-only.

One of the platforms was so ill-queued only a few stragglers had self-consciously sidled there into makeshift positions of arrival's order by mechanical memory-aid. They wondered if they were on the right platform, as they viewed the milling hordes on the opposite platform across the gleaming tracks. These few stragglers were evidently representatives of people who had already been to the Earth's Core—and, in some cases, were still there, never having returned in the rather undependable transitions provided by the early 'Heath Robinson' Drills that had prevailed heretofore. Their tickets were for specific journeys whereby they could seek and then reclaim their lost selves... an adventure or quest that would be both exciting and linear. Several trainspotters or twitchers watched them from various signal-boxes in the vicinity, giving themselves (and hopefully others) some perspective to the early beginnings of the platform stragglers' characterisation and potentiality within an unusually distinct plot-development.

A smartly be-suited Greg was a tall figure with pink chops sporting Victorian whiskers, which rather belied earlier sightings in other habitats of his working-class upbringing and work as a lorry-driver or amusement arcade attendant. Mike, Greg's alter-nemo, was possibly the wise counsellor Greg truly sought, rather than just another version of himself.

Beth, his wife, frowned but instinctively showed an equal balancing of love and caring beneath the brusque veneer. She would be his real-life counsellor, whilst maintaining a rather uncomfortable relationship with her own 'road rage'. Once beautiful (and her alter-nemo Susan was still present just below the surface of the skin in a far more acceptable silhouette of femininity), she now had frown-lines tracking the crows' feet on her face and (if revealed) the rest of her body.

The children Amy and Arthur would need to develop more naturally without being force-fed fictional epithets. Equally the older ladies Edith and Clare would be given even more shadowy roles than those granted to them in earlier days.

If Lope de Vega, Dognahnyi or Sudra were present at all, they were not among this shorter platform queue of so-called stragglers. They probably only had tickets for the more populous queues on other platforms. We perhaps shall never know.

This time, however, what was already certain, the main protagonists were due (by dint of the railtrack's pre-laid direction within Inner Earth) to by-pass Klaxon City, thus hopefully enabling them an easier path towards the goals they thought they sought.

Another or the same train disappeared with great whinings of fire-cranked pain (fed upon nuggets of blackened Angevin)... down the steep slope towards the centre of the Earth, ratchetting upon funicular gravity-braces. Aboard this corridorless vehicle, mock-timed for other eras when steam was the only motive force behind such iron beasts of transport, those in one carriage were immediately disappointed that there was no on-board lighting. Amy and Arthur were scared, but Greg managed to light a spill (one he used for his pipe). The glow upon their faces was more than just ghostly. It was comforting, too.

They felt the juddering of the gravity-braces as they slipped across the sleepers of time as well as of dream upon another set of sleepers: themselves. The Sleeper Express for the ends of the world.

In timely fashion they skirted a visibly far-stretching dune-curved lobe within a gigantic cavity, lit only by a subdued Sunnemo. Greg quenched the spill as they watched awe-inspired the glistening tracks vastly undulate into the numinous distance with a renewed flurry of choking smoke or steam: inferred to be thus choking since plumes of such emissions had only been cursorily test-run within mock-ups of these cavities or chambers, but the authorities had hoped for the best—in that the natural vents of an organic planet would naturally cope with such human interventions as fire-cranked transport.

Then utter blackness again, eventually dimly inflamed by another spill.

Followed, a few hours later, by a bright chink of a few seconds as the pyloned city of Klaxon was by-passed—viewed between the margins of a lightning crack in an otherwise unilluminated cavity of Earth's most elephantine junction of rail-tunnels. The train's whistle—becoming more like a siren by dint of the echoing cavity's configuration of space and sound—blasted out for the first time (with the shuddering imminence or immanence of seemingly religious 'antipodal angst') as the train continued its nigh unstoppable steam-driven course through a more benighted night than even those previously imagined.

Scene: Lecture Room of Earth Towers Hall, London. Delving further into *'Nemonymous Night'* as a work of fiction, many reviews have pointed out how the characters remain fluid, difficult to nail down, even *not always the same person!* Therefore sympathy or empathy with the protagonists remains elusive. Normally a disastrous situation for the efficacy of any novel or set of novels. A sign of failure.

Hopefully, they are sufficiently *al*lusive to warrant further consideration in the light of the author's intent (as far as I can ascertain without recourse to any debate on 'The Intentional Fallacy' upon which subject I currently keep my powder dry). That intent, then, however difficult it is itself to nail down (like the characters), seems to me—as I implied before—to stem from an attempt at making *any* empathy as untenable as possible. However, I've met this author head on (determined to play the game on my own terms) and I feel that one can put *yourself* in the role of Greg or Beth, whichever one is chosen to be more likely to be empathisable for you. The 'vexed texture of text' and/or 'a novel growing up as it is written with very little retrospective revision by the author except for typos or grammatical mistakes' help one in this attempt to empathise and become involved and to suspend disbelief in the—what is it?—SF novel within a Jonathan-Swiftian or Jules-Vernian or Marcel-Proustian 'Inner Ear' or perceived dune of trackable fictionality by drilling through for the oil of its plot. In other words, the empathy becomes more powerful from the fact there is little assistance by the author towards any empathy at all. You need, therefore, to insert yourself.

Before I came on to the podium here today, I scribbled out—at the last minute—with this small stub of a pencil (holds it up to applause) a few more notes as analogy and to serve as my own *aide mémoire*. I'll read them out verbatim: "The method of fiction in '*Nemonymous Night*'. Like trying to crawl through a long horizontal hedge. It's easier than you thought. Coming out at the end of the hedge—find oneself lodged on a cliff-face. No way forward. Yet, the hedge going backwards has turned itself against you. More nettles. More spiky obtrusions pointing in the wrong direction..."

The first regathering of its steam by the train within Inner Earth was at Whofage. It would be folly to pretend that this was anything other than a short cessation for reprovisioning or renewed fire-cranking or water/carbonised-angevin re-stocking. The passengers were intended to stay in the vicinity of the station awaiting announcements from the mini-tannoy system that had been set up merely within the hearing-range of the station itself. Whofage had no ambition to become another Klaxon, it seemed. Whofage's tannoys could hardly be heard, except for a pitiful cartoonish squeak punctuating the steam-burnished hiss of the mighty iron beast that still billowed visible smoky off-detritus into the crowded atmosphere.

It is also folly to use the word 'station'—as it was more like an old-fashioned halt from that idyllic period in English history depicted by 'The Railway Children'. Greg and Beth, together with their own two children, stretched their legs along the dark-roofed platform—amazed that a cavé was provided, one not dissimilar to the buffet used in the film 'Brief Encounter'. Steaming samovars of freshly-infused concoctions of Indian leaf, plus various tiers of cream or coconutty cakes. And a large old-fashioned clockwork clock that told surface time, for the benefit of the smooth throughput of surfaceers such as Greg and his family. Amy and Arthur shuddered in their thin-limbed smocks, because the station was merely a dank, troublous tunnel—such as those tunnels punctuating the canals of surface England whereby Narrow Boats plied their own ancient, sluggish, chilly, gloom-filled, chugging paths of broken water—and the *shyfryngs* were almost second nature. Even Beth felt the gnawing to the very bottom bone. They were all relieved to get into the relative cosiness of the cavé, where they could replenish their stock of good-will and pluck.

Upon their alter-nemos' first visit to Whofage, they had not been able to explore the city at all. In fact, a passing subterfuge of memory seemed to tell them that they had by-passed this city altogether in the Drill, just as, on this journey, they had by-passed Klaxon. Therefore, there was a temptation to leave the jurisdiction of the squeaky tannoys in the station and just poke their heads out for a moment and view the vistas available, including the previously unknown pyramid on the hill (equivalent in historical interest to Klaxon's Canterbury Oak or, on the surface, the Colchester Tree)—and, having discussed the chances of managing this without missing the train's departure (i.e. discussing these chances with the buxom white-overalled tea-lady behind the cavé's counter)—they took off on Poliakoff-type adventures within the purlieus of Whofage and beyond the catchment area of the station premises, let alone just its tannoys. And perhaps those adventures are worthy of a whole book in themselves.

They were surprised, for example, that there were many other passengers on the train—judging by the very short queue of them that had boarded on the train's first inward outward-journey. Many of these shadowy individuals eschewed a trip round the city, but a number did take the same risk as Greg and his family took. How many managed to get back to the train before it departed remains an exciting conundrum of rushed running and panting moments of dire stress. Each a book in itself.

The city was rather Eastern European in atmosphere, with a mighty cathedral on huge stilts that seemed to be around every corner they turned. No sign of the pyramid on the hill and there were rumours that it had toppled a few years before—killing three million citizens in the process. The city was a strange contrast to the close-ordered darkness of most of the erstwhile train journey—with muffled sirens from the front pullman—as well as being an equal contrast to the fleeting vistas of Sunnemo-lit dunes or lobes that took the continuously curving railtrack upon their backs. For something to be a contrast to two quite opposing contrasts simultaneously said a lot for the power of Whofage as a contrast.

By-passing the various books that will one day be available to tell of the adventures of Greg and his family in Whofage, they returned to the station just in time to hear the tannoy's announcement of their train's impending resumption of its journey to the Earth's Core.

After leaving Whofage Station, it wasn't long before the train came to a series of irritating halts... with intermittent hisses of brakes.

"Engineering works," suggested Greg.

Unusually, illumination within the carriage was a few notches of glimmer above pure darkness—thanks, it seemed, to a few uncertain chinks in the cavity-walls that allowed a thin effulgence from an ever-weakening Sunnemo... or so Greg assumed. His two children were sitting patiently on the opposite side of the carriage—far too patient to be believed possible, but they were probably over-awed by the novelties involved in this journey—as they had yet insufficiently evolved to be able to empathise with—or, rather, "wear"—their alter-nemos who had already travelled throughout Inner Earth during earlier times.

"It's a pity we couldn't visit Sudra this time," said Beth, the children's mother. Greg nodded, as she continued: "I hope her shoe business is keeping its head above water."

"Bound to be," said Greg, "with all those preparing for war."

"I don't know if she has military footwear in some of the displays."

Greg laughed, saying: "Well, those jingle-jangly ones are certainly not suitable for spies!"

At that point, the train began to travel forward more consistently, if still painfully slowly—leaving Sunnemo's dim light behind.

The two children took this opportunity—amid much fidgeting—to attend to some necessary matters of ablution or body-dispersal.

"Can't you do that a bit more quietly?" snapped Beth. Greg lit another spill, but the children had, by then, resumed their more natural sitting positions. Amy tugged up and down the padded armrest from its slot in the seat's back—as if rehearsing some future tantrum.

"That's enough of that," said Greg, as the train finally picked up speed.

The train roared through the tunnel cavities like dust through a vacuum's nozzle. Hours of wild churning passage (each chug having become a rough transition towards a uniform teeth-grinding surge) as the train's travel touched upon the fasttracks... with the carriage vibrating and each pair of points being crossed with surprising ease as the train plunged onward alongside the very close proximity of the black cavity walls that formed the untouching but closely-hugging tunnel-sides. The passengers became accustomed to their own nerves, as they attempted to sleep.

Eventually, the train emerged into a more consistent area of Sunnemo light, where the cavity walls widened sufficiently to allow the appearance of surface travel, the striated mould on the rocks even granting the terrain a feel of fields: dunes of traditional countryside vanishing towards the horizon where Arthur imagined an English village nestled with its churchspire prominent... but not prominent enough yet to see. The trees were mysterious figures—perhaps setting out for Dunsinane.

Soon, however, Arthur (yawning and rubbing his sleepy eyes) saw the terrain had become less 'traditional' and in a field of mould turned brown, if not black, he saw thousands of boys squatting: each with a single overgrown ear: surrounded by bottles and cans and packets: delving into the subcarpet of Inner Earth with trowels.

Upon a distant hill sat a giant Toilet Frog, as if overseeing the 'labourers'.

Arthur silently wept. He realised, frighteningly, that one could not escape the dream sickness—even here within Inner Earth, where they had all been assured dreams would be easily distinguishable from reality... as they had earlier been promised would be the case in the erstwhile zoo grounds of man-city, an area of the past which had been forgotten amidst subsequent events, forgotten not only by Arthur but, sadly, by us, too. Even fiction has its own version of pitiful senility amid the other realities to which it ever tries to cling.

Scene: Lecture Hall, Earth Towers Hall, London

"A new theory has emerged. We now need to proceed speedily from hypothetical literary matters concerning the use of Fiction as the New Magic in the role either of genuine cure or, at least, of constructively believable panacea. The Art of Fiction needs, therefore, to progress towards a stricter and more verifiable account of what happened or what will happen in the final war between humanity and a terrible foe and, subsequently, by extrapolation, to become a means to the end of neutralising the results of that very war.

"Heretofore, it was believed (and I am the first to admit that I was one of those believers) that the Core—aka Earth's Core, Mount Core, Sunnemo, Jules Verne's Centre Of The Earth—housed a single malignancy known as the Angel Megazanthus or the Infinite Cuckoo or other possible names that were listed by various protagonists. Gradually, however, queries began to crop up as to whether its initial appearance as a malignancy represented in effect a benign force in disguise. One that fought on humanity's behalf.

"Then, with even more powers of creative meaning and truth, it was proposed that the force inhabiting the Core had not *started* its life there but had always existed as a generally migrating form in a wider universe... but then it was plucked from its otherwise slow and self-occupied passage through space-time and transported to the Core—perhaps accidentally—by a means of public transport invented by humanity.

"It was a proposal coupled with a diverse concept of dream sickness, a sickness that yet enabled the potentiality for good to evolve."

Stub of pencil: Aide Mémoire. I'm getting stuck. The fact that a core could double up as a sun was probably the most crucial 'vision', when Captain Nemo—all those years ago—showed Sunnemo to Mike from the window of the Drill's corporate lounge. And I'm due to explain that the 'skies' of Inner Earth are beginning to be populated with vast machines that rival even Sunnemo in size and it must be wondered if these are related to the Unidentified Flying Objects that often pepper our surface skies. But a singularly outlandish flying-saucer hovers, currently, over Klaxon City, like a spinning wheel churning through soft earth as well as off-detritus. End of notes.

"The fish smelled!"

Arthur smiled as he replaced another divot above the body that he and his younger sister Amy had just buried during a solemn ceremony of childish reveration... marking a departure from life by one of Amy's loved pets.

"He didn't!" Amy dabbed at her eyes.

At that moment, a low-flying helicopter—vanes clacking fast—banked over the apartment towers, criss-crossed as in a display of aviation above the allotments and finally churned quickly into the distance. If children were able to feel their own paranoia for what it was, then Arthur sensed that his worst enemy was the pilot of that chopper spying on him... and, with the sensitivities that only children can feel but not understand, he somehow knew that the pilot was himself (Arthur) from a future he was yet to inhabit.

He turned to Amy, deciding to ignore his dark instincts with regard to the diminishing pinprick of the helicopter now being lost to the suburban horizon. While both their sibling feelings towards each other were typically abrasive he did, at heart, worry about her and, before being able to stop himself, he proceeded to quench Amy's tears regarding her recently deceased goldfish.

"You've still got a canary in a cage. And that fish really smelled!"

"It only smelled after it died." Her sobs worsened to the extent of giving her words an even higher pitch than normal.

When they had found her dear fish floating at the top of the bowl bloated like a human ear, the room was so filled with fumes, Amy's canary showed signs of soon choking to death itself had not the fish-bowl been removed forthwith to the outhouse. And, if not death, certainly some state between life and death which could not easily be defined.

Arthur stared at Amy, his immediate impulse caught between hugging her and scolding her for being so sentimental, but the words he used to convey this thought to his brain were much simpler than words such as 'scold' or 'sentimental'. He recalled their mother's story of dream sickness and wondered if it would be any use in comforting Amy by reminding her of it in words she could understand. Arthur himself had failed to understand their mother's version of it, but deep within yet another instinct similar to the earlier one regarding the helicopter, he understood the story quite well as he replayed it in his mind.

Once upon a time—their mother had begun by telling them—there was a country where people could not judge between the state of dreaming and that of experiencing real things while awake. A girl called Sudra lived in that country. Not a country of the blind, but a country of dream uncertainty. Sudra loved the new shoes that she had been given for Christmas. But how could she be sure they were new enough? Or even shoes at all in such a world? She decided to visit the wisest man in the country who happened to live in the same village as Sudra and her family. This man told her the shoes were not only new, but also real. She was relieved—at first. Until she worried if the wisest man in the country was a dream himself. Why would the wisest man in the country happen to live in the same village as Sudra? But he had to live somewhere. He had even claimed he was the wisest man in the whole world, not just the wisest man in this particular country. Did this claim not prove he was lying, and, if lying, did not the probability of this being a dream increase considerably? Or lessen? Sudra didn't know where to turn. The shoes were strange shoes since at the front and back of each one were little bells. And they were yellow shoes. Her parents said this would help them find her, should she get lost. But Sudra had never seen shoes like them before in the country where she lived. They must have been specially made. And the family was so poor how could they have afforded such bespoke shoes? She decided to test out the reality of her current thoughts by unthinking them. People got over deaths by unthinking them. They got over grief and pain simply by unthinking them. Yet she still smelled the countryside that surrounded the house, she still smelled all the common and customary smells of the house itself... and even with her eyes closed as she concentrated on unthinking all her doubts, the smell of the smells continued to smell around her. And when the parents entered the room to find her, she had vanished! Only the shoes remained, sitting silently on the yellow carpet. But Sudra's smell remained for her parents to follow.

A sad or inscrutable ending—their mother had explained—but one that had many possible meanings.

Indeed it did, thought Arthur, as he more simply retold the tale to Amy. And as Amy wiped the tears away, she even smiled. Now the whole world would be her fish. Just one of the tale's many morals.

They laughed as many other morals of their mother's fable took root.

Meanwhile, a huge spinning wheel appeared over the suburban skyline, constructed of many shining metal stanchions and cylinders, its central top cockpit filled with the biggest head of an unknown creature the children had ever seen. Soon, however, at a vast slant in the sky, it dipped towards the ground where its spinning edges began to delve: throwing up great cascades of earth like fountains of detritus towards the clouds that soon became gritty themselves. This Unidentified Flying Object soon vanished below the ground towards further skies it hoped existed inside the Earth—or it had simply grounded itself like a pitifully sick whale beaching upon the bank of a river.

"If the fish smelled anything," said Arthur, "it certainly can still smell you, Amy."

And he took her hand to go inside.

"Wait!" shouted Amy. And she picked up her favourite flowerpot nearby, in which sat her favourite doll, and she took this with her as she followed a now freshly unthinking, unthoughtful Arthur overland towards their home.

Scene: In Paternoster Square: just outside Earth Towers Hall, Klaxon City.

"There was no scene-setting," said Crazy Lope, "only the bare stage."

"Did anyone introduce Sudra?" asked Edith with the parasol. Indeed, she bobbed it up and down with the rhythm of her words.

"She did her best. Nobody knew what to expect." Lope was fascinated by the lady's parasol, if not hypnotised.

"What did Sudra say?" asked the matronly lady, still in tune with the parasol.

"Sudra, Sudra, Sudra, Sudra, why keep saying her name? There's only one person we can talk about at a time."

"Well, what was said?"

"Verbatim? You want it verbatim?"

"As far as possible."

The parasol remained dead still, despite a breeze, as Lope did his best to repeat, for Edith's benefit, the exact words which Sudra used during her speech from the bare stage:

"'*Speech needs nothing but the words and nothing outside of what was actually said. The explanation of my theory, therefore, will, today, be uninterrupted by scene-setting or, even, questions. I shall simply launch into it, as I have already done with the words about speech above, and then launch out of it before you have the chance to know what has happened. Indeed, a being's most significant sign of humanity is speech. Once upon a time, speech developed slowly but, at least, it did develop and only in rare cases did it remain in the realm of animal grunts. But, now, children are becoming less and less innocent with the onset of an increasingly modern civilisation. Their eyes become cowed with experience, as if they can foresee the sex in which they'll be forced to partake, by gratuitous choice or by love or by lust or by rape... or by a combination of any of these. Speech is part of this process, that and self-awareness, body-awareness, gender-awareness, genital-awareness... even before puberty. No wonder a sparkling infant soon becomes dowdy and bleary-eyed... with sorrow and sadness underlying the veneer of its happy-go-lucky speech. Another factor, too, is madness. You may feel the impossibility of self-madness. You may look at drunks or lunatics or any of the fringe people in the street mouthing obscenities or simply shouting nonsensical noises or grunting like animals. Indeed, as a side issue, have you noticed how even ordinary, clean-living folk are now more prone to mouthing uncouth words? Anyway, you may be confident in your own sanity but, then, completely unpremeditated, you find yourself shouting out... angry, say, at how the waitress is late with your order or, simply, the stress of an increasingly modern world finally takes its toll on you... and that is merely the beginning of uncontrollable madness taking you over as the language of speech once slowly took you over when you were an infant...*'"

Lope paused from quoting Sudra, with tears in his eyes.

"Is that all that was spoken by Sudra?" asked the dowager, wondering why she, Edith, was still holding up the parasol when the sun had long since vanished behind the clouds.

"I may not have quoted exactly."

"Yes, but was there any more?"

"I don't know. I had to leave the theatre in a hurry to meet you here."

"I wouldn't have minded if you stayed to hear the end."

"Well, I felt too sad to listen to more. I recognised myself in that bit about madness. And in that bit about children growing up too quickly."

"We all grow old too quick. There's nothing new in that."

"And we all grow confused and unsure of our bearings."

"And of who is speaking..."

"...to whom?"

"Yes."

"Well, maybe God meant it to happen this way."

At this moment, crowds began to pour silently from the Hall's entrance at the other side of the square. Many of them raised umbrellas over their heads as it was now raining. And many did not. Sudra, uniquely coloured, was among them pushing a doll—in a toy pram or wheeled flowerpot depending on the distance with which one was viewing it. A zoom lens would have revealed a stub of a pencil stuck in one of the doll's eyes, perhaps evidence of an earlier tantrum—also that Sudra was bare-footed. At least, one hopes that Sudra *had* reached the outside, because a giant complex UFO accidentally clipped a pylon and finally collided with the Hall where she had been speaking... followed by a roar of splintering off-detritus more suitable for a strapped-bomb christened Sunnemo finally imploding.

The waitresses were generously supplied, almost one for each table.

The tea-room was very swish, plenty of smooth freshly laundered white linen, silver napkin rings embossed with antlered deer and pentinent youths, sturdy chunky heavy-duty yet good quality cutlery... and large bowls of fresh flowers pricked out in bright colours and still drenched in dew.

He ordered a tier of cakes, licking his lips at the thought of the custard slices, cream cones, coconut pyramids, battenburgs topped with whipped almond, spicy bread-and-butter pudding baked to a rich brown crust, waffles dripping in wild honey...

The particular waitress attending to his needs was no older

than his own daughter, the prettiest of the whole bunch, he thought. She wore a uniform which, rather than hiding her figure, accentuated its more sensuous angles, as if an artist had finished off an otherwise boring portrait with the subtle pastel striptease of water-colour.

The skirt-length was below her knees, but the slender calves and dimpled ankles were all the more enticing for that. The stockings were of such low denier, they took nothing from the flesh.

The tea infused him, like a heady drug. The blends reached to the back of his throat, even before he lifted the bone china to his lips. And he stared dreamily across the tea-room, as the waitress turned her back to fetch from the display counter further cakes he had ordered. Her rear proportions were slight enough to retain the integrity of the skirt-length, but womanly enough to produce folds, pleats, flairs and a long sculptured quarter-moon down each side... that made him want to touch, if only fleetingly.

The other waitresses were nothing in comparison: mere bodies holding up their uniforms like clothes-horses for airing. One even had a face that reminded him of his nightmares... and she had the temerity to scold his own waitress for picking up the cakes with her fingers rather than with the tongs.

He half rose from his chair, as if to remonstrate: he could not wish for anything better than to have the comestibles handled by his waitress, to produce a new flavour, whether imaginary or not, that would backwash the roof of his mouth with the froth of love...

He thought better of it. The tongs would have to do. The winsome one returned with the second tier of cakes, smiling fit to take sunshine into the dreariest late afternoon.

Her skirt-length lightly brushed his arm, inadvertently, and he bit his tongue painfully to stop himself from...

She had gone far too quick. Evidently the end of her duty, disappearing into the kitchen, with not even a backward glance for her erstwhile loyal loving customer.

His teeth entered an angel cake, leaving daubs of red where his injured tongue had probed its texture...

He cursed and left the tea-room, paying the nightmare waitress; she worked the old-fashioned cash register as if she were issuing tickets for a dubious show in that other part of London he sometimes frequented. Being in so much of a hurry, he even forgot to retrieve the large gratuity he had left under the bone china saucer: it had been intended of course for the waitress with the sunny smile who, like him, had taken such a sudden departure into the gloom of dusk. Perhaps intent on catching a train before it left. Air-raid sirens permitting.

The view through the cockpit window—as the vast Circular-Saw penetrated the cavity-walls of Inner Earth—was not so much a panorama of the reality beyond the window but of a moment of strobe-history that the pilot who peered through the window was undergoing as he instinctively tussled with the controls.

His dream of strobe-history showed twin Earths that were on a collision course—through the wide vista of his vision. Instead of creating a huge explosion, they blended or merged in the same way that, once upon a time, the legendary man-city, having begun to bury itself beyond its own foundations, eventually encountered another city with initial splintering ricochets of architecture and hard core but then blended with it—thus making two places the same place but different.

The pilot of the Saw quickly regathered his present moment uncorrupted by any dream of strobe-history just in time to address the situation of a Drill making towards him.

My custom was to explore secondhand bookshops at the slightest opportunity. It needed guile to shake off Beth and the children—but, one day in Whofage, I had a rare success in subterfuge. We were about to traipse around a toy museum and, without giving them a chance to reply, I told them that I would be back in half an hour to conduct them onwards to the various amusements in the 'Klaxon City' amusement arcade that needed coins in the slots.

I had indeed spotted a wondrous curiosity shop on the approach to the toy museum, hidden to the view of my wife and children (and of most other visitors, too). But my expert tunnel vision having picked it out down a Sunnemo-less alley, I was convinced by my instinct that it would purvey a veritable trove of dusty books. And I was not mistaken. However, it proved not very different from what I imagined the toy museum to be, since in every corner there seemed to reside many ancient jacks-in-the-box, china dolls, jingle-jangly shoes, pop-up nursery rhyme books and colourful whips and spinning-tops—but here they were for sale rather than show. If I had known, I could have killed two birds with one stone by bringing my family here.

The books themselves were a dream. First editions galore with lightly pencilled prices on the fly-leaves, some even within the range of my purse. Others, of course, not. Many were Victorian, but mostly hardbacks (with original dust-wrappers) from the twenties, thirties and forties, children's dreams and adults' fancies.

I was surprised to discover an old stamp album: full of colourful squares, oblongs and triangles (and even one large colourful trapezium of a stamp from Agraska), carefully affixed with sticky paper hinges. I imagined a child (now grown into an adult more long in the tooth even than myself) meticulously wielding tweezers, positioning his prize specimens at the optimum angle and sitting back sighing with pride. This boy would have eschewed even birdsong or playtime in the sunshine for such a close-ordered activity.

My surprise was generated by the fact that such an article was stacked with the secondhand books, bulging as it was with well-hung stamps. Some of the stamps looked "rare", but many must have been gathered together from a lucky-dip selection which children used to obtain by sending off a coupon from the Tiger or Lion or Eagle comics. The stamps used to come "on approval". But there were some examples of stamps in this album that I had not been able to even dream about when I was that age.

I covetted that album more than anything I could recall covetting before. I held a whole childhood between my fingers. But there was no price pencilled, presumably because the fly-leaf was covered with a highly stylised map of the surface world. So, that was where Saar was. And Andorra, San Marino, British Honduras, Monaco and St Helena. Nobody ever seemed surprised that most of these small places had outlandishly large postage stamps. I looked round for the shop counter, fully expecting a wizened old man to be stationed behind it—one with pipe, toothbrush moustache and eyes bleary from poring over small print. But this was a day full of surprises—since a girl of surpassing beauty smiled at me from behind the counter, appearing as cool as her flowingly diaphonous dress of white…

I collected my family who were impatiently kicking their heels outside the museum. Apparently, it was a natural history exhibition. Why I had originally thought it was a toy museum, I could not now fathom. What was abundantly clear, my wife and children had been bored and decidedly crotchety at my lengthy absence from their party. I blamed it on having been cut short and the nearest convenience a fair step away. And it had not been a particular pleasure, I assured them, standing next to all those sweaty individuals and the many 'nervous little people' who followed us around in Whofage. But my family soon oozed forgiveness when I changed my remaining ten bob note for 120 pennies at the 'Klaxon City' arcade. The old wizened fellow who sat behind the towers of copper quarter p coins in the change booth actually winked at me. He looked decidedly unhinged.

As I tried my luck on the fortune-wheel, which was supposed to give some inkling into one's future love-life and luck, I suddenly wondered why stamp collections always used to be conducted by short-arse boys who did not have many friends with whom to go scrumping apples or building dens. I could not possibly imagine those unattainable angelic girls of my lonely childhood abandoning their china dolls and dressing-up hampers for such close-ordered activities as mounting stamps.

The fortune-wheel did not record any romance in store for me. In fact, the bad luck it indicated seemed to start with me somehow losing the stamp album soon afterwards. Like the beautiful ghost who sold it to me, it must have slipped through my fingers.

For an indeterminate period, Greg, Beth and their two children, Arthur and Amy, toured the streets of Whofage, but instead of relaxing during this interlude in their train journey they were beset with an antipodal angst which involved thoughts that they may not get back to the station before the train left for Sunnemo. This was an undercurrent that made all their activities fraught with an anxiety, an anxiety that soon grew tentacles (giving new worries leg room) including one significant nagging doubt that they had already travelled to Sunnemo before and finished their lives there during a dream—but now the anxiety became more relevant because they feared that *that* was no dream and the real dream was this their seemingly endless temporary stay-over in Whofage. If the latter is a dream, why worry? Dreams can't hurt you. Or so the parents told the children.

Other factors lengthening the tentacles of angst included the so-called 'nervous little people' that seemed to plague them at every turning of the city. They were seeking identities and, if this *were* a dream after all, then identities *could* be stolen and used elsewhere. So one remedy of an angst as a dream had soon created a new angst! These creatures—of human persuasion—nevertheless chirruped like chickflicks on continuous strobe. One or two even sported beaks instead of lips.

Another tentacle of angst: Sunnemo was looming closer and if it grew even closer as a dull light source or even a surrogate nemo-moon, then there would be no need to return to the train to reach their destination at all! Greg decided to shrug off the angst and ensure he and his family at least pretended to themselves that they were enjoying their stay-over. Pleased, too, to see that Sudra's Shoes Inc. had a branch here as well as in Klaxon.

Edith sat in the Proustian arbour, holding the stalk of a flower pressed between the backs of her hands, the red bloom of involuted petals held at eye-level.

She posed for both painting and photograph, unsure as yet which of them would do her full justice. She held the angles of her body at their optimum level whilst masking the ugly birthmark on her forehead with the bloom.

The painter was standing by an easel at the far end of the inner garden, the long brush held aloft, his artistic thought processes apparently taking their time to percolate, and the palette upon his other arm mounted with wormcasts of corruptive colour, all chosen for Edith's complexion.

Further over to the side, where the neatly manicured topiary began, there was a tall tripod bearing an instrument with a retractable snout and a black cape flowing from its rear and the legs of a man curved over from under the cape and a bulb to squeeze and a flash like lightning and...

Arthur, as a small boy, shut the pop-up book with a crack. He twiddled with his left ear absent-mindedly.

The front of the board covers was decorated with the only abstract image in the whole volume and, with the dying light of the nursery fire, he discerned a pattern more suitable for carpets than murals.

The book had been left with him as a peace offering by his parents who had departed in a horse-drawn carriage for an evening at the opera. He had heard the clatter of hooves disappearing into the echoey Klaxon distance, leaving him alone in the house—or worse than alone, since the only other person left behind under the same roof was the family's ancient nanny. She sat in the corner by the fitful log fire, knitting-needles clicking, her asthmatic lungs rasping. He watched the sometimes insect-like, sometimes bird-like silhouette moving only very slightly in unfaithful rhythm to her deft stitching.

He wanted to be a dare-devil. He wanted to stir her into realising that it was too dark in the nursery, since she could have blindly knitted on forever—and that her little charge was in danger of being snatched by the Angel Megazanthus who, to the boy's certain knowledge, lurked up the chimney.

So he broke wind. And a distant siren fortuitously boosted the noise.

She jolted in her wicker chair. Her neck creaked, turning a stern gaze upon him.

"Ptcha! There are places for such noises."

"I know, Nanny Edith, but my tummy-ache—and the fire's going out—and I'm worried sick about the darkness."

"I know what will sluice out your belly, young man, a good dose..."

At that moment, soot billowed from the chimney, as silently as an army's secret striking of camp at the dead of night. It caught his eyes, so he heard no more of her mad ramblings. She did however absent-mindedly brighten up the end of a candlewick.

He returned to the pop-up book to bury himself in its pages, whilst yearning to hear the hooves which bore his parents homeward from the Klaxon opera. He kept at least one ear pricked, despite the utter dread of what he expected to hear with it. Nanna's bones cracked loudly as she lifted herself from the wicker-claws of the chair to attend to the fire, perhaps to entice a few more flames from the glowing ruby embers...

...and Edith, elsewhere, elsewhen, had by now lowered the glowing bloom and positioned it between the points of her bosom.

That part of the face bearing the stain of the birthmark lacked features and, possibly, substance, too.

It was as if one could look straight through her head at the point which oriental mystics had once believed to be the site of man's invisible Third Eye or, at least, an optical illusion of one. And through it, could be seen the blacker eye approaching from behind.

The hair of the painter's brush was known intuitively to be manufactured from a dictator's moustache. He had dipped it in a generous mix of strange paints. It formed a colour but at the same time not any colour under the Zodiac.

The tripod camera had lifted the photographer's legs into the air like wings and was in the violent process of flapping around the garden, a huge insect-bird of a creature, clicking insanely. Nowhere to go, it could not bring itself to halt the wild careering—until it became entangled in the ivy trellises of the arbour. There it flinched for a few seconds, with fitful bursts of fire from its black beak and the squeezings of purple venom for a naughty boy's tummy, until it died...

...like the fire in the grate.

Nanna Edith had by now lit the oil lamp hanging above

the boy's cot. He could vaguely see the remains of a dead entity woven in and out of the wire fireguard. In disgust, he threw the book towards the fire and, despite falling short, it proceeded to pop and crack. He made his way to the cot to crawl between the covers. And, then, while he dozed, he imagined he heard hooves clopping on distant cobbles. As Nanna bent down to give him a little peck on his petally cheek, he heard her churning, phlegm-clogged breath and saw straight through her head—and through this head he saw a bloated spider-bird glistening in the crook of the ceiling. The little boy squeezed his eyes tight, praying for sleep; even nightmares would be preferable to such reality...

...and the man into whom Arthur was eventually to grow woke with a start. It was freezing in the garret and he had a job to do. Not before fulsomely farting, he quickly dressed in darkness, picked up his heavy-duty paintbrushes and departed into the shivering Klaxon square, to await the arrival of the bosses with the ladders. He stamped his feet to rid himself of pins and needles. He felt along his hardening top lip—yes, coming on nicely. Even rind-growth was, in itself, a would-be entity.

The Sunnemo dawn, when it painstakingly arrived, was colourless and cold. The hooves of the decorators on the cobbles could just be heard.

The man's ambition was to paint on palace walls in the manner of Hieronymous Bosch, whilst a thousand Popes screamed inside.

And nurseries exploded within him as the brain bloomed red. A bogus waking fetched the thud of his parents' hooves clopping up the stairs. He prayed they couldn't have fruited each other with him in the first place. The *real* frighteners, however, would come when the little boy stopped dreaming.

Though I never lived during that kingdom of war—the one that blitzed London—I could easily imagine the colourlessness (or, rather, variegated brown) in every wet afternoon, prefiguring the contrast of night's man-made lightning. Séances were being held amid the chintz of every blitz-free sitting-room; tears being shed in every outhouse; tender hands held, over and over again, in every beach hut and every park.

Well, for every every, amen. I shook my shoulders—not a shrug as such; more of a shudder. I tramped the back-end streets, wondering if I had been transported in time to those very afternoons when shapes emerging in fragile freedom from the night's shelters (the Underground included) became the slowly nudging together of lightly-fleshed ghosts in the hope that something worthwhile or tangible would emerge by this serendipity of touch. Ghosts, I guessed, were to be everybody, even you and me.

This was to have been a poem. But it felt like prose fiction, with all the trappings of a plot, albeit missing a beginning, a middle or an end, if not all three. I could have gutted this fiction of its protagonists, but then nobody would have been there to report its waywardness.

I met Sudra in one of the many parks where courting couples were more colourless than most, if less tearful. She was someone with whom I assumed an immediate mutuality. She smiled, wiping away her tears with a burnt hankie. Collateral damage, she said, from last night's bombs. I didn't take umbrage at her false modernity. I knew she joked; this was then, not now.

A fleeting image of an evening when Sudra and I did walk under a fleet of doodlebugs—and suddenly a thing like a plum-pudding bursting with a fiery sauce came down and a lot of glass fell out of the windows on to us.

"Good job we were not there": my first ever set of words to Sudra upon meeting in the park. My second: "Ghosts were simply the future."

"Ghosts will forever be the past," were my sweet Sudra's last.

But truth told no rhymes.

Crazy Lope's head was a camera, or it seemed like it to him; he saw everything as if framed for a motion picture. As a film, he had been given an adult certificate when he reached a relatively young age, but now, with the years piling up on top of each other, even that was not sufficient to cover the scenes he sought out.

One day, Lope discovered a backstreet of his home town he had not previously explored in which there was a tall disused warehouse with a faintly glowing signboard on the vestigial gantries. He could just peer through the misted up lens and see the letters spelling out SUDRA'S SHOES INC. He tried to pan round but his feet were rooted to the crumbling pavement and his neck had stiffened: he felt a movement on his shoulders as if a creature had lodged there, squinting through a slot in the back of his head. Whatever it was, claws were penetrating his overcoat and, finally, his flesh... fastening on to the blade bones like steel. He tried to shake it off. It was all well and good to imagine being a camera but here he was actually being used as one by some frightful inhabitant of the night.

His eyeballs revolved in the sockets, and the warehouse sign flickered out of freeze frame, scrolling like an old-fashioned black & white TV of the fifties. He desperately needed vertical hold: but that was the least of his worries: before long, he found himself going into cinemascope and edges of the scene he had previously not been able to view encroached and fluttered in from the sides:

things like wriggling hairs and, then, insect feelers which often used to blemish projections upon the flea-pit screens of the sixties; the technicolor oozed back, and a blood-red haze gave the whole vista a dream-like quality; like speech bubbles in comic strips, this was a token of dissolving ready-reckoner reality, a symbol of beliefs being suspended.

The whole vistavision screen was now acrawl with translucent bird-wings beating faster than the strobe of the frames. He could no longer make any assumptions about his own sanity. He turned his eyes downwards as far as they would go without detaching the optic nerve, to see his cylindrical nose extending forth from his face: zooming in on the entrance of the warehouse: where he saw a camera filming him filming it: but surely it couldn't be a real one, because it seemed to grow wonky and misshapen the more he stared back at it. However, he was pleased on discovering eventually that it was a female camera: but, as their noses came together across the street in some primitive ritual of a kiss, all he could see was the utter emptiness of his own backscreen soul.

That's when the thing on his back extricated itself from Crazy Lope's bones and scuttled off somewhere, abandoning the tickertape of the film to flap uselessly... as it reeled off the spool and tangled up the inside of his skull. Since it left no other room in there, his brain slithered out of the ear like a white worm in search of a bird.

The Saw circled: seeing the nightmare of identities and words blurring upon Inner Earth's texture of vexed text.

Angevin angevin sudra sunnemo agraska sunnemo mike amy arthur alter-nemo off-detritus man-city whofage klaxon siren-yellow angevin core hawling hawling hawling horla susan sudra hilda ogdon edith clare amy dognahnyi lope lope godspanker ogdon nemo sunnemo balsam clacton klaxon london weirdmonger blake swift dylan thomas mike jules verne proust sunnemo nemo-moon lovecraft hataz tho azathoth king in yellow angevin.

And gradually, as Greg and Beth (and their two children) concluded their stressful stay-over tour holiday of Whofage, not only their own human shape of deep and realisable characterisation emerged from the shuttling semantics, phonetics, graphology of that very italic list but also they saw—within the circular silhouettes of these laconic words—the emerging spectre of the halting-station and its still steaming burnished train of ratcheted carriages ready to take them on to Earth's Core via the customised hawling-tunnels. The antipodal angst.

If only one looked properly at any form emerging from traditional childish scribble, one would see the Angel Megazanthus also beginning slowly to glide from the adumbration or limning of meanings even if the very words 'Angel Megazanthus' were not overtly included as part of that once pencil-annotated list. They were, as words, however, contained in previous and later syntactical blocks of vellumed vexture.

Stub of pencil: "Most memories are false, but when I am faced with the only true memory, which is death, I have then no need of it."

My wife Beth and I have been married happily for as long as my receding memory stretches. Although being overbearingly carpet-proud, she actually forgot to empty the vacuum.

Now, in the quiet evening of our years, she has taken to strange doings. They are obviously harder to explain than merely to describe, so I shall only attempt the latter in the hope of finding a key to the mystery in the fullness of time.

Recently, with us both fast asleep following the customary early nights, she has woken up and extended her housework through the small hours, only to tell me in the mornings that daylight can only reveal the normal jobs. At night, she maintains, different dust emerges, slops and moulds gone unnoticed during standard waking hours.

"But, my dear, you're being absurd. I've heard of housewives spending all their days making everything spick and span, but disturbing your valuable beauty sleep...!"

"You think I'm mad, I know, Greg."

"No, of course I don't. But there's not nearly enough to be done in this house to keep you busy, anyway. It's only a two-up-two-down, after all. There's no need at all to get up in the dark when all godfearing people are asleep."

Then she repeats her claims about the night being more suitable for seeking out the otherwise unseen corners where real dirt worth its salt collected… not your mealy-mouthed daytime muck which masqueraded as encrusted food or merely as motes stirred by sunbeams.

So, I have decided to see for myself.

Often, she has been up and about without me having even broken the rhythm of my snores. Tonight, though, I tried to prop up my eyelids with the matchsticks of will-power, listening to her breaths becoming heavier and with longer gaps between. I heard the church clock striking ten which was more often than not the hour that acted as alarm for the Angel Megazanthus to spread its wings upon us both.

I pinched my lips between the teeth, almost to the gums... also attached a length of thread between one of her big toes and one of mine. She tossed fitfully, making the job harder than it would otherwise have been. Eventually, we were tethered in dreams…

It was no dream, however, when she awoke within the death-lull that night creates between both margins of nothing. My toe almost parted company with the bone which held it out like a stringless puppet. I followed her on the tips of my feet, wincing away the anguish in them.

Firstly, she proceeded to the broom cupboard under the stairs, whilst I remained on the landing looking down at her black felt house-cap. Several jointed broom-handles came out like giant spider-legs kicking.

Abruptly, I had the crazy notion that she must always spend the small hours crazily hoping to earn pin-money as a chimney-sweep in the neighbouring back-to-backs. That would explain everything, except the craziness itself.

Before I returned desultorily to our bed, she had bustled into the front parlour, cooing with delight at the layers of minced shadow she expected herself to sweep up.

I now lie cross-limbed, unmercifully awake. I can discern the still dented pillow next my own, for there is a dimness thrown by the street light feebly flashing outside the bedroom window in makeshift pleas for repair.

Almost without thinking, I lift up my own pillow and retrieve the old toothbrush I keep under there for lost fairies. I poke this into one of my ears and out the other, thus scattering dust in the air like dirty Angevin powder.

There is nothing I would not do for my dear wife, in these her days of crazy old age. In this way, I at least keep my own brain bright as a button while I leaf through the album of memories of our honeymoon in Whofage.

The train for Sunnemo eventually careered (as from a blowpipe version of the deadly sound-torch) through and out of the final tunnel into the empty light of Earth's most inward terminus: a train with many names on board, if not the people attached to the names. Absent or present, however, all of them managed to scream in sheer terror while each name was peeled from their skin along with the feathers themselves... and the pomegranate rind of the Core was penetrated by the final steaming thrust of forward rocket-motion from the front of the Hawler-train's spinning saw-drill.

Hataz and Tho yearned between the tears with which their eyes stared each other out before the Core's final implosion sucked them towards a nostalgic state of birdsong and childhood where they'd first fallen in love: he amid his own self-mixed music and she wearing, for the first time, her beautifully new overland shoes. Tricking the Above, the Below and the Across.

I cried more than most—as even these young lovers had become nervous little people.

Azathoth, the real name of the Angel, smiled.

Then laughed...

They all had names, but none knew any but his own. So, when one of them was accidentally lost in the dark, the others wondered what to call out.

And the lost one wondered whether to answer. It happened after one of those early frosts that often took sun-worshippers by surprise.

There was a summer which childhood made endless, when shafts of sunshine slanted across the meadows like the golden eye-sight of Ancient Gods. But this particular summer became accused of issuing a false promise akin to everlasting youth—until one among the disporters, called Lope de Vega, said that *he* knew all along that such sunny days could never have lasted, despite their seeming endlessness.

The questions with which Lope de Vega was consequently faced came thick and fast. Why had he not warned the others, if he knew? Surely, the unexpected frost had taken him by equal surprise? No, he maintained, since he had not considered it necessary to taint their holiday in the bright warm sun. Would they have otherwise raced between the makeshift see-saws and the prehistoric elfin hidey-holes, with such carefree spirit? Would they, indeed, have been able to make their laughter heard above the tree-tops? The sky could never be blue, Lope de Vega maintained, unless it had thermals of real laughter to feed upon and help it clear the clouds. And he laughed, as if to prove that he at least could still raise such laughter.

The others stared back at him, victims of their own hopes... until, from within, as it were, they reacted to the burgeoning need to work their joints, not in play, but in labour. Shelter was the byword, but none of them actually knew the implications of its meaning. They possessed some inkling that they needed to study the ramshackle hidey-holes which had previously been simple ingredients of their adventure playground. They clustered chatterless within the leaning shadows of cross-section chimneystacks which, for some odd reason, had originally been built taller than the trees. Many pointed and gesticulated—but none knew the reason for their own excitement. It was merely a component of their thought patterns which everyone accepted without the one obvious next step of asking... why?

Then Lope de Vega, who had known all the time that

this would happen, started to scale the nearest chimneystack, adopting a courage which should become a legend if any were left to remember it. The brickwork groaned as he neared the bright orange pots ranked along the rim of the stack, the climber's actions reminding many of the onlookers about games which they had once played amid the branches of the trees. His shape cast a lengthening shadow across the meadow. Once aloft, he straddled the pots and called out his own name... as if nobody had heard it before. The others called back and received only echoes for their pains.

The stars were reborn in a still clear blue sky—but it was a darkening blue: a navy blue without the sailor's uniform. The frost's colour, instead of depleting with the light, had seemed to grow whiter in desiccations of daisies. The grass crackled underfoot, as some of the onlookers heaved bricks from the prehistoric hidey-holes (except it was now known that "hidey-hole" was not the word to describe them) to another part of the meadow, to build their own—and Lope de Vega, who overmastered the campaign, still sat upon the smokestack which teetered further from true the more its foundations were unplumbed by the others. He knew, all knew, that, by night (and many now felt in their bones what was meant by the word "night") he was to die, death being the only real way he could obtain forgiveness for deception.

But he called loudly: How was he to have known they had wanted to be told? They had not asked him to tell.

But they had not known that there was indeed anything to be told that they could have asked him to tell, the others returned in answer.

If he had told, he shouted, they would have been miserable and not gambolled amid the sunbeams.

But at least they would have known (they retorted), and not

wasted their precious time in false, longing dreams.

At that moment, the stack began to topple. As did the other stacks.

Many were crushed by the masonry as they rushed to catch Lope de Vega—which carnage was Nature's only sure way of allowing the new hidey-holes to have sufficient room inside for shelter.

By this time, the sky had become a shade this side of indelible inky blue-black and the survivors crouched within their newly created ruins; the *shyfryngs* of cold thankfully masked the more insidious ones of fear.

Lope de Vega, who had laughed and climbed, could no longer be blamed nor even praised, simply because he was the only character in the legend who was fictitious. They had even forgotten his name, along with their own.

Thus, they who thought themselves elves or selves did not of course expect him to be holed up with them in the basements they burrowed—and indeed he wasn't. They made a few fitful forays into the cold wilderness in search of a nameless one who was lost, but they soon forgot the reason for their desultory quest; they thought it was purely for the stories that could be told later in the benighted huddlecot.

The new season felt both seamless and eternal.

But, wait—that had also been said of the previous season!

One day, the absurdity of it all might make them laugh out loud. But, by then, they would have forgotten what laughter might accomplish.

"We are not our names, not our bodies, not our actions—not our soul or self. Not even a segment of collective unconscious. Just dig and see, haul back what we find. And try not laugh or cry when, from the core of reality, we reveal the fiction that is each of us. Or not even a fiction, but nothing."

Or perhaps it is a fiction that we are nothing, because these non-attributable words at least remain.

Milton Keynes UK
Ingram Content Group UK Ltd.
UKHW012211140624
444015UK00006B/49/J

9 781913 766283